The Very Last Gambado

A Lovejoy Novel

Jonathan Gash

Constable • London

CONSTABLE

First published in 1989 by William Collins Sons & Co Ltd

This edition published in Great Britain in 2017 by Constable

1 3 5 7 9 10 8 6 4 2

A CIP catalogue record for this book is available from the British Library.

Important note:

The British Museum of course exists, but the characters in this novel are fictitious and no reference is intended to any living person.

ISBN 978-1-47211-950-6

Typeset in Berkeley by TW Type, Cornwall

Printed and bound in Great Britain by Clays Ltd, St Ives plc

Papers used by Constable are from well-managed forests and other responsible sources.

Constable
An imprint of
Little, Brown Book Group
Carmelite House
50 Victoria Embankment
London EC4Y 0DZ

An Hachette UK Company
www.hachette.co.uk

www.littlebrown.co.uk

For:
Sarah Kate, with love

To:
The Chinese God Wei D'To, protector of manuscripts,
this manuscript is respectfully dedicated.

Lovejoy

To the staff of the British Library and British Museum,
a thanks for unfailing courtesy and help.

Jonathan Gash

Chapter 1

Antiques and women, being passion, are the only living things you can depend on. Trouble is, they come with this other stuff called crime.

By three in the morning I'd done the burglary. It wasn't easy. Cycling down dark drizzly country lanes in the owl hours is not my idea of fun, but when the devil drives and all that. My gammy leg was killing me. I stopped at the lay-by, pretended to pee against the hedge – odd how you can't wring out a single drop to order – and wistfully left the pair of antique silver salt cellars as ordered, in a plastic shopping-bag under the hawthorn. They were idyll models, Victorian children with baskets selling fruit. Just over six inches tall, and as lovely as when they'd left the silversmith's magic hands in 1859. (Tip: a boy and girl pair quadruples the price of one.) The craze for these superbly detailed figures was actually given its impetus by the Great Exhibition of 1851 . . . Where was I? On my way to an alibi, that's where. As I remounted and wobbled off, sobbing at having to leave them, I heard a car start up. A real pro; and I don't mean me.

Back at the cottage I carefully dried my bike, changed the wheels for two buckled derelicts full of cobwebs, put it ostentatiously in the vestibule, and slept the transient sleep of the just, dreaming of antiques.

Tarzans age, don't they. Beauties wither. Civilizations crumble. Pasties go mouldy. When you think of it, everything's got a bad prognosis.

Except there's one entity which carries loveliness down the years in spite of politicians, wars, pestilence. It remains, blindingly beautiful as any far galaxy. Yet that cluster of mere things is within reach. It's here among us. You can even put some, so small, in your pocket if you're lucky.

That entity is antiques. Nothing else matters. Almost.

Dr Lancaster's surgery, nine o'clock on a drab rainy Monday morning. Four days previously I'd prepared this medical alibi by damaging my foot. I drove up and parked my old Ruby, and was limping in when this woman emerged. Blonde, slick, giving me a glance hard as nails. I sighed wistfully, but alibis called. I entered to wait my turn and sat, bored, looking round. Is limbo as dull as a doctor's waiting-room?

I play this game called People, my own invention to antidote boredom, that dreaded state. You play People this way: Invent a question, any question, about anybody. Like, 'What is she going to do next?' or some such. Then, you apply that question to whoever you next get a good look at. Simple, eh? No. Try it.

There were three of us waiting for Doc Lancaster's scornful cynicism this particular day, Corinne with her monster infant Joe, me, and a bloke. Corinne I already knew about; she serves in the village shop, always worn out. Joe doesn't count. He was making a noisy speech, unhindered by the lack of vocabulary, and tramping Corinne's thighs meanwhile. I envied him his succulent trampoline but left them both out of my People Game. You have to play fair.

The bloke, though, wasn't a villager. He sat motionless. Not a nod, not a smile. Faded pinstripe suit, frayed cuffs. And turn-ups, would you believe. Thin dark tie, shirt with washed-out stripes. He held a bowler hat on his knees with soft bleached hands.

Mrs Vanston emerged, ushered by Doc Lancaster's surgery nurse Anna. I smiled my most winning smile.

''Morning, Mrs Vanston.' She has a lovely early Crown Derby dinner service I've been after for years. She displays it in her front room window just to annoy me.

''Morning, Lovejoy.' She left, sadly a picture of health. I honestly most sincerely don't hope she pops off. But imagine her Crown Derby at auction . . .

The bell dinged. Corinne gave me Joe while she went in after Nurse Anna. Joe silenced momentarily, leaning away to eye me like they do. A faint sneer flitted across his eyes as recognition struck: *Lovejoy; antique dealer; scruff; penniless; no food as usual.* He resumed his speech and his march. God, he was heavy. God, he hurt my thighs. And God, he was noisy.

'Shut your din, noisy little bugger.'

'Lovejoy!' Anna reappeared for a file, swished her bottom out of sight.

'All right for her,' I grumbled, trying to encase Joe. Realizing that he was now on a lapless thoroughfare he became more energetic than ever, thrusting an occasional leg through so he'd risk falling. 'You'll tumble, you little nerk. Knock it off.' Joe thought this hilarious.

The bloke opposite ahemed. 'Children,' he pronounced straight out of an elocution class, 'are capable of adaptive learning from an extraordinarily early age.'

Eh? Silence.

Joe fell about, screaming with laughter. I could feel his belly shake. Struggling, I compromised by giving the bloke an expectant smile for him to chat some more, but that show-stopper seemed to be it.

Anxiously I prodded my dozy neurones. What had he said? Children's adaptive learning or something. How the hell are you expected to answer that, for God's sake?

'Er, aye,' I managed finally. 'Aye, very early.'

He gave a curt approving nod.

'I've always thought that,' I added helpfully. 'How very early they, er, do that.'

Pro-o-o-o-longed silence.

Well, I'd tried. Sulkily I went back to trying to control Joe's adaptive learning, but he was bloody difficult. Fifteen minutes into Corinne's consultation Joe reddened, concentrated on grunts, then started stinking the place out. He burst into celebratory song.

'Excuse me, mate,' I said. 'Could you pass his bag, please?'

Corinne has a pushchair – chrome protuberances ankle high, of course, to slash your shin. I'm sure women favour this sort from a kind of vestigial race memory, Queen Boadicea being a local East Anglian lass complete with sabre-toting hub-caps. A plastic bag dangled from Joe's chariot handle.

No answer. He stared into the middle distance.

Now I'm a polite sort of bloke, honestly, but I had to say it as I clutched Joe – God, the stench – and crabbed across the waiting-room to collect the bag.

'You idle rotten sod.'

Still not a word. I'm pretty good with most things, even Joe-sized, so by the time Nurse Anna sprung Corinne the only evidence of the problem was the terrible niff from the nappy I'd bagged.

'I couldn't wash him, Corinne,' I explained, adding nastily, 'No medical help, you see.'

Nurse Anna's amusement narked me as she shepherded

the prim bloke inside. Joe's din and Corinne's thanks dwindled, and I was alone with my People Game. I should have played cat's cradle. Safer.

In solitude, I asked the room loudly, 'What is she going to do next?' That had been my People question, and Mister Sunshine its focus.

Now, the game's cardinal rule is that you're not allowed to change the question. The subject was a bloke, not a bird. The rule said stick with it.

I pondered. 'What is she going to do next?'

Well, I reasoned, he must know at least one she, right? Auntie? Wife? Live-in lover? Seductress whore straight out of *The Blue Angel* with him the lust-lorn love-crazed professor on the balcony? Mother? He'd looked about forty. But she'd have turned his frayed shirt cuffs for him, and done better stitching than that coarse mend on his trouser-leg. I relegated Mother to a distant Lincolnshire nursing home.

Wife, then?

Not really. He was too clean. Oh, I'm a man of the world. I know everybody puts clean underpants or knickers on before going to the doctor's and scrubs themselves skinless. It's the way we are. I mean, I have a bath about six o'clock every morning but this particular day I'd had an especially vigorous double go. So it was only to be expected that Old Misery was spotless. But his cleanliness was the obsessional toenails-and-armpits hoovering of the loner. No doghairs. No chin stubble. He was the sort who'd be edgy if his pencil broke. Could any wife stand that? Doubt it. Women hate permanent extremes in a man. I've found that. Like, I'm a natural scruff, so women reflexly set about tidying my cottage beyond repair. They fail, but that's OK because they thrive on being annoyed.

Delete wife.

My old Austin Ruby still clung to life on the critical list where I'd parked it on the surgery's forecourt. Had Chatterbox come on the bus? Rule Two of the People Game: you can't wheedle help. I could easily ask Nurse Anna had she seen the stranger arrive. If I'd not invented the game I'd have broken the rules quick as a flash, but honour's honour and I didn't.

The village where I live's a few miles from the nearest town. East Anglia's depressingly rural, so word spreads with ominous speed about practically anything. Worrying, in a way. I should have heard of the prim bloke, if only by osmosis. So he wasn't staying in the village.

A sudden afterthought. I opened the door and limped round the side of the surgery extension (it's stuck on to Doc's house). No bike, no car. Aha. So he'd walked. Surely he couldn't have been dropped off by that gorgeous blonde bird just leaving as I'd arrived?

'On yon gloomy tower,' I sang from welling boredom, doing the *Miserere* bit in a deep voice accompaniment. The tannoy crackled, Doc Lancaster.

'Lovejoy? Is that you making that infernal row? I can't hear a bloody thing in here. Shut him up, Nurse Baker.' Over and out.

'This is your captain speaking,' I murmured, doing the flinty pilot's bit, but Anna sortied forth to ballock me in whispers.

'Lovejoy. You've been nothing but trouble ever since you came,' et medical cetera.

'Who looks after your patients' infants when I'm not here?' I shot back, stung, but she'd already swept out. Bloody cheek.

Thirty-five minutes Mr Helpful had been incarcerated. Odderer and queerer. I've only been to Doc Lancaster's three times and it's been haul in, submit, then be fired out. I began a finger-snapping, tongue-clicking accompaniment to that Lloyd Webber song about Sunday, humming gently in case medical marauders sallied out to exterminate Art. I'd have read one of Doc's magazines, but they're all nipple hygiene and tooth decay. Village doctors hooked on health are really disheartening. Doc tries to get me running to Bullock Wood and back, the maniac.

'Don't write a letter,' I sang, tapping, clicking.

'*Lovejoy!*' thundered the tannoy. I jumped a mile. See what I mean? Doc was probably only trying to listen down some tube or other, and lets himself get ratty like that. He's always been a bad-tempered swine. More yawnsome silence. You'd think they'd have a radio or a telly.

Then I noticed the bloke's bowler on his chair. Clue. Might there be a clue in that bowler?

A quick wrestle with conscience over the interpretation of Rule Two, and I was across the room investigating the hat.

Inside the leather band was a little bump. Only natural to put a fingernail down and lift the margin. Mere inquisitiveness, honestly not wanting to nick anything. A piece of ultramarine lapis lazuli lay within. And I recognized it.

Shaken, I returned and sat. I'd won the People Game hands down, or so I thought. Q: What would she do next? A: The she in question was his wife. And she would go and sleep in passionate ecstasy with Parson Brown. Mrs Shrouder, wife of Sam Shrouder the antiques expert. Now I knew who he was, I knew practically everything else as well.

Get set, go. Into antiques and women. And that other stuff.

Chapter 2

Sam Shrouder emerged after another forty minutes, slightly flushed. I watched him, fascinated. I did no more than give him a smile, because Sam Shrouder's been deaf as a post since birth. Nurse Anna, waggling provocatively, showed him out, then beckoned me in. Doc gave me his usual poisonous welcome. His grin narks me.

'Lovejoy, you're the noisiest patient on earth. How about I transfer you to Dr West at Ipswich? I've always disliked him.'

'Doc, I've been waiting five hours—'

'One, Doctor,' our favourite nurse said.

'One's nearly five.' I was all ice as I held out my leg. 'Hope you're as thorough with me as you were with old woodentop.'

'Who?' Doc Lancaster's innocence didn't fool me. He's obsessional about confidentiality. Anna angrily gestured me to the couch.

'I mean that other bloke.' Worth a try. If Sam Shrouder was seriously ill the antiques game round here would suffer.

'Bloke, Lovejoy? You're imagining things. You're my first case today. Trousers off.'

Nurse Anna drew the curtains, swish swish.

'Undress? It's only my foot.'

'Still down there at the end of your leg, is it?'

'Very funny.' I shoved Anna outside the curtain and undid my belt. I could hear her tutting. Well, it's all right for women, but a naked man looks stupid. Lamely I scrambled on the couch and dragged the blanket over.

'Ready.'

'Oh, for heaven's *sake*!' She came in, flicked the blanket away and ripped my sock off. My squeal of pain made Doc chuckle. A right haven of concern and care.

'I'll bloody report you both to the Minister of Health.'

'Please do, Lovejoy.' Lancaster came and stood as Anna removed the surgical dressing. 'Get me the sack, then I can go sailing.' Encouragingly he slapped my leg. 'Time those stitches came out, Nurse.' He went to wash his hands, whistling.

'She's too rough,' I said nastily. 'You do it, Doc.'

'Wouldn't criticize too much, Lovejoy. You're on the pointed ends. She's got scalpels, toothed forceps, dissecting scissors, needles—'

He kept chuckling. Oh, the medical merriment. I watched apprehensively as Anna started clashing instruments out of the sterilizer on to a trolley. The tong things she used to lift are enough to frighten you to death. I'm sure they only make them shiny to put the fear of God up us.

'It won't hurt, will it?' I asked, really casual.

'It's gruesome,' Lancaster said, scribbling happily. 'Wouldn't watch if I were you.'

She came like a white bat and gave me the whole bit, the towels, the sterile wash that stings you into a coma, the compound lights.

'How did you do it, Lovejoy?' Lancaster was asking, puzzled, as I wondered if ether was an aphrodisiac.

Anna's curved haunch was so near as she worked. No consideration. 'Drop a lead pig on it, I mean.'

'That's right – sssss!' Anna had struck.

'Keep still, Lovejoy,' she commanded. Why is it nurses think they have a right to get annoyed, when I was doing all the bloody suffering?

'A pig is a piece of cast bar metal, you daft—' I halted, and smiled weakly. Nurse Anna had paused warningly, turned slitted eyes on me. She loves Doc, which is unfair, especially to me.

'But why would the world's scroungiest antique dealer be working with lead, Lovejoy?'

'To, er, mend things.'

Anna's instruments clashed and snipped. I tried to keep a smile in my voice. As soon as I was free I'd clout her.

'What things, Lovejoy?' from Doc, the pest.

'Ask old Sam Shrouder!' I shot out in pain as something pulled a long agony from my foot.

'Who?'

Give up. I just lay and groaned, trying not to watch the reflection of my poor mangled foot in the massive round lights staring down at me with their hot gaze. Anna finished the dressing and angrily said that she'd told me twenty-seven times to keep still.

'Like a child,' she blazed, furious. 'You're the worst patient we have.'

'Shut your teeth,' I said, limping upright.

'Here's your clearance chit, Lovejoy.' Doc gave me a paper. 'Off you go. Do it to the other foot.'

Sympathy? Typical. Still, my alibi was established. I left, limping ostentatiously to show a high degree of infirmity. I remembered my walking stick.

Ten minutes later, rattling towards town in my Ruby at

a smart nineteen m.p.h. I thought about Sam Shrouder. In spite of his fame, I'd never before clapped eyes on him. What I'd seen intrigued me. Fakes, you see, in a way are an emulation of love, which is what life's about, and Sam Shrouder is the greatest faker of antique jewellery, furniture, porcelain, and practically everything else, in East Anglia. East Anglia includes me, so you can judge my concern.

His missus is reputed to visit Parson Brown (tell you about him in a minute) most days for purposes of, er, indoor recreation, while husband Sam slogs hard at his trade. The Shrouders live away beyond Melford but visitors are discouraged. Now, why was he on Doc Lancaster's list, miles from home? Slowly I trundled into the car park, thinking. That was when this uniformed bobby climbed in beside me and directed me to the police station.

'Knock it off, George,' I said wearily. 'Can't you see I'm a cripple?'

'Suspicion of shoplifting, Lovejoy. Or whatever.'

'A policeman? And you'd lie?'

He laughed as we entered Crouch Street. 'You're a card, Lovejoy, straight up.'

That cooled me. I hate hearing the Old Bill laugh, especially when I don't know enough of the joke to join in.

'You antique dealers are pestilential, Lovejoy,' Ledger said in the cop shop. I was barely over the threshold before he'd started moaning.

'And good day to you, Ledger,' I said. They loathe cheerfulness, so I grinned like an ape. 'That it? Can I go now?'

George shut the door behind him. Ledger isn't normally that careful. No policewoman taking every word down, either. This called for caution. I stopped smiling and looked obedient.

'Ben Clayton's in town, Lovejoy,' Ledger said. Pause.

'Really?' I said, polite but scared. I vowed to throttle Tinker, my drunken old barker. He's supposed to sniff out news of other antique dealers and their wares, and preferably let me know before every peeler in East Anglia hears. He'd be sloshed at the Three Cups, on his tenth pint by now. 'Ben Clayton? Staying long, is he?'

'Lovejoy.' Ledger rose, paced. He hadn't invited me to sit, so I stood like a rabbit before a stoat's hypnotic dance. 'Just listen, lad. You're the slyest, most pathetic nerk in East Anglia. You live off women, conning anybody dumb enough.' It was hard, but I let him rant on unopposed. 'About this old town of ours, Lovejoy. Lots of people, all decent subjects of our sovereign Monarch, believe it's *their* responsibility – the mayor, councillors, the town guilds. But.'

His silence was a prompt. 'They're wrong?' I offered helpfully.

'Correct, Lovejoy. This town's down to me.'

'I've nowt to do with Ben Clayton, Ledger.'

He stopped. 'Possibly true. But what about the helper he's got with him?'

Now I really would kill Tinker, drunken old sod. Ben Clayton's the ultimate in gormlessness, but he owns a psychopathic aide called Seg, whose knack with aggro can be very, very ugly. I once saw Seg do over three husky football fans in Tottenham, fists and feet. Ben Clayton prides himself on arranging scams in antiques. Word was that the Saxmundham robbery, Continental porcelains, was one of his, and the Warwickshire oil paintings, plus lesser goings-on. Seven scams in a twelvemonth. Wherever Ben Clayton took Seg, mayhem was sure to follow.

'Helper?' I bleated, sweating now, suddenly remembering.

'At last, Lovejoy. You've remembered the Russian Exhibition. Me too, lad.'

'Moyes Hall.' It's a delectable building in St Edmundsbury's Buttermarket, famous for its pristine survival for nigh on a millennium and its marvellous collection of antique clocks. Starting yesterday, it was hosting an exhibition of Russian antiques designed to illuminate darkest East Anglia. I was dying to see it, preferably when Ben Clayton wasn't lurking nearby – I'd get blamed if half of everything mysteriously vanished, that's why.

He tapped my chest. 'Right, Lovejoy. I appoint you suspect Number One, as of now. Any sparrow falls in the Eastern Hundreds and I'll have you, no matter what the evidence.'

I swallowed. He's a nasty, even for his ilk, but I'd never seen him quite so edgy. He'd got wind of something. Clearly he was scraping the barrel by having George the Plod snaffle me. I scented money and greed, and instantly cheered up. Alone, those two factors are pests; together they spelled antiques.

'What're you grinning at, Lovejoy?'

'Nothing, Ledger. Honest. Just had, er, my teeth done.'

'Anything happens, Lovejoy. Remember.'

'Right, Ledger.' I left, nodding to Ernie on the desk.

Now for the tavern, to strangle my one and only employee. In a law-abiding manner, of course, seeing I was under police surveillance. I'm honestly fair about most things, whatever Ledger says.

Chapter 3

Remember the Great Imperial Egg Fiasco at Christie's? It became Great because it was initially simple and finished up unbelievably complicated. And all because of a little thing called money. It's an innocent tale, and tells all that anybody needs to know about the wicked world of antiques.

Once upon a time in Imperial Russia, Carl Fabergé, jeweller of the day, worked happily. (You can tell this is history, modernity being ramjampacked with equality, so everybody shares nothing but dross.) Came 1885, and the Tsars got good old Carl to make jewelled eggs. Just that; birthday presents. Each was individual. Also, each one opened to show a figurine, a coach, even a scene – all in dazzling jewels. Carl made them until the 1917 Revolution. He did a mere 57 of these brilliant Tsarine ova, which isn't many, plus some ordinary cheaper enamelled jobs for well-heeled kulaks. You can guess how keenly antique dealers (and, yes, even thieves) drool at these rare valuable Imperial eggs.

And collectors.

Cut to 1977. Enter a millionaire, delighted to hear that Christie's at Geneva is auctioning a Fabergé egg! And what's more, it's none other than the very one Tsarina Alexandra gave to her husband Nicholas II, Tsar of All The Russias, as celebration of the three hundredth anniversary of the Romanovs. The Imperialist jewel of all time! Ecstasy!

Well, you can imagine.

Come auction day, the bidding soared. A delighted millionaire wins it, flies in to collect The Egg. He almost faints with horror when he sees it for, he says, it's junk, a fake, a bad egg, worse. Came the inevitable lawsuit, the arguing, the tabletop glares, the Expert Testimony. Finally the millionaire has to pay up. Sighing, he does and collects a Romanov jewelled egg.

Another leap and it's 1985, and now the millionaire decides to sell. Where else but at That Famous Auctioneer's of Manhattan, where all the best jewels go? And here comes the crunch, because immediately all hell's let loose. *They now refuse to sell The Egg.* And why? Because Expert Testimony says it's not The Egg they previously thought. It's not a rare Imperial egg after all.

Asks the baffled owner, How can this be? Genuine in 1977, duff in 1985? *The same antique?* The same Expert Testimony? Sure, says any auctioneer, cool as a cucumber, why not? We can change our minds, for heaven's sake. The lawsuits look likely to run into the twenty-third century. A fiasco, no?

The lesson is that the buyer – you, me – must suspect the worst. Once you buy, expect no sympathy and precious little apology. You're alone with your antique – fake, genuine, copy, repro, look-alike, whatever. It's yours and good luck. This is the world I live in, my normal scene of risk. Now read on.

The pub was almost crowded. Pretty Helen Maybanks was in, long of leg and wearing an ultramarine woolly. It reminded me of Sam Shrouder, which reminded me of Helen and Sam. I limped over, flopped groaning on a neighbouring bar stool. She offered me a drink. I accepted. Smilingly she scribbled air over everybody's head at Ted the barman. He nodded in compliance. That really narks me. I have to shout even to be ignored.

'Seen Lydia, Helen?' Lydia's my apprentice, prim, pure and palpable. She's always got some do-gooding scheme on the go.

'No. Should I have?'

'If you see her, I want her.' I planned my tactics. 'Who re-did you that oil painting, love?'

'Last autumn.' She lifted her chin, deerlike, plumed cigarette smoke at the low-hanging lamp. 'Sam Shrouder.' She held my gaze, not difficult for a bird like her. 'Even you admired it, remember? Botticelli copy.'

'So I did. Did he use true ultramarine?'

'Mmmh. Cost the earth.' She spoke with anguish. 'Sam's an artist. But if you want work done, Lovejoy, you're too late.'

'Eh?'

'He's gravely ill, maybe even passing away. Hasn't taken a single nod for ages.' A nod in the antiques game is an acceptance to do restoration work. This includes forgery, repairs, copying – anything a craftsman can get up to.

'Hell fire,' I exclaimed, wondering what on earth was going on. As well I might. I'd just seen him looking fit as a flea. 'I only want a piece of jewellery copied. Nothing much.'

Her eyes ignited with the brilliance greed brings. Casually she reached for my hand. 'At Sam's prices, Lovejoy? Your piece must be a dazzler.'

'No, honestly.' Denials always confirm a woman's suspicions, so I gave her a few sincere ones. 'Pity, though. I hadn't heard he was sick. What's he like, love?'

'Physically?' Helen described the bloke in Doc Lancaster's surgery to a T, and added, 'But reclusive. I've only met him once, and that was accidental, years ago.'

'Wasn't he a friend of Parson Brown?'

She looked evenly at me through smoke-wrinkled fug. 'So they say. A complicated arrangement through Mrs Shrouder, to coin a phrase.' Her gaze swirled past me. 'Speak of the devil.'

Casually I glanced at all available mirrors, and there Parson Brown was: lanky, poplin tie, monogrammed buttons, leather elbows and cuffs to his salt-and-pepper tweed. Pipe clenched in firm white teeth. He chortled as he came, some joke with cronies. I caught his glance bouncing between mirrors while he ordered at the bar and decided to ask Helen more questions later in a quieter place. Lydia shyly arrived, breathily twinset and pearls, matching handbag. She always looks at the floor in pubs. Beats me how she sees where I am.

'Good morning, Lovejoy,' she said. 'Good morning Helen.'

''Morning Lydia. See you later, Lovejoy.' Helen drifted knowingly.

'How is your poor foot, Lovejoy?'

'Very sore.' I raised my voice for the world's witnesses. 'Lucky the car's back on the road.'

'You poor thing.' She sat, all sympathy.

Strike while the iron's hot. 'Pain makes you thirsty, love.'

'Oh. I'm so sorry. Do they do coffees here?'

'No, love.' She's like this, eternally astonished at life's methods.

Tinker shuffled over, grubby, whiskery, bubbling with every breath. He's a drunken old wreck, but barkers don't come any better. 'A posh fat geezer's asking after you, Lovejoy. Saloon.'

'Oh, aye. Soon as I'm fit I'll throttle you, Tinker. You didn't warn me. Ben Clayton and Seg.'

'Sorry, Lovejoy. Bad 'flu this morning.'

A hangover by any other name. 'That Aigina necklace, Tinker. Did we get it?' I'd sent him to the local auction, more in hopes than anything else.

'Nar, mate.' He coughed, a long gurgling riff which shuddered the walls and silenced marsh ducks for miles down the estuaries. He takes a minute to recover, clinging to the bar rail. I don't know how, but he never spills a drop. 'Went for a frigging fortune.'

I groaned as Lydia returned. She'd brought Tinker another pint. 'Are you in pain, Lovejoy?'

'Not much, love.' I was so noble, but I was sorrowing for the lost antique. The ancient Minoan civilization left jewellery which doesn't look much at a distance. But put it on a woman and it is beyond words. The Aigina Treasure was a rich Cretan harvest, say 1700 years BC with a spread either side, of these triple layer cornelian and amethyst bead necklaces. They're 'fellow-strung', as we say in antiques, meaning the cornelians on one string align with the cornelians on the other in shape – beads, tubelets – colour and size. Lovely, but illegal to export from Crete's archaeological sites, ha ha.

'Helen got it, Lovejoy. Thought she'd've said.'

I caught Helen's eye. Sweetly the cow raised her glass, smiling, guessing Tinker was reporting in. She was talking to Parson Brown – and telling him what? Someone interposed.

'Howdy, pardners!' And there he was. Doom, squared.

Some people have a terrific impact, don't they. Put this bloke down on paper and he sounds humdrum – stout, breathless, wheezily hot, too many clothes. In fact he behaved like a slammer, vigorous, a human dynamo.

'Hello, friends. Ray Meese, to youse!' He patted us all and descended, calling loudly for service. 'What's your pleasure, men?' We were troops resting by some road and here came the officer with orders for the platoon of me, Lydia, Tinker.

'Pint, guv,' from Tinker.

Not me, ta,' I said.

'No, thank you kindly,' from Lydia.

'Same again, Ted,' Meese yelled, and would you believe, Ted served him?

A babblemouth if I ever saw one. He beamed, fat and florid, through these thick hornrimmed specs. 'You're Lovejoy. Am I right or am I right?' I was to learn he only gave the world the two choices. I said nothing, already knowing who I was.

'Ta, guv,' Tinker yelped, draining his ale and giving his gummy grin as Ted fetched drinks from behind the bar. I stared. East Anglian barmen simply do not emerge, not ever. I didn't even know Ted had legs. He avoided my eye, deposited glasses and a bottle of plonk, some foreign label crammed with a gothic coat-of-arms. Unbelievable.

'Lovejoy's the only divvy we got,' Tinker gravelled out, wiping his mouth. His mitten still had his breakfast sauce. I gave him the bent eye to shut up.

'Ray Meese, six movie awards, Lake Bayon Enterprises. President, producer, director, financier.'

'Wotcher, guv.'

This was getting out of hand. 'Shut it, Tinker.'

'Ted,' Meese called, pointing a finger imperiously. Tinker shambled off to the bar to swill more free ale. Loyalty, like morality, often ends peed against some alley wall.

'You and me, Lovejoy, are in business.' His pudgy hand pressed my arm. The ring was Roman, genuine, on a glittering modern gold carrier ring. I felt my chest go bong. Either he was a true caring collector, or he'd done his homework.

'Are we?' I said, cold.

Lydia edged closer at the sound of my voice.

'Friend, you're joining the movies!' He fell about laughing with great vertical shakes. He poured wine into three glasses, raised his in sudden solemnity. 'To Lovejoy. May he prosper. May he attain his pinnacle—'

'No, ta,' I said, as opener. Lydia stirred.

'A mere no?' Meese kept his beam, hands outspread. 'A mere denial?' He switched to soulful. 'Lovejoy. Your average fee's a pittance. These inferior antique dealers take advantage of you. They need you, but don't pay. Why, with your special divvying skill you should be exalted in the Sunday supplements, featured in a drossy glossy—'

'Lovejoy is highly thought of, Mr Meese,' Lydia cut in sharply.

'Certainly, my dear.' His voice sank, its timbre phoney episcopalian, suggestive. Was he about to ask if he could finger her pretty necklace? 'Let me add to that. He deserves – you deserve, with him, dear – reward for talent. Examine him: a divvy, with your superb support. Doesn't it merit a proper financial reward?'

'Well, of course,' Lydia said. 'It's only fair.'

'Not fair, my dear.' His face throbbed with emotion. 'We want – did I say want? *Demand* – due recognition. For genius.' His voice caught. 'For beautiful, truly, genius.'

For Christ's sake, I thought. I'd never ever seen anything as phoney as Ray Meese. I'm a born fraud so I should know. But when a gold, possibly new, carrier ring dazzles as much as his, it's the handiwork of Miracle in Coggeshall. Yet the bloke was a stranger. How come?

Meese leaned closer, misty of eye. 'Lovejoy – and I'll

only die if you refuse – please be advisorial consultant in antiques, for my new movie. It's going to be the greatest movie ever made! Is this Ray Meese begging? Indeed, indeed!'

'I know nowt about cinema.'

'But movies need you. Simply be available, on the phone, six weeks.'

I was still worried about advisorial. And did people actually call films movies?

'You want money talk? I got money talk, Lovejoy.' He never stopped beaming, glistening on overheat, gushing sincerity. 'A year's salary for your advice.' He almost sobbed. 'Stay home, with your magnificent lady. Live. Love. But help, contribute. Give my movie your guidance – nay, friendship. Nay again – your love.'

'When?' I was wary. For all I knew they might all be like him.

His podgy hand with its Roman ring squeezed my arm. 'When? You decide, Lovejoy.' He raised a hand, snapped his fingers. His eyes were still radiating soul as a tall bossy girl appeared – I really do mean appeared – in an instant. She gave him a paper from a folder. I felt Lydia stir, but it didn't signify. Women always sense coming wars.

'Statement of Intent, Lovejoy.' Meese pointed to sparse clauses. 'Agree. And let me rejoice. It means – heartbreak time if it ever came to it – you can change your mind.' He raised liquid eyes to the girl. 'Lorane. Will there be a way to live beyond the pain if Lovejoy spurns Lake Bayon Enterprises?'

'We shall have to, Mr Meese,' she said.

'But at what cost?'

'All right,' I said, in case heavenly violins started and made us all fill up.

'He's accepted!' The nerk really did announce it.

Everybody in the pub looked round. 'I can live!' He wrung my hand, beaming. 'We'll phone. It will be soon, dear friend. Soon.'

'The limousine awaits, Mr Meese,' the girl said. Honestly.

'Very well, Lorane.' He straightened, eyes straight ahead, simply walked out, to a scaffold at the very least. I expected him to say that This Is A Far Better Thing bit.

His bird chucked an envelope on to the table. 'Cards, Lovejoy. Agreement. Addresses. Start dates.'

'Ah, look, love,' I said quickly. 'My case comes up tomorrow.'

'Case?'

'An unfortunate misunderstanding, love. Nothing dire—'

'Just follow the schedule, Lovejoy,' she said coldly, not heeding. She flung money at Ted and strolled. Women never listen to a word I say.

Lydia was subdued. 'I'm very proud, Lovejoy. In films!' See? Not movies. 'Yet I'm somewhat disturbed.'

'That pal of yours has a frigging Rolls.' Martin, a young antique tableware dealer new to the trade, paused to speak in awe. 'What's he collect? Tell him I've a lovely Woodward claret jug, 1875, six hundred. I'd chop commission, Lovejoy.'

News to me. I gave Tinker a glance of pure fury. He looked sheepish, as well he might. He'd told me less than a day ago Martin had nothing. Claret jugs – wine wasn't always mystique with bottles to impress the ladies – have grown in price steadier than almost any antique and are still underpriced. Horace Woodward made the best cut glass silver-mounted pieces in Birmingham in the 1870s. The whole world's chasing them. Knowing Martin, it would be mint. At that price it was a gift.

'He's something in films,' I said to make him go away, then gave Lydia my attention. 'Look after things if I'm not back from Hereford, er, soon. OK?'

Her lips went punitively thin. 'What you did there was highly irresponsible, Lovejoy. You must stand trial. Society deserves an explanation.'

I sighed. They've got paid magistrates to ballock me. I could do without freebies from my apprentice. 'I'll go. I'll go. If I'm found guilty, I'll meet you in Coggeshall about four tomorrow afternoon.' Miracle lives at Coggeshall. I could find out about that newly mounted Roman ring.

'And if not, Lovejoy?'

'Optimist.'

The lads watched Lydia pass, jeering at my limp. As soon as the taproom door swung to behind us the hubbub returned louder than before.

Chapter 4

Hereford's nattily neat, and pretty famous for not being famous, if you follow. I thought this pseudo-deep thought while waiting to go on trial before their magistrates. Hereford makes even your thinking antique.

Nell (really Eleanor) Gwynne was born in Hereford's Pipe Lane. The great barefister Tom 'Spring' Winter came from hereabouts, I recalled; he became champion in 1824 by finishing John Langan in seventy-seven rounds. I'd originally paused in Hereford to see the country's largest chained parish library. It's in the church of All Saints in Eign Gate. I honestly wasn't interested solely because I'd heard its security was duff and would be easy for some criminally minded antique dealer to knock off. No, honestly. I'd honestly dropped in to admire it. And the huge gothic Mappa Mundi, which the cathedral wants to sell to fatten its priests. And David Garrick was baptized there—

'Call Lovejoy.'

My stomach sank. The crunch. A bobby shook his head for me to leave my bag. I'd brought my few spare clothes in case justice was as crooked as ever and unfairly condemned me to prison. I stood for the preliminaries while a few bored spectators, presumably sheltering from the rain, cleared throats and shared cough sweets.

'Er, one thing, ma'am,' I interrupted. The boss magistrate shuffled her papers and glared through bifocals. She looked fresh from some tiger hunt. 'Could I have my train fare back? Only the early express is so expensive—'

'What is he asking?' she boomed to her aides, geriatric colonels along for the flogging.

'Fare money.'

'No,' she intoned, read impatiently, looked down at me from her exalted desk before the royal coat-of-arms. '*What's* this charge?'

'Burying a Crusader, m'lord,' I explained. 'Er, m'lady.'

'Breaking and entering, and wilful damage,' a clerk corrected.

'That's not true, Your Honour,' I put in, narked. 'I repaired it.'

She shut us up and had the charge read and expounded. This led to considerable silence. I tried to look honest and indignant while she scrutinized me. Twice she had a go at a sentence, dried up. I smiled encouragement. The two coppers who'd nabbed me frowned on the benches.

'Let me get this straight, Lovejoy,' she managed eventually. 'On the date in question, you broke into the Museum of the Knights of Saint John in Widemarsh Street?'

'Entered by the front door, Your Worship, doing no damage—'

'Quiet, Lovejoy. And then you buried . . . ?' She laid the papers aside. 'Tell the court in your own words.'

'There's this Crusader, some old Knight.' My anger grew as I told her how he'd been laid out under glass paving. 'He's like a tomato in a greenhouse, spotlighted starkers. Visitors walk over him, poor old sod – er, soldier.'

'I don't understand how the museum's displaying an ancient Knight's skeleton concerns you, Lovejoy.'

'It concerns Hereford,' I shot back, nasty. 'I painted the

glass black. Filled in the grave with soil from outside. Disconnected the floodlights.' I went all modest, because for once I'd done a really nifty job. It had nearly killed me, not being the world's best handyman, but you could have eaten your dinner off the museum floor when I'd cleared up. 'It's as it should be. Then I fell asleep.'

'Where?'

'On a bench in the rose garden outside. I was knack—er, fatigued, m'ladyship.'

'What did you steal?'

'Nowt!' I said indignantly. That's a bird for you, jumping to conclusions.

'Lovejoy.' She leaned over the high desk. 'Why did you *do* this? With your appalling record of antiques robberies, arrests—'

'Here, missus. You watch your tongue. I'll have the law . . .' I adjusted lamely as she glared, 'Er, police records are unreliable. But if you want to know, it's a bloody disgrace.' The magistracy's silence was a sure invitation, I guessed, and surged on. 'Civilization's vanished. It's kaput, gone. The nearest we get to it these days is fishing up bits of galleons wrecked on Goodwin Sands so we can flog the crud to the highest bidder. Everything's for sale. Love's dwindled to drunken snogging with strangers and one-night stands. Compassion's history. The family's a vestige. So what do we do? We rob graves and call it archaeology. And pop some poor old bugger's skeleton into the limelight to gawp at, for pennies. When that old geezer's probably the last human being we'll ever clap eyes on who had principles, honest convictions he died for. And we make him a peep-show. It's pathetic. So I buried him.'

Silence.

'Well,' I said defensively. 'It's a disgrace, Your, er, Honour.'

'He means it!' the lady said to her team, astonished.

They prattled among themselves, occasionally pausing for odd bits of evidence, a curator, electricians, somebody from Hereford Council. There was a brief flurry when I was made to admit that I'd stuck a notice saying PLAGUE! KEEP OFF! on the grave to discourage resurrectors. A doctor said I was deplorably sane, as if doctors know the difference. A copper said I'd not resisted arrest. He made it sound like capturing King Kong. In fact he'd had a hell of a time waking me up.

They sympathized with the Knight's predicament, approved of my compassionate attitude, and awarded me a massive fine, plus two months in gaol. Well, the only time Christ went to law they gave the verdict to a mob, right? As I was led out a pretty tawny-haired lass in the public benches gave me a tilted hard-luck-that's-life smile in which rue and regret mingled. Odd, because I'd never seen her before. Twenty to seven I was sprung by two suited lawyers bent on appeal at some date unspecified. Bail equal to the National Debt had been arranged. I tried telling them there was some mistake, I had no money, no prospects, was told to shut up and taken to the cop shop. From there the lawyers phoned a Miss Lorane in London and reported they'd followed instructions to the letter and good evening. They left without a glance. I waited alone. Zilch.

'Er, mate,' I said eventually to the bobby nodding at the desk. 'What happens now?'

He looked up, sniggered. 'You get out of town, Lovejoy.'

I sighed at the mysterious ways of Justice, got my bag and plodded out into the drizzle heading for the trunk road. With luck I'd cadge a lift on some lorry at an all-night caff. I honestly never know what the world's up to these days.

* * *

By three next afternoon I was waiting under Coggeshall's clock tower. The postcardy little place still has a free car park. My Ruby was in it, so Lydia was around somewhere. You cut through the ginnel to see a dozen antique shops, the tea-house, and Miracle's shop across the road. Ledger was waiting. My limp worsened instantly.

'Hello, Lovejoy. Who's bailing crooks out free these days?'

'Wotcher, Ledger. Lost, are you? Turn right on the A604—'

'Shut it, Lovejoy. A robbery, night before last. Lavenham. Can you account for your movements?'

'Oh, sure.' I limped a pace, leaning on my stick. 'I got this microlite, parachuted down and—'

'Gold hunter watch and its watch stand. Pair of silver figure salts. A small Portuguese ivory votive carving. A Russian ikon, approximately twelve by eight inches, dated 1804.' His notebook went flap in the silence. 'You look astonished, Lovejoy.'

'Well, who wouldn't be?' I'd only nicked the two silvers. What was going on?

'You can still drive, I see.' Ledger kept his eyes on me.

'Oh, that the theory is it? I drove my noisy old Ruby in great secrecy through the sleepy Suffolk night . . . ?'

'Sir? This was in his motor.' A constable handed Ledger Ray Meese's manila envelope. I'd cast it unopened into the car as we'd left the tavern. It seemed months ago.

'Here, Royal Mail's private.'

The bobby was smirking. Ledger slit it open. He showed the envelope. 'It's not stamped. It just says: British Museum Robbery.'

'It's a film,' I said. 'They hired me.'

Two Coggeshall drifters paused to gape. Ledger scanned the enclosed paper, reluctantly returned it. 'I'll check, Lovejoy.'

'Please do.' I limped off into the tea-shop to get away from the blighter. Lydia found me there as I ordered and said what had gone on. Best not to call on Miracle until the Old Bill had scarpered. We had crumpets, then small Battenbergs. I had hers because I quite like cake, on the rare occasions it comes within reach. Anyway, women are always slimming. They think it's good for them.

Half an hour later, Miracle told me he'd mounted a plain Roman ring on to a gold carrier ring. Three days ago, would you believe.

'I made a miracle, Lovejoy.' Everything Miracle does is a miracle, hence his name.

'I saw it, Miracle. Mr Meese, ah, er, thought I should pop in and say you're terrific.'

Miracle's so bald he looks bald all over, if you follow. He's close on eighty. His daughter only lets him work for two hours in the afternoon. He secretly teaches his great-grandchild about goldworking tools so skill can escape.

'Thanks, Lovejoy. Parson said the same.'

I paused on the way out. 'Any old parson, or Parson Brown?'

'Brown. It was his Roman ring, see? The fat chap bought it.'

'You sure?'

'Parson got it from Steve Sanders, a local lad who'd shown it me a week since. Steve . . . found it one night.'

'Oh. Right. Still, nice work, Miracle. Cheers.'

Hereabouts there's plenty of finds, especially now everyone seems to have electronic metal-detectors. They go about the fields in droves. We were once a massive Roman colony, the first-ever in the Kingdom. But Parson Brown was connected to Sam Shrouder via his wife, and now Meese knows Parson and I'd seen Sam this very morning and what was going on? There seemed to be a lot of Sam around all of a sudden, for somebody reportedly dying in health, that is.

With Lydia complaining about the cold I sat and read the envelope's message. The film was about a gang who rob the British Museum of unspecified treasures, as if that were possible. It involved gunplay. A gun hire firm was mentioned. A cheque was enclosed, my first week's consultation fee.

Meese had had it all worked out, me included, before we'd even met.

'Lovejoy, I think I should warn you,' Lydia said as I dropped her at the bus stop by the chapel. 'Miss Sandwell is of course perfectly acceptable as a colleague.' I nodded for her to race on to the all-important *but*. 'But,' she went on, polishing her specs like mad, 'on occasion, her manner encroaches on over-familiarity.'

'Do you really think so?' My frown was in place, my voice riddled with doubt. You have to humour them.

'I'm afraid I do, Lovejoy.' She replaced her glasses, assembling her handbag, gloves, swung her hair out. 'I detected quite a gleam in her eye when I arrived.' The gleam in Liz's eye had been pure murder. It had happened the previous Wednesday.

'You're marvellous, love. Rescuing me in the nick of time.' I pressed her hand fervently. 'Thank you.' In fact, once I could have strangled the silly cow. She'd almost caught us. Liz had yelped and hurtled to the bathroom while I'd dressed cursing behind the alcove curtain. We'd made respectability by a millisec.

Lydia moved her hand and went pink. 'In public, Lovejoy!' She's the Miss Prim of East Anglia, twenty-three years old, and conceals her delectable succulence under sensible clothes. Since becoming my No. 1 apprentice she's stopped wearing her hair in a bun, but that's depravity for you.

'Sorry, doowerlink,' I said. 'I forgot myself.' Strangling was nothing to what Liz will do to Lydia one of these days. 'Look. Excavate Parson Brown's dealings lately. Oh, and see if you can come up with anything by Sam Shrouder, the faker – jewels, furniture, paintings, OK?'

'Very well, Lovejoy.' She descended from the Ruby. 'And thank you for agreeing to participate in the hospice charity.'

'Eh?' I said, but she was already off. She looked delectable crossing the road, a symphony of skim milk and bran flakes. I waited until the bus hove in view, then blew her a kiss. She reddened, stared firmly at the approaching vehicle. She'd have the precise fare, no change necessary, and would ballock the driver for being two minutes late. I sighed and coaxed the engine into its usual wheeze. I ask you. Why does a beautiful young bird, shapely as they come, wish to pretend she's dowdy and twice her age? I shelved the problem. I had others.

Nurse Anna Baker hadn't been on the bus, so good old slave-driver Doc Lancaster had kept her at it. She lives at posh Frinton, two bus rides and change at the town station, so she'd be glad of a lift. By a fluke I was driving past, third time, as she emerged from the surgery and flagged me down.

'Oh, Lovejoy!' She affects these high heels and has to run with her knees impossibly together like most do. 'Be a pet. Give me a lift to town. I've missed the bus.'

'Thousands wouldn't,' I grumbled, letting her in. 'You were bloody rude to me this morning about old Sam Shrouder.'

'Mr Shrouder's not old, Lovejoy. And I was perfectly polite . . .'

Bingo. I did so well winkling information out of her that I carried on and drove her all the way home. We chatted. Her bloke's a jealous axe-wielding forester who keeps regular hours, so I meekly waved her indoors and drove off, a picture of chastity.

Penfold's auction house at Earls Colne has late-night viewing on Thursdays, so naturally I was there in good time to irritate Penfold by 'shading' – this means going about muttering that everything is rubbish. All antique dealers do it by reflex, so don't be put off if you hear them snigger as you pause to admire a chaste Wedgwood jasper jug you particularly want. They try to dissuade all genuine buyers, not being used to honesty. I got a true auctioneer's welcome.

'Nothing here for the likes of you, Lovejoy.'

'True, Pennie, true. It's all gunge.'

He did his frosty reproof. Folk say he was quite a womanizer in his day. Now he's a crusty middle-age widower with a row of pens in his waistcoat and a white moustache. His belly's chained to a watch which has to be inspected every few minutes, checking when to put you in your place.

'Then why are you here, Lovejoy?' His specky gaze took in my attire, contempt.

Smouldering silently, I drifted. Nerk-confounding quips have never been my particular strength, but one day I really will think up some and shatter smugness everywhere.

There were not many in, for a fair evening. Doris was, a brittle grey grandma with castanet teeth and a crocodile handbag full of IOUs. She's been hunting that genuine stray Rembrandt for forty years. (I keep telling her to steal the Dulwich Gallery's Rembrandt instead. Why not? Everybody else has.) She gave me an impish grin with her pot teeth and waved. I like Doris, and not only because her lovely daughter Elsa is a scrupulous pay-on-the-nail blonde antique dealer in childhood ephemera, dolls' houses, toys and the like. Chris Masterson, arguing with Margaret Dainty, shouted over – silver hammered coins, Saxon to Charles I, are his sole reason for living. I waved absently and slid quickly among the heavy furniture because I still owed him for some Northumbrian skeats. I'd sold the tiny bronze coins for food, the height of criminal self-indulgence. The woman I was seeking, *pro tem*, was in, to my delight. Suki Lonegan, Parson Brown's partner, hadn't seen me and strolled off among the paintings. This means of course she really had glimpsed me but, womanlike, was too clever to let me notice. Triumph made me careless, and I got caught by Margaret and Tinker simultaneously. The former's a dear lame friend, older and wiser than most.

'Lovejoy,' Tinker began, gallantly ignoring the fact that Margaret had come up and smilingly taken my arm to speak. 'That big brown pot cost us a frigging fortune. Wasn't worth it.'

'Where is it?' All barkers pong of armpit. Tinker's worse, living as he does in a shed by St Peter's churchyard.

'Left it in Gimbert's. You pay the deposit tomorrow.'

This was becoming one of those days. 'Lend us a fiver, Margaret, love.'

'Answer me one question, Lovejoy.'

I passed the note across to Tinker. 'I need a Victorian lace bertha and a pair of framed embroidery samplers by ten tonight, so get going. Oh,' I added quietly as he shuffled off, 'and suss out Parson Brown and Sam Shrouder.'

He paused, cackling. 'You after shagging his bird too, Lovejoy? It'll be like Piccadilly Circus in yon bed.'

Weakly I smiled at Margaret. 'Apologies.'

She pulled me round so I had to face her. 'Lovejoy. Focus, please.'

'I'm focused. Want a share in a water bottle?' Gimbert, a swine, would cancel the deal if I didn't have the deposit. She seemed doubtful, so I explained. 'Salt-glazed, commemorative stoneware. It's 1750, used for carrying water from the Iron Peartree in Godstone, Surrey.' I waited hopefully as doubts flickered across her face. Named bottles are currently doubling in value every year. 'London folk paid thirty pence for the three gallons; good water cured gout, see?'

'Is it genuine?' She quickly corrected herself with a headshake. 'Sorry, darling. Only, it's a risk, isn't it?'

'I've a ticket. The London Science Museum.' A ticket in antiques means a promise to buy.

'Very well. Tell Gimbert I'll stand deposit.'

'Marry me.' I clasped her to my bosom theatrically, which made her laugh – and let me peer about and see where Suki Lonegan had got to. And Chris Masterson.

'Yes,' she said unexpectedly, and laughed as I leapt away startled. 'Incidentally, isn't Sam Shrouder terminally ill? I heard so from Jessica.'

Two in favour of Sam's incipient demise, one mere eyewitness against. Jessica's a wealthy dealer who cohabits with – some say on – her son-in-law Lennie in a vast house down by the Blackwater estuary. She's as bright as Lennie's thick. They're mostly oriental porcelains and Regency stuff.

'Lovejoy.' Margaret halted me as I pulled away. Suki was showing signs of moving. Still inspecting the paintings, she'd taken her car keys from her handbag. 'Will you scan for me?'

'No.' I was off. Suki's wasp waist casually drifted towards the door.

'Remember the deposit,' Margaret called.

That stopped me. I groaned. 'All right. Tomorrow, tennish.' I hate divvying. It's a kind of psychic examination of assorted gunge. Divvies can pluck out the one hidden genuine antique, using supersensory vibes alone. I'm one of that rare and vanishing breed. If Sotheby's and Christie's had any sense they'd clone me, or build me a stud farm. I could charge a fee. Imagine! A million zlotniks for every pupped infant divvy, with a fee payable for a genuine thoroughbred certificate embossed with—

'Lovejoy. You're in a mood today.' Margaret passed a hand before my eyes so I came to. 'Mrs Lonegan's no good for you. Don't say you weren't warned.'

'Eh? Her?' I chuckled convincingly. 'No, love. You're wrong. I've, er, forgotten to tell Tinker something.'

'Lovejoy.' Chris Masterson's voice boomed, too close. 'Those Northumbrian skeats. You owe me—'

'Back in a minute, Chris,' I said, edging away at limp max. 'I'll just catch Tinker—'

Not often you are saved by a creditor. I was too late to catch Mrs Lonegan. Two or three cars were pulling away as I hopped out. I cursed. If it hadn't been for Margaret and her kindly warning . . . Bloody women. I limp-ran to crank the Ruby.

'Hello, Lovejoy.'

Mrs Lonegan was sitting in it, cool as a cucumber. She laughed at my surprise.

'Ah, oh. Hello. Want a lift?'

'Hurry up, silly. My feet are like ice. I'm freezing.'

It's a man's instinct to do as the nearest woman tells him, isn't it. They have this knack of stopping thought. For once I should have cerebrated. But I grinned oafishly at the beautiful woman, and daft as ever, hurried – towards the death of innocence. And the vanishing of her partner, Parson Brown.

Chapter 5

Point of info: All news isn't. I'm the only person on the earth who's never called a press conference. True. There's a prevailing opinion that the world is desperate to know every detail of everybody else. It's cock. The majority of everything nowadays is modern, hence worthless rubbish. So what's to know?

Yet I find even boring things are fascinating. I once had this bird – correction; she had me – who was daft on skiing. We went to this Swiss dump packed with snowy Alps, and for four days stood in a blizzard among an ululating crowd watching women ski downhill. The crowd donged little cowbells by way of applause. It was a real yawn, not an antique anywhere. But a kind of odd interest eventually seeped through: how come these birds, more or less identical sizes in sprayed-on rubber suits, went at different speeds? After all, skiing's only standing still, isn't it? The slope does it all. I asked Evadne this but she only laughed and called me hopeless, then got mad. She came third. Later she pointedly sent me a card from the Olympics. She ski-raced for Austria, or one of those yodelling countries which win all the Winter golds. I'd meant no offence. But things like this prove that it's best to ration your interest. Spend it with care, because innocent old interest can get you into hot water. Unless of course antiques are involved, and even then it's wise to be on your guard. Inevitably, I wasn't.

'I got your message, Lovejoy.'

'Scared of your mouse?' She'd seen my nervous looks as I cranked the Ruby.

'Lydia? No. She thinks I'm in my infancy. Or dotage. I don't tell her most deals until they're done.' We zoomed off.

'She's clever,' Suki said. 'Watch her, Lovejoy. Pure Little Innocence comes with claws, hooks, chains.'

Lydia, for heaven's sake? My foot was flat down. The Ruby whimpered up to fifteen m.p.h. 'Got anything?'

'Miniature porcelains, a few. And personal silvers, a couple.'

'Great. At Parson's drop?' Cunningly I brought in the name of her partner.

'No. The shop.'

'Right.' I swung up towards Sudbury. 'Been busy?'

'Not as busy as you'll be, filming with Ray Meese.'

'Oh. You know him?' See? I'm cunning.

'By repute. We're all very impressed, Lovejoy, the company you keep. Hollywood, then the world.' She sounded strangely bitter.

All right. No deep problem there. Parson could have sold Meese the Roman ring through a trillion intermediaries, anything. 'The picture's about the British Museum.'

'Did you do that robbery, Lovejoy?'

Swerve, correct. 'Eh? No. Ledger had a go at sticking it on me, but being crippled's a good alibi.'

'You sprang into the car after cranking it, Lovejoy.'

'I used the other foot,' I explained quickly. Caution, Lovejoy. Suki did that I'm-not-really-smiling gaze which meant she was inwardly finding lies among my truths.

An open Jaguar overtook us at a roar, dangerously close. I clung to the wheel as the air wake slammed the Ruby sideways. Parson Brown waved his calfskin gloves as his car dwindled ahead. Once a prat, always a prat. I didn't say so. The palpitating Ruby resumed its chug on the lonely road.

'Here, Suki. He any good?'

'Parson? Excellent on Regency furniture—'

'Not as a dealer, love. I know he's nerk at that.'

She stared out over the fields trundling past. 'As a person he's a bit . . . undecided, what he wants. Can't settle.'

Oh dear. That bad. Worse than I'd feared. Partners to the ultimate. Suki's really nice, keeps within herself. She and I made smiles one Christmas, and I have a soft for past smilers. This isn't true for birds, though. I knew this woman a year gone who—

'You've gone past, Lovejoy.'

'Eh? Oh, sorry, love. Daydreaming.'

The shop's smallfish, fronting the road with no pavement like so many in East Anglian villages. I parked at the side of Parson's liner. My Ruby looked ashamed, especially when this girl laughed at it. Lavina is Parson's daughter and was just on her way out, dolled up as only a sixteen-year-old can doll. She propositions me, sometimes; I'm holding out. She looked a blizzard at Suki, eyed me smiling.

'Out of prison again, Lovejoy?'

'Shut your teeth, you little cow. It was a misunderstanding.'

She swept past on her stilt heels, her perfume wilting trees for miles around. Suki sighed, gave me a bleak smile.

'Lavina's a problem, Lovejoy.'

'Mmmmh.' I'd heard. I honestly don't know what happens to females between sixteen and twenty-two, but it's odd that the younger batch always hates the other, and v.v.

'Mam, Lovejoy called our Lavina a cow!' a little lad bawled.

'She called me a felon, Jules,' I bawled towards the back yard, where a wooden fence encloses a patch of grass with a swing and a shed. 'Fair's fair.' Jules is six, Parson's second attempt to purify the race. The Browns live at the rear, a brick cottage. We went through. Jules was digging to Australia, his head showing as he flung soil up. I went to look. He was down to gravel and clay. Trench? Atom shelter? Maybe these littles know something we don't.

'Do come in, Lovejoy.' Winnie Brown I've never seen without her apron. She's forever wiping her hands in it. Desperation's in her like the spring in clockwork, essential and generating tension. She's late thirties. 'Walter's just gone through. Hello, Suki.'

'Hello.' Suki hurried ahead.

'Here, Winnie.' I paused. You sometimes never really see people properly until circumstances project them into relief. There's a farmer in Ardleigh, not far, who never knew of an ancient pre-Roman burial circle of the Trinovantes on his land until freak weather caused his crop to fail, whereupon a circular patch of wheat grew tall and beautiful. Passing motorists spotted it from the road and one called to ask. See? Circumstances. Winnie was mechanically returning to doing the washing and turning back to me, anxious. 'What were you?' Suki and Parson were talking in the shop.

'What was I? When?'

'Keep calm, sunshine. Before. Teacher? Typist?'

'Oh.' She gave that woman's half laugh, brushed hair

from her eyes with the back of her hand. 'You won't believe it. I was a dancer. Professional, Equity card and everything.'

'Do you do it now?'

'Of course not, silly. Where on earth would I get the time?' She was laughing, piling clothes into the machine plumbed in by the sink. Her eyes kept checking Jules.

'Hello, Lovejoy.' Parson emerged. 'Trolling for minis and silvers, eh? Sorry, but we've nothing in that line.'

'Already sold them, eh?' I shrugged, pretended a glare at Suki who was being all uncomfortable behind Parson. 'Treacherous, that's the trouble with you dealers.'

Parson laughed to show his clean, even teeth. He seemed straight off a vast country estate, pink gins at the hunt ball. 'Sorry, Lovejoy. Our turnover's picked up a trice. You're too slow. Now, an hour ago . . .'

'Aye, aye,' I said, sarky. 'Anything else I might, er . . . ?'

'No, sorry.' He was so affable. And firmly between me and the entrance to his shop. 'Sold out. Container, export order to New York. Better luck next time.'

'Woe, woe. You jammy arab. Why does it never happen to me?' I said tara to Suki, avoiding my eyes, and to Winnie smiling from her sink, and left past Jules' obsessional dig. 'Oh. Did you hear I've got a job on a film, Parson?'

'They said at the pub. Any idea what it's about?'

'Something about the British Museum.'

'Good grief, Lovejoy. You're in the money!'

'Aye. I'll expect it when I see it.'

'Sorry about the antiques, Lovejoy.' Suki came beside Parson to wave me off.

'Next week, I'll have a thirteenth-century English wooden crucifix, Lovejoy. Genuine. I'll keep it for you, eh?'

'Great, Parson. Love to see it. Cheers.'

'Up, up and away,' he joked as I cranked the Ruby into a promising clatter and limped – limped, note – into my blast-off position.

And off a-trundle towards Sudbury's squarish church tower. Well, all in all a casual, if vaguely disappointing, unimportant journey. That's what happens every day in this game. You go miles because X has promised to keep you a luscious antique, and when you get there he's sold it to Y. Tough luck and struggle on.

Except sometimes.

The drizzle began again and I had to stop to light my headlamps – I carry matches – because of a sea fog coming in. The hood doesn't quite reach all the way to its latchings, so I tie string through its holes. This all takes about twenty minutes. By the time I was back in action I was soaked and perished. Air squeezes in through every crack and orifice when the old crate's moving, so I didn't get any warmer as we clattered homewards.

It's really strange,' I told the car, for somebody to talk to. I'm not one of those who give names to objects. Whimsy's pestilential. But explaining to a void's daft, and I was alone in a wet gale. 'Suki leads me out there to see some incidental antiques. Why? Parson pretends he's no longer got them, yet I know he's not done a container shipment for weeks. And he implies he has no idea what Meese's film's about. Yet Miracle said Parson sold that Roman ring to Meese – whose film plans are as secret as the nine o'clock news. Worse, Parson and Meese didn't even speak in the pub. Why not?

'There's one thing this creaking old Kingdom of ours lacks, pal,' I prattled into the sewing-machine noise as we made the A133 roundabout. 'And that's a genuine English wooden crucifix of the thirteenth century.' There's none in the UK. The nearest one's in Norway. The reason is that History's thugs served God – the Puritans, Lollards, the destructive Catholic Franks of the Fourth Crusade licking their lips as they entered exquisite Byzantium in 1204 AD. Had they all ignored Him there'd be more of mankind's superb artistry left. God's zealots burned and smashed religious artefacts – statues, paintings, buildings. And wooden crucifix figures. It's called holiness, though definitions vary.

'Parson got that phoney idea from some magazine,' I muttered on. 'He must be desperate to keep in touch with me.' But why did he say next week? I wasn't doing anything except hang around Meese and his cameras, a real bore. And wasn't it an odd coincidence that Parson had streaked home to be there, really casual, when I arrived with Suki? 'Yes,' I answered myself – and promptly forgot all about these musings in the search for Sam Shrouder.

OK, I admit I was worried about this film business. I didn't know what to expect, and I'd heard they were all lunatics. Anyway, emissaries from the antiques underworld began to turn up about then. And a lovely lass called Laila.

Guess who was most trouble.

Chapter 6

Everything, I long since decided, is worth more. Like, Shakespeare got £5 for *Hamlet*. Five measly rotten quid for a whole play. Not being literary, I've no way of gauging its value, but it must be worth at least double (joke). Van Gogh's masterpieces you could have got for less than fifty dollars – once. And most of the antiques I've sold were underpriced because I was starving and needed luxuries like food and warmth. And I mean just look at the effort I was putting into buying Laila's horse glass – 'cheval' glass, if you want to sound posh. This is a tall rectangular mirror, over five feet tall, pivoted about its middle within a lovely mahogany frame. A really good one will have ebony inlay and be on four genuine castors. Some antique dealers can be diddled into selling a cheval cheap because the rectangle is only half-filled with glass. Innocents assume there's a piece missing, that it's a cheapo, or something's broken. Wrong. All things being equal, it's worth four times the value of a full-glassed model, because it's older and cleverer and, therefore, of course more beautiful. The glass slides up and down on counterweights like old-fashioned sash windows. The reason is that sheet glass was difficult to make. By 1820, though, tall horse glasses were being made full-length. Laila's lovely piece was a half-glassed affair, mint and delectable. I'd spotted it in her bedroom, never mind how.

There was a lot of urgency about Laila's cheval, because her husband wanted to sell up and move house to where he could fit out some suburban nook with new Scandinavian pine grot. Laila was fighting a desperate delaying battle. And so was I. I knew a good dozen dealers who'd snap the mahogany mirror up and marry the legs to a mahogany plank for sale as a 'genuine Georgian mahogany sofa table' (the usual trick, so watch out). They'd make a fortune, and yet another glorious antique would be lost for ever. To me, loving Laila was a crusade for righteousness.

I reached my cottage to find a note from her saying meet for supper at the new Italian restaurant by the art gallery. And a note from Lydia, my apprentice:

> Lovejoy,
>
> Miss Lorane of Lake Bayon Enterprises suggests that she call for you in her conveyance one hour before the commencement of the meeting. Lydia.

Meeting? I chucked it away and forgot it. Only Lydia could call a motor a conveyance.

Plenty of time before my evening meeting with Laila, my 1822 French-style English carriage clock said. Which gave me time to feed the budgies, play fingers with them a minute, brew up and go over some old notes I keep about likely fakes, dealers' activities and who was ripping off whom. Only two, possibly three, hints of Sam Shrouder's neffie activities. My one fixed point was the piece of lapis lazuli I'd got and sold him. It's precious to all artists and fakers, being the original perfect blue; Old Master painters in their heyday accepted commissions which stipulated the actual weight of genuine true lapis lazuli they were to use in their masterpieces. It's very rare, precious stuff.

Thinking, I washed my spare shirt, and underclothes and hung them on a string in the kitchen alcove. More pottering, then I opened the door to drive to town. Tinker should have dug out a few facts about Sam by now—

Ben Clayton stood there. He's your friendly soulful baldy little bloke, a born book-keeper if there ever was one. You'd buy a used car from him any day, if Seg was there to lend encouragement, like now.

'Why, hello, Ben!' I sounded really pleased to see him. Terror added warmth to my greeting. Seg, his trained psychopath, is given to unnatural explosive laughs and sullen glares, and puts the fear of God into me just saying hello.

'Hello, Lovejoy.' Seg spoke with malice.

'And Seg! Come in!' I'm pathetic. I sounded scared sweaty.

Ben glared in scorn. 'Not into that shithouse. Lovejoy, there's an exhibition on. Mine. Seen it yet?'

'Yours? Those lovely Russians?' I spoke fervently. 'I've heard it's really wonderful, Ben! How marvellous of you to sponsor such a tremendous contribution! I'm going to see it first thing tomorrow.'

Ben shook his head. 'No, Lovejoy. You're not.'

My chest squeezed. 'No? Well, actually, I was thinking of giving it a miss . . .'

'No, Lovejoy. You're to put it out of that fucking rabbit warren of a mind you've got.'

'Altogether,' Seg said.

'What exhibition?' I said, smiling a cardboard smile.

'That means no barker, no Tinker, no quiet little visits from your specky apprentice lass. Follow?'

'Sure, Ben, sure. Honest. You have my word. Sure you can't stay for a cuppa . . . ?'

'Motor,' Seg said.

'Right, right.' I walked to their car and climbed into its cavernous interior, conscious of the dusk down the lonely lane. Ben goes for big white Fords. Seg always drives, very badly but experiencing little difficulty with cross motorists.

We drove maybe forty minutes. Nobody spoke except as we parked, in some leafy lane near the main A12 where it turns coastward. Seg asked a voice box, 'He still there?' It croaked a yes.

We waited ten minutes. Another car approached, pulled on to the verge as Seg flicked our headlights in recognition. A beefy stranger alighted. Ben Clayton beamed at me while Seg and the hood talked between the vehicles.

'You're going to drive, Lovejoy. That.'

'I've a bad leg, Ben,' I croaked.

'It'll hurt, then.'

Surprisingly, it didn't, because I was so frightened I felt nothing as I crashed gears and kangaroo drove. The nerk sat behind me, directing by thumping my shoulders with his fist. Ben and Seg stayed behind. I was wet with terror when told to halt after about fifteen minutes of juddering through the countryside. Apart from a hamlet I didn't recognize I was quite lost, except for the great neon necklace of the A12 trunk's lights ambering the night sky nearby to the east.

We were only a mile or so from it when he said, 'Stop. Get out.'

'Look, mate,' I bleated. 'I've got money. If you let me go I'll—'

He slung me from the car one-handed and wedged

behind the wheel. 'Pathetic,' he said, *and drove off.* My mind went but my neurones fired relief so fast I sank to the grass as my legs gave way.

The car lights vanished. Silence. I wasn't executed, beaten up, maimed. Just left here out in the countryside, for no reason.

Within five minutes I was walking towards the lights. Two police cars and an ambulance went past in the opposite direction as I got a lift on the southbound carriageway from a Dutch lorry-driver who talked football. Stupid as ever, I thought nothing of the hurrying police. The lorry-driver supported Eindhoven, poor bloke.

My petrol tank was only quarter full, but I had good old Ray Meese's grand cheque to cash in the morning, and Laila was giving me supper tonight so all was well until one of Big John Sheehan's men flagged me down by the railway bridge and thumbed a new direction for me. It was becoming a habit. The station car park. I stopped, climbed out and ostentatiously limped on my stick towards the huge black Jaguar where Big John sat smoking a cigar.

'Wotcher, John. All right?'

'Fine, Lovejoy, fine. You?'

'Fair to middling, John.' Two big Jags, undertakers' models, six henchmen with witty Ulster faces. They waited chatting idly.

'You did all right the other night, Lovejoy.'

'Aye, John. Piece of cake. You got the silvers all right?'

'Thanks be to God, Lovejoy.' Here, I thought. *I'd* pulled the lift, not the Almighty. And where is He when you need a leg up? 'But what's all this about other items gone missing?'

'Ledger told me that, John. I reckon the householder's

pulling a bookie.' A bookie in the antiques game means pretending that more's been nicked than really has – and charging the insurance for it.

'Ah. Thought as much. You didn't touch anything else?'

'No, honest. You said not to, John.'

'Good lad, Lovejoy.' He drummed to the radio's melody. 'What did Ben Clayton want? Social call, was it?'

'Warned me off the Russian exhibition, John. I'm not to go. Not even buy a catalogue.'

'That definite, was he?'

'Very, very, very definite, John,' I said fervently.

He pondered a second. Then, 'I might want you to do another jemmy job, Lovejoy.'

'But John . . .' The world halted. His lads silenced watchfully, hoping for a hint of rebellion. I swallowed. 'Any time, John.'

He smiled. 'Right, boys. We're done.' His blokes got into their cars. I saw the car park man approach with his bag, already clipping tickets. 'Don't break this old gentleman's legs, d'y'hear?'

The wise old bloke stopped, pouched his tickets and plodded on past. I wished I could do that. Shakily I drove into town. Odd. Nothing for weeks, then all of a sudden the world wants me to play pig-in-the-middle. Anyway, I'd soon be having a quiet supper with Laila, hahaha.

Car parks are a modern destructive epidemic. I avoid them like the plague they are.

I had to park down Roman Road's old wall because of traffic, which was my one stroke of luck. I caught sight of Lydia waiting by the war memorial. She was tapping her foot, which meant ominous tidings. Beneath that camel hair coat beat a voluptuous heart. I just wish it wasn't so uncompromisingly devoted to my interests, that's all. So

I ducked through the rose garden and was soon seated with Laila in a restaurant's nooky alcove.

This new place was plush, shadowy. It was also crowded, but cleverly arranged so you weren't ostentatious. Good old Laila. A score of couples dined among candles in tulip glasses. We spoke of incidentals – how are you, this dreadful weather – for a time, which was champion because I was starving. I was just reaching cruising speed when Laila put the dig in.

'We have to talk,' Laila said, pale and intent. We hadn't even reached our pudding. I'd been hoping for trifle first, but her tight voice spelled doom.

Quickly I filled my mouth, no time to waste.

'Yes, love. About your cheval glass—'

'Not that, Lovejoy. I mean your attitude.' She toyed with her fork. 'How long have we . . . ?'

'Five weeks?' Hopeful.

'Eighteen.'

'Really?' I could have sworn it was less. 'Wasn't it at that fête where your husband—?'

'Don't bring him into it. I mean us.'

Nothing for it. And I'd given her the best ten days of my life – well, nine maybe. I gazed past her, tutting in annoyance. 'What the hell's Enrico want now?' Two waiters were standing by the serving door. I gave a wave. 'Ignore him, Laila. Go on, darling.'

'You're hopeless, Lovejoy. Your mind's always on other things, never on our relationship.'

'I see.' I went all quiet. 'So that's it. You think I'm insincere.' Irritably I gazed over her shoulder again and said, 'Bloody waiter. It'll be some message. Sorry about this, love. I'd best see what he wants.'

I rose and crossed to the waiters. 'Sir?' one said, worried by my waving.

'What is it, Enrico?' I asked, loudly.

'I'm Paulo, signore,' he said, mystified. He'd never seen me before. With luck, he never would again.

'Telephone? Through here?' I entered the kitchen. Watched by two silent cooks and a waitress, I hurriedly filled a plate with cooked rice, chips and a dollop of some stew thing. The back door opens into an alleyway leading to the Castle Park. I paused, shoving bread rolls into my pocket. 'D'you do pasties?'

'No, sir,' the cook said.

Typical. I stepped out into the darkness. You can't depend on anything these days.

Some days I need rubbing out and starting again. Relationships – God, how I hate that pompous-arsed word – are the same. Me and Laila, for instance. I cut along the alley, steadily putting myself on the right side of my plate of victuals. It was coming on to rain. The streets were glistening with that exquisite black shine every born townie loves. I finished the grub with a gulp except for a bit of gristly stuff I left for a penniless cat which chanced by, and balanced the plate on a shop windowsill before plodding across Maidenburgh towards the George.

Don't get me wrong. Laila's not at all bad. I mean, she loves sacrifice in noble causes, which is really great. But if you happen to be the flavour of the month you finish up being her particular Noble Cause. Bad news. Her husband's the most influential engineer here in East Anglia, and can bend an ear or two. He pollinates decaying factories into productivity for a living. She's early forties, slenderly pretty, with an unerring eye for stylish clothes. Age never troubles me, because a woman's potency transcends a few wrinkles – an obvious fact, this, though you try convincing a woman that age is unimportant. They're obsessed by everybody else's youth and their own age.

And Laila's wealth honestly didn't mean a thing. No, honest. I'm more concerned with spiritual values of people, fairness to all. Same as any antique dealer, when you come to think of it. In this state of smug ignorance Lydia caught me and finally made me go to a meeting about making movies.

Chapter 7

Condor Hall lay beyond Long Melford, a vast brick rectangle lit by those vigilant anti-burglar lights which automatically illuminate the known world when you step into the garden. Where has trust gone? Lydia was still furious with me, though I'd explained times beyond number that I'd not realized the meeting was tonight. The Ruby tried to hurry, but was almost clapped out.

'It's no good sulking, Lovejoy,' she blazed. 'A left here, please. You knew perfectly well. I left a message. I also saw Lorane give you the envelope with my own eyes.'

'No, love, honest—'

'No, Lovejoy.' She was endearing hunched inside her coat, lovely knees together and gloved hands firmly keeping her skirt in place. 'Lorane waited an entire hour at your cottage. I shall not accept your explanation for an instant!'

You have to give in. 'All right, love. I admit it. I was trying to keep out of her way.'

'You were?' She turned her specky gaze on me.

'Yes.' I swung the Ruby beside the eight saloons alongside the mansion. The engine cut with a chesty burble. 'I rather felt that she's, well, you know . . . So I was looking around for you to come with us.'

Uncertainty diluted her stern expression. 'Why, Lovejoy?'

'Predatory. I'm not blaming her, of course. It's this modern age. It influences people.' I sprang down, caught myself and limped back for my stick. 'But that doesn't mean I should, well, succumb.'

'Well, Lovejoy . . .' Still doubtful, but I was slowly winning. 'If that's the only reason.' We ascended the steps. A butler appeared at the door as we approached. Six exterior alarms, every window and door. Absurd to be so defensive, though the thought honestly never crossed my mind. 'All the same, you could have telephoned their office.'

'I just feel better when you're along.'

'Shhh, Lovejoy,' she said, pink. She moved apart and said good-evening to the butler.

'Good evening, miss, sir.' He looked middle-aged but pretty sprightly. More bad news for burglars. 'The meeting is in the large library.'

I left this bit to Lydia, who's a born nuisance but useful on these occasions. We were ushered through a massive hall – no antiques – to double doors which opened on a meeting in a library. A lay curia? I'd never seen anything like it.

Chairs were arranged in an ellipse. Ray Meese dominated the room, Lorane next to him. Half a dozen blokes and birds were there. I'd never seen so many maniacal hairstyles. For once I felt really orthodox, and Lydia looked the token shop-window straightie. Everybody had clipboards. I glanced around as we entered. The books were Russian, if I'd sussed the lettering.

'Miss Lydia, ma'am. And Lovejoy.'

This elderly lady, one of the ellipse, was perched on cushions, maybe to stop her tiny frame being lost among the antimacassars. God, she was a titch. You've seen small people with disproportionately large feet, hands, faces? Well, this dowager was everything miniaturized. She had lovely ancient eyes, seen it all, which hardly gave Lydia a glance. I found her hand, shook it gently. She wore a black Victorian dress, high neck, mutton-shoulder sleeves, and a plain niello locket. Anastasia, at least.

'Please ameetings,' she said in a distant whisper.

'Eh? Oh. Pleased to, er.'

'Lovejoy.' Lydia went all subdued at this encounter with a Prominent Personage. She led the way to our chairs. We sat. I was disappointed. A big mob like this, you'd have thought the old crab would have laid on a bit of grub, but there was no sign.

'Glad you made it, Lovejoy.' Meese gave a munificent wave, rose and halted. Specs hung on chains about his neck.

'About time,' Lorane said, ice.

'We do apologize,' from a Lydia in panic. 'But—'

'Peace, pax, glasnost, folkeroonis,' Meese appealed. 'Lovejoy – our own Big L, soldats – is the necessary input. Lorane, baby, let's be on . . . *amalgam.*' He repeated this formula, delighted with his turn of phrase. 'Vance. Recaperooni.' He really talked like this. I wondered if this lot had ever tried decaffeinated.

One of the hairy woollies stirred. He sat crumpled in his chair, somehow sideways on. 'Yeah, well, like I mean, see, mate, this movie like this surge a trollies gointer rip off the BM, y'know, like a blammer, balls-up from sex and blam goes el fuzzo and SAS, Christ knows, OK Corral time, y'know?'

'Thanks, Vance,' Meese said with humility and admiration. I'd not understood a word. 'Vance, Lovejoy. Our main – did I say main? Our principal, our prime mover.' He gazed fondly at Vance, who now seemed worn out by his effort. 'We've got – nay, evolved – a start date, time, team, Lovejoy!' He was so thrilled he smacked his hands in time with each word. 'So go-go-go!'

People said, 'Yeah,' and 'Right on, Ray,' and suchlike. One slender girl with long swingy hair radiated adoration of Meese. The mood was ecstasy.

'The actors are on,' the thin girl said.

'Honey wagons, technicians, services, food?'

Various people said everything was covered. Meese began firing questions, reading from a clipboard list. 'Rails? Auto-gantries? About lighting services – has to be the back entrance, the university side? – get a window shifted, right? What's in a window, for Christ's sake . . . ?' Occasionally he froze and everybody went into tableau as he pressed his temples to communicate with some astral plane.

Lydia was fascinated, taking it all in. She looks bonny with her coat off. I caught the old lady's eyes on me. I shrugged, gave her a discreet grin. A woman seated behind her was murmuring in the shadows. Translator? Odd sort of production meeting, this, I thought. Why out here in the wilds if the film – movie, sorry – was in London?

My interest wobbled further off course. The old dear's locket was genuine niello, that lovely black and silver which Old Russia did better than any. (Tip: you can still buy these genuine Russian antiques for a song, because people think they're modern Thailand copies. The old Russians look more matt when held at arm's length, and are worth umpteen times more.) The matching chain was original too. I glanced about, though books never mean a great deal to me unless I can get between the pages. No paintings. No lovely antique furniture. No marvellous porcelains, tapestries, vases, statuary. An old Russian family fallen on hard times, having difficulty keeping the family retainers in vodka?

'Gunsmiths?' Meese was snapping on. 'Climbing tackle?'

Uneasily I glanced at the enraptured Lydia. I especially didn't want my apprentice consigning me to a shoot-out while dangling from the British Museum's upper floors. Then I remembered I wasn't in this, only advising.

Niello. It never really caught on as decorative jewellery here in our dozy old Kingdom. But on the Continent niello was always highly desirable – pendants, brooches, 'body furniture' as antique dealers call personal jewellery nowadays when they want to justify yet another price increase. I followed the locket, chain, and found my eyes meeting the old dear's amused gaze. Hastily I looked away, concentrating. Meese was in heavy dialogue with a duffle-coated bearded spindle called Max: 'Can we have a rewrite, Max? Any lesser creativity I wouldn't dare ask. But you, Max' – with a fervent handclasp in semblance of prayer – 'I'm positive – nay, convictionary – you'll deliver. On time. To perfection.' A revivalist meeting, podgy Ray doing Elmer Gantry and Lorane a dilute Jean Simmons. Why this feeling I'd seen it all before?

Max was making deprecatory gestures. 'I'll try . . .' Applause.

'Now, cameras . . . ?'

One faint bong in my chest had worried me since we'd arrived. Not the locket. Even though I could see nothing in the shadows behind the oldster my body kept being polarized. A wall decoration? Some exotic ancient Russian silver samovar? One of those peculiarly Russian costume uniforms straight out of pre-1812 Tsarist times, hanging concealed in a cupboard?

'Pay attention, Lovejoy.' Lydia, whispering.

'I'm listening, for Christ's sake.'

'Language, Lovejoy.'

She only speaks to me so I'll reply so she can tell me off, if you follow. I was fed up, irritated by that black glow feeling from behind the old duchess and not being allowed a closer look. Anyway, what was an ancient Russian crone doing in a movie think tank? Some vestigial Garbo-type resurrected for another remake of a remake?

'. . . by Lovejoy,' I heard, and came to with a clang. 'Eh?' Everybody was waiting expectantly.

'Be guided by you, Lovejoy,' Lydia prompted in a furious whisper. 'What antiques to steal.'

'Eh?' I gave a doubtful smile all around. People shuffled.

'From the Museum. For the film's story.'

'Ah,' I said. 'As long as this is let's pretend. The British Museum's impregnable. Well, there's a world to choose from.' Pause. At least half had lifted their pens in eagerness. I invented desperately, 'We can go for the prints gallery at the top. It's enclosed. Or the Far Eastern stuff, near the back, first floor. The, er, Egyptians are a dead loss because, er . . .'

'He doesn't know,' Lorane glowered. Lydia's face was flaming. I'd catch it for this but how the hell could I be expected to make their story up for them? They had more writers and assistants here than the parson preached about. Why turn on me?

'He certainly does!' Lydia shot back.

'Then what's this ho-hum crap? We *know* antiques are all over the frigging place.'

'Your outline was insufficiently specific, Lorane.' Good old Lydia.

'Lovejoy.' Max had his head in his hands. 'That's in the script, man. Vance has just explained.'

'You're here to tell *how*, dummy.' Lorane's sweetly withering scorn included Lydia.

'Hang on, doowerlink.' I'd got it. I was so relieved. 'You

only want to know *how* to nick a McGuffin from the Brit Mus? Sorry. That's easy.'

'Easy?' Max stared, Vance stirred, Ray Meese starred in a display of sudden heartfelt tears.

''Course.'

'But you weren't even listening!' Lorane wasn't going to let go. She wanted me executed. 'There are guards, alarms—'

I lost patience with the lot of them. 'Shut up, you silly cow. Ask me, and I'll answer.'

'Lovejoy! Language!' Lydia was aghast, mortified. 'Apologize this instant!'

'Well,' I said, 'birds like her nark me. All mouth and moan.'

'Of all the—!' Lorane was on her pins, enraged.

'You'll apologize, Lovejoy! And no sulking. This very instant.' Lydia's gloves were in her hand, tap tap. Everybody was looking. I felt a right prat.

'Looka here, folkeroons!' Meese tried bouncily. 'Lovejoy only—'

'No, Mr Meese.' Lydia was pale, stern. With a sinking heart I recognized the matter-of-principle speech looming. 'This is a Matter of Principle. Courtesy preserves civilization.'

It can last a full quarter-hour even on a good day so I cleared my throat. 'Sorry,' I said at the carpet. Threadbare. Now how come a mansion's carpet is threadbare? One day I'll strangle Lydia.

'Thank you, Lovejoy.' The gloves stilled. Lydia recomposed herself. 'Mr Meese, rest assured that no better person than Lovejoy exists to advise on security faults in the British Museum.'

'All . . . rightee!' from Meese. He was overcome, probably an all-time first. I could have dived under the floorboards from embarrassment. I sweat when my face goes red. 'Vance, Max, Lorane, get together with Lovejoy. Gimme a report soonest, okayee? I like tomorrow noon. At the Museum. You call it, Virginia.' The thin girl moved ecstatically in her sheath of lank hair to signify compliance.

He sank into his chair, beamed at the old lady. 'Madam, I have this inner gut feeling. You're going to be dee-lighted, deedy deed!' Tears of ecstasy flowed down his cheeks.

'Thankings,' the crone fluted. 'Everyones thankings.'

The signal for a dispersal. We all rose and slowly scattered. Meese was the oldest, by far, the dowager Russian lady excepted. The youngsters, all trendily shopsoiled, straggled out chatting noisily. I crossed to the crone.

'Ta, lady,' I told her. 'Sorry that tart lost her rag. Only, your things here are really, er, nice and I was interested.'

This guff gave me the chance to peer behind her. A gallery ran round the higher library shelves, good quality Edwardian ironwork, with a scrolled staircase creating further shadows. I was still squinting when the lady piped a Russian reply. The interpreter came a little forward.

'Would you please come to tea tomorrow, Lovejoy? Four o'clock.'

'Eh? Well, I'm busy—'

'Thank you,' Lydia cut in firmly. 'Lovejoy is pleased to accept.'

I was staring. The interpreter was beautiful, thirties, dressed in cardigan and sombre tweed suit, but with that lit-from-within luminosity some tempera paintings have. Her face held a hint of Slav, but the eyes were rounded and astonishingly blue.

'Yes?' the interpreter was asking, worried she'd missed some vital subjunctive.

'Oh, er, nowt, love. Four o'clock, then.'

Lydia was moving me bodily out of the room with those clever oh-so-accidental nudges women have off to perfection. Meese clapped me on the shoulder as we milled down the front steps.

'Lovejoy. You are salvation. You know it. I know it.' He waved an arm expansively. 'Soon the world will know it.' He blew his nose, dabbed his moist eyes, replaced his hornrims.

'Do you get the feeling,' I asked Lydia when our lamps were lit and the Ruby's engine was tugging us laboriously out of the drive, 'that we're actually in some 1940s threepenny B film?' I'd never seen so much phoney emotion since the Gunga Din/Lassie re-rereleases.

'Stop complaining, Lovejoy. These people are exceedingly creative.' She sat primly, so serious. (She's only ever made two jokes that I know of. Tell you one if I get a minute.) 'They are subject to artistic tensions. It behoves us to be understanding . . .' et cetera.

'What's the old Russian lass in on it for?'

'It's rude to ask that sort of question, Lovejoy, without invitation.'

So we shelved the problem and drove on. Events proved me right, in a wrong sort of way. I wish now I'd listened to me and nobody else, just for once.

Chapter 8

Museums and galleries the world over have had their ups and downs. Except one. That one is the British Museum. It's always definitely on the up. Famed in song and story, it stands there in its narrow London street, grand, quiet, and impregnable. It looks smug because it has never – repeat never, ever – been effectively done over, burgled, or ripped off. It is unique. And impregnable.

Mind you, it always was queer. Its strangeness survives to this day. I mean, everybody knows how Sir Hans Sloane, posh doctor of Queen Anne's London, left his antiques collections to the nation for £20,000 given to his heirs. When he popped off in 1753, God rest him, Parliament enacted a lottery to raise the gelt. All 80,000 objects the top doc had hoovered up in his 92 years were crammed into a wilting dump called Montague House and, fanfare please, the institution opened to the world a couple of weeks into 1759. (They were fast movers in those days; we take two decades to open half a shed.) Massive libraries – Cotton, Harley – were added to Sloane's stuff. And it grew and grew: George III chipped in his wonderful antiquarian collection, others did the same. Over the years the paintings were hived off, then natural history, and ethnography ('wood-and-feathers' to antique dealers) and lately library. It's the greatest refresher on earth. I defy anyone to go in tired, downhearted, bored, and not come out radiant. It's an exaltation, a spiritual uplift. In short, it's paradise. It welcomes everyone and shows them wonderment. Free.

Lydia dropped me at the station, gave me the train ticket for London, some bad news, a warning, and a note.

'I have taken Mr Meese's cheque, Lovejoy. It must go towards your outstanding debts.'

'You've *what*? For God's sake, debts *are* outstanding. It's what debts do.'

'Also, Tinker informs me that four dealers lately have dealt with Mr Shrouder. And here is a note concerning one such. Professor Desai. He is supervising an art activity today.' Frowning with concentration she gave me a photocopied page, a site inked in red. 'This indicates Professor Desai's location. Making this photocopy from the commercial A *to Z Geographia* has not infringed the Copyright Act . . .'

I took my headache on to the train.

We formed a moody quartet at Tottenham Court Road tube station. Lorane walked her disdain on ahead while we three tried to keep up. Max the writer apologized for a hangover. Vance spoke, affably I think, in starts and grunts, only saying good morning or something. I had no real way of communicating and found myself talking back in the same like-wow stuff.

'Let's move our arses, for Christ's sake,' Lorane commanded. 'Fortunes hang on this movie.'

'Fortunes?' I asked, trying to be chatty. 'How much does a, er, movie cost?'

'More than you've ever heard of. All that old lady's wealth plus a bank or two.' And that was that. We made the British Museum main entrance in silence.

She shot us down the entrance hall, past a long thin bookshop, then into a wall door where a couple of blokes seemed to expect us. Uniforms make me edgy. We don't get on. The last time I'd worn one people kept shooting at me. We were now two corridors and three doors from the safety of the public galleries. Admin territory.

'Oliver Bracegirdle,' a cheerful man said, striding up and shaking our hands. 'Security Officer Visitor Activity Liaison, SOVAL.' He laughed a regular laugh, ha, pause, ha, pause. He was tall and tweedy, brilliant teeth under a moustache and looked very pentathlon-before-breakfast.

'Max, Vance,' Lorane introduced. 'And Lovejoy.' She made me sound beneath contempt.

'Greetings.' Merrily he conducted us down drab corridors. 'Photographs.'

Lorane flashed a plastic folder and Bracegirdle acknowledged her exemption with a ha, ha. 'Registered!' he boomed. I realized he'd never yet spoken a word without a capital letter.

A fat bird photographed us conveyor-belt fashion and we filled in a form.

'Gracious!' Bracegirdle exclaimed, reading over my shoulder.

'What's up?' I said, narked.

'Lovejoy Antiques, Inc., Bercolta, East Anglia.' He shook his head in admiration. 'Proprietor?'

'He's supposed to be an adviser.' Lorane withered me with a glance. 'He came in a job lot.'

'Ah, telephone number . . . ?'

I reddened. 'Er, well, the line's down.'

Lorane snorted. Bracegirdle tutted sympathetically. 'Just leave it blank, then. It's unimportant.'

Miserably I stood to one side while Max and Vance were photographed. Lorane had as good as announced that I'd been cut off for non-payment. And Lydia had nicked Meese's cheque to waste on non-essentials. I was upset. I could do without Bracegirdle's tact.

'Right!' The eager security man rubbed his hands. 'Now. What's the jolly old drill?'

'Lovejoy's going to explore,' Lorane said, venom-sweet. 'While we look on admiringly, he'll then tell us how to break in and rob your museum.'

'Splendid! Splendid!' Bracegirdle made his staccato ha-has for a moment. Joke on the way. 'Remember I've counted the Rosetta Stone! Ha . . . ha!'

Lorane's flat tone mocked, 'Where to, Lovejoy?'

'Anywhere you like.' Antiques are antiques. Already the invisible radiation of the place had me walking on air. I only stayed on the floor for the sake of appearances. And they were making the bloody film, not me.

Lorane exploded. 'You've been fucking paid, Lovejoy!'

'Hey,' Vance said. 'Save'n'rave, paisanos. Like-a ooze 'n'choose, compo?' Something like that. He made a slow flapping gesture.

'Vance the Prance, I agree.' Max pronounced the words *ex cathedra*, and that was it. With Lorane bound to disagree with whatever I suggested, I was outnumbered. Democracy had done it again. They stood aside for me to lead the way. I shrugged, not knowing what I was supposed to be doing.

'Fuss ain't no wuss.' Vance sang the words.

'What did Horace say, Winnie?' Bracegirdle chortled. To my blank stare – maybe Vance was catching – he began explaining. 'That was the catchphrase of an old radio ventriloquist . . .'

He walked with me. A bonny lass in the uniform of a security guard, her badge identifying her as Gabriella, trailed us smiling pleasantly. I looked, but said nothing.

Gabriella was the girl in Hereford magistrates court who had given me that tilted smile. Hell of a coincidence. I thought Lorane was unbending slightly as we started out into the lovely Greece and Rome galleries, until I heard a click from her shoulder-bag and realized she was taping every cough and quip. Trust.

'I'll perhaps begin by describing the layout, shall I?' Bracegirdle must have been a military man. He strode, easy and in command, uniformed attendants straightening as he hove into view. 'The trouble we have with American visitors! Our *ground* floor's their *first*, you see? So – ' he twinkled merriment – 'if we all agree we're on the ground floor! Now, think of a square building enclosing a rectangular quadrangle, and that's the British Museum. The central quad's now partly covered by Antonio Panizzi's great dome – the Reading Room. The rest is an exterior yard, of course, for services.' He paused, saw my uncertainty, smiled. 'When you're ready, Lovejoy.'

'Oh. Right.' I tried to look thoughtful while Lorane sneered.

Naturally I felt a bit of a fool, promoted beyond my class, but strolled in the direction of maximum pull. It was difficult, what with wondrous antiquities all around bonging me almost insensible, but you have to start somewhere even with bliss. I soon forgot my companions and drifted on regardless.

The ground floor's what used to be called antiques proper, artefacts from the Old World as such, Rome, Greece, Egypt, Assyria and the like. It's spread now to include Western Asia, Islam, plus Southern Asia and areas that nowadays you aren't supposed to call the Far East. The porcelain is magic, out of this world. As I went, I casually clocked the tall rectangular windows. Each had an expanding metal grid of the lift-gate kind which is a pig to cut through without a ton of oxyacetylene. I smiled, remembering a time me and Eddie the Oil from Sunderland once tried to do a golf clubhouse near Blackpool for its display of ancient golfing silver cups, and . . . Bracegirdle's steady eyes were in my way all of a sudden.

'All right, Lovejoy, old chap?'

'Er, yes, ta. All books down here, eh?'

'The British Library has Rooms Twenty-Nine to Thirty-Three now. That's the ground floor, right-hand side, from the front entrance. And the Reading Room, of course. Manuscripts, everything originals from the Lindisfarne Gospels to Shakespeare's signature and the Codex Sinaiticus, in the Saloon.'

'Can anybody see them?' I already knew.

'Of course. Just walk through the King's library and you're there.' He was really proud. People milled about, families, crocodiles of school children, the lot. 'The display cases are guarded of course. Plus inbuilt alarms. Maintenance of relative humidity's vital, you see. Even for stamps—'

'Postage stamps?'

'Yes. George the Fifth was the world's leading exponent of philately. Then the Department of Printed Books has whole sections – maps, newspapers, music, official publications and philately – each with a separate library. Has to be, for efficiency. Ha . . . ha! Can you imagine having to wade through sonatas and Penny Blacks to see Jane Austen's handwriting? Ha . . . ha.'

You've got to hand it to the old BM. They're pros. Whole sections were arranged as particular displays. The bronzes and terracottas from Rome and Hellenistic Greece, the development of writing, a temporary exhibition of coins and medals, the superb clocks in the subdued confinement of Room 44, everything was a brilliant stage production unique to itself. Lovely, a delight.

Except for a custodian in uniform in every doorway and gallery. None was kipping. One or two were women. One or two walked to and fro. No information desk was vacant. All windows were gridded. Extra guards floated casually by the great Sutton Hoo treasure, looking our way as we ambled through. I smiled and said hello. They smiled and said hello. Well, hellos cost nowt.

But Lorane increasingly narked me. As we moved from the Chinese jade to the Ephesus gallery, from Roman glass to Nimrud ivories, she began making know-all remarks. 'Lovejoy'll know all about these,' and, 'Tell us about this silverware, Lovejoy,' and, 'Lovejoy hasn't said a word yet about these funny gold coins. Well, Lovejoy?' I don't say a lot, best of times. When I'm being publicly ridiculed by neanderthals I'm just like Tom the cabin boy, saying nowt. Occasionally Bracegirdle tried to override her anger but even he gave up and merely ticked off the room numbers as we went along. We were given maps, explanatory booklets.

We must have walked through every public room three times before Lorane's patience broke. Furious, she hauled me to a standstill facing her.

'All *right*, Lovejoy! What, if anything, do we get from your gormless meandering? We've wasted hours here while you've enjoyed yourself, grinning like an ape.'

'What's there to say?' I was amazed. Visitors wandered by, looking at us with curiosity. We were by the steps leading down to the Chinese pottery from the map gallery.

'Perhaps we can use my office,' Bracegirdle said, less cheery now.

'No, Oliver! Let's settle this here and now!' She was spitting with rage. Oliver, eh? So she knew him from yore. 'I was against you being taken on from the very start! You're dross, Lovejoy.'

'Coming here wasn't my idea, love,' I said, narked. I cast about for help but Max and Vance were missing.

'So you admit you're useless! Right! Now we know exactly where we stand, Lovejoy! I'll tell Ray to strike you off.'

She marched away, heels stabbing the flooring. I ahemed apologetically. 'Sorry, mate,' I told Bracegirdle. 'You were great. It's my best outing in years. I guess I'm not much of a communicator.'

'Never mind, Lovejoy.' He gave his giant grin. 'It's a pleasure to see somebody enjoy our exhibits so much.'

We began to stroll down the oriental collections, Room 34. 'Hope it hasn't been a waste for you.'

'Certainly not, old chap. Security's the game, what?' he sized me up. 'Well? See any blind spots?'

'A little weak on Turkestan. And Maya, Inca antiques are so difficult to come by—'

'No. Security. Breaches in the defences.'

That old thing. 'Not really. You've got it all sewn up.'

He looked pleased. 'Glad to have your views, Lovejoy, especially from one so experienced. Divvy chap, aren't you? I can tell. It must be marvellous to have that facility.'

What? I came to. 'Experienced?'

'With your record, I mean. Nothing wrong, old chap,' he added hastily. 'Certainly no offence intended, or taken, I hope. But having you give us the once-over's like a jolly good security audit, what?'

I looked at him, possibly for the first time. This breezy bloke was no nerk. 'You dug out my record?'

'Apologies, Lovejoy. My job. Gabriella got a printout.'

She was still trailing us, still smiling innocently. 'But we'll keep mum about it. Not cricket. Confidentiality's the game, what?'

'Ta for that.' We went to the rear entrance, Islam and Japanese porcelain to the right, Official Publications and Music Libraries to the left. 'If you see Max or Vance, tell them I've gone.'

He pulled a tiny electronic thing from his pocket and tapped it a couple of times. Gabriella, now by the entrance, came over immediately. 'The two film gentlemen are waiting by the Great Russell Street entrance, Major.' She carried a lookalike gadget. Major. I should have known.

'Thanks, Gabriella. Want to catch them up, Lovejoy?'

'No thanks. I've a bloke to see near here. I'll cut off.'

We made noises of pleasantry and farewell. I liked the look of Gabriella, and Major Bracegirdle wasn't at all bad. I didn't like their nasty little electricals, but they'd be no real problem. Anyway, burglars can't be choosers.

The thing was, I now knew the world's greatest and last impregnable museum was easy. I could go in and out like a fiddler's elbow. Any time I wanted. Security or no security. I was enjoying this. Designer robbery, with the approval of almost everybody. Good idea for a film, or even a movie, no?

Oaf Desai. We call him Oaf because he's bright but Lebanese and says 'Oaf cowerss . . .' even with denials. He teaches art, as if anybody could, which suggests maybe he's not as bright as all that. I found him, as Lydia's copyright map directed, in Bedford Square. There's a shapely pavement at its south-west corner under the spreading giant London plane trees. I watched him for a while. He was creating a wooden circular pit filled with heaps of slate. Actually, he stood idle while dishevelled students plodded up a ramp discharging baskets of slate from a lorry, Chinese building another Yangtse dam. It palls.

'Wotcher, Oafie. Sculpture?'

'Oaf cowerss, Lovejoy.' He cut his smile and screeched abuse at a girl who'd cast her load too near the planking.

She burst into tears and ran behind the lorry to weep. Barmy, really, because the circle was a good twenty feet wide. An extra ton either end would have made no difference. I mean, a slate-filled pit is a slate-filled pit, but I knew better than to say so. Artists and criticism don't mix. The students trekked on, the lorry-man shovelling slate into their baskets. He caught my eye. I knew what he was thinking.

'Done owt for Sam Shrouder lately, Oaf?'

'Oaf cowerss, no.'

'No?' A few other besmocked artists were building what looked like a plank summerhouse at the far end. I spoke up over the hammering. No moquettes, marble fragments, porcelain chips?'

Oafie gazed at me. 'Oaf cowerss, just a liddle piece of porphyry. That bitch wife of hees telled you, no?'

'I heard, that's all.' Oaf's art school is in the next street to the British Museum, and he has winning ways. 'Oafie. How did he contact you?'

'Phone call, oaf cowerss.'

'He speak to you himself?'

'OC, no. Hees wife. She pay on the nail both times.'

'Both . . . ? Then how'd you know the porphyry was for Sam?'

'OC easy. First time she tell me an address. I sent it to Sam. Second time a different Post Office box number, but same bird. I sent a piece of clay. Too cheap. I should have charged her more.'

While the students trekked on I learned the clay was a quarter-ounce piece from an Egyptian figure, an ichneumon. This is a praiseworthy little four-footed creature which relished crocodile eggs, so was adored by Ancient Egyptians. The tiny porphyry was a hand fragged from a Rhodes statuette, Greek, late sixth century BC. I thanked Oafie and wished him good luck with his sculpture.

'What is it, Oafie?' I couldn't help asking.

'A spiritual rejection of weather, oaf cowerss.'

Silly me. 'Looks great, Oafie. Cheers.' Phew.

Chapter 9

'Now, Lovejoy,' Lydia began. It was nearly four and the Ruby was chugging dispiritedly up the mile-long incline towards Condor Hall. From her voice I was about to get the You Have Obligations speech. Just when I wanted to work things out.

'Yes, love?'

Quickly she moved my hand from her knee, though it was honestly accidental. 'Behave, Lovejoy! In public! You Have Obligations. I mean proper social behaviour. My sentiments towards Helen are only moderately friendly' – (they could strangle each other) – 'but you must not let Standards Fall.' She rummaged in her handbag. 'You must send her a birthday card.'

'Eh?' I swerved. She tut-tutted and pointed remindingly at the road.

'The envelope's addressed. And stamped.'

Birthday card? 'I never send birthday cards.'

Her face set, cross and determined. 'For tomorrow, Lovejoy. Next week is Mr Bateman's, Frank from Suffolk is fifth of next month—'

'What is this?' I cried. 'They never send me one, for Gawd's sake.'

'Failure on the part of one does not permit . . .' Et

Lydia cetera, her Backsliding Just Will Not Do speech. Chip them on stone and future archaeologists will think they've struck a new religion. Where do people get these notions? As if there weren't enough problems in the world.

'I don't even send Christmas cards!'

'That's another thing . . .'

I kicked the Ruby sullenly, trying to make the damned thing get a move on, but not a single erg above eighteen m.p.h.

'Give me a breast, then.'

'Lovejoy! How dare you!' She was aghast, outraged, apoplectic, plus whatever else is in the lexicon. 'To resort to blackmail *and of a carnal nature . . .*'

Naturally I'd said it without hope, just to shut her up, and signed her stupid card with a wheel-wobble as I drove. Then she wonders why I'm narked. I mean, she's supposed to be my apprentice. One of these days she'll go too far and I'll sack her and it'll serve her right. I'd have done it before now except she'd forgive me and one thing would lead to another.

'Lovejoy. What are you doing? And stop muttering.'

'Eh?' We were stopped at Condor Hall, Lydia already on the steps. The butler was waiting. 'Oh. Sorry. I was just thinking, er, how smart your frock is . . .'

'Afterwards, Lovejoy.' A smile forced itself over this threat as she led the way through the good afternoons and that to a large drawing-room. A fire was laid, logs plus draughts. The crinkly lady and her luscious translator were there. A side table was laid for tea. Isn't it odd how two women, simply sitting in a parlour, manage to indicate their pecking order? There was no doubt the crone was boss, her word bird some stray kulak.

''Afternoon.' I did my best, didn't trip over the carpet – a mock Tientsin affair; you could still pong its newness.

'Welcoming boths,' said our hostess. The translator made a subdued greeting.

'How do you do.' Lydia smiled, glared a prompt at me.

Cue. 'It's so very kind of you to invite us, missus,' I said as I'd been rehearsed. 'We're looking forward to the pleasure of your company.'

The old dear said something to the translator, who offered a tour of the house. 'The Countess Rumiantzeff invites you to see the humble dwelling.' Countess? Then how come the furniture was modern self-assembly clag, the pictures mail order prints? Hard times, that's how. Which raises the question of how films are funded, right?

'How lovely!' Lydia was thrilled. Nothing chuffs a woman more than the chance to delve round another bird's place. 'Isn't it, Lovejoy?'

'Eh? Aye, great, love.' I tried not to look bored out of my skull. I wouldn't have come except for that funny feeling that a lustrous antique lurked in the study where we'd whiled away yestereve, and the Countess's locket. Wisely, she wasn't wearing it now.

'This way, please.' The translator rose and ushered Lydia, prattling rooms.

'Er, I'll stay with Countess, er, Rumania, to keep her company.' I smiled sickeningly sweet, showing Lydia she should have realized the oldie wasn't up to a sprint around the attic.

'Oh. How kind.' But the translator only said that after getting an almost imperceptible nod. I watched them go, sat when bid. The door closed and their voices receded, talking simultaneously like women do. I cleared my throat and looked into those ancient bright eyes.

'Look, Duchess. What's all this welcomings crap?'

'Beggings pardon?'

'Shut it, love. My budgies do better.'

Suddenly she smiled, elfin and dimply. It illuminated her visage. I grinned, embarrassed because she might easily have been upset, getting caught out.

'Countess, actually, Lovejoy. Not duchess. And Natalia Rumiantzeff, please. Rumania's a country. Once a Russian colony.' Her voice was dry, witty, stylish as her dress. Upper crust all right. 'My name in Holy Russia is exceedingly famous. Catherine the Great honoured Count Peter Rumiantzeff with personal gifts for his wars against the Turks.'

'Any left?' Catherine the Great's ancient gifts are renowned, bound to be worth a fortune now.

'Alas, Lovejoy. Times change.' She gestured, see my modern gunge.

'Aye. Like the old joke, even our butler's poor. 'Where's the antique in your library, love?'

'Ah, my locket? I caught you staring at it last night.'

'Admiring, Countess,' I corrected. 'No. The one hidden in the books.'

'Goodness gracious, Lovejoy! How very perceptive! I'd heard, of course. Divining?'

'Divvying.'

'You're obviously the right person. They said so. Agafia explained it, but I am at a loss to understand how you do it.'

Agafia? 'Me too, love. It just happens. What's the game?'

'You've learned that I am financing the film.' Casually she rang a small glass bell. That casual, you've to be certain serfs will hurtle to answer.

'Yes. Lorane told me, British Museum this morning.'

'You are surprised?'

'Well, yes.'

'The majority of my possessions – heirlooms, antiques, furniture – have gone on the project, Lovejoy.'

'Isn't it a risk?' The butler came, was talked to, withdrew.

'I'm assured not.'

Well OK, but a nerk begging money never says he's on to a sure loser. 'You sussed these film people out, love?'

'Investigated? As far as possible.'

'And?'

'They are talented, have a successful record, and have contributed to the film's costs themselves.'

'Oh, aye. Good of them, seeing the money's going their way. But don't' – I fended her annoyance off with flat palms – 'er, no, I'm not knocking the pictures, love. I'm just dubious. I mean, they seem scatterbrains. Worse than me.'

'You and I are simply unused to their ways.'

'That's probably it, love.' I was relieved we'd not fallen out, what with Lydia having treacherously snaffled the cheque to settle my debts, and the cake between me and the Countess being so tiny we'd all have belly rumbles before the pubs opened and I made it to a couple of nourishing pasties. The butler returned. Bong went my thorax.

I don't know if you've ever seen a kovsh, but it's a boat-shaped scoop thing with a flat handle one end and a little knob or loop at the other. This was nearly a foot long. They were Russia's normal drinking receptacle until Peter the Great decided to ape Europe. Cups came in after this, but the kulaks downwards stuck to their old kovsh. Hence, you find beechwood or base metal kovshs around fairly commonly. This was silver, nigh on three centuries old. It was patterned with vines and a coat-of-arms, and had a Cyrillic inscription.

'Beautiful.' I was looking at wealth, loveliness, art.

'One of my ancestors, 1725.' She was pleased at my delight. 'I have – used to have – an oil painting of him, actually holding this.'

Have? Had? Provenance makes a kovsh rarer and pricier. Within reach of a year's luxurious holiday anywhere on earth. I asked, 'Can I . . . ?' She let me hold it.

Thus Lydia and Agafia found us, me smiling at the kovsh and Countess Natalia.

'Lovejoy saw through our deception, Agafia. Apologies, Lydia my dear.'

'I hope Lovejoy hasn't been any trouble, Countess.'

'Have I hell!' I said, narked. 'You said be on my politest.'

The Countess patted Lydia's hand. 'Perfectly well behaved. Now, both of you. About my little deception. It was an entirely defensive response to the film magnate and all those frayed children who attend on him. I must say I rather enjoyed it. Forgive me.'

'I do understand, Countess.' Lydia's forgiveness can be worse than assault, very intense stuff. 'Entirely natural. Media people are so aggressive.'

'As kind as you are pretty, my dear. Thank you. Now, tea.'

Lydia coloured up and avoided my eye. She did really look delectable. She wore her pastel blue suit, pearls, matching shoes, gloves in her handbag. Her top coat was with the butler. I felt quite proud of her – praised by a countess! Agafia wore a plum velvet calflength dress which gave lustre to her long auburn hair. Her features were as dark as Lydia's were fair. How to choose? The butler came to serve.

'While we're having tea, my dears, perhaps you'll tell us about your robbery.' The Countess smiled her wrinkly smile. Agafia did the cake business. I got a microchip of it. Hopefully I glanced about but Lydia's lovely lips were warningly set in a line. I concentrated.

'Well, I'm still not sure what they're planning to nick. Though I suppose Max has already decided.'

'Max? Decide?' she said. We all paused. I tightened my stomach to stop my belly rumbling. 'But your visit to the Museum today . . . ?'

'We did nowt. Lorane was in a bad mood. Max was fed up. Vance rabbited on, God knows what about.'

During the silence I stared at the remaining minuscule chunk of Genoa. I'd be lucky to survive. Tea came in anonymous cups. What a life. I mean, Russia's had superb glassmakers since the eleventh century. For God's sake, it had 140 Russian glass manufactories when Napoleon came a-roving. The St Petersburg Imperial Glass Factory's products are the ones to watch out for – eighteenth-century, with silver covers. And their Art Nouveau vases are superb . . .

'?' the world was saying.

Forlornly I held my empty plate but nobody rushed with more. Life's hard, and politeness doesn't make it any easier. I mean, a houseful of women and no grub. 'Eh?'

Agafia had joined in. 'What exactly do you advocate, Lovejoy? The object you steal in the film.'

Glim dawned inchwise. 'Something Russian, you mean?' I shrugged. 'Well, the BM's not actually got much Russian stuff. Oh, there's the odd ethnographic thing in the Mankind branch near Piccadilly, a canvas or two in the National Gallery. Not much in Manuscripts. That's it.'

My eyes were on that fragment of Genoa. I came to, aware of doom and gloom. 'What's up?'

'The purpose of the film has not been explained to you, Lovejoy?' Agafia asked.

'Vance says a lot, but not so's anybody'd understand.'

'The film is to be a romance. About a great, precious and noble culture.' Agafia's voice became husky with fervour. 'Nowadays, here in East Anglia, it is impossible even to imagine Russia as she was. Even little Ukraine stretched its influence from the Black Sea to the Baltic. It was unique. Great nations invaded and pillaged, and yet we survived under regimes so annihilatory, so cruel, that no words can describe. The Countess Natalia Rumiantzeff has – may I, Your Highness? – given her family treasure to bring to the attention of the West our immense cultural heritage. Mr Meese's film will achieve this.'

'Christ, love,' I said, awed. 'Tall order.'

'Language.' Lydia spoke reflexly, worried sick.

Agafia spoke on. 'The story is that certain robbers, interested only in money, raid the British Museum to steal valuable Russian antiques. A hero and his girl, descendants of Russian immigrants, are moved by sentiment to prevent them. Wounded from gunshots, they courageously succeed. The morals are plentiful and clear.'

'Then you're on a loser, love. Sorry. It's scraping the barrel somewhat. Egyptian, yes. Oriental, yes. But Russian . . .'

Countess Natalia interrupted. 'Are you saying there isn't enough material in the British Museum?'

'Aye, love. Sorry.'

She and Agafia exchanged stares. 'But it *must* succeed, Lovejoy. You do not understand refugees. Where can we go? America, that land without nuance? Eire or the Continent, countries which live on silly myths? Back to Russia, where the dullest unison has murdered melodious counterpoint? No. It is my final wanderer's song, Lovejoy. It must be heard.'

We all thought. The cake bit sat there, within reach but out of grasp. The film story should raid other places, maybe the V and A even . . . Hey, what about the Russian exhibition at St Edmundsbury? I drew breath to bawl this genius of an idea to the world, then stilled. I'd been warned off, hadn't I? Very forcefully. By Ben Clayton and his psychotic Seg. Plus the peelers, Ledger and his merry band of Plod.

'You were about to say, Lovejoy?' Agafia said.

'Can I have some more grub, please?'

The wahwah overtook us as soon as we trundled on to the A12. We were invited to pause in a lay-by. This meant a vast white car surmounted by toffeebar lights frightened us to death with its mad siren. I pulled in, shaking. Lydia was enraged. She had been furious with me since we'd left Condor Hall. In a way I was glad of the police. At least they interrupted her. She was playing hell about my manners. Everybody weeps when Oliver Twist asks for more. Me, I get Lydia'd. Ledger was in the passenger seat, the nerk.

'Mr Ledger, how dare you drive in such a manner!' His particular et cetera was a Lydia special. Responsible Persons Should Always.

'Sorry, miss,' he interrupted, his head out of the window. 'Lovejoy was driving at such a speed we thought he'd get away.'

The police driver snickered. He'd decelerated from eighty to nil in about five yards. The Ruby was still gasping.

'Escape?' I was bitter. 'Do I need to?'

'Sam Shrouder'd be glad we nabbed you, pal.'

Pal? My heart sank. 'Sam? What's happened?'

'That's the point, Lovejoy. He can't tell us, not any more.'

Ledger disembarked, stretched and watched a family car go sedately by, little faces at the rear windows admiring this posh big police saloon. One kiddie waved. Ledger waved amiably back, turned to me. Lydia grasped the nettle.

'I hope no harm has befallen Mr Shrouder.'

'No good hoping, miss. Statement, Mr Burton.' Sarcasm.

The uniformed nerk came grinning to do the notebook bit. 'Name and address, Lovejoy sir.'

Sir and pal? Worser and worserer.

'Get on with it, Burton. Time, place, date. I'll vouch for his identity.'

'Lovejoy.' Constable Burton laboured over his pencil. 'Your movements in the past twenty-four hours?'

'What for?'

Ledger answered. 'Sam Shrouder was found dead in a lay-by such as this. And you've been asking all over the universe after the deceased. Why?'

Lydia attacked bravely. 'Lovejoy is not required to make any statement, on the grounds that it may incriminate him. He pleads the Fifth—'

'Amendment? That's America, lady. This isn't.'

Pale but game, Lydia kept going. 'We demand his right to one telephone call—'

'That's the USA too.' Ledger took an hour to light his pipe. PC Burton grappled with the next word. 'Where were you earlier, Lovejoy? Ramming Sam Shrouder to death in a stolen car?'

Gulp. I began to summarize: Auctioneer Penfold's late night viewing at Earls Colne, Suki Lonegan to Parson Brown's, a drive to my cottage for a wash and change – omitting Ben Clayton, Seg, and that horribly inexplicable journey in that nerk's saloon. Avoiding Lydia's eyes, I included supper with Laila, the film meeting. 'Then today London. British Museum.'

'Witnesses?' Ledger jerked his chin, shoving smoke high.

'A film production team,' I said quickly. 'And BM Security.'

'And I met him off the two-thirty express.' Lydia nearly reached for my hand, halted the orgy in the nick of time. 'I drove this motor to the station.'

'Witnesses at the train?'

'He was helping a family with a pushchair up the station steps. A lady with a baby. She took a black Austin taxi, giving an address in Great Bentley.' I stared at her. She tapped the scribe's arm. 'Please treat that information as confidential, Constable.'

'Yes, miss.'

Ledger quelled Burton with a bent eye. 'Since which?'

'We drove straight to tea at Condor Hall with Natalia, Countess Rumiantzeff.'

That stymied him. 'Did you indeed?'

'Yes, we did indeed.' Lydia tapped my arm. 'Let us leave, Lovejoy.'

'Just a minute,' Ledger said. 'Your fingerprints are all over the car which crushed Sam Shrouder to death—'

'So? I get lifts in strange cars ten times a day, Ledger.'

'You've got to explain—'

'No, Mr Ledger,' Lydia was white, Joan of Arc at the stake and just as sure of herself. 'You are usurping authority.'

Meekly I gunned the Ruby's asthmatic cylinders and moved off, shrugging apologetically to show all this was none of my doing. Ledger walked a pace or two alongside, still working out what the hell she meant. Lydia's meanings have strained stronger cortices than his.

'Shrouder's catalogue's being dusted for your dabs, Lovejoy. I warn you. If it's positive, you're for it.'

The bobby also trotted, concentrating. 'Here, Lovejoy. How d'you spell . . . ?'

I did a frisky sixteen m.p.h. in forty seconds. Jaguar, Inc., look to your laurels. Lydia was still being defiant and breathless, which gave me a few minutes. Sam Shrouder dead? Catalogue? I can never afford the damned things. Once, they used to give you them free at museums and exhibitions, whereas nowadays . . . Exhibition. Ledger said he'd warned me. The Russian antiques exhibition at St Edmundsbury? But I'd obeyed, steered clear, hadn't I?

The obvious link was Countess Thingy at Condor Hall, Russian as ever was. Or maybe the lustrous Agafia? But where's the connection with Sam Shrouder, now RIP?

I said something or other, but I'd already decided to ask Suki Lonegan new questions about Sam, mostly while Parson Brown was absent. I'm not scared of Ben Clayton, honest. And I honestly wasn't trying to bolster my alibi with Ledger. Just curiosity.

As we neared civilization and horrible countryside gave way to lovely paving and dwellings I wondered if I could get hold of a catalogue of that Russian antiques exhibition. Not by going there myself of course – Ben Clayton would make Seg break my legs, and Ledger'd gaol me. The Plod can withdraw your licence to drive. Ben Clayton can withdraw your licence to breathe. I glanced at Lydia, thinking. If she took the risk instead of me, I'd stay safe, right? Anyway, she wasn't indispensable to Lovejoy Antiques, Inc. I was. Therefore it was only right for her to risk everybody's brutality, instead of me. Logic's wonderful stuff.

With a fond smile, I said, 'Lydia, doowerlink. I want you to run a little errand . . .'

Chapter 10

A film studio's the most lunatic place on earth. For a start, it's not a studio. And nobody seems to be filming. There are also millions of workers not working, writers not writing, directors not directing, producers doing nothing but hold their heads, cameras not photographing. No other place can compare. And everybody predicts disaster.

Now, I didn't know any of this until much, much later. I might have been more perceptive, except that Lydia had ditched me at Colchester station after a blazing row. I'd been handed the money to go by train.

'I see that you are too inattentive to tolerate my company, Lovejoy!' She'd exploded this megaton just when I was thinking something really complicated. I found myself in the station car park, a couple of notes thrust into my fist.

'What's up, love?' I was astonished.

'Possibly you are thinking over your forthcoming encounter with Lorane, Lovejoy! Or your evening tête-à-tête with Laila! Very well! Go alone! And may your experience be as pleasurable as your anticipation!'

'But—'

'I shall not meet you from the train, Lovejoy . . .' and so on. She went, head high and shoulders set. Indomitable.

So. Alone at the studios, other side of London, no protection. And a doubting security goon letting me in only when Lorane came to collect me.

'Much good you'll do us, Lovejoy,' she said, striding on in her thigh boots. 'Since you're here, have a word with Max, Vance, and see Stef in action.'

'Who?'

'Jesus. Are you always this dumb? Stef Honor.'

'What's he do?'

'Jesus H. Christopher. You *are* always this thick! He's like the star of this great epic movie. Star. You know star?'

We hopped among blokes carrying wooden sections, bits of furniture, crossed a gang laying some sort of narrow railway line. People were hammering, shouting. A gathering of sobersides dined inelegantly on the hoof round a couple of huge pantechnicons which were doing fry-ups. I instantly grew hungry but Lorane strode us on past. A bloke whistled after her. Disdainfully she raised two fingers, a reflex.

'Star,' I echoed obediently.

'The love interest's provided by Saffron Kay. She's a bitch. Acts only in moments when she's temporarily not on heat. Incidentally, keep your prick to yourself. She costs us a mint every day – and twice as much when she doesn't turn up because she's being serviced by some stray meat. We don't want our schedule buggered. Follow?'

'Follow.' I was out of my depth among this lot. Safer back in old East Anglia between hoodlums giving me contrary instructions on pain of death.

'This specimen gets access, Warren.'

'Righdee, Lorane.' A guard slid corrugated metal aside, admitting us to a cramped bedlam.

Imagine a sort of vast aircraft hangar, people milling aimlessly. Now imagine a room, looking quite like an unroofed cardboard cut-out from a giant cereal packet, set in the centre space. Unutterably phoney. Stick a score of menacing black cameras and lights round the edge, creating a bright island. Trail cables everywhere and there you have it, a film set. Put canvas chairs outside the epicentral pool of chalky light. Add a couple of cabin rooms along one hangar wall. Honest, that's all it is.

'Vance to the right, Lovejoy. Max is in conference with Ray, far office. Shooting an hour from now. See me any problem, OK? Ciao.'

'Er, Lorane, what am I here for, actually?'

'Exasperatio!' she said. 'I don't frigging *believe* it.' And left rolling her eyes in exasperation. Lovely lass, ruined by having to live among mere mortals. Halfheartedly I wandered across cables, darting out of the way of the occasional maverick trolley. Vance was there in a canvas chair, holding forth to a couple of intent birds who were noting his pearls of wisdom. I tried saying hello but he was oblivious of all except his own nebulous thoughts.

People were starting to surge slightly faster, some inner clock activating them. I saw Ray Meese emerge from his cabin, immediately gain a trio of sycophants which Vance and Lorane joined, plus sundries. Quite a team trailed behind him as he headed for the cardboard set. He talked volubly, sweatily gesticulating and pointing. Furniture was moved. I was too far to hear, but whatever he was saying people listened and obeyed. A good trick. Wish I had the knack. Well, I asked myself, looking around, where's the glamour? Is this all it is?

Waiting to me's hell. I went out, wandered away from this hectic non-activity, and soon found myself lost among a group of fork-lift trucks, trailer wagons and caravans. I heard a squeak from a caravan and knocked to ask how to return to civilization. 'Okayee,' sounded deeply from within. I opened the door. And stood. My breath left me gently.

This bloke was spread on a bunk. Two birds straddled him, rocking. Naked *in flagrante*. And, I swear, he was reading the paper. I couldn't even see which way round the birds were. He looked up, quite casual. The birds paused, staring. He swatted them with the paper to restart them. I recognized his face. An actor.

'Yip?' he said. 'Not due yet, hey?'

'Er, no sir,' I improvised weakly. 'About an hour. Thank you.' I quickly closed the door, retreated. Despairing, I knocked on the next caravan, opened it when a man's voice said, 'Yes?' This bonny girl lay sobbing her heart out on her bunk bed, fully clothed, thank heavens. An elderly suited man sat alongside, legs crossed, taking notes. She saw me, screamed herself into a tantrum, all limbs thrashing. The gentleman was unperturbed. 'Yes?'

'Ah,' I said, aghast. 'Sorry to, it's one hour, er . . .'

'Very well.' He said to the girl, 'Saffron? You're soon due in make-up . . .'

She howled, thrashed about. Discreetly I left. Saffron Kay, star actress. Her name was on her caravan door. So was Stef Honor's name, in his equally demanding bunker. Their faces were on all the studio posters. God, I was sweating. I followed the sound of hammering for guidance back to the set. What a world. What a team.

'Lovejoy. Am I glad to see you.' Max stood there, reeling in the maelstrom.

'Wotcher, Max. Look, is this shambles normal?'

'In movies it's tranquillity itself. Got a minute?'

My services were not urgently required so we went into the near cabin, me watching Max suspiciously. He seemed kaylied, drunk, ataxic. The two steps presented difficulty. I gave him a shove, and we were in a plush interior. I mean excessively affluent, velvets and ghastly modern cocktail cabinets, sofas, strip fluorescents, a minuscule desk with a typewriter. The air hung a faint blue fug about us. Cloying. An undergraduate's college room aroma. No wonder Max was wobbly. I was dizzy after half a breath.

He poured us coffee from a bubbling glass bulb thing, sank with a sigh. He was dishevelled, sunken of eye.

'Thank God you're here.' He lit a slender wilting fag, offered me one from his wallet. 'No? Sorry. These keep me calm.' His fingers were trembling. Even my reflection in his spectacles quivered.

'What's up?'

'This movie, that's what's up. We shoot the last interiors this week. Next week we're scheduled on the action, British Museum, the gun scenes. Everybody's giving me a rollicking.'

'Why?'

'Why, Lovejoy?' Until he emitted that bark I'd never known exactly what a hollow laugh was. 'Because wolves, animals out there, are crowding me for the frigging screenplay, that's what.'

'What's a screenplay?'

He stared, shook his head just like Lorane. 'Jesus, Lovejoy. And *you're* going to advise *us*? Here.' He lobbed me a manuscript thick as a Bible. 'A screenplay's every instruction for every actor in every scene. It's camera angles, shots, where and when they're filmed, every word uttered.'

'So?' Bored, I read half a typed page, much of it terse with abbreviations and capitals. The actors seemed to say very little. Every sliver of script seemed numbered. Odd sort of prose, if prose it was. Naturally I looked for the Museum bit. Blank.

'Where're the Museum scenes?'

'You noticed.' He reclined, feet on the coffee table.

'But the robbery. You must have some idea, Max.' I'm not so dim as to believe that financiers rush to throw money at a film company which hasn't worked out the story.

'Oh, don't worry, Lovejoy. I've written the Museum robbery. Sure. The trouble is I've written twenty. Every one different. Every one a reject.'

'Who does the rejecting?' I asked it wearing innocent puzzlement. As if I didn't know.

'Mmmmh? Lorane. On Ray Meese's orders.' He smoked, swigged. 'I'll give you my best version, Lovejoy. Try this: the blackhats, a trio of ex-SAS disgruntlers, do the plotting. Two men, one tart. I've good contrasts there, not bad. Gogogo so far. Hero Stef Honor and heroine Saffron Kay learn of the plot. They're Ruski descent, met at some Ukrainian thrash.'

'Great,' I said, making to rise. 'Well, thanks for the—'

'Sit. Hear the really good bit, Lovejoy.' He blinked, almost tearful. 'The robbery's done by a stolen helicopter. Stef happens to work in the City helicopter terminal. He gets a flame-thrower.' Max began to glow, painting hand pictures before my eyes. 'Saffron's a game girl – comes with him – nightmare dash through the West End – will they get there? Yes-yes-yes! Stef shoots down the whirly-bird! Flames, explosion, kapow!'

He waited, thrilled at his vision. 'Good, Lovejoy?'

I cleared my throat, nodded a bit. 'But what if—?'

'Nononononope!' He imploded, collapsed holding his head.

'Sorry, Max. But you did ask.'

He got a bottle of sherry, drank from the neck, lit another shaky flaky, swallowed the smoke. 'You know what words I hate most in the English language, Lovejoy? *What if*. Hateful words. Those two words I'll hate for ever and ever. Me, a writer, for Chrissakes. These last six months they've killed me.' He pulled himself together slowly, sucking at the bottle, drawing on the reefer.

'OK, Lovejoy. Version Two: Hero Stef loves-hates-lusts-rejects Pretty Bitty Saffron. She works at some crummy bookshop, Museum Street. What does she see, whiling her time at the counter, but a mysterious unexplained van. Get the picture? It comes, goes, comes. Cut to van interior – our ex-gaolbirds and their women, plotting. Saffron tries to warn people – they're crooks, plotting something! People laugh, derision-scorn-dismissal time. Hero Stef says hey babe, you're right. She melts. All's love-lust-randy-insight. They realize it's tonight. For Christ's sake!' He leapt, paced, gestured, swigged. 'And guess what?'

'The crooks've dug into the sewers underneath the Museum?'

He froze, sagged. 'Oh hell.' He recovered, turned to jab a finger. 'Maybe you'll like Script Twenty: they've—'

'Hidden on the roof during a daytime tour, abseil down in the darkness?'

He wept instant tears, gulping and coughing, so I took his sherry off him and docked his fag. 'Lovejoy. They're murdering me out there. Every shagging hour assistant producers come pounding. Meese won't speak to me. That cow Lorane badgers me night and day. Three phone calls before five this morning.'

'Why didn't you ask Major Bracegirdle for an idea?'

'I took him ten – that's T-E-N, Lovejoy.' He sniffed, rummaged for a hankie, wiped his snotty nose on a sleeve instead. 'He nearly pissed himself laughing at every one. Said the thieves wouldn't get two yards with any. The critics'd maul the movie rotten.'

So this was it. At last. Firm confirmation of my reason for being here. And Lorane's hatred, her decision to have me sacked, Vance's evasiveness, my chill reception – all because this film mob identified me with Max their duff writer.

'Max, if you had a definite foolproof idea, how long would it take you to write this screenplay thing?'

He looked, hope dawning. 'If necessary I'd overlap it, do it day by day as they shot. There's time as long as I got the idea approved, Lovejoy.'

I hesitated, thinking.

'Then there's no problem, Max. I'll tell you how you get your tea-leaves into the Museum, so the goodies can do the gunfire bit. Tomorrow be OK?'

He gaped. 'Straight up, Lovejoy? You know how the thieves can enter undetected—?'

'Easy.'

'Believable? So the story's credible, Lovejoy?' He didn't trust his relief. 'If it's not, it's Toytown Time instead of a heartstopper. And I'm negged for life. This is my one big chance, Lovejoy.'

'Oh, I see all right,' I said with fervour. Because I really did, that something here was terribly, horrendously wrong. And it involved me. I'd have to move a lot faster than I'd thought. That quiet peaceful day in the pub admiring a stranger's Roman ring now seemed a long way away. Danger to me is a stink. You pong the stench long before it comes round the corner. Like now.

'Ray Meese'll buy it? Be convinced?'

'He'll have to, Max.' I tried for confidence. 'No other way.'

Somebody knocked. A familiar-looking lass stood there, still smiling. Gabriella, from Bracegirdle's security squad.

'Hello, Lovejoy.' She was so bright. 'They told me you were here. I've got a day off to watch the filming. Mind?'

'Delighted.' I meant it. 'All right, Max?'

'Sure!' He came, jubilant. 'Lovejoy's got a screenplay!' He babbled my praises as we headed for the cardboard room and the camera mayhem.

'Has he, indeed!' Gabriella slipped her arm through mine. She was so friendly. 'Can the world be told?'

'Sure!' Max's relief and my deceit made me feel a twinge of guilt. 'It's plotproof! Ray'll be over the moon!'

'Won't he just!' She hugged my arm. Her eyes met mine with candour. 'And so will we, Lovejoy.'

Evading her gaze, I said, 'Hey, Max. Is it true there's a valuable collection of antique movie cameras at a firm called Samuelson's? How about a deal . . . ?'

The filming was a disappointment. I expected action, lights, a fireworks display of technology. Instead, me, Max, Gabriella stood there like lemons while people milled among cables and cameras round this cardboard centrepiece. Max tried describing the happenings, but gave up in the face of my incredulity.

'Why's everybody an assistant?' I asked him. You've never seen so many assistants in your life. There were assistant grips – whatever a grip is – and assistant cameramen, assistants to first, second and even third thisses and thats. I learned Lorane, personal assistant to Ray Meese, was a power in the land. Vance, first assistant to the director, was if anything bigger still.

'Don't ask me details, Lovejoy,' Max said. 'Just remember the lighting cameraman's God. Hello, they're going.'

'It's Stef Honor!' Gabriella was ecstatic.

I made a mistake. 'I didn't realize Stef Honor was that old. Ouch!'

Lorane had trod on my foot. 'Keep up the tact, Lovejoy. You won't make it to tea-break. That's the great star himself.'

Stef Honor, the paper-reader from the caravan, his bored above-it-all look telling minions that a deity had come among us, doing Planet Earth a favour, sat on a stool while serfs poked at his hair, his clothes, showed him a script.

'What's up with his face, love?'

'Keep your effing voice down.' Lorane's grip on my arm hurt like hell. 'It's make-up. On film it'll seem exactly right.'

I'd seen him years ago in cops and robbers B raters. Must be in his forties.

'Ooooh, Saffron Kay!' Gabriella whispered to me how famous the actress was. 'Imagine! Discovered as an infold pretty only last year, and now she's a star!'

Beautiful all right. It was the girl who'd been having psychoanalysis. She sat at a dressing-table, surrounded by lasses doing ministering touches. God, what a life. Folk forever poking your face, hair, peering in your ear-hole. In contrast, she seemed nervous, edgy. She snapped at a peasant wielding a hairbrush. I caught the look of exasperation which passed among the suffering villeins. The new star was trouble. Same as Stef Honor, but different – his six aides were simply resigned but had to keep serving the mighty, for bread. Lorane caught my look, shrugged, moved us for a camera's priority.

'Stars are stars, Lovejoy. The bastard public's so frigging fickle. They want a particular dumb blonde – and I mean boneheaded – you've got to give them her. And pay her a fortune for the privilege. Flavour of the month, everybody wants a lick.'

'How do you know the film'll be a success?'

'You don't, Lovejoy.' She sounded angry. Nowt new, of course, but I was starting to wonder more than somewhat about Lorane. 'You get the right ingredients, hire the best, lay retainers on half the industry. Then you pray the public doesn't walk away.'

'Why don't you work it out first?'

She uttered a sardonic laugh. 'Lovejoy, don't go into movies. Promise?'

The stars entered the lit area. Folk were beginning to shout urgently. I worried about being blamed for getting in some mega-assistant's way, but Lorane said we were fine. Stef Honor was moved about by Vance. Saffron was in a chair by the cardboard fireside. Ray Meese appeared, hasty and wheezing, his hornrims glinting, pointing and talking to a soberly casual bloke among the cameras.

A run-through's a kind of ignored rehearsal. The actors ignore each other most of the time, until their lines come up. Then it's the teeth, the beamy smile, all attention, words. A sort of synthetic life. Instant coffee, with self-love and animation stirred in as an extra-offer ingredient. Wonderful asset for some con merchant. Why don't actors turn to crime more often? They'd make a killing.

'Are these lights all right?' Stef Honor called at one point. 'Only my best side's . . .' He was instantly reassured with a chorus of, 'Marvellous, Steffie darling!' and, 'Superbo, Great One!' and suchlike. Really nauseating. Eventually the galaxy was ready for creativity to strike. Things stilled.

'We're going for a take, world!' Vance yelled, his first-ever intelligible words. So he did know the language after all.

'What's he—?'

'Shhh!' a million assistants hissed at me.

Instant silence. You've never heard such. Even at our

distance – twenty yards or so – I heard Stef Honor's shoes on the carpet, the glug of the drink he poured while he said hello to Saffron. She was being all lovely and flouncy in her chair. Max nudged me, swelling with pride. His immortal words, his screenplay recorded for all time on film.

'What *can* they be *up* to, Stanislav?' Saffron fluttered.

Stef paused. Deep-in-thought acting vibed out to the universe. 'I don't know, honey,' he intoned, being strong, determined. *'Yet!'* He crossed, gave her a glass, stared soulfully from the window.

'Stanislav. *Promise* me you *won't* . . . do *any*thing risky?' This girl had a way with emphasis.

'Risky?' He gave a hollow laugh, turned full face. 'Bernice, risks are made to be taken—'

'Cut,' somebody yelled so suddenly I jumped. Turmoil began. The sober bloke was looking at an instrument in his hand, pointing to a far corner of the vast hangar. Meese was infarcting, sweating, furiously ballocking people.

'Somebody moved over far right,' the sober bloke called.

Puzzled, I stood on tiptoe to see over the scrum. Nobody there, except a few screens placed haphazardly. A couple of birds poked their heads out.

'Sorry. We were just arranging—'

'Cut it out,' various people screamed. In the hullabaloo while the miscreants were shot or fired or something, I looked admiringly at the quiet middle-aged bloke who'd spotted the movements through solid screens.

'How'd he do that, Max? Magic?'

'The light,' Max said. 'Jim Boyce, lighting cameraman. If somebody behind him moves about silently he'll know. The light's quality changes. It shows on camera.

Imperceptible to the rest of us, even to the light meters. To him it's like a cloud covering the sun.'

'Honestly that good?'

'Try it,' he said. Then joked, 'No, don't!'

'Ha-ha,' I laughed politely. But what a nasty unpleasant skill to have, I couldn't help thinking. Especially troublesome when robbing the British Museum is uppermost in a person's mind, no? Solely for fictional purposes, of course. 'Here, Max. Your story. Have to be daytime, does it?'

'Any time.' He showed anguish. 'Problem, Lovejoy?'

'Problem? How do you spell it?'

He laughed with relief. 'Shhh!' a million assistants went. Another take. And another. And, yawn, another.

That's filming. A kind of hectic boredom with squabbles, hatreds interspersed with grovelling admiration, and insecurities toppling egos in the ferment.

Which meant I had to talk to Ray Meese about make-believe. Worse, it also meant I had to go through with concocting a believable robbery of the only impregnable museum on earth, with security people opposing my particular fairy tale every inch of the way.

It came to me then that the only thing to do was to do it properly. Go for gold. Fiction can be anything. But if you concoct a real scheme it's got to be believable, Max said. Even under the eyes of countless cameras and filmed from every angle for posterity, it must be true. I could see that, and why Max and Meese were panicky. The trouble was I now had a zillion jobs for Lydia, who wasn't speaking to me. And I needed help from sundry hard men, all criminals of sour intent.

Just as I was starting to feel really down, something odd happened, which delighted me at first but returned to worry me later. A tall bruiser beckoned me towards a line of vans, asked me if I was Lovejoy the antique dealer. He said he was Bri, a gofer.

'Only, I've just picked up a winner here.' He was so pleased with himself, said he'd paid a hundred quid for a genuine antique table. 'What d'you reckon?'

Behind one van stood a long table. Thick solid oak, a surface patina honestly 150 years old, dark with age. Sadly I ran my hand over the top.

'Sorry, Bri. Fake.'

'You what?' Frantically he yanked a book from the van's cabin, Gloag's *Short Dictionary Of Furniture*, began flipping the pages. This bit always breaks my heart.

'No good, Bri. See this plug?' I showed him where a plug of wood, three-quarters of an inch thick, interrupted the lovely even graining.

'But that's to hold the table top firm . . .'

'Three massive planks, each one foot wide and eight long. Looks fine, Bri, but notice the three-inch extra piece, as margin all around? And that plug, really ugly showing in the middle of the top? Victorian furniture makers were better than that.'

'But those oak legs, Lovejoy . . .'

'They're always modern, when the table's made from old chapel pews.' For a while it was our commonest fake furniture, especially in London and provincial showrooms. So many chapels and churches were sold, demolished or made derelict in our great post-war retreat from religion that anybody could buy a dozen splendid solid oak pews – wearing the luscious dark patinas acquired from a century's devoted polishing for tenpence each in the early 1960s. A few wise guessers stored some, making a killing when the antiques boom began. Years ago I was practically moved to tears, seeing builders in Colchester burn Wesley's original chapel wood furniture to ash, all for the want of a few shillings . . . I told Bri this. He was outraged.

'I've heard of you antique dealers. Bastards.' He flung his book away. 'You'd say that, just to make me think it's worthless. Then you'd get it for a song.' Like I say, disillusioning an antique hunter breaks your heart. I retreated, sighing, and went to watch them do more filming.

Did I say odd? Yes, odd. Because ten minutes later I saw Bri having a cigarette with Lorane. And they were chuckling. Bri's sorrow instantly forgotten in the lustre of Lorane's company. Or had it been real? I put the incident from my mind. I'd enough oddities to be going on with, without worrying about somebody who couldn't care less about having bought a pig in a poke.

Chapter 11

The day's best bit was they fed us from portable wagons in the yard. Good hot grub, as many pasties as you liked.

Later that night I was frying bread and marge over an oil lamp when the door received a discreet knock, rap rap. Lydia, must be. With the lane in darkness – no street lights in our village – latecomers tend to be aggressive doorbenders.

'Come in, love,' I bawled.

'Light, please, Lovejoy.' Lydia's faint voice.

Sigh. I hunted for an oil lamp, lit it from my candle, carried it to the door to illuminate the outer darkness. She waited while I hung it on a nail in the porch. 'Why don't you just come in when I shout?' She narks me more than any bird I've ever known, which is megatudinous.

'That would be improper, Lovejoy. Darkness suggests surreptitious.'

'Nobody'd see,' I said, reasonable. 'And God did the darkening, not me.'

'Don't blaspheme.' She entered unsurreptitiously, high heels clicking on the bare flags.

Can a fact be blasphemous? I followed, then leapt with a cry. 'My frigging bread, you silly cow! It's burning!'

The swine of a frying-pan does this, stays resolutely

cold until the minute I'm distracted by somebody making her bloody illuminated arrival, then goes nuclear critical. Coughing from smoke, I banged the charred mass into the sink and started scraping. Lydia opened the windows and admonished me. My two budgies, inside because of the outside cold, fell about laughing. I got wild and shoved a fist at their cage threatening fire and slaughter if they didn't shut up.

'Canaries die in this sort of smoke, you two little buggers. Thank your stars you aren't—'

'Lovejoy!' Lydia gestured helplessly at the room as the fug lessened. 'This . . . mess!'

Luckily the subdued light, two candles, concealed most of the untidiness. I thought it wasn't too bad, but Lydia always had to be furious at something. Or, indeed, anything. Spoils my nosh, then plays hell because a sock's out of place. She started tidying, ruining the place.

'What is that, Lovejoy?' She paused, holding a cushion. God, but I could eat her. Now I wish I had.

'Bread.' I demonstrated, stage magician's gestures. 'Margarine. Pan. Source of heat. Presto! Fried bread!'

She moved closer, candles in her spectacles. 'That isn't enough for your supper, Lovejoy. Why don't you cook something more wholesome?' She marched into my grub alcove, opening the fridge, the cupboard, drawers. And stood in silence. I kept going with my frying. A slice in the hand is worth any two of Lydia's theories. She's got more theories than an expectant dad.

'Lovejoy. Don't you ever go shopping? It's poor housekeeping.'

'No, love. It's poverty.' I shoved the bread around the pan to sog up. 'Caused by apprentices nicking cheques and misapplying funds.'

Long pause. Lydia's a lovely lass, but filled with health

and stiff moral motive. I'd have asked why she'd come, except Why is the most useless, pointless, all-less question on earth. Motives simply aren't. I mean, people drop in on me all the time giving out reasons, explanations. None withstands scrutiny. Motive? There's no such thing. It's words made up to eradicate doubt. Why Lydia dresses fifty years old when she's less than half that beats me, and it's no good asking. It all adds up to morality disguised. In practice, it compounds the eroticism of which she's oblivious. I looked round, forking the bread over. She was doing the handbag rummage, frowning in concentration.

'Lovejoy. Why did you not simply explain?'

She's been my apprentice fifteen months, and now she notices she's never been paid and I'm starving. 'You'd have said no, love.'

'Most certainly. But I should have loaned you money.'

'I already owe you, love.'

'Necessity alters cases.' She checked the room with rapid glances, making sure we were still alone, then held out a folded note, palm pronated so non-existent throngs wouldn't see. 'Please take this. A loan, you understand. I insist, Lovejoy.'

'Very well, doowerlink. Thank you.' I gave her a buss, friendly.

'That will do, Lovejoy.' I might have stripped us naked and grappled. 'Now to business. Or shall I wait until you've had your supper?'

'Go on, love. Want some?'

'No, thank you.' She went and sat, watching me for a minute while I started on the one and got another going. 'You know, Lovejoy, offering me your meal when it's so paltry reveals a very generous spirit. It really goes some way towards ameliorating your unsavoury aspects.'

'Eh?' I halted, mouth full of fried bread. What the hell

was she on about? I honestly have to function on guesswork these days. 'Nark it. King George the Sixth loved fried bread. I do it dead right. And less of that frigging unsavoury—'

'I've been thinking there are problems. First, Mr Ledger wants you to visit him at ten o'clock tomorrow morning. Second . . .' She sat, intent on the notebook resting on her lap. Lydia's a candle lady, though I challenge you to find a woman who isn't beautiful by candlelight. She was waiting expectantly; must have finished yapping.

'Er, well.' I thought, looking shrewd and planning. She'd go berserk if she realized I hadn't been listening.

'Is it,' she asked carefully, 'that you are still unhappy associating with Lorane?'

'That's it,' I cried. She must have been on about the mad movie lot. 'You've spotted it, love. Maybe I'm old-fashioned?'

Lydia nodded, ticking her notes. 'Then I'll accompany you instead.'

'Oh, right.' Out of the frying-pan into Lydia's moral-fuelled fire.

'And Tinker's found poor Mr Shrouder's last five local contacts.' She passed me a few pages. 'Lastly, Tinker's deals. He said he had spoken with you of a long thin wooden mallet, painted figures on the handle. He purchased it in Lavenham, apparently on your orders.' She folded her notebook, polished her glasses. Reproof was heading my way. 'Lovejoy. I understand you hadn't even seen a catalogue description—'

'You didn't countermand it, then?'

'Certainly not!' She was indignant. 'But—'

'Thank God. It's maybe more than a mallet, chuckie.' I got up to turn the next bread. 'Back in 1869, some cavalry officers stationed at Aldershot read a magazine. *The*

Field. It told how British planters in North-East India had taken up a ball-and-stick game called *pulu*. The local Manipuris had been experts for centuries. The cavalry formed teams, and called the craze Polo. Now and again you come across old pulu sticks, decorated with Indian scenes for presentation. Not many wooden mallets have long thin handles, love. But all polo sticks do. Worth a few bob to find.'

A pause. 'Very well, Lovejoy. Tinker's also bought a weathervane.'

'Good for him. Wish it was the one at Etchingham.' England's oldest weathervane's the copper one at Etchingham's old church in East Sussex, 1387 AD. Vane was once 'fane', the pennant on a knight's lance, flag. You needed a royal licence to set up a weathervane in the Middle Ages, because fanes depicted a family's coat-of-arms. These were rallying insignia, and therefore politically dangerous. Hence a personalized weathervane indicated you enjoyed royal favour. Tinker had described a copper coat-of-arms vane, which might be a modern repro, but I wouldn't know until I touched it and felt those lovely antique vibes.

'Tinker gave your IOU for that also, Lovejoy.'

'Right. Tea up in a minute.'

'An eighteenth-century wooden tankard, standing eight inches on four squat feet, with inside levels marked—'

'No, love. Not wooden. Birchwood. Tinker's never wrong on woods. That and beer's all the old devil knows. And not any old levels. It's an old Scandinavian tankard, for sharing. You swigged in turn, drank it down one level.'

I balanced the kettle on the spirit stove and came back. 'Did he get the fruitwood eggcup stand?'

'No. He says Liz Sandwell bought that. Six cups, the stand thirteen inches tall, described as early nineteenth century.' Her lovely mouth set for the bad news. 'She also bought the lady's toy shoe, three-and-a-half inches long.'

Groan. Liz Sandwell's my old – i.e. young – rival. 'That's the trouble. Those two items were slotted for the afternoon, and Tinker'd be sloshed by then. And it wasn't a toy shoe. Snuffboxes were fashioned in so-called amusing shapes. The ankle would hinge. How much did she pay?'

Lydia took out her calculator, dabbed expertly. 'Two months, Lovejoy. Was that your estimate?'

It takes me ages to educate people about prices. Saying 400 quid or 600 dollars means zilch, because inflation comes along and the bank rate plunges or soars and your figures are a hoot. Like those 1950s Italian novels where the baddie murders for a thousand lire. But take the national minimum wage, express the price as a fraction of that, and suddenly your comparisons are significant. So, if an antique costs one-sixth of a year's average wage, even if you keep an antique for ten years, no matter what happens to money you've a firm guide on how much to pay.

'That is all, Lovejoy.' She folded everything away and sat there. 'Have you instructions?'

'Aye. Find out why this film's story concerns a theft from the British Museum of tons of Russian antiques it hasn't got.'

She thought. I thought. We found ourselves for a while gazing at each other, doubtless thinking. She coloured slowly, and maybe I did too.

'May I telephone for a taxi?'

'No telephone, doowerlink. You take the Ruby.'

'Will you not require it?'

'No. She only lives a couple of furlongs.'

'She? Indeed.' She rose instantly at that, donned her coat, got her handbag, gloves, the Ruby's key. 'Very well. I obviously mustn't delay your next assignation—'

'No, love. You don't understand. She's only the lady at the bungalow. I just—'

No use. I got the 'Please don't apologize' saga. Women are born hanging judges. Wearily I went and cranked the engine and lit the front and rear lamps for her. I stood and watched.

'Good night, Lovejoy. I shall be along for you at nine a.m. – if you're home by then.'

I called, ''Night, doowerlink,' went inside, blew everything out, locked up, and walked the couple of furlongs down the dark hedgerows to my night job.

'Lovejoy! You're here! We're late!' Eleanor opened the door, blinding the world with glare. She's pretty, dimply, given to flared skirts and manages to make them look fashionable whether frills are in or out. She's never stopped screaming breathlessly since she was born. Everything's uttered at a desperate yell, and she always claims everybody's late. Tonight decibels were a *sotto voce* effort because Henry, my charge for the whilst, must be a-kip.

'I'm not late, even if you are.' I went in, bussing her face, and said wotcher to Colin, her husband. He's a publisher to the penniless, so is pudgy and affluent. He was sitting, resignedly suited, before the television. Nine o'clock news.

'Hello, Lovejoy. All well?'

'Aye, ta. How's the King Emperor?'

'Henry's fine, thanks. He went down an hour since. Our other two are at my dad's. You'll have a quiet evening.'

Eleanor rushed in screaming softly, head tilted to do an earring, modern. Sometimes I despair. Edwardian semi-precious jewellery's even cheaper than the new gunge, but people never listen. 'Lovejoy! His teething bar's in the fridge. His drink's in the usual place. Help yourself to anything. Just look at the time!'

'The time's OK.' I was calm. 'I'm here. The trouble is, so are you.'

'That's *right*, Lovejoy! We should be gone!'

'I'll get the car out.' Colin said so-long and went. Eleanor flashed me a brilliant smile, twirled fetchingly.

'How do I look, Lovejoy?'

'A million quid. I wish I had it. I'd buy you.'

She laughed, ruffled my thatch. 'Silly. No woman's worth that much.'

The real joke is that every woman is, but they always run themselves down. I grinned along. She said she knew I'd be hungry and had left me a plate of dinner, with instructions how to work the microwave. I told her ta. She was spinning out her farewell, the way women do.

'Look, Eleanor. Either send Colin wassailing on his own and jump me, or clear off.' She enjoyed that, laughingly scolded me. I shut the door behind her, listened for Henry's even-spaced little snores, and went to brew up and work out how to enslave the microwave. Me and Eleanor used to be sort of friends, sort of, before she went straight. She keeps hoping to marry me off, as if marriage and antiques could coexist. I'm the one to know. And, I suppose, Sam Shrouder knew it too. I should have thought of that earlier. Henry's one of the six village infants I babysit for. He's at the chew-all and dribble stage, a gnawing gummy marauder. He has a liking for songs I sing him, which proves he's intellectually bright beyond his years, year, but he's physically strong. I've never known a baby pee so high. I think those idle doctors should do research on him, maybe harness the power and wean us off North Sea oil.

Waiting for Henry to rouse – he yodels awake eleven-ish for a nappy change – I noshed the grub and swigged tea, and thought. Henry reminded me of little Joe in Doc Lancaster's surgery. And poor Sam. Which made me take out Lydia's sheaf of notes. Sam Shrouder's five local contacts, excluding my lapis lazuli stone fragment but including Oafie's tickles. Nothing much, really. Typical antique restorer chunks and lumps. There were all little bits. A small brass cogwheel Sam bought from Mannie our local timepiece maniac; sundry snippets of silver from Big Frank from Suffolk; a fragment of Roman glass sold to Sam by Roberta Murdoch, a tea-lady (translation: a lady antique dealer who's in it for pin money). The best frag was a whole page of parchment, with two extra tiny pieces, which Martin sold him after mucho haggle for nearly a fortune, though every dealer will say that. No clues there, I thought. All the same, I'd best pop over and see Roberta, Big Frank, Mannie, and Martin.

A small wail sounded. I went about my duties.

Next morning Tinker astounded the universe, himself included, by shuffling up my path before eight-thirty. He entered while I was shaving.

'What's that pong, Lovejoy?'

''Morning, Tinker. Fried tomatoes, bread. Want some?'

He rummaged, groaning, found a bottle of beer – I hate those tins which open with a sound of striking snakes. He was stained, filthy, stubbly.

'Got a lift on Jacko's coal wagon.' He swilled back the ale, Adam's apple rollicking in and out of his muffler. Jacko conveys villagers to and from town when the buses thrombose. 'I give him your IOU.' Jacko's vehicle is fuelled by my IOUs. 'Big John Sheehan says call him. He's a job for you.'

My heart leadened. Things were already as wrong as they could be. 'Did he say what?'

'Not to me.' His bloodshot eyes roamed, gauged the distance to my one remaining full bottle. His brain urged him it was worth the effort and he wheezed over to grab it. 'The bleeder said you knew.'

Burglary? Same as last time.

'Job for you, Tinker. Suss out Mrs Shrouder.'

'Yon bird Lydia's done it.' His scrawny throttle ecstatically pumped the beer down. 'Hey, Lovejoy. Her's got grand knockers. Aincha stuffin' her yet? She'd be a real good—'

Give me strength. 'Listen, Fauntleroy,' I said patiently. 'Lydia moves in different circles. See? So you try, as well.'

'Keep your hair on. You know she shacks up with Parson Brown. I hate that bleedin' poofter. Fancy motor, posh handmades, and starvin' childer. Time somebody topped the bastard, 'stead of honest workers like Sam.'

'What's the word on Sam, Tinker?'

'Somebody he knew, maybe. Runned down by some motor, folk say. Sam wouldn't hear a motor running at him, him being mutt an' jeff.' Rhyming slang, deaf. He wouldn't of course. 'Police are terribly quiet.'

'Suss that out too, eh?'

'Need ale money, Lovejoy.'

'Come into town, Lydia'll be along after breakfast. I'll cadge a note.'

'Right, Lovejoy. Got a drink to be goin' on with?'

They made me view Sam's body. It looked serene, stitched like a sailor's swag bag. Then Ledger made me read the pathologist's post-mortem report. It hid horrendously behind gruesome words. Lydia sat beside me, still unforgiving. Only her consciousness of being in a police station made her marginally more my ally than theirs. I put the report down feeling green. Odd. It was worse than Sam's corpse. But for those three pages of typescript, Sam might never have existed.

Ledger was in one of his moods of poisonous affability. I was glad to see he'd nicked himself shaving. It's not all bad news. He put his feet up on his desk, struck a match, fouled the air with smoke. 'Well, Lovejoy? Sam, you observe, has departed from this life. Views?'

'Bumped by a vehicle, the doctor's report said.'

'Bumped, Lovejoy?' He pretended consternation, walked about, re-read the relevant bit in silence. 'Doc said nothing about bumped. Crushed, yes. By a vehicle at speed against the solid wall of a service station. More than a mere bump, Lovejoy. More of a splatter, wouldn't you say?'

'Suppose so.' I took stock. The policewoman was idly eyeing Lydia through the office glass, taking in shoes, attire, speculating whether this prissy missie was a secret raver and who with. She caught my glance and looked to her dictating machine. 'When then, Ledger?'

He made an irritable gesture. The WPC settled back on hold. 'Off the record, Phyllis. I'm going to do Lovejoy a favour. I'll stop pulling him in, leave him alone, let him about his lawful business, all that.' Ledger glanced into my eyes. He knew I knew. 'In return, I'm asking Lovejoy's cooperation.'

'Yes, sir.'

I cleared my throat. 'Somebody speak to me.' I felt like a Wimbledon umpire, side to side. 'Sam owed me for a piece of lapis lazuli.' I gave him my most sincere lie. 'It's a semi-precious stone classifiable as a gem. Ancient artists used it as a true ultramarine blue. And before you start thinking nowty thoughts,' I stuck in as he drew breath, 'no, I hadn't commissioned him to do a duffie.' A duffie's a fake made to be sold fast as an original. Usually furniture, unless otherwise stated. The Continent's littered with the damned things.

'A lot of trouble over a bit of pot,' Ledger said, probing.

'I took a hell of a lot over finding it.' I was narked. 'You've no idea of the realities of life, same as all you Plod. It wasn't your streaky South American crud. It was genuine—'

'Second, Lovejoy. Where'd Sam live?'

He'd spotted it, crafty sod. I looked innocent. 'Bradfield St George.'

Ledger raised his eyebrows. 'You have Shrouder's address, yet you're still hounding the poor man out. Why?'

'Sam's elusive. Ask around. He'd put out an order, always some post office box number, always different. Anybody in the trade'll tell you. We hear by phone secondhand or from some pub message.'

'The Scarlet Pimpernel of fakers, eh?'

'Antiques restorer, please, Ledger.'

'Of course.' He gave a lazaroid grin. 'Apologies to the departed. You were very slick to locate him.'

'My apprentice. Mrs Shrouder's registered address is Spere Cott, Bradfield St George, Suffolk. Under her maiden name of Baring. Electoral registration officers maintain a list. It's available in all public libraries. And local council treasuries are always up-to-date with their rating returns. Tell your Phyllis here they can be very useful, and impose no fee.'

Ledger was turning puce. 'She'll bear it in mind,

Lovejoy. Actually we already knew. What I'm getting at is, why didn't any antique dealers know? What exactly did Sam have to hide?' He relit his pipe. 'Mrs Shrouder's statement on the point, Phyllis.'

The WPC activated, read in a bored monotone, '"My husband was secretive about his antiques work." In answer to my question by—'

'Cut the cackle, Phyllis.'

She hurried on. 'She said Sam went off on public transport on working days. Often stayed away two, three days consec. Return by bus. Never revealed where, distance, activities—'

'See my difficulty, Lovejoy?' Ledger was back into calm water. 'Sam gets a bus from sleepy old Noddyville, picks up a few scraps of antiquery from various accommodation addresses around East Anglia, disappears, returns home. He tells his missus who to pay, how much, who to invoice. Even those transactions were via similar drops, post office boxes, the like.'

'Careful bloke, Sam.'

'Not careful enough, Lovejoy. So find answers to questions A and B, Lovejoy, and the forces of law and order will be very grateful. A – where did he do his, ah, restoring. And B – what was he doing in the lay-by, besides getting killed.'

'Tall order, Ledger.'

'Isn't it!' He smiled with pleasure. 'B is more vital than A, remember. Because his unnatural death is incontrovertible proof that he met his murderer there. You see, Lovejoy, my lads are scouring the A12 trunk road. If I find somebody who gave you a lift along it the night Shrouder was killed, you're done for.' I swallowed. I'd forgotten that. My Dutch wagoner, after Seg dropped me close by.

We parted then, me full of promises, Ledger giving me the bent eye but being all Sir Galahad with Lydia. WPC Phyllis was still all speculation. I shook my head a little and shrugged. She didn't quite giggle, but didn't believe me. Ledger had the last word.

'Enjoy the filming today, Lovejoy,' he said affably. 'Western, is it?'

We were leaving when a woman hurried past us down the cop shop steps. As we passed she glanced at me sideways. I'd seen her before, once and swiftly. She was fairish, a little plump, not excessively young, smart. She and Lydia exchanged that hostile up-and-downer women use. I felt a displeasing prickle between my shoulders and turned. Sure enough, Ledger was at his window, smiling in a cloud of pipe smoke. He gave a nod, indicating the woman, winked.

'Love,' I asked Lydia. 'That woman. Do we know her?' We went a different way.

'No, Lovejoy. And without a proper introduction—'

'Are her clothes expensive? How's she dressed?'

'The height of expensive fashion, Lovejoy.' She disapproved. 'I'm not at all sure about those stockings with fawn shoes—'

'That's enough.' Odd that she was leaving the nick exactly when we did. Almost as if the timing was deliberately arranged, say by some scheming neffie Old Bill. But why? Maybe because she was the same woman who'd been leaving Doc Lancaster's surgery as I'd arrived for destitching. Which further meant maybe Ledger had pulled me in to be scrutinized by her as a possible suspect through some hidden panel, a kind of illicit off-the-record identity parade? The penny dropped. 'The rotten swine.'

'Who, Lovejoy? The lady?' Lydia was nonplussed. I must have spoken aloud.

'Sorry, love. I meant Ledger, subjecting you to this.'

'Don't worry on my behalf, Lovejoy. I shall of course draft a letter of complaint to the Chief Constable.'

'Great, love.' Help never helps.

'Lovejoy. Where on earth are we going?'

'Bradfield St George.'

The trouble was, I realized as we went through the shopping arcade, I'd forgotten my People Game. As I limped and fumed, its crucial question returned to niggle: What does she do next? Now that she was free of poor Sam, and looking singularly wealthy dressed unmournful?

'Wait a sec, love.' The woman crossed the road by the post office. A snazzy Jaguar slid alongside. She gave it a bright smile, showed her legs off to the assembled multitudes, got in and was whisked away, Parson Brown's sleek motor looked better every time. We'd just met Mrs Sam Shrouder. And without a proper introduction.

'Is this it?' I wasn't really asking. You know that rather gaunt appearance a house acquires the minute its inhabitants leave? Well, this place looked down, spectroidal. A house without folk's so sad. I honestly believe they have feelings – well, maybe not feelings as feelings, but getting on that way.

'Certainly, Lovejoy.'

'Looks empty.'

'We must call, Lovejoy. We can't stay here in the lane.'

The house stood back from the narrow road. Trees, hedges, a pond, extensive shrubberies somewhat overgrown. Birds were plentiful, pretty confident. I scanned around. No houses nearby, no pubs. The village school we'd passed half a mile off as we'd left the nearest village's outskirts. Sam Shrouder's place blended in all this neffie countryside.

'It must have been a farmer's house once, eh, love?'

She consulted notes. 'Gamekeeper's. Traditionally, this area is associated with three farming families, of which this—'

'Ta, love.' I drove into the gateway. She'd probably got the species of local wheat listed in her bloody notebook. I peered in the windows ('Lovejoy! That is disreputable behaviour . . .' etc) and through letterboxes. No dust sheets. No wonderful antiques visible from any angle. If Lydia hadn't been with me I'd have eeled in somehow and looked around.

Odd, but the house didn't feel like Sam Shrouder's at all. Daft. But Lydia's never wrong. I walked the garden.

'What are we searching for, Lovejoy?'

I gave her a glance. 'What sort of woman is she, love?'

She never answers this kind of question immediately, so I strolled. The drive was macadam, hard surface all round the house. The garage was bare, apart from the usual stepladder, the odd tin of household paint. The shed held hedge-clippers, odd planks, pieces of an old wheelbarrow, a rake, hoe, a rusty saw. Nothing. Long blots of engine oil near the rear of the house. Nil.

We regained the car. Lydia said, 'Mrs Shrouder is . . . unreliable, Lovejoy. She is about to move.' Trans: whore, restless.

'Move?' I stared at Lydia. 'Before or after she knew about Sam?'

'Oh, before.' She looked back at the house. 'I don't think she saw this place as home.'

We drove off. The question was, did poor Sam have any interest in it, as a home? OK, his workshop might be in a top-floor garret or something, but I guessed not. Fakers operate in very defined circumstances, and very few of these circumstances are domestic.

No workshop, not at this address.

'Love, suss out Mrs Shrouder, would you?'

'But why, Lovejoy?'

I yelled, 'Use your bloody head, for Christ's sake! Gawd, do I have to do every bloody—'

'Control yourself, Lovejoy!'

Whoever heard of a classy faker without a workshop? Not me, for sure.

Chapter 12

Here's how you burgle any building, palace, hut, castle.

When you think of it, everything is the sum of its edges. A person, an antique, anything from a tidal wave to outer space. That brilliant intrinsic luminescence of a Sisley painting is created by attention to edges, the so-clever juxtapositioning of different colours. That yacht winning the America's Cup is the one whose surfaces meet the sea with kindliest touch. See? Edges. Museums are included.

Which is why I contemplated edges when I walked round outside the impregnable British Museum.

The principle is to stroll at the object of your heart's desire from a totally unusual direction. Don't do what all tourists do – which is head for Tottenham Court Road tube station and plod in a crocodile to the imposing front entrance. Do it different.

Emerge from the tube at Euston Square, maybe. Drift southwards down Gower Street, and you come to Bedford Square, whose trees lean at the north-west corner of the British Museum's rectangle. Russell Square's trees do the same at the north-east corner. The main entrance is to the south in Great Russell Street. Bloomsbury Street, a dull street of little hotels, marks the west and Montague

Street, equally dull with similar hotels, demarcates the east. That's it, except for this observation: the street lying to the north, Montague Place, is the widest. It's also the one with a building tall enough to overlook the Museum's dour quadrilateral. That building is the Senate House tower of London University. Well, worth a thought. Edges.

Luckily, London helps any penniless crook worth his salt. How come? – because the whole city's riddled with history. Where history rules, no street's straight, no rectangle's perfectly square. And no museum is in the safe and full possession of all its edges.

By four o'clock the traffic had thickened, stenosing Bloomsbury. But the two Montagues, Place and Street, were virtually empty. Not many folk use the north entrance – no shops lie adjacent. The pavement space is empty, which is why occasional coaches use it as their private terminus. I started there, walked east along the Museum's north face, counting windows in a casual and disinterested manner. Eighteen of the great things, not counting the central one over the doorway. Cunning old Bracegirdle had put two-inch mesh net over each window's twenty-eight panes, especially in view of wondrous oriental displays inside the Edward the Seventh galleries. You wouldn't notice the netting from outside. If I hadn't already seen it from inside . . .

'Hello, Lovejoy.'

'Wotcher, Gabriella. Doing the rounds?' This girl was full of coincidences.

'Not really. Saw you strolling, thought I'd come along.' She smiled impishly. 'The idea of the netting is that if anybody got on to the roof and lowered themselves down on a rope—'

'—they couldn't get in even if they managed to smash the window?'

'Spoilsport. You guessed!' She nodded across at Senate House. 'But it'd be quite a job, Lovejoy. Rope and pulley, perhaps. Hang-glider. A manned kite, even. Otherwise it's the rocket-driven ladder.'

'SAS stuff's not in my line.'

We walked round into Montague Street. Hotels on the left, low dwellings on the right stuck to the BM's dark exterior.

'Museum activities in the first few houses here.' Gabriella pointed up the steep steps to the doorways, and down steeper steps to cellars beyond nasty railings. 'Note the padlocked cellar gates, Lovejoy.' She was laughing at me, yet not cracking her face an inch. I was narked.

'Where's trust gone?' I said smiling. 'Did Max consult you, writing his twenty screenplays?'

'Only when he was suicidal.'

'They seem to live under terrible tension, film folk.'

'Understandable, isn't it? You drop a Ming vase, you can manage somehow. But a film maker's like a general at war – only as good as his last battle.'

'Interesting thought.'

'These, Lovejoy?' She paused, almost as if I'd asked about the first few houses before the Montague Hotel. 'The BM research laboratory, a separate unit. The trade union. Further along's the BM education place.'

'Eh?' I pretended to wonder what tack she'd gone on for the moment. 'Oh, these houses?'

She was falling about. 'There is a way into the BM through these premises, Lovejoy. But you probably noticed the railings and wall-top stoppers as you walked along Montague Place earlier. Old-fashioned, but very effective.'

'Mmmmh? I'll take your word.' Laid back old Lovejoy.

We reached the Great Russell Street corner.

'Open space within the railings here, Lovejoy. That

Portakabin's hired. Your villains could of course hire one, try to get it into the grounds by deception.'

'But?' Becoming my favourite word.

'But it's the basis of Max's sixteenth rejected screenplay.'

'No good?'

'It's been tried in real life, Lovejoy. By real crooks. They didn't even get past the gate.' Gabriella was merry with interest. 'We security people want something that really would work. Mr Meese told Major Bracegirdle to judge it as real.'

'Repairs at the far side, I see.' Crowds were milling in the courtyard still.

'Yes. Reinforcing part of the structure.' She smiled. 'Lot of workmen, aren't there, Lovejoy?'

Funny, but I was just thinking that. 'Mmmmh? Oh, aye, love.'

'The question is,' she said innocently, 'which three are disguised Security, isn't it?'

'Gosh, Gabriella, you're clever,' I said in a bored voice.

We walked along Great Russell Street, past the vehicle gate next to the corner bookshops. I eyed the massive iron obstruction. It looked borrowed from Holloway Gaol. Two special constables on guard said hello to Gabriella. We turned right up Bloomsbury Street, more small hotels stuck to the Museum. Traffic crawled in inches.

'Plenty of witnesses on this west side, cars and buses, Lovejoy.'

'And the hotel people,' I pointed out. 'This near Shaftesbury Avenue they'll all tend to be night owls, theatre goers, late-night revellers.'

'That condemned Max's eighth screenplay. He had a hijacked bus ramming the Great Russell Street vehicle entrance.' She was friendly now she had the upper hand.

'What ditched it?'

'Night drivers have two-way radios and presser bleeps.' She indicated the crawling traffic. 'Daytime buses can hardly manage walking pace, let alone work up enough speed to batter through a steel gate. Even if you forget the permanent police guard.'

'Poor Max.'

'Some of the houses become Museum property at the top corner.' Gabriella was pleasant, fonder of me as every pace proved me a failure at least as hopeless as Max. 'You see your problem, Lovejoy? Their back entrances are double guarded. Access is voice-printed, ID carded, photographs warranted.'

'That's the spirit.' I added bitterness to my voice. 'Cheer me up. I'm supposed to be helping the poor buggers, not rubbing their faces in it. And so are you.'

'Don't take on, Lovejoy.' She hugged my arm in delight, jokily putting on an official guide's monotone. 'Moving to the northern aspect of this great museum, ladies and gentlemen, we see once more the Edward the Seventh entrance where we commenced our circular tour. Enterprising crooks should note the two vehicular entrances, respectively east and west, in this aspect. Portcullis gates of reinforced steel, always under permanent live guard day and night. Duplicate, of course, on a non-recurrent rota.'

'Don't forget the autocameras.'

'Banked panels, triple sweepers, Lovejoy.' She mimed little-girl disappointment. 'That was one of my surprises.'

'A central control room?'

'Of course. And enough flyers – spare security men – on instant bleep. Ruined four separate screenplays, one after the other.'

'Good girl. No chance of infiltrating your security cadre, I suppose?'

'Hardly. We're screened by every shrink in the Kingdom. We're printed, weighed, photographed, everythinged. Selection for Security takes a lifetime – one of our sayings,' she added modestly.

'Glad to hear it. How about this: the baddies impersonate honest members of the public and—?'

She groaned. 'And hide inside some duct, sewer, case, office, secret panel? Hasn't that been done to death, Lovejoy? I mean, every cheap crime novel has—'

'Yeah, yeah. Your lads'd laugh, I suppose?'

'They'd fall about, Lovejoy. A million laughs every screenplay. Well? Ideas?'

'Well.' I looked up at Senate House, grinning as we came to a halt. 'Have to be the balloon, I suppose.'

She eyed me quizzically. 'You serious? I told you, aerial assault's been rejected.'

'Serious? Never more, love. I'll give you details.' I bussed her and said so-long, walking away from the guardians of our national treasures. Guardians? I've shot 'em, as the antique boyos say. It's a phrase indicating derision. I could go through the museum like a dose of salts.

Now, ballooning's not my game. Which meant I didn't want to do any. So I'd need Three Wheel Archie, and a little bit of help from my friends.

Chapter 13

I got the help all right. It was the usual sort – nothing but trouble.

The train turfed us out of the station less than an hour late, which is space age stuff for East Anglia. I got the bus into town and found Tinker at the Ship on East Hill. He was sloshed as usual but very pleased with himself, trying to spin his tale out for maximum beer volume. I cut him short by prophesying a drought.

'Give, Tinker.' Three pints, lined up on the table. With mine, four. His rheumy old eyes brightened. He looked about. A dozen barkers were in from the auction rooms and the local antique shops, plus strangers. Town was busy.

'Fuss, Lovejoy, there's a run on Victorian furniture. Small stuff's vanishing, bein' bought up rotten.'

'Why?'

'Word is Ben Clayton's syndicate, wiv some Brighton lot.'

'Clayton? You sure?' More worries.

'That's the word, Lovejoy. Got a prile of tonners. Yanks are buying again.'

'*Three* container loads?' Nobody had bought on this

scale for months. No wonder so many barkers were in. Good times lay ahead for brewery stocks at this rate. 'Clayton's spending that much?'

'Aye. He's called in a lot of favours to get them. Even bought a Yankee tonner customer from that Sussex mob.'

'Christ.' I did a Stef Honor smile, showing the hawk-eyed barkers I was hearing nothing but good news, Lovejoy can cope. But my knees were knocking. A tonner is the antique trade's nickname for a sealed container load. The container of antiques, skilfully packed, goes unopened from the dealer's place to delivery point overseas. It's all above board, Customs and Excise doing their stuff, everything recorded. Much of it's speculative buying. The overseas purchaser trusts the local dealer to assemble a full load of honest antiques, pays up, and doesn't clap eyes on them until they arrive. One tonner costs a king's ransom. It's no farthing Lucky Dip for the fainthearted.

When money's plentiful, or desperately sparse, local dealers start buying customers. That is, they'll pay a dealer for the privilege of supplying the container load ordered by his next customer. If the dealer agrees and is certain the antiques will be just as good as those he himself would supply – it's money for jam. Why? Because he does nothing except sit and twiddle his thumbs while the money rolls in. Purchasing a customer costs one-third of the total value of the shipment. Minimum cost: eight times the national average wage.

A prile is three of anything. Tinker's news therefore meant Ben Clayton had spent at least twenty-four years' wages, plus commission, plus swap fees and God-knows-what else, to buy into the tonner trade all of a sudden.

'Tinker,' I said, still grinning showily, 'what the hell's going on?'

He indignantly nicked my pint, having already quaffed his own. 'Don't ask me, Lovejoy. Thinking's your job.'

'Give me a for-instance.'

He coughed mournfully into the empty glass, raising a gravelly echo. I flagged Patty to keep the ale flowing. She obeyed but held up three fingers, silent scolding for being three weeks behind on the slate. Fascist cow. 'Well, son,' Tinker said, returning. 'That Welsh dresser in Foggerty's at Wormingford – gone. Chandler's mahogany commode that you went daft over – gone. That Sheraton worktable you was after from Liz Sandwell – gone.'

'Stop.' My grin was getting cramp. 'Big spend *and* big buy?'

'Told you, Lovejoy. I knew you'd go spare.'

A Welsh dresser in oak, genuine 1790, is a gift almost beyond price. They're among the loveliest pieces ever to come out of these old islands of ours. Foggerty, a renegade priest, got this beauty from Carmarthen, and had been teasing us for weeks. The reason they're so popular is that you can stick a Welsh dresser anywhere – living-room, restaurant, pub, an ancient creaking rectory – and immediately it's at home. It'll live in perfect harmony with its surroundings because it has design magic: three long shelves above cupboards and drawers, all in lovely symmetry. At first sight a little too rectangular, it harmonizes with any decor, however daft the colour schemes. A Welsh dresser'll add class to any jerry-built modern dross. The commode was in so-called 'plum-pudding' mahogany (from its grain) and cross-banded with pale satinwood. Only four drawers, with splayed-out legs and a bellied apron shape, it screamed 1795 or so. Dealers call the style Sheraton, but at the time furniture makers called the tiny out-curving legs 'French feet'. When I'd seen it for sale in Chandler's window my chest had bonged out Hepplewhite's name, for it was so like his designs. The Sheraton worktable was a slender little—

'The good news is I got a bloke as seed old Sam afore he got done.'

'A witness? You've actually found a witness?' I went and got him a refill and two pasties with chips and a fried egg. He shed tomato ketchup over the plate and began eating, sometimes even using the cutlery provided. His stubbly chin undulated. His mittens added new to ancient grease. I tried to look away but needed to know.

'Go to the lay-by, son. Opposite's a lay-by on the other lane. Duffie's caff stall.'

'Duffie? Didn't he tell the Old Bill?'

'Leave off, Lovejoy. Duffie's not barmy. Watch out.'

I looked around. Lydia's shadow was on the vestibule's frosted glass. I sighed. A faint knock sounded. Patty the barmaid gave me a sweet smile.

'A lady wants you in the porch, Lovejoy.'

'Great, Tinker. See you.' To jeers and catcalls I rose and reported for duty, my ears burning.

She glanced about. 'May I invite you to tea, Lovejoy?'

Must be life-threatening. 'Er, well . . .'

We have a sedate restaurant – only one – called Jackson's, not far from the war memorial. Resolutely it maintains standards: white tablecloths, crumpets, Dundee and Eccles cakes, a choice of muffins, white toast. It doesn't go far if you're starving, but since women never are they love the place. Me and Lydia faced each other. The waitress, astute diagnostician, had given us a table for eight so we were apart rather than together. Lydia ordered, being terribly brave about something.

A few false starts later, 'Lovejoy,' she said.

'Look, love. I'm sorry. Whatever I did, I apologize.'

'No, Lovejoy. Please.' She sat, turgid, prim, gathering resource. It looked like yoga from where I sat. She was charming, a smart dark suit, cardigan, a brooch by the Frenchman Froment-Meurice – gold, white enamel, amethyst, two emeralds – on her left lapel (a lady's left is also correct since Liz II, Lydia once tartly rebuked me when I'd asked). 'I must ask your forgiveness.'

'Eh?' This was new. I scrutinized her for guile, but she lacked it as always. 'Well, er . . . yes. Of course, Lyd.'

'Lydia, please,' mechanically. Then, gentler: 'I had no right to imply, utterly without foundation, that your interests in Lorane were of . . .'

'Yes, love?' Lorane? I'd no notion what she was on about, but you must go careful.

'. . . of a carnal nature, Lovejoy. There. I've said it.'

'Lydia! Really! I'm shocked . . .' My playing up was a joke, but I find you can't joke much with them. Lydia closed her eyes, hands and handbag on her lap.

'You're right to be upset, Lovejoy. All day I've felt remorse.'

'Me too, love,' I said, wondering what about. 'But it's all past.'

'You're generous, Lovejoy. I'm grateful. Especially when you were so desolated by your dear friend's tragedy.'

'Ah, well.' The grub had come by now, its aroma fighting for attention.

'To atone, Lovejoy, I have excavated details of the film company.' She rummaged in her handbag. Safe in the knowledge that this was an indefinite process, I scoffed a load of muffins and started on the toast and marmalade. 'Here.' She passed me a spring notepad filled with her methodical handwriting.

'Everyone envies me, Lyd,' I said truthfully, though I didn't tell her why. There isn't a dealer in the province wouldn't give an antique Spanish vargueno for an hour's chance alone with Lydia. I've even had blokes—

'Here,' I said. I'd been flipping through her booklet. 'Where'd you get this balance sheet? Biographies, reports on the principal assistants. Ray Meese. Lorane. Vance. Max.' I gaped at her in wonder. 'You gorgeous tart. Aren't you the clever one, then!'

Her colour heightened. Womanlike, to disguise it she ballocked the waitress for letting my plate get empty. 'I also have your catalogue, Lovejoy.' She laid it on the linen cloth. 'The expense! I told the director of the St Edmundsbury Trust that there's simply no need for prices to increase exponentially when production costs rise arithmetically . . .' etc., etc. 'Mr Sheehan agrees.'

My jaws froze on a gnawed muffin. 'You saw Sheehan?'

'Since he wishes to retain you in antiques, we agreed he should pay an advance.' She placed an envelope on the table. Today was suddenly Christmas. 'I also bought in groceries for you.'

'In your handbag too?'

The quip sailed over her head. 'Of course not. In the cottage. I made sure the villagers were fully aware of your absence when I visited.'

To save my reputation, no less. 'Thank you,' I said gravely.

An hour later I trundled the Ruby along the bypass to Duffie's roadside caravan caff, having sent Lydia to tee up Three Wheel Archie. All of a sudden things were quickening too much for my liking.

Incidentally, a vargueno's a decorative front-hinged writing chest on an elaborate framework. And Lydia's worth more. Except that now she'd hired me to Big John Sheehan. I've never known him pay in money, only blood.

Chapter 14

The A12 trunk road's a trickster. You get a few miles of safe dual carriageway, then it's back to nasty little windings between fields, woods, hedgerows. It was in one of these remotish stretches that Sam Shrouder died.

Duffie – not Duffy, note, but some contracture of a name as yet unknown – is typical of the unlicensed roadside caff. Usually unshaven, unwashed, filthy apron older than him, he operates from a drop-sided caravan. It's motorized for a quick getaway should the Old Bill come calling. No licence means he'd be fined every ten minutes. His chipped and weathered caravan stands in a lay-by, those grotty macadamized nooks wherein weary motorists can park and kip. Duffie's the only facility. No toilets, no warmth.

As I arrived he was just packing up for the day. One bare bulb lit the lay-by. The occasional car swished past in the drizzle, lights on against the murk. I parked the Ruby. The caravan's wall lifts to form a shelter for customers.

'Wotcher, Lovejoy. Thought you'd be along. Tinker's been worrying me, dog-a-bone.'

'Good lad, him. Tea, Duffie. And a pasty, please. How's trade?'

He served, slapdash and grue. Hot pasties, scalding

sweet tea, pouring rain. Paradise. I paid, grumbled about the price.

He leaned on his elbows. 'I didn't see it happen, Lovejoy. Sam.'

'Ledger's busy lads come nosing?'

He glanced a crooked glance. 'Anything ever happens, it's always the day I stayed at my daughter's.'

'Wise old Duffie.' He's never been a witness to anything. And when the prowl cars call he usually slams his caravan sides and claims he's just pulled off the road for a pee. 'Tell me certs, then possibles.'

'You know the lay-by, Lovejoy?' He nodded at the hedges opposite, painting me a mental picture. 'Opposite the service station fifteen miles up. I use the lane this side. Posh nosh, petrol, loos. I know the gaffer, rotten sod. Bubbles me.'

'Has you moved on, does he?'

'Complains I take away his trade.' Duffie lit a fag, coughed in the general direction of his uncovered seed cakes, hawked phlegm and spat downwind. I could see why he and Tinker got on. 'Never groused about Sam's bloody bus.'

'Sam? Didn't know he had a motor.' Ledger hadn't mentioned one.

'Not motor, pillock. Bus.'

I'd misunderstood because bus is slang for an ordinary car. 'Bus as in bus?'

'Mmmmh. Good customer was Sam. Quiet. Deaf as a post. Tell you something secret, Lovejoy.'

'Yes, Duffie?' I was all eager.

'Sam had a sweet tooth. Always bought my rock cakes. A connoisseur.'

'Oh.' Well, Duffie was bound to have a different world view than me. 'You ever see inside?' This was queer. I couldn't imagine Sam, reclusive faker, driving a blinking bus about, all hours.

'Once. He pulled in close, avoiding football charabancs. I saw. You never seen so many tools in your life. Lights. I could've sworn I saw a lathe, no bigger than your fist. And a painter's easel, wood and all that. Lamps down its length. I never asked him.'

'A workshop.' No wonder nobody had the cunning old devil's workshop address. His given locations were all temporary drops, post office boxes. From Oafie's accounts I knew Mrs Sam Shrouder was compliant. But why had nobody known this? I asked Duffie.

He chuckled. 'Where d'you hide a brick, Lovejoy?'

'On a building site.'

'And a bus? You put *Special* on the front. Park it in odd lay-bys, never the same twice. Black the windows—'

'—Spray it obscure colours.'

Duffie laughed, his laugh a creak behind bad teeth. 'Maroon and green. That was how I realized it was his bus. The colours were a visiting team's, by accident. Some Ipswich coaches started crowding him. He was scared stiff. Plonked his bus so close I thought he'd ram me.' He described it: a single-decker, oldish, snout-nosed country roamer.

'You hadn't known it was Sam's? You said he was a regular.'

'He was, now and again. But never with his bus. Maybe I'd notice it pass, maybe not. Occasional like, he'd park it a mile off, no lights. I'd see it along some lane as I passed. Sam'd walk up, have a nosh, walk off.'

'Ever get a lift?'

'Nar, not him. Though the lads'd offer, like. That was how I placed him, deaf as a post.'

So that was Sam Shrouder's life. Up in the morning, drive to some remote area, park his bus, start his fakery work. Occasionally call at a country post office to collect the antique restorer materials he'd told his wife to order. He'd work all day in his mobile workshop, nosh at some roadside caff like Duffie's. Then home. From Duffie's account Sam'd been careful not to be identified with his mystery vehicle.

'Sam's big day, Duffie?'

'I'd help you if I'd seen, Lovejoy.' He meant it. 'He'd parked near three charabancs, far as I remember. Called for his dinner an hour or so later, took it with him. Y'know, Lovejoy, I think Sam really appreciated me keeping shtum about his wagon. Never said much, but I got the feeling.'

'What's happened to this bus, Duffie?'

'Saw nowt, heard nowt. First I knowed, the lorry lads were on about a bloke getting smudged. Wasn't until the local paper I knew it was him.' The local advertiser, next morning. 'His bus was still there when I went home. It was standing on its own.'

'Ta, Duffie. I owe you.'

'Then pay me, you mean sod.'

We parted, amicably. Friends have to do without payment.

On the way home I made a detour, a million miles out of my way. No bus in the service station. I stopped and walked round among the parked cars. There was an ugly scrape of damaged brickwork on the garage wall. Gulp. Which raised the question where Sam's bus was. No wonder Tinker had been pleased. For this I'd owe him beer now till New Year.

So it was that, in command of more info than anyone, I chugged my Ruby homeward in a feeling of high jubilation. Towards its final doom. It was making its last journey on earth, in its present existence.

* * *

The garden was drenched, its grass marked by tyre ruts. A great car stood askew before the cottage. Ben Clayton was emerging from the – my – porch. Seg stood, watching me arrive. He posed as a mad gorilla does, itching to batter.

'Wotcher, Ben. OK?' I cut the Ruby's clatter to stillness.

'Come here, Lovejoy.'

My path was suddenly twice as long. I plodded up it, heartsunk.

'What did I tell you, Lovejoy?'

'Er, when exactly, Ben?'

Seg belted me in the belly. I folded, vision blurred and retching. God, nausea's terrible stuff.

'Don't leave marks, Seg.' Ben was in high good humour. 'Lovejoy's in deep with Mr Ledger and his nasty plods these days. We don't want him running telling tales, do we?'

God, but I hate the first person plural. Teachers, bullies, psychotic crooks exacting vengeance – hear it, you know fascism's singled you out for torture.

'What's up, Ben?' I croaked, hoping some lie might cavalry to my rescue.

'Wait.' While I tried to recover he went to the Ruby, felt around, brought Lydia's catalogue. 'Recognize this, Lovejoy?'

'I can explain, Ben, honest—'

Woomph, thud, thud, thud. I assumed my retch-and-spew kneeling position, head on gravel, arms hugging my heaving belly. Sweat broke out of every pore. My skin crawled in pain.

'Who sent his popsie to the exhibition when I'd said not to?' Ben paced a step or two. 'Right, Seg.'

That plural made me brace myself for more kicks, even harder blows. None came. But something smashed, metal on metal and glass shattering. Skewed, I looked up, hoping it'd be something else not me. Seg was at the Ruby with a massive sledgehammer. Did the maniac travel ready prepared for demolition, tools and everything? He did in the lanterns, doors, screen, crashed the steering-wheel on to the grass. The bonnet, boot, the engine. Hugely elated, muscles bulging and a-gleam, he was an extra-terrestrial from some science fiction film. Maybe ten minutes later he rested. I hadn't moved.

'Here, Seg.' Ben tossed him the catalogue. 'Burn this. We don't want Lovejoy to waste his energy, do we?' Oh-ho. Plural.

Seg lit the catalogue with a match, dropped it by the driving seat. Smoke and flame spread instantly. Seg had been thoughtful with petrol.

'His cottage, Seg,' Ben said, admiring the flames.

'No! No! Ben, please.' I grovelled, crawled, screeching pleas. 'My budgies are inside. Please, Ben.'

He beamed, really shone down at me with delighted fascination. 'Not burn, Lovejoy. Only . . . shuffle things a bit.'

Seg went inside. Crash and bash. Windows shattered outwards. He made merry to the sound of my ignited motor's crackle.

'See, Lovejoy, it's like this.' Ben sounded so patient. 'I've an interest in that Russki exhibition at St Edmundsbury. It's a lot – repeat, el mucho – of gelt. Out of your tinpot league, Lovejoy.'

'I've done nowt, Ben. Honest to God.'

'Correction, Lovejoy. You *will* do nowt.'

The crashing stopped. Crunching glass fragments, Seg appeared in the porch. He nudged the splintered door, which fell with a crash. He was carrying my budgies' cage. They were fluttering in fits and starts.

'What'd I do with these, Ben?' Seg called.

He thought a second. 'Leave them, Seg.' He shone his hearty face at me. 'We'll have pigeon pie when we torch Lovejoy.'

He jerked his head, got into his saloon. Seg chucked the cage on to the grass, the budgies spilling out. Seg trudged over, took the driver's seat. I watched them go. Tarry smoke swelled into the sky, mercifully away from the cottage. I got myself upright and started making my tweeting noise. It's a half-whistling sound made with my lips padding rapidly together.

Nock was cheeping in the apple tree nearest the cottage. Egg had decided laziness was the better part of valour and stayed where he'd fallen in the grass. I got their cage, removed its floor by unlatching the clips, and hung it in the tree.

'Home time, lads.'

Nock came on to my finger straight away. Egg, always trouble, was half an hour in the catching. Wouldn't come on my finger, strutted away every time I came close.

'I'm in frigging agony here, you burke,' I groaned, crawling after him. Finally a couple of village children caught him, visiting to be awed by the burning Ruby. Nock nodded off but Egg was pleased with himself at his escapade, cheeping and showing no remorse. I showed him my fist.

'I'll smash your teeth in, you little bugger.'

'Ooooh, you sweared!' one of the kiddies said, Elsie.

'No, I didn't. It's budgie language. It means Bless You.'

Six children came at the finish, sweeping up and generally making the cottage more of a mess than Seg but taking longer about it. Some loon had called the fire brigade. I sent them away in a temper, yelling had they never seen a car on fire before. The children were thrilled by everything happening, burning car, smashed-up cottage, fire-engines, the budgies, a row with the fire brigade. I could see I was famously entering village legend. I wasn't sorry when they cleared off.

Alone.

Some of Lydia's supplies were intact, though jam, flour, frozen stuff, a cake, mostly were smeared on the broken furniture. My divan bed was in smithereens. Shelves dangled, table de-legged, chairs were fractured. Still I managed to brew up and fry some bread and a couple of slices of apple, ready for a long think. I sat on the floor to dine. By now I needed light because dusk had fallen. I found two candles.

The trouble was, armies of merciless helpers were homing on me like bomber waves. This disaster was a typical example. I'd started this particular adventure sitting peacefully in Doc Lancaster's surgery. Nurse Anna then helped me. Then Lydia helped, several times. Then Lorane, by giving me a film job. Then the Countess, with tea and sympathy. Then Big John Sheehan, paying me for that burglary. And here I was, still on fried bread, but further sunk in abject poverty with my motor in meltdown, my cottage marmalized, and myself bruised every inch. The fact I didn't look injured was no . . . Hang on. I rose, gasping, found a sliver of mirror, peered at my face. Beautiful as ever. 'Don't leave marks, Seg.' *Why not?*

Ben didn't mind the world – well, the village – knowing I'd been done over. He didn't mind that the fire brigade might be called. He didn't mind frightening me to death.

But carefully, meticulously, he did mind two things. One, he minded me seeing that exhibition. Two, I was to remain as pristine and unsullied as ever. My usual dishevelled self stared in puzzlement from the bit of mirror. How very odd. After all, I'm no film star. All right,

I don't go short of women, but that's more good luck and their barminess than any magnetic charisma I possess. Hang on. What was that? *No film star?*

Well, well, I thought. And went back, finished my nosh.

An hour later I'd done what I could – clearing up's faster unaided – and got my jacket. I nailed bits of wood across the windows, but left a two-foot gap at floor level for the badgers to come in. They're born scroungers. They'd nosh anything within reach, save me more of a job.

'Come on, you two. We've a long way to go before morning.' I'd parcelled the budgies' spare seed, millet sticks, cuttlefish, and half-emptied their water dropper for the journey. I have a green cloth for night cover, and draped it over their cage.

Jacko wasn't too pleased being hawked out on a chill wet evening, but I made him. He drove me the hour to the Alconbury lay-by on the Great North Road. I said nothing the entire trip, just sat thinking, carrying the cage. He always sings light opera when he's driving anyway, so talk's not worth much.

Another twenty minutes and a huge night-hauler's headlights saw me standing in the rain, arm raised. It slowed and pulled in ahead of Jacko. A pleasant stoutish bloke leaned out of his high citadel and called had I a job.

'Aye.' I ran, fetched the cage, climbed and handed it up. He was delighted, couldn't resist peering under the cover at Nock and Egg.

'Budgies, eh? I breed canaries.' He was grinning as he took the paper on which I'd scribbled my cousin Glenice's address in the North, and joked, 'Hardly show birds, mate.'

'They're thoroughbreds,' I said upwards in the rain. 'Too good to go on show.'

He looked at my face. ''Course they are, mate. That's what I meant. To Lancashire, is it? That'll be one frog. I'm to Edinburgh.'

'All right. Ta.' I paid him. A frog's a transfer of the illicit parcel, load, whatever, to another long-distance wagoner who's going nearer the destination. Each such shift costs extra, since every leg of the journey requires a new lorry-man to risk his job for carrying unauthorized clobber. 'Be good, Nockie, Eggie. And don't give Glenice any trouble. OK?'

'I'll watch them,' the man said kindly. 'So-long, mate.'

'Thanks. So-long.' I stood while the vast lorry snorted on to the wet roadway, blew my nose, and went back to Jacko.

'Home sweet home, Jacko.' I raised a finger when he drew breath to start one of his notorious grumbles, and we departed, not peacefully, but in peace.

Now, on that return journey I pulled out Lydia's tidy little notebook. While Jacko bawled selections from *The Desert Song* and *Cavalcade* and his one functional windscreen-wiper threshed hypnotically, I read her meticulously classified notes by the dashboard's faint gleaming.

It was something I should have done yonks ago. By the time we hove into the village I was a far, far wiser idiot than I had been since my trouble began. I'd been thinking antiques. I should have been thinking movies.

Chapter 15

Tinker found Three Wheel Archie an hour before they shouted last orders in the White Hart. I got a lift from Margaret Dainty who owed me for divvying a porcelain fire mark – these wall plaques identified householders as insured by particular fire brigades, 1830 onwards, and are highly collectable. Pricey at an average month's wage, it was genuine all right. The trouble was it belonged to her and not me.

Three Wheel never grew much, though his head's the right size. On account of being a dwarf, he travels on a canopied tricycle. Tinker proudly showed him to me, then complained he'd had to buy him a pint to keep him in the tap room till I'd arrived.

'Cost a frigging fortune, Lovejoy.'

'All right, all right.' I gave him a note, raised a finger warning him not to (a) spit phlegm into his empty glass, (b) not to spit over me, and (c) not to bawl gravelly-voiced questions about whether I'd found Duffie or not. He went cackling in glee to drink his silly old head off.

'How's the new motor, Archie?'

'Beautiful, Lovejoy.'

'Much on the clock, now?'

He grinned at my sobersides joke. His new car's

actually old, never having burned rubber. Or petrol either, for that matter. It's housed in a palatial garage and gets trundled out for serious cleaning in sunny weather. I can't see the point because he can't reach the pedals, but Three Wheel Archie can so that's all right.

'How do I get the measles out of an Indian paper print, Lovejoy?'

'Gawd, Archie. Be careful.' Measles is trade nickname for 'foxing', those brown spots – actually a micro-organism – which trouble books, prints, and water-colours. 'If you're sure it's Indian paper it won't like water. Shake some ether with hydrogen peroxide – you buy it about four per cent. The ether takes the peroxide out of its water, floats as a layer. Then you use that with a cotton tip.'

'What if I do get some water on it?'

'Chuck in pure ethyl alcohol, fifty-fifty. It cuts out most of the water attack. Remember me when you sell the print. Anything interesting, Archie?'

He gazed levelly at me, not easy for a pint-size on a pub chair. 'Not as interesting as your proposition, Lovejoy.'

To business. 'Do you like open spaces, Archie?' For all I knew a titch might have ingrained aversions or something.

'Take or leave 'um, Lovejoy.' He was puzzled.

So far so good. 'What about confined spaces, then?'

His brow cleared. 'An oliver? It'd depend what for.'

An oliver's a robber's trick named for Oliver Twist. In the course of burgling, you pop a small being, usually a kiddie, through a fanlight into a house. The little quietly trots around, opens a door from inside, and lets in his team of burglars.

'There's gelt, Archie. It might be two hours, cramped up. Dry land throughout.'

'And who lets me out?'

'It's your hand on the lever, start to finish.'

'Straight up, Lovejoy?'

'As God's my witness, Archie. You can step out any time and home you go. I give you a story to prove you're innocent, in case.'

'OK, then. As you tell it.' We sat in silence for a while as the pub revelled all about. 'Ether and peroxide, eh?'

Tinker hove over with an empty glass, a continual source of distress to him. 'Here, Lovejoy. You helpin' these other wallies for nowt again?' He's always on about charging for my advice. A wally's an antique dealer. Funny-odd that it's general slang for a buffoon. Or maybe not.

'On me, Tinker.' I gave him enough for a couple of refills for himself and Archie to show the matter was more complex than it seemed. 'Anybody going by Parson Brown's?'

'Get you somebody, Lovejoy. Ten minutes.'

A matronly lady later dropped me at Parson's place in the dark. She was on her way to her sister's down the estuary. The price I paid for the lift was considerable – I had to admire her crummy modern bejewelled gold infallible Rolex watch for the entire journey. And she coyly gave me her phone number. I ask you. Accept a lift to lend them your company and they want blood.

Winnie was alone watching telly, a game show where the cliffhanger's whether some bird wins a washing machine or a weekend in Reykjavik. We made polite how-are-you-but-don't-for-Christ's-sake-tell-me noises. She brewed up, coming intermittently to see the whooping studio audience greet the Second Coming. She still wore her apron, and her a dancer.

'Did Parson leave a message, Winnie?'

'Walter?' She dished tea up, eyes wavering between me and the screen. Contestants were showing elation, running out of the audience, waving both hands. Unnatural and phoney. 'No. Should he have?'

'When I called. Remember? He said about a valuable crucifix. He's going to sell me it.'

'Oh dear. I knew this would happen.'

'Good heavens! She's won a camera!' To lessen her anxiety.

Winnie was instantly back into a smile. 'She'll go for the golden gong. You see.'

We watched the balderdash to its merciful end, then had our tea as the news started.

'He's never here, you see, Lovejoy.'

'Just recently?'

'Oh, years. Weeks at a time, months even.' She indicated her home with a lethargic flap of an arm. 'He has such commitments. I sometimes wonder how we had Jules.'

'Been busy lately, I expect.'

'Lately?' She pursed her mouth, rueful. 'He's chasing some scheme, Lovejoy. Always had to have a faster car, snappier clothes, bigger deals. He only wanted me because I was in some chorus line he thought glamorous.'

'We're all a bit like that. Magpies.'

She eyed me candidly. 'We women know. We make allowances. But it can go too far and destroy people, even families. I feel you understand, Lovejoy.'

I was beginning to feel uncomfortable. 'What'll you do, love?'

'I've a brother in the West Country. His wife's lovely. They know how it's been. As if Lavina and Jules had no dad. And I know he plays around. Keep secrets in this village? My brother's got a travel agency, with a spare flat above it. Just think, a little job. I'd meet people. Walter wouldn't even notice us gone, probably be glad.'

'And you?'

'Yes. Relieved.' She'd made up her mind, did she but know it. 'Is your crucifix really important, Lovejoy?'

To this day I don't know what made me say it. 'And urgent, love.'

'I have a number I can call, Lovejoy. I can't let you have it, but I'll ring him as soon as you're gone.'

'Great. Ta.' I'd known she would have. Police and insurance companies are big on out-of-hours contact for antique shops. I bussed her a so-long and caught the country bus from the coast on its last town run for the night.

That's how it's done. Execution.

Ever wondered about emotion? It's dicey, of course; it fluctuates. I don't mean individually, like you're sad one minute and happy the next. No. I mean I really do believe we all surge together. We're all more inclined to be down in concert, or jovial as one. Scientists say it can't be true, but what do they know? So I wasn't surprised to find Suki Lonegan with her eyes all red and a hankie balled in her hand.

'Refugee Lovejoy, love. Chance of a cuppa?'

She turned and walked in. Well, swayed. Her house is set back from the road, in town about a mile from the Arcade. I followed warily. No husband, no other visitors. I brightened.

'Hungry, Lovejoy?' She sounded tight, angry.

A table was set, two twisted red candles, floral table centre, lazy susan loaded with dishes of bits. Sambals? Curry scented the air. Cutlery receded into the distance. Romantic elegance was everywhere, and somebody hadn't come.

'Well, if I can help . . .'

'You bloody well can. Open that bottle.'

Wine, in a sloping basket. A corkscrew. Uneasily I walked round the lovely supper setting. Romance was called for. She'd drawn the short straw, scruffy battered Lovejoy instead of Sir Gawaine.

'You mean this wine, Suki?'

'Get on with it!' Dishes clattered, an oven door slammed. Women get madder in kitchens than in bed, even, which is saying something. Suki had already started on hooch out there. Obediently I popped the cork, replaced the bottle, stood waiting like a spare tool. I decided *on* light chitchat.

'Er, Suki? You can still get one of those antique dusting-brush corkscrews with a side lever, patented, for less than a hundred quid. Why don't you—?'

'Lovejoy!' Suki flung back the kitchen door with a crash so loud I winced my ribs into stabbing pain. She stood there, glaring. A wisp of hair was loose on to her forehead. 'I want to hear nothing – nix, zero, bugger-all – about antiques. Understand? Mona Lisas, Virgin of the Rocks, Venus de Milo. *No* antiques.'

I swallowed. For romantic elegance read fury. 'Right.'

She advanced on me, threatening. She was dressed lovely, long skirt, white lace blouse, bishop sleeves, a piqué-bead necklace sweeping below her frothy lace throat. She clutched a wooden spoon.

'I love your necklace, Suki,' I said brightly. 'That's tortoiseshell, isn't it? Gold and silver, too, unless I'm mistaken. It's usually only papper mashie—'

She screamed, 'Shut fucking up!'

I backed away. 'Sorry, love. I was only—'

'Sit *down*!'

'Er, thanks. Only I can't stay too long—'

She slammed me into the carver chair, head of her pretty table. Two goes to light the candles, but she did it. I sat in worried silence, eyeing the distance to the door.

Breathless from sheer rage, she quavered, 'Now, Lovejoy. Move one fucking inch I'll hunt you down and kill you. Please pour.' And she swept into the kitchen, slamming the door.

I'd come for sanctuary and found Castle Perilous. Crashes sounded from without, just like me and the cottage while Seg demolished my home. I was just working out which was worse when she yelled, 'Lovejoy! Have you poured?'

'Yes! Yes!' I scrabbled, poured shakily, got the bottle back in its basket without a drop spilled. My prayers answered, the first time ever. I sat some more, thinking hungrily of her piqué necklace. Ivory or tortoiseshell beads, inlaid with gold and silver points, leaves, star shapes, are called 'true' piqué, and usually date from before 1855. Later stuff was made of any old rubbish. Pakistan, Bangladesh, and Taiwan turn out fakes – bits of gilt and foil in blobs of resin you can spot even without a handlens . . . She entered, flung down a tray of stuff, swept out, returned, did magic pointing with a remote control to start a seductive Vivaldi from the wainscoting, served us vichyssoise soup, rushed dizzily to the mirror to adjust her hair, hurtled back.

'Now, Lovejoy,' she panted, composing herself. 'Cheers.'

'Your health, love.' We toasted with the best grace we could manage in the circumstances. 'And thank you for your kind invitation.'

'Not at all, Lovejoy. My pleasure.'

'You, er, look beautiful, Suki.' Well, it's standard but it often works.

'Thank you, Lovejoy.'

'I'm sorry I'm not classily turned out. You deserve better, love.' I'd thought that safe too because it's true for all women, but mistake. Tears ran down her cheeks. We continued in a silence broken only by her chokes and sobs.

'That was luscious. Any chance of some more?'

She paused, nodded, rose and did the woman's second-best giving. Second course dressed globe artichokes. She didn't finish hers, so I helped her out. I find women don't eat much. We got the main course, curry, the rice properly done to my delight. It was great. She partook very little, finished up drinking us into a second bottle, elbows on the table, fingers laced pretty beneath her chin, just watching me. 'Wild strawberries, those, Lovejoy,' were her only words, used when serving a strawberry and chocolate roulade.

'Never mind. Just as good.' Maybe the shops had run out. She almost reached a smile at that for some reason but didn't speak until the coffee. It was done in a complicated gluggy thing, very American.

'Lovejoy. You have women. But why haven't you got a woman? Or have you?'

Dangerous talk. I got served some more. She resumed her stare. I start worrying in case I'm a noisy eater, which is repellent.

'They don't think I'm up to much, love.'

'Including your smarmy little cow?'

'Lydia? With her morals? The Pope might stand a chance, not me.'

'But you have plenty of others, haven't you?'

'Best ask them, love. Not me.' It's my policy.

'I'm glad you don't gossip, Lovejoy. I'd heard so.' She refilled her glass. 'What about me, Lovejoy?' Now I knew she'd definitely had too much. 'Am I attractive? Truth.'

'You're what blokes dream about.' It was true.

'Then what stops a man from coming, Lovejoy?' Tears started. She led us to a couch, Vivaldi still giving out sensuous living. No lights, just candles. She blotted her eyes, sat with her glass. This was all getting too much. I was replete with grub, but a lovely bird in these surroundings makes for new hungers. 'I mean, a man shows interest, it's wonderful. Then he falls off, doesn't arrive on time, gets ratty.'

'Work's often the trouble—'

'When work's going superbly?'

She meant Parson Brown. 'Then he's worried about something.'

'Don't try to be kind, Lovejoy. It's another woman.'

This is the way a woman'll behave. She'll tolerate her bloke's wife, work, his family attachments. But let him flirt elsewhere and she's Murder Inc.

'Ever since this film thing started he's been off his head. It's that Lorane bitch. She shoved herself at him right from the start.'

Who? 'She's not a patch on you, love.'

'Isn't she?' Suki held my hand. 'Truly, Lovejoy?'

'Couldn't hold a candle. Is it Parson you're on about?'

'Walter, yes. We were friends all year.' Bitterness crept in. 'All those special jobs I did for him. Crazy artists in London, arranging silly bloody post offices all over three counties, signing anything he shoved at me—'

I bit my tongue. *She* was Oafie's telephone contact? *She* did the arranging for Sam? 'Maybe he's just got some special job on tonight.'

She shivered. There was a gas-log hearth. Her face gilded in the firelight. She spoke looking into it. 'I'm scared, Lovejoy. A woman knows when a man goes mindless.'

'Wasn't he, well, big with Sam Shrouder's wife, once?'

'Her? Oh, Walter explained all that. Only business. He had to have these things made that only Sam could do. And he was never away long. Always came back to me, where he belonged. She's bedridden, you see. That was why Walter's had to drive up there so much.' She gave a half-smile. 'I keep telling myself this crazy film can't last for ever.'

Bedridden was a laugh. Sort of. 'He'll be back, love,' I reasoned. We held hands, absolutely only reassuringly. 'He'd be daft to pass you up.'

'Oh, Lovejoy. You're so sweet. Having supper. Listening.'

Well, it's true. And I'd saved my own life in the bargain, for she'd have killed me if I hadn't.

From there matters intensified in a time-honoured way. I dare say some folk might blame me, say I was taking advantage of a sorrowing tipsy bird seeking solace. But I don't see it like that. I'd no home to go to, no means of going. And I too was alone and sorrowing. No. I definitely see it as helping out in a compassionate and caring way. And if it's passion which is eventually the driving force, so what? I learned something more, too: if Parson ditched Suki Lonegan for that Lorane, or any other bird I could think of quick, he really was off his trolley. She was worth any ten of most.

As a precaution I locked the door. Didn't want Parson arriving for his delayed tryst while Suki and I were swapping compassion. I had to be in good nick, for tomorrow we filmed.

During the night I found myself awake in a lovelock yet thinking of Lydia's notebook with its disturbing details of the film people. I'd always thought that filmmakers depended on their track record, like football teams – you're only as good as your last game. A dozen successes followed by one dud means you're a has-been. Ten flops followed by a smasher means you're God's gift.

'Yes, darling?' Suki misinterpreted my fidgeting, which ended abstruse contemplation. Ecstasy called. But a film team made up of deadlegs plodding through the undefined screenplay of a failed writer is heading for certain ruin, no? *Unless it's really not.*

'Yes, doowerlink,' I said.

Chapter 16

'You see, Ray, a balloon's logical. Everybody can understand it.' He listened, wheezing and forever poking his hornrims up his nose.

Broad daylight. We were in the little tree-lined square in Malet Street, looking up at London University's mini-Kremlin, Senate House. Cars drifted hither and thither, hub deep in traffic wardens. The occasional student strolled past scratching dozily. It was all happening.

'It seems a lot taller than it really is. The Bolton architect who designed it had delusions which matched the times. I mean, he also made Hanger Lane tube station. Just like God would have built the Vatican, if only God'd had the money.'

'The gang fly from there on to the Museum?'

'Aye. Hot air balloon. Simple.'

'How do you get them in?'

'The story is, they register as *bona fide* students, assumed names, false photo cards. Once you're in, you're in.'

'Max had all this in a screenplay I rejected.' He spoke accusingly.

'I know.' I exuded confidence. 'So a couple of points, Ray. There's a canteen in Senate House, third floor. Seats a couple of hundred, more. Even the public go in – coffees, dinners, teas. Access no problem.'

'Winds, noise, night ballooning?'

'Noise – it's raining, see? Night ballooning's not difficult if the balloon's tethered. And wind? Cinch.' I pointed into Russell Square. 'Montague Street's got hotels, right? Here's my story.' I was being really patient. I'd already given him a written outline, damned near filling a whole postcard, but these film people couldn't read. 'If the wind's in the right direction, OK. If it's not – and my story says it's not, more dramatic, see? – then your baddie takes a room at one of the hotels. Goes to the roof. Has a child's balloon, shop-bought, one of those advertising balloons shops give out, anything – on a string. He lets it out, until it's over Senate House.'

'Got it.' Ray was looking up. 'The balloonists are up there. They catch hold of the pilot balloon, pull in a stronger rope—'

'—And your hotel baddies simply haul the balloonists over the Museum!'

'How much power does it take?'

'Plenty,' I admitted. 'A gas balloon can lift several blokes, so some winch thing would be needed. The hotel baddies hold the guests and managers at gunpoint.'

He liked that. 'Real real real!'

'They're disguised as workmen, take in a winch once the hotel's commandeered. Max can write in bits of tension with a guest awaited at some assignation—'

'A Cabinet politician shacked up in a hotel bedroom!'

'That's been done, Ray,' I said tiredly. I didn't want it ludicrous. 'And remember Senate House was used in *Day of the Triffids*, so watch it. I reckon better a *Rififi* picture than a *League of Gentlemen*. Don't you?'

He was more pleased. 'Awareness. Insight. A-okay, Lovejoy.'

'What if the wind's south-west, Lovejoy?' Gabriella, now in uniform, stood beside us. We made greetings as if popping up everywhere unannounced was her normal means of arrival.

'Then you use a hotel along Bloomsbury Street instead. You can even use two.' I'd looked it up. 'It's called resolution of forces. Pull the two bottom corners of a triangle, its apex moves down in a straight line.'

'It's good.' She smiled at me. 'Lovejoy's right, Mr Meese. A balloon is logical. And everybody can understand it.' An exact quotation of me. Somebody was recording every word. Thank goodness.

'And once the baddies are over the roof?' from Meese.

'They land on it. Break in any old how. Pull the snatch. There's a gunfight – which you said has to be included. The thieves try to escape. Stef Honor and Saffron Kay, the goodies, thwart them, save the priceless MacGuffin. The thieves, shooting away, get to the balloon, cut its tethering cables. Disaster. It crashes into some building. Horror, flames, bodies falling. Tata!' I made a trumpet sound.

'I like it. I'll call in the stunt arranger. Max in on it?'

'I'll see him this afternoon.'

'One thing, Lovejoy.' Gabriella was at her charming best. 'What exactly is it that the baddies are going to steal? Only in the story, of course.'

'Tell you later today,' I said. I can be as charming as her any day. 'Only in the story, of course, Gabriella. Can't be done in real life, can it?'

Between boredoms, an assistant called Hal brought me an antique. Water in the desert.

He produced this dirk. Imagine a big knife sheathed

in a decorative blackish scabbard, with two tinier hilts protruding lower down. I was delighted.

'The boar badge of the Campbells. Well, yes.' I pulled out the smaller weapons. 'They're knife and fork, see? But genuine silver, 1881, no later.'

'That's a genuine precious stone, isn't it?'

These Scottish dirks have an orange stone at the top of the hilt. Folk call it a Cairngorm. 'Genuine orange glass, Hal. Sorry. They're just set on silver foil, which shines through. You almost never find a genuine stone.' Fakers use the same trick nowadays for 'the beautiful and elusive lady', as Aussie miners call the opal. So watch out.

The worst part of antiques is handing out bad news. He went, downcast. But why? He'd got a genuine Argyll and Sutherland officer's dirk, well over a century old. What does a bit of glass matter if it's the real thing? I got narked. People want jam on it.

Me and Meese went to the Three Greyhounds off Cambridge Circus for a bite. He was beginning to have doubts, firing questions about my story, so I got fed up and decided to have done and tell him.

'Flaws, Ray? There has to be.'

'Has to be?' He almost fainted.

'Yes. The balloon ploy doesn't have to work, see? The real gambit's elsewhere, from within.'

'Two assaults?' He went still.

'My story has a traitor within the gang. He pulls a lone scam, maybe with some tart along for love interest. You can still have your shoot-out, Stef and Saffron can do their stuff, but it makes the balloon's flaws credible, even desirable.'

'Hey, Lovejoy the natural! What's the other heist?'

'Didn't want to tell you while Gabriella was there. More

of a test for her security services if we keep it secret. You and me, eh?'

He looked at me. I looked at him. Suddenly we were both pleased, I hoped for different reasons.

'Agreed, Lovejoy. We may not need the second scam, though, right?'

We did more smiling when I said, 'Alternatively, we may.'

He seemed to live on pink gins. I began to worry in case I hadn't enough gelt for my shouts. During the next hour he became maudlin. I asked about actors, something to talk about. He unbent.

'Frigging cattle, Lovejoy. Ninety per cent of them are trash.' He tapped my arm. 'Know what that cunt-struck ageing Romeo costs me? Double.'

'Double what?' He meant Stef Honor.

'Double the book costs. He wants some popsy hired as his make-up girl – we hire her. You know that fucking trailer he has, his private living quarters? It's his old derelict. I've to rent it *from* him *for* him, two thousand a week. Would you believe it? A has-been like him, thinking he's here on talent. Yesterday's news. Truly truly. Had to fight his agents like hell. Those vampires wanted a percentage of the gross. He came aboard on a fixed salary, thank Christ.'

There was more of this, all in-fighting. Vance was always stoned. Max didn't know his arse from his elbow. Saffron Kay was nobody's news, stuntmen were bleeding him dry, technicians' unions were subversives who made anarchists look like clergy.

We parted vowing eternal friendship, mutual support, respect and total commitment to The Cause. He was almost in tears, so moved was he by the alcohol consumed. Lorane's limo arrived about twoish and he was whisked away. As he entered the car, though, something odd happened which stuck in my mind. Ray said a word or two to her. She paused, slim and trendy, holding the limo door, looked back at me, and smiled. I hadn't known she could. That's all. Not much, but odd.

With time on my hands I crossed to the British Museum and had a wander. Beautiful. The best acreage on earth. In fact I was so entranced by those satisfying vibes from everything that I almost forgot to suss out possible Russian antiques for the film to let's-pretend steal. With less than an hour before my train left I did a sprint along the upper floors, the entrances and the ground floor.

And found what I'd been looking for, in the tiny little Temporary Exhibitions Room 31. Its walls and display cases glittered with priceless dazzling ikons, silverware, illuminated gospel manuscripts. All were ancient Armenian. And Armenia's a Soviet Russian Republic.

Rejoicing, I headed home, caught my train in good time to be arrested for complicity in the disappearance and probable murder of antique dealer Walter Brown, a.k.a. Parson.

Chapter 17

'Ever noticed, Lovejoy,' MacAdam asked as I nearly made the town bus at the railway station, 'how patterns recur?'

'Yes. In antiques, they're often constant. Furniture designs, artists' use of colour, Celtic jewellery designs—'

MacAdam smiled, nodded. He doesn't go in for this pacing game Ledger adopts. He just sat there in his police car, too pudgy even for a peeler. 'Aye. In behaviour, too. Yours.'

He was obsessional as only a Stirling man can be. I wished he was none of those. Also, I wished he was elsewhere.

'Nice philosophical point, Mac, but I'll miss that bus.'

'You've missed it, Lovejoy. In, please.'

I got in the rear seat. He's something below Ledger in those unknowable ranks they have, but plainclothes. He rated a driver.

'Give you three guesses where you're going.'

'I'm not psychic, Mac.'

We drove down the coast road. A strood runs to Mersea Island, passable at low tide. The car paused on the island side. There, where the road runs up out of the estuary on to dry land again, another police car waited. A photographer was pondering. Plods measured and marked. A

Jaguar, familiar, was half-embedded in the muddy swark below the roadway.

'Is that Parson's motor?' I asked.

'Aye, laddie. With blood on the inside.'

'Is Parson OK?'

'He's missing, Lovejoy. This was reported, midnight. Its lights were on, doors open. A Peldon man going home from the Rose pub. No sign of Walter Brown, Esquire.'

'Swam out to sea? Made it home?'

'No, laddie. Coastguards have combed and swept, hunted and trawled with all the skills at their command.' He descended, beckoned me after. We walked up to where the road curves right to West Mersea village, paused to look down at the sea. The tide was swirling fast about Parson's car. 'Tides are funny things, Lovejoy. All imperceptible changes of speed, direction. Look away a minute and it's up your legs, marooning, rushing, aye, and drowning. Terrible swiftness. Get the picture?'

'No.'

He pointed. 'Somebody knocked unconscious in a crash – or clobbered senseless by a criminal, let's say – can easily vanish for good in yonder ocean.'

'And I went calling at Parson's house?'

'Guessed first time, laddie!' He moved to the gaggle squad. I walked with him. 'The phone number was his car. His wee wife passed on the message about your desirable antique cross. I'm reliably informed there's no such crucifix, Lovejoy. Brown told his wife so in no uncertain terms. She gave us chapter and verse. And timed the call by a telly programme. Bit late to be making a routine visit, wasn't it?'

'Antiques never sleep, Mac.'

'You procured a lift from town, Lovejoy. To inquire after a rare crucifix which doesn't exist. There's not a rare thirteenth-century crucifix in the whole Eastern Hundreds.'

'Well, that's saved a penny or two.'

'Watch it, laddie.'

'Best find Parson and ask him what's going on, Mac. Hasn't he a partner?' My heart was in my mouth, where it tends to be most days. 'You could call on her.'

'Suki Lonegan. Aye, a pretty lass. She was hostessing him last night, supper cum business, her place. He never turned up, Lovejoy. She dined alone, retired early.'

Tension lessened somewhat. 'And the dealers?'

'Neither hide nor hair, last sighting around sixish. The town antiques Arcade.' We reached the place where the car had plunged off the roadway. ''Course, Lovejoy, there's always some hero decides to streak across the strood at high tide. Silly accidents happen. But blood front and back seats? It's almost a flagrant exhibition of a non-accident. Some murderer announcing to the rest of his associates: Watch it, keep in line.'

'Who, though?' I said, all innocence.

'You, maybe.' He leaned on the rails, foot lodged on the bottom strut. 'You got an alibi, Lovejoy?'

'For when? I caught the last bus into town from Parson's. Then I went . . .' Whoops, Suki had deprived me of my alibi. Ensured her own safety, of course, in doing so. A dear girl, but costly. 'Home. Had to walk. I'd missed the last bus.'

'No car, Lovejoy?'

'An accident burned it. The fire brigade has records of exactly when.'

The sod knew. 'And your cottage all smashed to blazes.' He tut-tutted.

'Vandals. I went for a walk down the lane, and some vandals broke in, ruined the place, set my motor alight.'

'So you hired Jacko's coal wagon to run you to the Great North Road. With your budgies.' He judged me, patient. 'Got rid of them to some lorry-driver, I hear.'

'I'd forgotten.'

'Let me try this, Lovejoy. Parson did over your place, burned your Ruby. You threaten him, gave his missus some cock-and-bull message. You follow him, gain access to his motor, bludgeon him to death. And rig this.' He indicated the marshes, the car.

'Holes all through it, Mac.' He knew it, too. 'I spent the night peacefully at my cottage, trying to clear up.'

'Aye. That's a point in your favour. The place is the worse for wear, but cleaned up all right. Must have taken a few hours. But you're in here somewhere, Lovejoy.'

'Eh?' I'd left my cottage in a shambles.

'So you're under local arrest.' He sighed wearily as I drew breath to speak. 'I know there's no such thing, Lovejoy. And so do you. But you are. Understand? Set a whisker out of the Eastern Hundreds and I'll arrest you on a hundred and one charges.'

'All right, Mac. But can I visit Security at the British Museum?'

'Aye. But phone me first.'

'Ta.' I glanced around at the remote marshes. 'How do I get home, Mac?'

He too scanned the estuary. 'God knows.'

As I started walking, I thought that my visit to Big John Sheehan was long overdue. And a call in on Hymie the goldsmith was becoming at least as urgent.

Lydia for once must have helped right. Sheer accident, of course. I got to my village by a succession of buses and lifts, reaching there on time. I'd put a note in the

Arcade for Tinker to drop word down the vine to Big John Sheehan, could I see him about nine, urgent.

Sure enough, Snow White's little forest animals, or Lydia, had done the necessary. The cottage was swept. New bulbs cast light. A new kettle replaced its crushed predecessor. Food supplies had been replenished. The phone service was miraculously restored. I checked with the operator. Yes, sir, the outstanding bill had been paid. I celebrated by telephoning Lydia, her answering machine only. I said to find me soonest, that I'd be at Hymie the goldsmith's in Wyre Street at five, and hoped to meet Big John later.

She'd left me three pasties. The oven was working and spotless though battered. I hotted them up, made two pints of tea, filled myself, fed the sparrows their afternoon cheese, put out pobs for Crispin the hedgehog, loaded up the net sock with peanuts for the bluetits, then hit the road, worn out.

Hymie the goldsmith works in a shed off Wyre Street. He's an escapee from Whitechapel's fraternity of artificers in precious metal. His workshop's quite small, in a wooden upstairs in an outfitter's yard. You go through a narrow ginnel to reach it. If you don't know Hymie's down there, you've no way of finding it. He wants it that way. You ring an old clonker bell by pulling a string, then knocking patiently at intervals until he yells to come in. You don't dare vary this, because his work is precious, sacred, and very, very private. He was fifteen minutes letting me in.

'You hiding a woman in here, Hymie?'

'Women make idle. I'm a busy person, Lovejoy.'

'That's the spirit, Hymie. Romance all the way.'

His workshop could be straight out of a Diderot

engraving of the eighteenth century. The bench has bays scooped out, with brats, leather aprons, fixed to the underside of each bay to catch the lemel – filings of precious metal – in his lap. The flooring around the traditional oak workbench was covered by claies, wooden grilles. Gold dust and chips which happen to fall settle into the claie openings. They also scrape any valuable lemel which sticks to the soles of his leather slippers. Every year, Hymie lifts them – the grilles are still made over in Montreuil – and recovers enough to make a wedding ring.

I sat on the floor away from the claies and watched. He's a lovely worker, methodical and tidy. Lydia would approve. Like all good goldsmiths, Hymie is precision incarnate. He has six different patterns of Bunsen – fans, straights, side-vents – for various work. Three tiny bench kilns, umpteen lens systems and lights. He'd do as Father Christmas for a Yuletide card. He works with a MacArthur microscope, sensible man that he is. I know for a fact he paid a fortune to have MacArthur himself make a special, up in his Cambridge cottage. It's no bigger than a box of fags, and does everything but predict the Derby winner.

'Well, Lovejoy?'

'Got the time to make me a gold antique?'

'The time God allows. The gold you provide.'

'A Russian samovar, tray, the lot. Orthodox saintly and patriotic inscriptions.'

He stared. 'Russian? And saintly? Lovejoy, you not heard about Jews and Jesuits? Russians and refuseniks? Oy vey! In he comes, wants I should make for the Tsar already!'

This is only Hymie's way of saying talk gelt. 'Don't give me this crap, Hymie. Yes or no?'

'And anti-Semitic, yet.'

'I will be when you tell me your price, Hymie.'

'Lovejoy. Dear idiot. Listen to Uncle Hymie. Gold plate is—'

'Solid gold, Hymie.' That shut him up, made him stop work. He was doing battle with a lovely cream jug, splendid with Regency elegance. My chest quivered and hummed. Genuine.

'That Sheffield plate, Hymie?'

'Yes.'

'You replating a seam?' There are no seams in modern fakes. The trouble is that people worry when the base copper starts showing through where the silver layer has worn in long years of handling. Nowadays there are silver creams and electroplating methods which give a homogeneous bright gleamy colour, but it's bad news. Old Sheffield plate tends to take on a faint creamy colour or even a pewterish tint which makes for loveliness. The only way to restore a worn area on a lovely original is to silver leaf it, matching the original thickness of the silver plate with your leaf, and then wear it down anew to blend with the entire piece. It's a man's job. That was why Hymie had taken so long to let me in. Gold and silver leaf is applied with gentlest breath. A door wafting open gales precious metals into outer space. Tip: examine phoney joins in oblique light and you'll spot the fakes.

'Who made it, Hymie?'

He nearly grinned a grin. 'Boulton, Birmingham.'

Well, I laughed aloud. It's one of the antiques trade's cruellest permanent jokes. When Sheffield plate was invented by Thomas Bolsover in 1743, he didn't really develop it to the full. His apprentice Joseph Hancock wasn't so reticent and launched into full-scale rolling mills. By 1784 Sheffield plate makers were registering at their local assay office – and the great Birmingham silversmiths who started up this new manufacturing process had to register their plate at Sheffield. Birmingham's never recovered that lost face. We still pull Brummy silversmiths' legs over it.

'Gold, Lovejoy, stands at a fortune an ounce.'

'Still not cheap, eh?'

Silence. He worked something out. 'Very minimum, two hundred ounces. Thank God for Japanese calculators.'

One gold ounce standing at an average monthly wage gives . . . gulp. 'My cottage deeds, Hymie. My Ruby's a collector's item. And I'm earning good money helping out on a film. My deeds are worth the gold as a building plot alone. Land prices are through the roof.'

He pondered, eyeing me round his shoulder. 'Aren't you in trouble with the constabulary?'

'Not really. Misunderstanding.' How the hell had he heard?

'Cost'll be the metal plus a third.'

'Don't be daft, Hymie. Tenth.'

We haggled, settled on a seventh, the decimal points to fall on his side, thieving swine.

'How soon, Lovejoy?'

'Very, very fast, Hymie.' I rose, dusted my trousers, which is only polite in a goldsmith's. 'Days rather than weeks. And make the inscription about 1870. OK?'

'Russian Orthodox, yet!' he mourned. 'One condition, Lovejoy. Don't tell my Hester I'm working for the Cossacks.'

That encounter cheered me up. I left promising to deliver my deeds at Hymie's next morning, with the Ruby's log book. Problems there, nowt new.

Big John works from, sometimes stays at, runs, a hotel near Great Tey. I arrived in good time and was let into the long upstairs lounge folk call his office. He was in an armchair, humming along with a telly pop song. Four goons in cuboidal suits hung about plotting tomorrow's race cards or just gaping with the vacant serenity of their kind. I waited until the song ended. He applauded genially. His nerks applauded. Wisely I joined in, though I thought it a rotten tune.

'Ah, there's your man, Lovejoy. Sit down.'

''Evening, John.'

'All ready to go?'

'Yes, John.'

'Give him the address, Logie.' An especially truncated punter brought me a page torn from a notebook. 'An estate agent. Southwold. He collects these paintings. He won't sell us his Constable oil, will he, boys?'

'No,' the neighbourhood growled in anger.

'We've tried peaceful ways. Haven't we, boys?'

'Yes,' the psychopathic quartet gravelled, cracking knuckles.

I tried to look convinced and outraged.

'So there's nothing for it, Lovejoy. This next weekend. Right?'

My throat dried, my tongue pasted to my palate. I couldn't even swallow to get going. The nerks swelled, staring at me in astonished rage. Anything less than instantaneous total agreement with Big John was beyond belief.

'Well, John,' I croaked out, sixth go. 'There's a slight problem. I would like to but—'

He seemed amused. 'But, Lovejoy? Harry, Logie. Is Lovejoy giving me buts now?'

'He'd better not, John,' Logie said.

''Course I'll do it, John. Only, is it all right with Ben?'

Silence so long and protracted you could hear the

music downstairs in the dining-room, the muted clatter from the bars. Ben Clayton and Big John's lot are mortal enemies. I'd mentioned Satan in Paradise.

'I'll—'

'No, Logie.' Big John flicked a finger and I was thrust on to an upright chair. Sundry nerks placed one for John. He sat at me, rather than opposite, staring into me with curiosity.

'Clayton? Is it you's pally with Clayton now, Lovejoy?'

'No, John. But he came and shambled my cottage, ashed my Ruby. Threatened to kill my budgies, then my apprentice.'

John snapped fingers for information, eyes still on me. Logie responded. 'His apprentice is a bird, Lydia. You've seen her, John. Singing in the choir. Churchgoer, St James's Protestant. Honest, youngish. Nice enough.' He snorted. 'Thinks Lovejoy's a reprobate, lowlife.'

Big John nodded approvingly at all this biography, especially the churchgoing bit. 'Indeed. A bonny lass. Always looks worried.' He eyed me some more. 'And well she might, eh?'

'And then me, John. Ben said.'

'If what?'

'If I burgled anywhere. For anybody.'

His eyes were blue, his face square, fair. He always looks affable, but then so did Genghis Khan. 'He know you've done a little for me, Lovejoy?'

'Dunno, John. He said nothing.'

His fingers snapped once. Logie advanced, penitential. 'Not heard anything, John. Last Clayton did was a big buy at the Nottinghamshire sales. And a load of art nouveau furnishings, Brighton.'

Big John turned slightly, looked up at Logie. The

bruiser shuffled uneasily. I breathed easier. Somebody else was in trouble. John replaced his attention.

'Tell, Lovejoy. Everything, mind.'

'Something's afoot, John.' I told him I'd been placed, under virtual arrest for Sam Shrouder's death, then for Parson Brown's disappearance. Ledger and MacAdam I gave a brief but bad press, very satisfying. 'I think Ben Clayton's financing the Russian exhibition at St Edmundsbury – God knows how or why. But he's chopped into at least three container loads. Big money. For Yanks, I heard.'

He silenced me with a palm to ponder. It took five minutes. I fidgeted slightly, stilled when Logie raised an eyebrow.

Then, 'Go on, Lovejoy.'

'He said I wasn't even to visit the St Edmundsbury exhibition, not even get a catalogue. Bought from some old Russki countess. My apprentice got one, only doing her job, routine like. He did me over for disobedience. Seg. Probably scared I'd wrong-foot his picture.'

'Logie. I'm hearing all this for the first time.'

Logie paled, visibly shrank a few cubic feet. 'Yes, John. But—'

'Picture, Lovejoy?' Sheehan's voice had softened, a sign of his terrible anger upping a gear.

'There's a film crew doing some cops-and-robbers thing. They hired me. In the story they rob the British Museum.' I pressed on over the hiss of sharp inhalations all around John's mob. 'Not real, y'understand. Only on the pictures.'

'What's this to do with Clayton?'

I had to strain to hear his words, and him only three feet away. Sheer fright set my right leg trembling all on its own, quiveringly hinting to get the hell out of here. 'A guess, John. I was scared to ask. But I believe he's financing the film someway, whole or part. It wasn't me killed Parson. Nor Sam Shrouder.'

'Parson's a dealer,' Logie put in, anxious to win his badges back. 'Sam's a faker—'

'Lovejoy?' John whispered, choked on anger.

'Don't know about Sam,' I said shrilly. 'But I feel Ben Clayton or Seg disappeared Parson. Maybe a mistake.' I told him of my custodial bout with MacAdam, the car in the tide off the strood causeway, how the Plod had me marked over some innocent question of a crucifix. 'Y'see, John, I went asking after a cross. Parson'd promised it. His missus phoned him my message. I think somebody was with him when he received it, assumed I meant some crucifix nicked from Clayton's Russian exhibition. So put Parson out of the way.'

'Not quite enough, Lovejoy, is it now?'

So quiet I had to guess the words in the sibilance. 'No, John. I think it's much bigger than all these local goings-on.'

'Tell me.' Magnanimity showed through. 'I'll not have you cindered for being wrong.'

'My guess is Ben Clayton's setting up to do the British Museum, under cover of this film.'

The world halted. I swear the band, chatter, drinking stopped all over the Eastern Hundreds. Big John breathed in, exhaled a long breath so slow it lasted for ever.

'Why?'

He meant reasons. 'Nowt else's big enough to go topping people for, John. He's called in favours, put the elbow on dealers – all to collar container loads. They're the only big advance payments in antiques at this level. So he needs money. He abducted me, dumped me in the countryside, trying to bubble me for Sam's murder – then realized he could use me in the movie robbery some way. My apprentice did some delving on the film company. It's genuine, but on its last legs. The writer's hopeless, the main assistant's a druggie, the lead bloke's a has-been, the heroine's a scatty beginner, the producer's an ageing wonderkid who's never fulfilled promise . . .'

'And what're you doing in it?'

'I think I'm now cast as the fall guy – that's Americanese for somebody set up—'

'Will you get on, Lovejoy.'

'Because they hire me in good faith, see? As an antique dealer with maybe some understanding of antique scams. Kindly they ignore any evidence of my shady past. Then they have me along, let me even make up part of the story – having carefully vetoed all twenty-odd storylines their writer's thought up, only to accept the first rehash one I contribute.'

'What're they after?'

'John,' I said sadly, 'been to the British Museum lately? Nick anything good and you're in clover – not meaning me, you follow. But film crew's like a Bedouin caravan – more vehicles, people, boxes, than the parson preached about. The trouble is, I'm not sure what they'll pinch.'

'And you're there to take the blame?'

'So they think, John. I want out, but Ben Clayton won't let me. He won't allow anything to go wrong with the film because it conceals the scam.' I paused, but most crooks are slow thinkers, so I added, 'It's everything to him, you see. With the Museum's staff in his pocket he'll be the biggest bloke in antiques ever.'

'So he will, so he will.' He rose, stood by the fireplace, clicked his fingers. A filled glass magically appeared in his hand. He sipped thoughtfully. None for poor sweating terrified me, note. 'Shit or bust, eh?'

'That's as I see it, John.'

'Would you be seeing any way to spoil his game, now? You being so shrewd and all?' A goon snickered, froze when Big John tilted his head inquiringly.

'Oh, aye. Easy.' I nodded around at his army to show confidence. 'You get your lads to rob a valuable antique from his Russian exhibition, John. That's the first thing. It'll make him edgy, flail about, maybe make him goad the filming on, stir him up. It'd publicize his involvement in the Russki show too much for his liking. That'll show you where his aim really is.'

'Not bad, Lovejoy.' He smiled kindly. 'So do it.'

'Me?' I was aghast, terrified. 'Please, John. Ben'll kill me. Please. Let your lads—'

'Do it, Lovejoy. And soon.' He was so pleased he rubbed his hands. The goons also rubbed theirs. 'Want a drink?'

'Ta, John,' I said as shakily as I could, still pretending sheer terror, almost overacting. Honestly, these crooks. Worse than the Old Bill for slowness. I thought we'd never get there. Masterminds of the bloody obvious.

Chapter 18

'I don't believe this.'

'Ballooning's perfectly safe, Lovejoy.'

'Not with me in a bloody flying basket.'

'You told me to arrange it.'

'But not with *me* inside.'

We were on a large field. Cars were parked nearby, rows on meadow. Assorted lunatics milled about huge – and I mean mega-huge – multicoloured sacks on the grass. Each one needed a score of blokes to hold the damned thing down. Two had already flown, ascending with elongated grace into the heavens to applause, one pair of daredevils per wicker. Daft. The balloons looked colourful but life-threatening. Lydia was furious because I refused to fly. A cretinoid called Dave was equally disappointed. I'd met him once before.

'What's the matter, Lovejoy?' He was mystified, congenitally unable to see why any normal bloke wouldn't want to dangle perilously in a trug strung at umpteen zillion feet with no parachute. Maniacs don't change.

'This sport's the matter. Go if you like, but don't ask me.'

She was exasperated. 'Our sole purpose was to give you the actual encounter, Lovejoy. The dedicated writer experiences what he writes about.'

Does he indeed. 'Let Max.'

Dave's mates, lunatics all, laughed as I walked off, Lydia trotting after, reproaching furiously. She'd borrowed her mother's car for our trek into literary creativity. Max was just emerging from his motor, a dishevelled but dedicated writer if ever I saw one.

'Hello, Lovejoy. I read your ideas outline. Did the balloonists say it was practicable?'

'Yes, Max.' I spoke out, avoiding Lydia's eye. 'They're thrilled. They wanted to show me the practical details, but I've given you pride of place.'

'Honestly?' he said. 'Really?'

'Well, it's more important that you have the living creature experience, Max. I'd really like to go, but you're the one who has to cope with the stunt arranger.'

'Lovejoy, that's really decent of you.' He clasped my hand, soulful. 'I'll dedicate my screenplay to you. You're terrific. And generous.'

He went towards the balloons on the grass, the gas jets burning hot air. Two were steepling vertically, their brilliant hues in the weak sunlight making gaudy silk cathedrals. Lydia came, narked and angry.

'That was despicable, Lovejoy. Pretending—'

'Look, Lydia.' I halted, held both her hands. She snatched them away, glancing about in case any stray balloonists had noticed this unbridled sex play. 'What was in your notebook?'

'About the film company? It is almost defunct.'

'Go on.'

'It desperately needs a major success during this fiscal year. Its financial resources are virtually nil.'

'And Max?'

'My film industry informants are mystified as to why he was chosen. He is regarded as a writer of minimum inventiveness, mediocre talent. Especially with this film being the Lake Bayon people's possible swan song.'

'So. How can I best help Max?' I opened her passenger door and got in, wound down the window and spoke with sorrow. 'I'll tell you, Lydia. By helping Max. Giving him every chance.'

'Lovejoy,' she tried, but I spoke on.

'Which means giving him my place in that balloon, Lydia. I could have enjoyed myself, been self-indulgent. But no.'

'Lovejoy. Perhaps I was hasty—'

'No.' I nearly did a stage sob but decided that was probably going over the top, so maintained a low intense voice. 'No, Lydia. You're determined to see only the worst in me. So be it.'

By Maldon she was apologizing, saying she was only concerned to see me higher in both our esteems, trala. On the whole I was pretty gracious, finally forgiving her and being really pleased with myself. Especially when thinking of nerk Max in that frigging balloon up in the stratosphere. One little bit of help escaped, thank God.

The building society was open when we reached town. Lydia pulled in by the war memorial.

'Could you do an errand, love?'

'Yes, Lovejoy.'

The deeds of my cottage are in the Camulodunum Building Society. I need them withdrawn. I'm making a will at last. The lawyer needs to, er, initial them.'

'Oh!' Her hands flew to her face. 'There's nothing—?'

'No, love. Only . . . I downcast my gaze, tried to blush, but you can never manage the damned thing when you want. 'I have someone in mind to leave my cottage to.

Only foolish sentiment, Lydia. But since you and I are so close—'

'Lovejoy! You mustn't think of it!'

'I'll feel so much better. Please.'

'Very well. But I think this whole thing needs discussion, before such personal committal . . .' Et cetera.

'I promise. But get a move on. They close in an hour. Ask for Phoebe, under-manageress.' She'd better. It was old Cranfield's day off, her obsessional old boss. 'I'll wait. I've a phone call to make. I want to commiserate with Mrs Brown. I'm really worried about her.'

'How kind, Lovejoy. Please convey my regards.'

Luckily I got Phoebe third go, an all-time record for East Anglia's degenerate phone network.

'Phoebe? Lovejoy. I need my deeds for half an hour, please. My lawyer's calling for them, Miss Lydia.'

Phoebe's normally pliable, but she'd obviously heard of my current woes. 'Lovejoy. Your cottage deeds are in entail because of that illicit triple mortgage. There's a fraud claim—'

'For Christ's sake!' I yelled. Everybody's got suspicions like an epidemic. 'Phoebe, on my knees. Ten minutes, and I'll have them back in your hand. Honest.' I sank to a wheedle. 'Look, love. I know I'm not always straight. But deception's for others, love. Not for you and me, Phoebe. Not after . . .'

'All right, Lovejoy. You can borrow them. Thirty minutes. Lydia, you said?'

Five minutes later Lydia came with the deeds, all pleased. 'Did you get through, Lovejoy?'

'Eh?' I was shocked for a moment. Had she realized?

'Mrs Brown.'

'Oh. Yes. She said thanks for your, er, felicitations. Right, love. Drop those deeds in at Hymie's workshed.

You know it, Wyre Street. And this other envelope.' It contained the Ruby's logbook. 'I've to call at Hammer's—'

She paused. I sensed propriety. 'Hymie the goldsmith?'

'Yes, love.' I blinked innocence. 'I've changed lawyers. To his nephew. The lad's just qualified from law school. What little business I can put his way won't help much, but—'

'Lovejoy.' She stood there on the pavement, radiant, brimming with happiness. 'Sometimes I'm quite moved. Of course I shall.'

Bashfully I waved her off into the traffic. I was really moved myself. After all, helping some poor struggling nephew, worrying about Winnie Brown, altering my non-existent will because of fondness for my apprentice – they all revealed a ton of deep, deep compassion.

For a county without much rock in its basic flooring, East Anglia's got quite a team of specialists in geology, archaeology, soil merchants. It's not all the consequence of North Sea oil exploration. Hammer's one of these. He's a grave-digger, as antique dealers call archaeologists who specialize in burials. A long thin sandy-haired bloke in cotton duck trousers and bush shirt, he's in a permanent state of readiness for a quick safari. I found him at a ring burial out beyond Ardleigh. A middle-aged bird from the Castle staff gave me a lift. You approach digs quietly and don't interrupt, so for a while I stood watching. There were three of them digging under a crude tarpaulin canopy. Hammer, a nice plump woman with Lady Godiva hair that kept falling into her dug bit, and a gnarled crone sweeping soil from a stone. Ring burials abound hereabouts. Farmers are forever turning them up. The great hope is of course a gold cache, Celtic torcs or the like from some Ancient British tribal kings.

Eventually Hammer looked up, smiled, stopped work.

'Cymbeline at last, Hammer?' Everybody's Number One contender for spiritual bliss is King Cymbeline. Local folk dream of finding his tomb like the Holy Grail. He'd died just before Claudius the God came conquering.

'Wish it was. Some minor king, probably early Roman.'

'Anything?'

'A few artefacts, nothing much.'

'Better luck next time.' We went and stood apart. 'Celtic crosses, Hammer. What if I wanted one?'

He stared over the fields. Six miles off is the sea. Celtic crosses are big monoliths carved in early Christian times. They're a feature of the North, the West, Ireland.

'You never ask anything easy, Lovejoy.'

'Don't grumble, Hammer. I only want to hire it, not sell, not buy.'

Now he stared at me astonished. 'You joking, Lovejoy?'

'There's no jokes in antiques, Hammer,' I said patiently. 'A genuine ancient Celtic cross, carved, just discovered, embedded in rock.'

'Well, they usually weren't—'

'I know. But this one must be. A big chunk of granite, or whatever that solid stone is. Can you?'

'Does the insertion have to be authentic, or can I marry the cross to any piece of granite?'

'Do what you like. And hollow it out.' I waited, letting it sink in. 'The base rock, not the cross.'

'How hollow?' Now he was worried. 'Those stone crosses were landmarks, Lovejoy, hell of a size. You can't just stick one upright in a jamjar.'

'I did say a big chunk, Hammer.'

'How big, exactly?'

Nowt but questions, these scientists. 'Big enough to

hold a man, crouching.' I didn't say or a titch standing. 'With an exit latched from the inside.'

'Here, Lovejoy. If you're up to something—'

'It's for a film. You haven't heard? I'm retained . . .' He listened. I suggested he phone Ray Meese at the film studios if doubt lingered. His worry transmuted to entrancement. Mentioning the movies is our modern philosopher's stone.

'And it really will be in the final picture?'

'Cert, Hammer. So it must look right. Weight it with a thick lead shell inside or something. And don't give the game away. Keep mum. A rival film company would give anything to hear the plot . . .'

'I understand, Lovejoy. Complete secrecy. Now, how big's the cavity, did you say?'

I held my hand at Three Wheel Archie's fullest height. 'That big.'

And promised Hammer my Ruby, as deposit. I'd have stayed to watch the dig, but burglary called.

Chapter 19

Alibi time.

The day of my burglary was also a big day for Lake Bayon Enterprises, Inc. A conference was called for noon at the studios. Obediently I phoned the Old Bill, left a message for MacAdam saying where I could be reached. On the way through London I stopped at a street market and bought some gear, stowed it in a dark blue sports holdall. At the studio I spoke to everybody I could. The meeting began almost on schedule, by some fluke.

A sparse room by the hangar was crammed with freeloaders. Pecking order ruled as the pundits arrived. First came Vance, floating on high, with a cluster of assorted floaters at least as stoned as himself. Then Max, anxiously toting a few folios of distilled genius, waving with cheery anxiety – I was beginning to like Max, never having met anyone as gormless as me before. Several birds hung around with clipboards. People were guzzling wine, noshing windy little eats that give you not an erg of nourishment. Then Ray Meese and Lorane swept in, to acclaim of Roman proportions. That was the signal for the sundries to fade and leave us of the think tank at the feet of the guru. Stef Honor kept his two birds to minister maul. Saffron Kay flounced, bewildered as ever.

Meese began by recounting Max's new story. A calm bloke in corduroy, Hank, was served a few swingers right at the start.

'Balloon off the big Senate building, Hank,' Ray announced, drawing the process in the air with his hands. 'Stunts include one tumble to ground from a trailing balloon rope.'

'Special rate applies.' Everybody but me said it with Hank, falling about laughing. Max, next to me, whispered, 'Hank's stunt arranger. He negotiates wage rates.'

'Winches, hotel extras with support, evil-doers double up in black outfits, guns. That's the hotels. We do most cased, but day footage in two Montague Street and Bloomsbury hotels, all right?'

'Sure, Ray,' people chorused. Notes sped from clipboard to clipboard, assistants gesturing approval to each other.

'Time sheets out, Beth?'

'Done, Ray.' Beth was as fat as a sumo wrestler. I'd seen her before, always on hand, calmest of the lot.

'We're over budget, proles.' Ray's voice bled on us all. 'No Spielberg crappisms about costs, spin-overs. Stef, Saffron, you do indoor set action, second unit in studio. Ten days, the massacre scene in the Museum. No headaches, broken legs, hangovers, religious conversions or other snafus, OK?'

'OK, maestro,' from Stef and a bewildered 'What?' from Saffron.

'Peasants. I wanna go in ten feet tall.'

Everybody, still less me, assured him he'd be at least twelve. A pair of enthusiasts called, 'Go, Ray, go!' I listened, watched, not knowing what the hell was going on. A dark-haired bloke opposite me grinned, winked. He'd not done much shouting either. Ray Meese continued down his roll-call of duties. Cars, services, food canteens, cameras, electricity supplies, all were summarized by assistants – ready, Ray, ready – even loos and booze. A brief battle occurred over something called an Elemack Mini Jib, when a grim hulk of a man swaying near the drinks table suddenly erupted about designer assistants and costumes.

'Lancelot Lake,' Max whispered, worried sick. 'He's the criminal in the movie. He has a grudge against society, see? Wants to punish the world's culture. A lost love's embittered him . . .'

'Lancelot, Lancelot,' Ray wheezed expansively. 'Would I ever let you screen less than exotic, perfect, magnetic? Nonono!'

'I dunno, Ray,' Lancelot was genuinely disgruntled. 'It's the same blackhat crap, y'know?'

'You and I talk close-ups, Lancelot,' Ray promised, which made Stef Honor raise his head sharply. 'Okayee?'

'Well.' Lancelot settled sulkily, holding out a glass to be filled instantly by diligent serfs.

'Who's the dark bloke opposite?' I whispered to Max.

'Pal Trevelyan. Trajectory man, weapons, our shootist.'

'Right, right.' Translation: gunsmith.

The meeting lumbered on. My interest faded. It seemed that many scenes would be shot in a mock-up, some false cardboard lookalike gallery in the studio hangar. Why, when there was the perfectly good genuine Museum itself ready, willing and photogenically able? The actual robbery scenes would have to be done there anyway . . . I yawned a couple of times, grinned when Pal Trevelyan caught me and nodded in sympathy.

Time. I occupied it by trying to make sure everybody on earth remembered me there. Inwardly I was planning my real genuine robbery with far greater precision than they were planning their story. The meeting broke with an announcement that tonight's celebration dinner-party would be in the Novello Room. I made a point – several, indeed – of telling all the assistants I would visit during the afternoon and see where they worked. They said, 'Hey, right on, do that, man.'

I left the back gate of the studios telling the gate man I was just getting something from my car. A taxi to a tube station, and in an hour I was winging my way on the express. It's pretty empty that time of day, and I chose my compartment with care. I didn't want too many folk noticing me sewing buttons on to a dark blue serge suit I'd got in my holdall.

If you stand in the centre of St Edmundsbury, looking at the so-called square with the main row of shops descending to your right, the hall in question stands to your front and right. A bus station of unpleasing aspect lies across an intervening pavement. Otherwise, it's a posh shopping area. The hall's ancient, very noble in a tiny kind of way, and has an unusual safety feature: its prominence is its security. No garden, and it can be seen from almost every direction. It abuts on to the pavement which in daytime heaves with pedestrians, shoppers, bus passengers. Youngsters go in and out of the fast food place over the ginnel next door. Nasty tall street lights add to the problem. Pubs and taverns summon still further throngs. Who says country towns are dozy?

Pinching a car's never a problem, but choosing the right one is. I finally selected a little black mini from the social club by the railway. A lady's handbag lay on the passenger seat, silly woman. Crooks could have come by and nicked it. Enough fuel, thank heavens. Ladies' bowling teams gather there when they play away. They frugally arrange car pools, and leave most of their cars outside the clubhouse.

I drove to Bury, passed through once, then paused on the bypass. It was nearly dark, the early edge-of-light town sort which lacks the terrible intensity of countryside midnights. Unobserved, I tilted the driving mirror to inspect myself. Black crash helmet with SECURITY 43 stuck on to it. Only kiddies' transfer numbers, but imposing in conjunction with my blue suit. I'd transformed it with silver buttons, a metal shoulder flash, a police whistle and chain. An imposing bunch of keys, from a Berwick Street market barrow, swung from my belt. Gloves under my left shoulder tab. Black boots. I looked so sombre I was thrilled, especially with the toy badge pinned to my chest. I was a children's science fiction thing. A transparent visor pivoted from my helmet. I carried a truncheon. I'd clipped a bobby's shiny torch to my front, the sort which stares forward, one-eyed, leaving both hands threateningly free. I was the business. My reflection put the fear of God in me. My handy mini-recorder was fixed up with an aerial, nicked from another car and black-taped on. I'd done the recording waiting for the train, when I was still a civilian.

Ten minutes later I'd checked that at least one of the phone-boxes near the exhibition hall was working. I parked my car behind a hotel – better than a pub, safer and less conspicuous – and walked portentously along the pavement towards the hall. A light was on outside, two spotlights bragging of this lovely town's ancient architecture. I walked, keys jingling, counting pedestrians. Twenty, plus a couple emerging from hamburgers. The joint was still heaving, but its big windows, so full of diners, looks out across the hall's face rather than directly at it, so that was OK. Had to be now.

Phone. A 999 call. 'Emergency operator. Which service, please?'

'Police,' I snapped, voice gravelly.

'Police-can-I-help-you?'

'Private Security Guard Four Three reporting a broken window. The exhibition hall. Am on site. No intruders identified. Three children reportedly perpetrated the act. Permanent continuous private guard ordered to remain until morning. No police action required. Over and out.' I was pouring with sweat. I walked quickly to the car, got in. The hotel yard was quiet. I stuck a magnetic blue lamp on the roof, leaving it switched off, and drove purposefully at speed round the corner, halting in front of the hall. I marched into the alley space. Nobody. A bus just leaving, and me out of view. The small ground floor was leaded, barred. The equivalent window of the floor above wore a sill of out-curved miniature palings, points downward. This left the top half free for access.

I slung my hook up, less than a dozen feet, hauled myself up to it, nutted the top of the window in with a blow from my crash helmet, and squirmed through only partly stunned. But not too comatose to notice two kids in the alleyway staring up as I pulled the rope in after me. Nor to remain deaf to the din of a million alarms whooping and clamouring inside the museum.

'What's up, mister?' one of the kids yelled.

'Did you see any lads chucking stones at this building?' I yelled down authoritatively.

'No, mister. Only you breaking the window.'

'Did you see anybody with a car trying to ram the front door?'

'No, mister.'

'Go round to the front. Make sure nobody gets out.'

They scampered off. I coiled the rope, lodged it and

the hook round my waist under the jacket, switched on my chest lamp and calmly descended the stairs, clicking every light on as I went. It took me an ugly two whole minutes finding the night alarm switch, even though the control box was clearly labelled in the foyer. Shows what a state I was in. Silence descended. I opened the front door to find my two heroes waiting in awe. I tried to loom larger than life.

'Anybody come out?'

'No, mister. What's happened?'

I gave them both a quid. 'Three kids were reported vandalizing. Right. Well done. Off you go.' I marched across to my car, set the blue rotating light going, returned. An elderly gentleman was passing.

'Anything amiss, Officer?'

'No, sir. Thank you. Just a group of scamps throwing things. I was along pretty quickly.'

'Sign of the times, Officer, sign of the times.'

Five more minutes and, restless, I phoned the police station, not using the emergency number, made a report. Still no squad car. Had I been too convincing? Or were they resting in some hostelry and couldn't be bothered?

The squad car came after another ten minutes. By then I was almost worn to a grease spot from worry. Two pudgy uniformed constables alighted for a smoke and a chat. I was on the pavement by then, having closed the door, switched most lights off.

'No damage except a window.' I pointed. 'Some kids. Means I'll have to be here all frigging night now.'

The two nodded, asked me how much wage I got, were there any perks. I said it was all confidential, grinned and told them a fortune, precisely doubling what I guessed was their salary. 'Free car, too,' I said. 'Not this crap heap.

Recreational use permitted. And home-buy assistance, two per cent mortgage.'

They whistled, envious. This would fuel grumbles in the police canteen. I added more money details, keeping my crash helmet on and standing with my back to the street lamps.

'Hang on a sec. My squawk box.' As they talked and made comparisons I went to the door where I'd left my tiny tape-recorder hanging. 'Hello. Operator Four Three. Come in.'

Click on. 'Report now and time, come in,' my falsetto voice crackled back at me.

Click off. 'Police car's called. Nothing missing. Am on standby until eight a.m. as directed.' Pause. 'Wilco. Over and out.' It sounded good to me, anyway. I tried to sound bored, faintly irritated, as I rejoined the two police. We chatted a bit more, until I said my half-hourly check was due. We parted, grumbling. I turned off my whizzer light and waved as they sleepily left to cruise the bypass and clock up more unearned inflation-proof pension.

I re-entered the hall, closed the front door and locked it. And rested a second, breathing and sweating hard. A lot of effort and risk, but I was inside with the approval of the Plod.

The item I quickly chose was selected with my sense of irony uppermost. A fine tea service of silver, St Petersburg, tea urn, teapot, tray, sugar, cream, the lot. It was glorious, but heavy as lead. I packed it with supreme care and put it in my holdall.

An hour later I was on the train, in my own clothes. Sensibly I reached the platform by climbing the hoardings bordering the unlit car park, avoiding the ticket bloke. Not many people heading for London at that hour. I left my blue serge suit, buttons and other clobber removed, near the café in Euston Station's concourse. It would be nicked within an hour. And the boots outside in the garden. Some wino would benefit. The mini tape I'd erased on some train and slung out on to the dark embankment. The mini recorder I left on the tube train, a gift to the gods. Badges and buttons I dripfed into litter bins with my sewing set. The crash helmet I left on a Central line tube platform, having scratched off the transfers. No fingerprints. My gloves I simply discarded as I walked towards Wardour Street. The holdall with the Russian silver I put in a drop near St Giles's Church – a restaurant whose owner knew Big John. He telephoned Sheehan's men the minute I handed the stuff over.

The Novello Room is highly posh. It actually belongs to the British Library, a part of the British Museum conglomerate. Though the British Library's central offices are in tiny Sheraton Street, you enter the Novello Room through the much grander doorway at 160 Wardour Street. I like Soho, with all its quirks. It has atmosphere. I was embarrassed because the Novello is probably the poshest banquet suite around there, and I never look well groomed at the best of times. I positioned myself in the hallway awaiting Lydia. I'd combed my hair and done my nails in the loo, and was clean if a bit curled at the edges. As Lydia entered, I called to a group of trendy assistants assembling for the nosh, 'Oh, thanks for the lift, er, Jay!' so she'd hear me, and went towards her.

And stopped. My breath was gone. I stared.

'Good evening, Lovejoy.'

Pause and silence, the hubbub from the film people in the anterooms a sort of unheard din.

'I do hope I'm in good time.' As if there was any question of that. She's never late, a right pest. The pause stretched. 'Have you been waiting long, Lovejoy?' I got my breath going in useful volumes. 'How did the noon meeting go?' In the absence of response she resorted to complaint. 'Your tie's crooked.'

'You're beautiful.' My voice was a distant bleat.

'Now, Lovejoy.' She coloured up, beautiful times three, times any number.

She wore a dark silver dress with a high frill collar. Her arms were ensheathed in a lace material of the same colour. Her blonde hair was unbunned, a seemingly casual asymmetry. The jewellery was a complete suite of necklace, two bracelets, earrings, aquamarines on silver. OK, that closed-setting French style of 1760 isn't fashionable now, but that's only because women lack the elegance to wear it properly matched with the right hair and form; stridency's the game nowadays. Each principal stone in the necklace, some forty, had its own subordinate pendant stone. Each bracelet aquamarine had two pupped stones, the earrings three. She'd never told me she had a suite so delectable, lovely enough to move you to tears. She was a heart-stopper.

'Shouldn't we be joining the others?'

'Look, love.' I went red and glanced in. The anterooms were filled with wealth in every size and shape. 'They're grand in there. It's a whole banquet.'

'Of course. It's the celebration for last stage of the film. Brookes are the caterers!' She was impressed.

'But I'm a scruff, love. You're exquisite. Shouldn't I get Max for you? He's on his tod.' I'd already seen him, looking out of his depth but in a dinner jacket.

'Certainly not, Lovejoy.' She had a matching stole and drew it round her. 'Without you this film can't progress. You're the divvy, not they. They need you. Come.'

And in we camed.

Lydia was a sensation. The assistants for once were outdone. Some had dressed over the top, others had dressed down. Variety was the order of the day. Oddly, Lydia fitted with uncanny ease into every group. Noisy technicians tanking on beer accepted her with open admiration and quickly-moderated language. Dressers and the props girls, kaleidoscopically trendy in every dress from period costume to mod pops and full lengths, instantly asked opinions. She even chatted with Vance's gaggle of bafflers, and had them listening and laughing. It was astonishing. I was really proud of her. Saffron Kay, who fetched her psychiatrist as companion, anxiously sought Lydia's company. Stef Honor tried to move in, but Lydia must have given him some steely put-down because people nearby grinned as Stef retired sulkily to a trio of worshippers. Until Lydia arrived I'd thought them stunning. Lorane hated Lydia, I could tell. She made a couple of scathing remarks to Ray Meese, but he only pursed his lips and looked from Lydia to me. I glanced away in time, and shoved my way through to Pal Trevelyan. He was with Hank the stunt arranger.

'Here comes Lovejoy,' Hank said. 'You two met?'

'Yes. At the meeting today.'

'Spare tool, more like,' I said. Pal seemed friendly and laughed.

'Well, you've got your Equity card.'

'Eh?'

'Equity. Actors' union.' Hank pretended to be the Hunchback of Notre Dame. 'You can even do stunts now.'

'What do I want an Equity card for?'

'To act.' Pal nodded. 'Not me. I'm only the gun man. But if you actually go in front of the camera—'

'Who, me?' I was suddenly anxious. That bad feeling was back.

'Yes. You're in the robbery scene.'

Me? 'Are you sure?'

'Typical cock-up,' Pal said, laughing. 'No wonder movies go over budget. It's them silly bitches of coordinators. You're in the script. One of Lancelot Lake's merry men.'

I went cold. 'That frigging balloon?'

Hank fell about. 'No. Actors don't fall, tumble, hang on high. They neither crash nor do they die. It's my people, me, who do that. We dress so we'll look the same and do the stunts.'

Not me, then. 'Praise be.'

Pal added, amused, 'When you're caught in the crossfire, Lovejoy, it's Hank will tumble off the gallery.'

Tumble? From on high? *'Off what balcony?'*

'Isn't there some tall gallery railing running round the Museum room where Lancelot Lake does the robbery?'

'Round the King's Gallery, yes. Not the Temporary Exhibitions place.'

'How high is it?' Hank asked. 'That influences the price.'

'There's a running shootout.' Pal was pleased. 'I hate single handgun stuff. No real interest. And those bloody sprayguns everybody uses since Viet Nam are a real yawn.'

I wanted to get this really clear. 'So no ballooning? No rope-climbing?'

'You run across the floor.' Hank was amused at my fear. Such merriment. 'Check the script Lorane'll give you.'

'Dinna fash, Lovejoy,' Pal added. 'You'll find you're superfluous, like the rest of these pillocks, truth be known.'

Before dinner was called, I edged into Lorane's charmed novinary of admirers and humbly asked for a word. She looked attractive, but slick rather than pretty, and hard as if bevel-edged in her long gold lamé dress. Not a patch on Lydia.

'What's this about me acting, Lorane?' I asked.

She was not smiling as she turned, hugging herself. It wasn't that non-smile smile women have perfected over the millennia. It was the cruel secret no-smile, which they've also perfected but which is a very different thing. Lydia sometimes does the former, which means I think she likes me deep down. She'd never smile like Lorane in a million years. 'Oh. It's Lovejoy. Yes, Ray wants you to be one of Lancelot's baddies.'

'Me? What for?'

'Dunno. I'll find out if you like.' She looked me up and down. 'Don't worry, Lovejoy. Your elegant features won't be noticeable. You'll be encased in a hooded black assault suit.'

'Maybe he'll act us all off the screen,' some pill warbled, laughing. He had a severe tan and was in a cream dress suit with a gold bow tie.

'Maybe he's worried about his sartorial image, Baz,' Lorane added. I was red and stuck to the floor, wanting it to open.

An arm slipped through mine. 'So sorry to interrupt, Miss Lorane.' Lydia to the rescue. For once I was glad. 'But can I borrow Lovejoy?' She stayed there, though I was ready to hurtle into the multitude for safety. 'It's only a small question, Lovejoy. One of Ray Meese's lady guests has heard that you were here in person, and has asked me about some German-silver alloy statuette—'

Safe ground. 'Packfong's its proper name. So-called white copper. Actually Chinese. You sure it's an alloy, love? Zinc, copper and nickel alloys like those come pretty rare these days.'

'Could you explain in person, Lovejoy?' Lydia smiled apologetically at Lorane's camarilla, somehow managing to omit Lorane herself. 'She's so eager to meet you, having heard of your amazing feat in the Vatican.'

And drew me away. Lorane's admirers' admiration trailed after Lydia. Lorane was decidedly put out. Even I could tell.

'Which is she, Lyd?' I whispered when we'd eeled clear.

'Lydia, please.' She stood before me in the loud press, eyes downcast. 'I'm afraid it was subterfuge. There isn't a real problem question, Lovejoy.'

'Why?' What was going on?

'Lorane was being deliberately vindictive. I suspected she would.'

'Oh.' I looked at her. No spectacles, eyes deep and blue. You could go for a swim in those. 'I was glad you . . . subterfuged. Thanks.'

'The least an apprentice could do.'

'Did you hear I'm to be in this film?'

'Yes. Your Equity card's arranged.'

We'd had many a stilted conversation since I'd taken her on, but I'd never found myself struggling for words before.

'I don't do much, apparently.'

Halt. Tongue-tied. I felt like an awkward kid, simply ridiculous. I mean, my apprentice, right? And I'm shuffling and embarrassed. But what for? A waiter broke the spell, hawking me out to find one of MacAdam's nerks in the foyer just as places were called for dinner. It wasn't anything important, just routine inquiries. It only took a minute. I rejoined the party, sat beside Lydia. 'Nothing, love,' I said. 'Somebody burgled that Russian exhibition in St Edmundsbury.'

'Did the police catch the criminals?'

'Not yet. The Old Bill came to check I was still here. I explained I've been with the film people all day, including the noon meeting. They'll check with the production assistants.'

'I sincerely hope they do, too,' she said, on my side but interrogating me with a glance.

'Tell me how to eat this first course, love.' It was mussels.

As Lydia did so, I thought of nasty old MacAdam's attempt to catch me out. A woman's car had been taken from a social club. Her handbag had gone missing from the car, alas. This was my cue – he'd hoped – to say I hadn't touched it. Then he'd have pounced. I'd just said, 'Naughty people around these days. If I find it, I'll ring in.'

I ate heartily, for strength when Ben Clayton came calling to wreak vengeance. Proving alibis to peelers is one thing, to the Claytons of this world different entirely. Odd that he hadn't yet showed up, but he would, he would.

Chapter 20

Would you believe, but a film company limousine drove us back into East Anglia. By then I'd recovered from that awkwardness, partly at least. Lydia took time off from being glamorous to upbraid the driver – surely the provision of motor cars for guests was a wholly unwarranted expenditure? Et cetera. He was startled even more when, two hours later, he dropped her off at her mother's, then drove me to my village. Normality sails under many flags. It had been odd saying good night to Lydia. She'd almost hesitated, disembarking, then hurried on up the path without a backward glance. I felt really strange.

No vicious Seg or vindictive Ben Clayton was waiting, thank heavens. The phone was ringing when I entered. It was Lydia. A message had been left on her answer phone. Tinker, no less.

'He says to tell you Duffie has discovered what you wanted to know, Lovejoy. That is all.' And went quiet. 'Lovejoy?'

'Aye?' Sam's bus, found.

'A year ago I was about to . . . to sojourn at your cottage. To care for you after you sustained injuries. If you remember.'

'Aye.' My voice cracked. 'Your mother intervened.'

'I wish you to know that, should circumstances require, I'd be quite prepared to stay, as we provisionally agreed then.' Her euphemism had been housekeeping.

'Er, that's very kind, love, only—' A sleeping-bag on the bare flags?

'I feel responsible, Lovejoy. It was my visit to the Russian exhibition which led to the damage done by Clayton. I shall make restitution.' She paused for me to express thanks. I did so, feebly. 'In your right jacket pocket, you will find a call sheet. It lists you as acting in the robbery scenes.'

'It what?'

'Keep calm, Lovejoy. I thought it wise to avoid discussion in the film company's driver's hearing. I suggest that tomorrow you meet Ray Meese and Lorane as agreed, and adopt the following tactic . . .'

No Ben Clayton in the misty dripping dawn.

Ray Meese brought Lorane to the Three Greyhounds. Polite, I praised his posh party.

'Truly on a par with that Paramount thrash,' Meese wheezed.

'Er, nice.'

'Not super excessively so, I guess?' from sweet Lorane, looking distastefully round the pub. She had an infallible way of narking me.

'This call sheet.' I showed it.

'Miss Prim too busy during the night to decipher it, Lovejoy?'

'What she's got, love, you couldn't even spell.'

She tried to backhand me but I deflected her swing and let her overbalance. The crash shut everybody in the pub up for a second. Meese helped her up, staring hard at her for control. She recovered, hating me.

'Not hurt, dear?' he boomed, setting the scene. She could have killed me, probably would if I didn't look out.

'She overbalanced,' Meese intoned. The pub resumed its talking. One or two muttered drunk-again jokes.

'No offence intended,' I said, rejoining the pleasantries. 'It's that famous line from, wasn't it a Bogart film? The one where—'

'I sense unhappiness, Lovejoy. Give give give.'

'Not really. I don't understand this call sheet.' It was full of art/props and camera/grips and scene numbers and fisher boom splices and dolly tracks and instructions to wardrobe people. But what griped my entrails was on page five. 'I'm not going to be in your film crew, that's all.'

He groaned slowly. 'Lovejoy. Give me a hundred sound reasons for raining destruction upon my aching brow.'

'Giving advice on filming an antiques robbery in a Wembley mock-up set, yes. The same in the British Museum, yes. But this says I dress up and pretend I can act, shoot, rob. No, Ray.'

He placed an avuncular hand on my arm. 'You mean yes, Lovejoy. Truly truly truly.'

'I mean no, mate.'

'The shooting's elementary, Lovejoy. In my hands, can people fear? We've constructed a British Museum Room 31 set in studio. Correct down to the last antique. All those crazy Russian Armenian scrolls, silvers, paintings. Perfect. At a cost of Jesus. All you have to do is trot with Lancelot Lake and his two hoods across that set, in costume. Lancelot says words. All in studio comfort, truly. You pack the studio props into studio sacks on our perfect studio set. It takes ten minutes, for fuck's sake. You are paid a fortune. And still say no?'

'Definitely. No.'

'Why not?' Lorane had recovered. Somehow I wish she hadn't.

'Because if I do the studio filming in Wembley, I'll have to do the British Museum bit.' I fumbled with my call sheet. 'It says here—'

'That we shoot the BM footage in the BM.' Meese held his head. 'Apocalypse wow. My head, Lorane.'

She passed him a shake of three white pills. He gulped them with a swirl of vodka and lime, sent her for another double.

'That's because the British Museum is the British Museum, Lovejoy.' He sounded broken. I began to feel really sorry for him, and not a bit narked that Lydia had put me up to this. 'And the movie's about robbing the British Museum. Get it?'

I said I couldn't see why everything was so desperate. Meese blinked. It was one of those odd moments when truths will out.

'Lovejoy. You don't know the movies.' His eyes shone, owled in those glass discs. 'There's what we call The Ratio. For every hundred movies planned, fourteen get financed. Three get finished. And one's *The Guns of Navarone*.'

'Not bad odds.' I felt I had to explain, their silence being so full of blame aimed my way. 'Compared to antiques. Our odds are a thousand to one for the tiddlers, but a million to one for a Cellini gold work or a Sheraton bureau.'

Meese listened me out. The man was transfixed. I felt weird, uneased by the fervour in his eyes. I've seen it before and hated it every single time. It's a kind of selective insanity, as if his brain was sending some terrible signal: *in all else I am sane; but better go along with me because in this I'm mad.* He spoke in a whisper, still as a pike in a pool.

'But don't you dream, Lovejoy? Of that one great antiques scoop, that triumph which will make you a legend?' I had to lean to hear, so low his voice. 'Movies have the same fable. We all strive for that one superb movie which has everything. The truly last gambado – superbly original, something never been screened before, the whole adoring world howling to see it. Fame. Fortune. Its creator pedestaled, immortal. Among the gods.'

Pause for re-entry. 'And your picture's it?'

'Has to be, Lovejoy. That's why the British Museum, the last great impregnable antiques fortress on earth. Impenetrable, inviolate. I'll ravish the ultimate virgin . . .'

And so on. I went along with the barminess, nodding my asinine smile to earn my wage. But deep down I knew I wasn't witnessing a mystic transport of some latterday St Francis; I was sitting in on dementia. It's stuff that kills. Time Lovejoy got out from under.

Lorane returned and weighed in. 'The balloon shots are being done on studio sets mostly. The stuntmen – not you – will do the rest on the London University tower. And Lancelot Lake, one prelim take. That's it. You won't even see the balloon, Lovejoy.'

'You've got to teach Lancelot Lake how to handle these things. It's not a simple snatch, Lovejoy. Not for Russian Armenia's entire priceless heritage, right?'

'What if something gets nicked, Ray?' I was chatty, offhand. 'I've a police record. Any of your million assistants pinches a light bulb, the constabulary'll slam me in the clink and forget.'

Meese moaned. Lorane took up the argument, exactly as Lydia had predicted. Almost. 'Lovejoy. In what capacity were you hired?'

'To advise on antiques.'

'Right.' She lit a cigarette. 'You signed a contract, cashed the cheques. Fancy a visit to our lawyers?'

'Lovejoy. Lorane.' Meese smiled. 'Peace be unto you.

I'll die if you quarrel. How about you two get together, resolve those conflicts. Let Ray Meese live again, hmmm?'

She spoke before I could draw breath. 'Very well, Ray. We'll give you a definite.'

Meese prayed to heaven. 'Lord, let it be soon.'

No Ben Clayton stalking me in the streets of Soho. No maniacal Seg flinging me from the train. Quiet life.

The East Coast has ugly patches, God knows. Most of them are caravan sites – called Perfect Paradise, Trailer Park Supremo, some such. During our miserable wet summers they are occupied by legions of holiday-makers. These desperate resorts are situated hard by gale-swept shores, centred on clapboard bungalow-style buildings, pinball arcades, bingo parlours and the like. Out of season these areas degenerate into drab loneliness. They are honestly awful.

The saving grace is that, as holiday crowds dwindle, nearby villages revert to normalcy. Pubs cautiously creep back to a pleasant indolence. Shopkeepers start smiling. The one village bobby nods off. All is well. Even the itinerant hotdog stands and roadside icecreamios give up the ghost. The few diehards who stick it out do quite well, but have to travel further for the same number of customers. So it was that Duffie's brother Gus, combing the caravan parks near Great Yarmouth, saw a lonely bus on a concrete acre. It answered Duffie's description. I phoned MacAdam with a lie: the studio wanted me to plan a scene. Then I borrowed Lydia's car to run out, late that evening. I didn't want anybody following.

The East Coast can be malign, wet and full of nasty gales. It was misbehaving energetically this particular night. I only discovered the bus by a fluke, though Duffie had given me precise directions. The holiday camp half a mile away was mostly silent, except for one building trying to pretend it was a live disco. A light showed here and there. God, it was desolate.

My torch showed Sam Shrouder's bus. I cut my car's lights, hunched my collar, and effected entry to the cabin which was partitioned from the passenger's area by a sliding panel with an unbeatable – for the moment – lock. The engine fired first time I touched the wires. Sam must have kept it in pretty fair running order. He'd have had to, of course, needing it every day. I couldn't open the rear door. I relocked the cabin, drove a million leagues to find a phone-box, and got Lydia. I told her I needed her to drive her car home, gave her directions.

'But you already have my mother's car, Lovejoy. How on earth can I—?'

'Lydia,' I said wearily. 'Come. In secrecy. Forthwith, if you please.' And rang off. Every time you want a woman to really get her skates on she gives you a load of lip. Ever noticed that? I went and sat in the car on the seafront until she came. Three hours. Three bloody hours. I ask you. Is that cooperation?

She came trotting over, exasperated and tilting herself against the wind. 'Lovejoy!' she began, breathless. 'I've had to tell such fibs to get a lift from my friend Rosalyn! I said that my aunt was ill—'

'Good old Rosalyn. 'Night.' I gave her the car keys and walked off, ignoring her yelps of outrage. Ask a favour, they moan you've sucked blood.

I drove the bus through the stormy night to St Michael's ruined church, near Myland. Not much cover except for a small wood, but it was handy and I was worn out. I put a 'Police: Do Not Attempt To Remove' sticker on it, which I'd thoughtfully stolen while passing through Great Yarmouth, thereby saving some motorist from an unexpected infarct. And trudged home, three drenching miles and the rain teeming.

The outside light was burning. Ben Clayton at last. A white saloon car blocked my gravel drive. Praying he'd give me time to prove my cast-iron alibi before setting Seg on me, I wearily opened the remains of the door.

'Welcome home, Lovejoy,' Lorane said. 'Any way of heating this place except sex?'

There wasn't as it happened, and I'm not proud of that or of what happened next.

'You see, Lovejoy,' Lorane said in the early hours. 'It mayn't seem much to you, because you're one of Mother Nature's simpletons. But believe me, 110 minutes of movie takes an average of forty tons of electrical equipment *a minute*. It'd take a man ten years to pay for that single minute of shooting, every penny he earned. It needs nine dozen support staff minimum, thirty vehicles basic plus a dozen specialist carriers. Wardrobe staff alone are two dozen, full-time.'

'You keep on telling me this.' She occupied a hell of a lot of the sleeping-bag, but two's warmer than one. And less restful. She'd proved that.

'One defective cog means the machine doesn't work, Lovejoy.'

'So get a substitute.'

She was all knees as she turned round, shoving her bum into my belly and wriggled backwards to get to my warmth. Typical. 'You're on the payroll because you're a divvy. The Museum insisted there be an antiques adviser. You're it.'

'In a black assault suit with a kid's toy gun?'

'Able to tell us how to snatch precious antiques convincingly, Lovejoy. Any idiot can jemmy displays off a wall.'

'Does it matter?'

'It matters, idiot. Authenticity wins Oscars. Lack of credibility loses them.'

'Couldn't I just show the actors how and let them get on with it?'

She sighed. 'We're so frigging dicey, finance-wise, half a day's shooting can push us off the wire.'

'You know, love. All that action – cameras, crew, cops-and-robbers stories – it makes you think, eh?' I felt her stiffen. Her hand had reached for me. Now it stilled.

'You, you mean? Pull a real robbery?'

'No, not really. Honest, no. But you can't help thinking, can you?'

'Stupid, stupid Lovejoy.' Her hand resumed its steady work. She shivered – once – and murmured as the inevitable happened. 'More warmth, Lovejoy?'

You don't get to be proud of everything, I find. People say contracts haven't hearts, and they're right. But more and more I find myself simply doing as women say. It came to me that I was committed to obeying Lorane. The darkness clasped us anew. In the last second before reflex ruled, that same old thought nagged: Ben Clayton still hadn't come, but Lorane had. *Why?*

Ecstasy and out.

Before she left next morning I asked when I could next see her. She smiled at that, tugging on her long boots.

'You want to? In this doss house?'

'It's the only place I've got.'

She came close. 'For you, Lovejoy, OK, while the going's good. You'll shoot the scenes?'

'Aye. Anything you say.'

'And what is it Miss Prim's got that I can't spell?'

'Nowt, love.' I smiled most sincerely. 'Truly truly.' I could lose her in sincerity, any day of the week.

Chapter 21

'Honest, John. It's the truth. I've no idea.'

Dejected and scared, I sat in his motor confessing ineptitude and failed compliance. Both hanging offences. We were in a farmyard near Saxmundham, too far from civilization for my liking. The place had a look of dereliction, no hens, dogs, people. The fields seemed to be growing nothing, the trees dejected. Countryside at its ghastly worst. Two carloads of the Sheehan mob seethed nearby, ominously bored.

'You're sure Ben Clayton's financing this Meese?'

'I believe it, John. Clayton's scraped his kitty to raise the gelt.'

'Just to make a picture?' He made it sound outlandish.

'Some folk do, John.'

'And they're going to rob the British Museum.' His statement, my responsibility.

A dry swallow. 'I think so, John.'

'What of?'

'Maybe the Armenian collection. I dunno.' I shrugged, staring out through the windscreen. Is there anything more desolate than an empty farmhouse? 'That's what the film story calls for.'

'But you said they're filming it in a Wembley studio, using bodged replicas.'

'That's what they say, John.'

'And the balloonists?'

'They'll be filmed mostly in the studio, with mockups on a London University building.'

'Glory be.' Big John shook his head, amazed. 'Will it look real, then?'

'They say so. Confident.'

'You've done a wander, Lovejoy?'

I sighed, nodding. 'John, I could walk the British Museum blindfold, in the dark, and not knock over a single pot. I just can't see how they'll pull it off.' His laconic glance told me he was having me watched.

'Kick that thin lassie out of your sleeping-bag, Lovejoy. You'll sleep the sounder.'

'And no Ben Clayton, John. No Seg.'

'Tch,' he tutted. 'That's a strangie, Lovejoy. 'Deed it is.'

'Right.' I spoke with feeling. 'He should be breathing fire and slaughter, demanding proof I didn't nick that Russian silver from his exhibition.'

'Maybe he's heard from the peelers you've an alibi?'

'That wouldn't stop him. He'd do me over from habit.'

'True, Lovejoy.' He pondered, curious. '*Can* the Museum be done, Lovejoy?'

'Honest?' I shook my head. 'Impossible, I reckon. Oh, I could nip in and out anytime you like. But so what? So does any nonagenarian taking his ten great-grandchildren on a cultural outing.'

'Know what's worrying me, Lovejoy? Robbing the British Museum's the biggie. It's the one great remaining scam. It's Everest, the Lost Continent, the original moon walk, rolled into one. Been tried a million times, never been done. It's the big gambado. Whoever pulls it off is a legend, Lovejoy. The Topkapi rip'll look like a Woolworth shoplift.' Meese had said that. John's gaze turned thoughtful. 'I'd not appreciate Ben Clayton and a bunch of camera clickers becoming everybody's heroes, Lovejoy.'

His hailstone eyes said I'd catch it if that happened. I took a minute to answer.

'John. Honest to God, I'll do what I can—'

'Shush.' I shushed obediently while he whistled *Lillibulero* through his teeth. A minute passed. Two. Four. 'Lovejoy,' he resumed, drumming his fingers. 'If *you* were trying the Museum, and couldn't suss it yourself, who would you get?'

'A moler? Well. That Sunderland bloke did a good job for the Dulwich scam.'

'Name of Andy? He's inside.'

No arguing with Sheehan's knowledge of recent events regarding gaols. 'Well, there's Footer. Getting on a bit, but sound as a bell. Does security advice for shops in Southampton. Or Ankles Benedict – she uses her cousin's baby. Then you might try—'

'One name, Lovejoy. Not a roll-call.'

'Tooter, then. But he's gone expensive—'

'Lovejoy!' Sheehan said quietly. I shut up. 'Tell Dutch to hire Footer. Then send him to Spain for a month. Immediate.'

I drew breath, finally decided not to speak and got out of the motor to transmit Sheehan's orders to Dutch, a fatty in the first saloon. The sun brings old Footer out in a terrible rash. Spain would be hell, but that was his problem.

Maybe there was a clue in the bus.

The bus was untouched, as far as I could make out

from a distant glance from the hospital road. There aren't many ruins left, but St Michael's must have been a grand gothic church once, to judge from the size of its mounds. People have stolen stones over the centuries, and now only kids play there and the odd badger doing its silly gambolling. Nobody about, not even a twitcher – birdwatchers are always a problem. I'd chosen St Michael's because no houses overlook it. You can just see the railway in the distance.

Nobody along. I opened the cab, climbed in. Nothing touched. I sniffed the air. Nil. Reassured, I had a go but failed to enter the bus itself. That was clever Sam Shrouder, may he rest in peace. Of course, half the problem was myself. I was scared. Parson Brown's body was still not found. I didn't want to be its finder, especially if it mouldered inside a motorized vehicle of which I was the sole and illicit possessor.

Give up, Lovejoy. What can be in a derelict old bus? The killer would have removed all possible clues anyway. I began to feel edgy, certain now I could niff decaying antique dealer. I locked the cab and left the bus secure in its isolation.

It seemed hardly worth going home. I could have had a nosh in any pub in or near town, seeing that Lydia was now letting me keep two per cent of my – that's *my* – retainer. This would suffice for luxuries like food. But I spent valuable coins of the realm in travel, and with casual pride revealed to a busload of villagers that I was flush.

It was worth it. The rough sketch I'd made of a Celtic cross embedded in a big chunk of granite wasn't exactly where I'd left it oh so casually – the patchwork cushion underneath which I'd positioned it was wrongly aligned.

My drawing showed the granite hollowed, giving crude dimensions in feet and inches. I'd scribbled TIMELOCK and HINGED FLOOR ACCESS VITAL on it, with 3WA TO CONTROL. I must say it looked pretty convincing, for a truly secret secret. A card by the phone on the bare floor reminded me to phone Tinker and bring the stone cross's date forward. The card was undisturbed, but face up it could be read by any passing intruder.

Satisfied, I burned card and sketch in the fireplace and crushed the ash. Now Lorane and Ray Meese knew part of my secret plan. Quite good going. I mustn't forget to leak the rest later. I caught the town bus, to find Tinker and tell him I wanted Sorry Malone. He does locks.

They call Footer Footer because he's daft on football. He says he played for Sheffield Wednesday, Liverpool, all over. Never did, of course. He's lame, has been since birth. But if making up the odd unbelievable fantasy was the worst this wicked old world got up to, it wouldn't be in quite such dire straits, would it?

We met up at Dirty Dick's, near Liverpool Street Station in London. Recognized each other instantly, though we'd never actually met. He was drinking bitter, a long-faced lanky old man just this side of shabbiness. I had a pint of shandy.

'Knew you straight away, Lovejoy.'

'How do, Footer. All right?'

'Yes, son. All well.' He pulled me along the bar to where it met the wall, a cautionary sign I liked. The bar was moderately empty; we weren't overheard. 'You could've knocked me down with a feather when Dutch dropped by, Lovejoy. The old BM! Christ, the boys'd never believe it.'

'They'll never hear, eh?'

'No, Lovejoy.' His rheumy old eyes were sparkling. 'Dutch agreed a price. They say you're straight as a die on the old gelt.'

'You'll get it, Footer. But a holiday to Malaga's written in.'

'Malaga?' He was astonished. 'Where the bleedin' hell's Malaga?'

'Spain, Footer. Sorry. Big John said.'

'My frigging skin, Lovejoy! I'll peel like a frigging rabbit!'

'Orders is orders, Footer.'

'OK. Today, is it?'

'Don't go home, Footer. Just deliver, then away on the Great White Bird. Dutch'll be waiting at Marble Arch.'

'Tch! Beer's rotten overseas, Lovejoy. I'll die.'

'Dying from poor ale's not the worst thing on earth, Footer.'

'True, Lovejoy.' The worst thing on earth was Big John, and we nodded in knowing synchrony. 'Well, son. I've sussed the Museum out for you. It's not good news.' He shrugged. 'Even though you could go through that place like a dose of senna pods.'

'Aye, but so could anybody.'

'Well, son, here it is. The easy places are the nosh spot, where staff turnover rate's one every couple of months or so. Warders – sorry, attendants – the same. And the info staff. Then there's the British Museum Society. Join it for a shekel and you get private evening views. They even have a private members' room, and special closed tours round the admin and research departments. For a tenner a year you're virtually a trustee.' He said trusty, but he's done time. 'Everybody trusts a trustee, eh?'

'That's their purpose, Footer.'

'Aye, son. Well.' He sounded cynical. 'There's the book

stacks below the Reading Room. But they've person-detectors down there for after hours. I ask you. Who'd want to nick old bloody books? Some are the size of a frigging desk. All dust. Them book cellars go all the way under London to Holborn. Christ Almighty. You'd think people'd have better things to do, all that readin'. Then there's the lorries.'

Gabriella had mentioned vehicle entrances. 'What lorries?'

'They arrive each day. Six from Micawber Street, three runs from Woolwich. That Micawber van – you seen the frigging mess them planners made of City Road, Lovejoy? – it's not important, only antique maps and things. The main one's the Woolwich wagon. Starts out from the Army. Reserved books – too many for the Museum to hold any one time, see? – are under guard down there. Royal Artillery base. Mean bastards, they. I remember one time we was in Egypt, me with the Loyal Regiment—'

'The lorries, Footer.' He reminisces.

'Two drivers. Sealed in by the Army, all the way. Unsealed in the Museum. It drives down the ramp. Codes and bleeps are changed every day. That Bracegirdle, security, tells only one bloke. He's a maniac. Always busy, always around. Checks it personal. Nasty sod.'

'Does he now.'

'Has a young tart, stickler for ticking things on lists. Nasty.' Gabriella. Nasty in our game means incorruptibly honest, and therefore unfair. 'Electrical staff are another hole, Lovejoy. Sewage not too good, though. It's so old-fashioned it's a dead risk. They have the same sewage men, doing it for years. First name stuff, so forget it.'

'Any other way in?'

'Grub supplies to the restaurant, daily delivery.'

'Roof?'

He raised his eyes to heaven. 'Leave off, Lovejoy.'

'I'm only asking, Footer. And you're being paid.'

'Aye, Spain.' He was miserable about Spain.

'Lots of ways in. And out.' We both knew what was coming next; the bad news. 'So what stops all the precious exhibits walking?'

'People, Lovejoy.' He was really gloomy. 'Everywhere there's frigging warders. The bastards are counting you half the bloody time, pocket clickers. And you're never out of sight of two. The old double direction game. The buggers signal central control and each other if you're on your own in a gallery for more than half a minute.' He gave me an envelope. In it I would find details of staff numbers, duty rosters, food suppliers' addresses, the usual gunge.

'Ta. Electronics?'

'Vibrators, sensors, closed-circuit cameras, the lot. Noise detectors go on automatic after lights-out. Thrystor detectors – a touch changes the electrical charge so all hell's let loose. Doors double crosslocked. The display cases tripled. A right pig, Lovejoy. Fart, and you set off some frigging alarm.' I bought him a fresh pint. 'Three cop shops have two special peelers on full standby, including that dozy load of bleeders up Theobalds Road. Frigging ridiculous.'

All this was routine cackle, but quite good news. 'Obstacles, Footer?'

'What I really didn't like, son, is them detachable turn-handles fer them rolling brass doors. The bleeders shut the Map Gallery, then take the handles away. I call that a dead liberty. You can't get through without handles – and the Old Bill'd spot you carrying a foot-long brass turn-screw at midnight. Ridiculous.'

I knew how peeved he felt. His job was making thefts easier, not more difficult.

'But there must be something positive, Footer.'

'Not much. There's a glass roof, by the kiddies' shop near the nosh bar. And the dining area's got tall windows, but it's Pilkington's special glass, the swine. You'll raise the dead scratching it. Though it abuts on tall trees, back of Bloomsbury Street.' He was so apologetic I felt sympathy. 'Sorry, Lovejoy. It's not Springheeled Jack stuff.'

'Did you notice if there's a high walkway gallery round the Temporary Exhibitions room?'

He gave me an injured stare. There isn't. He knew I knew and was just checking that he'd been thorough.

'Do leave orf, son. I was doing this before you was walking. No. Ceiling's too low. There's one all round the Manuscript Saloon where they keep all them gospel cases. It's the only road out. And in the Grenville and King's rooms too, but you'll have difficulty getting round the corner pillars. The high walkways have lockable glass doors, see?' He shrugged, looking quizzical. 'You come running out of that Temporary Exhibitions room, Lovejoy, you've got to go left or straight on. No other way, worm or sparrow. I hate the way they always keep them big window blinds drawn. It's not natural. What they got against frigging daylight?'

'All in all, Footer, what d'you reckon?'

He contemplated. 'Ways? You could try the Lost Sprog, with Ankles Benedict. It's done wonders in its time, not been used for ages. Or the Londoner? But they'd be wise to that. There's a fire exit by the kitchen.'

'Right, mmmmh, right,' I kept saying, but I was not really listening. I'd only asked from politeness, to make the old man feel better. The Londoner's an old trick – you pretend or start a fire; it's named from the child's roundelay, London's Burning – then nick your heart's desire in the pandemonium. The Lost Baby's best for fairs, small theatres, shops. The BM could take that ploy – or any other – in its stride.

When he'd done I asked, 'Verdict, Footer?'

'Rather you than me, son. But good luck.'

'Have a nice holiday. Here.'

'What is it, Lovejoy?' He took the pot.

'Barrier cream, Footer. My apprentice says it's just right for sunshine. Cheers.' Like I say, dose of salts.

Chapter 22

Disappointment is total. There aren't fine shades, I find. Disappointment's always top gear, on max. And making movies is it in boring spades, the ultimate yawn.

We were at the studios, the big hangar. I'd been kitted up in some black outfit like ballet dancers wear except it had a hood with eyeholes. They gave me a toy gun on a belt. I felt terrific. Two girls processed me, even worrying about how my eyes looked.

Then I sat down. For an hour. During this hectic time birds and blokes drifted about, pausing for a smoke, chatting, doing things with cables. I was joined by two other black-garbed nerks, Nick and Lofty. We could see one another's eyes and talked through our tight black cloth hoods. They too had popguns, belts. Nick wore a coil of rope. We talked. They had a fag. Lofty told me of his daughter's wedding. They talked about past films they'd done, mostly getting shot or throwing grenades from helicopters.

And another hour. After this exertion, worn out, we knocked off for a cuppa. Somebody went to the loo. Much talk of Lancelot Lake, a born duckegg who was Past It. Stef Honor never should have got the part. That Saffron Kay's real name was Jennifer Something, neurotic lass the cameras didn't like.

'You aren't confident, then?' I asked. We were watching the hangar slowly fill with blokes carrying wood. This was the famed movies?

Lofty chuckled, nudged Nick. 'Tell him.'

'It's a dog. A turkey. Sorry.' Nick was grinning. 'The Yanks'd say it's a bomber, Yank-speak for a flop.'

'A flop?' I was mystified. 'But Ray Meese is confident. And they've spent a fortune—'

'F-l-o-p, Lovejoy. Dud. Smell them a mile off. Why they keep going beats me.'

'Think of your mortgage, Nick,' Lofty said, getting a laugh. 'Soon be dinner-time.'

One bright spot did occur. I was in the queue for nosh – a degrading business. Shirley, an assistant, showed me an antique cloth. It was a delight, well worth losing my place for. I was so happy. Civilization here, right here in a film studio of all places.

'A darning sampler!' Imagine a piece of linen, eighteen inches square, with darning stitches in different coloured cottons spaced separately all over it. Each coloured area had a date and initials, E. J., 1780.

'What's it worth?' People's cry since the dawn of Man.

'Not as much as you hope, love. The price of one good meal.'

'Is that all?' Shirley was outraged.

'Embroidery, lace, needlework are the orphan children of antiques. Hang on to it for a few years. It's beautiful, Shirley.'

Antiques come in convoys or not at all, like London buses. One sets off another. Quite an avalanche started, six asides in quick succession. I suppose an antique dealer's like a doctor at a party – at risk of hearing about everybody's operation. Two were gems, though, and made up for the disappointments. A camera crewman,

Tel, brought a so-say Georgian black bracket clock, about sixteen inches high. He was dejected when I said it was only 1908 or so.

'Not true Georgian, Tel. Listen to it – Cambridge chimers weren't available in the eighteenth century.' We call them 'revival' clocks. They're skilled first-class replicas of the earlier Georgians, complete with gold finials and ebony case. 'You'll get a good second-hand car for it, though.' He perked up and made way for a plain lady from accounts carrying a long cardboard box full of a tissue-wrapped brown silk dress.

'Lovely,' I told her in delight but grieving, knowing what was coming. 'Bell sleeves, brocaded silk, concertina pleats, a shaped vee bodice, black-fringed peplum, black tassels. You've really got something here. About 1860.'

'My great-grandmother's,' she said, pleased at the crowd of girls coming to ogle.

'And handworked silk buttons down the bodice! Superb.' It was mint. If there'd been anybody on the set with a slender enough waist they could have worn it to a ball instantly. Quietly I told her its value.

'But I earn that much in a week, Lovejoy! Are you sure?'

'Sorry, love.' It's heartbreaking when you think. So much skill, so much valuable silk, worth only the odd groat. It'll change, as our so-called civilization loses ever more of its skills. But right now genuine antique garments are close to give-aways in the trade. This game breaks your heart.

We began filming at two o'clock in the afternoon, having waited since nine. Five hours of inertia, yawnsville. The trouble was, it got worse.

They'd built a series of dark panelled walls by then. Us baddies were to emerge from these doors – not quite the same as those to the Museum's exhibition room but it'd do in gloom and smoke I suppose. Vance came with six assistants. They pushed and pulled the three of us in position, and made us run, hunched, carrying these great black bin-bags. Lancelot Lake sat and watched us, in mufti.

'The idea is you've stolen the entire collection,' somebody told me when I asked, a pretty lass called Tina. 'The sacks are weighted.'

'Run, run, do run, say yeah?' Vance called.

'Ready,' Tina called. 'Good luck.'

'Action!' somebody yelled. White smoke billowed. Lights glared.

The three of us ran, hunched, carrying the bags. We held our pistols in a threatening manner. We made it into the clear space of the hangar. I pulled off my hood. I was drenched with sweat but grinning, pleased it was all over.

'Cheers, Lofty, Nick,' I said. 'See you around.' They just stood there, eyeholes aghast.

'What the hell's he doing?' Meese's voice boomed, loud and electronic. I couldn't see anything for white fog pouring everywhere.

'Eh? I did it,' I called indignantly. Tina trotted through the fog.

'Lovejoy. Where are you going? It was a rehearsal.'

To run? To carry a sack? You rehearse? For *King Lear*, I could see rehearsals might help. 'I've been running carrying sacks since I was seven, love.'

'One more time.' Tina was exasperated.

Actually she meant three more times. Plus three. Plus three more after a tea-break. Then still more.

'They haven't even got frigging cameras,' I complained to Lofty and Nick. They fell about. By then I was the butt of much leg-pulling. Assistants came with electricians and carpenters to stare at me and crack jokes at my expense. We ran slow, we ran fast, hunched, less hunched, very much more hunched, unhunched.

Twenty-nine rehearsals – I ask you – then they started working a camera. Truly truly, we actually started filming.

'They'll go for a take soon,' Lofty predicted at four-thirty. By then I was gasping for air and worn out.

'We're doing no bloody different,' I grumbled.

'One more time, please!' I now hated Tina's cheery cry. More drifty white fog.

'The smoke's the wrong colour anyway,' I groused to Nick. 'It should be thick brown greyish stuff.' They train the army with great thunderflashes and smoke canisters which fume out great clouds of the stuff.

'Cameras couldn't film through that, Lovejoy. And everything's for the cameras, pillock. Not us.'

Let the record show that three of us were filmed forty-six times running ten yards through artificial smoke, and that it took thirty-five specialist staff nine hours to accomplish. Let it now show, though, that Three Wheel Archie came as instructed to find me during a break. He caused a commotion when he found I wasn't yet ready to leave. In fact I was summoned to Meese's position, a chair soldered somehow to cameras on a tall crane thing, to quieten Three Wheel.

'Hello, Archie,' I said. 'Three Wheel, please meet—'

Archie really let me have it. 'You said you'd be finished by now, Lovejoy!' He was blazing. Everybody was gaping at him, so tiny among the beautiful people. 'I've been waiting two hours!'

'Now, Archie,' I said reasonably. 'They can't do it right.'

A few laughed. Others were furious. I was ballocked by Lorane and Vance's crew for stepping out of position, and apologized to Archie, said to go on home if he couldn't wait. Three Wheel marched off the set with a great show of indignation, and we returned to our cliffhanging.

It wasn't all waste. For as we reassembled I saw Lorane glance up at Ray on the gantry. He was looking after Archie's retreating form. Then he swivelled, looking for Lorane. Their eyes met. Neither smiled, but they were both very, very glad. For them my part in their scam was complete.

Worn out by doing nothing all day, I reached home at eleven. The phone rang at midnight on the dot.

'All right, Lovejoy?'

'Exact, Archie. You did great. Best acting they've ever seen.'

'Thought I'd overdone it.'

'No, Archie. Dead on. Cheers.'

Now it was all set up. Lorane and Ray Meese would believe that Three Wheel Archie was somehow involved. It took no intellect to match Archie's diminutive size with a certain spacious hole in a Celtic cross's granite base, as seen in a tatty sketch clumsily unconcealed in my cottage. I felt superb, for once ahead of the game.

Well, I would have done, but for one nagging anxiety. I still for the life of me couldn't understand why I was so necessary in all this. They could have done all they'd done so far without me. And probably done it better, faster, cheaper, less bother. Yet, when I'd threatened to duck out, Lorane steams over and forces me into submission.

That night I made a couple of phone calls. By next evening a local paper would carry details of the discovery of a Celtic cross, embedded in solid granite. It would be found somewhere very rural; the location would be unnamed for security reasons. Its import would be a source of considerable dispute among archaeologists and experts. I'd already seen to that.

Chapter 23

About Woolwich.

Woolwich isn't as simple as it looks. Down in that untidy corner of London there's all sorts of buildings, areas, parks, waterways. It has quite a history, so is best approached by river. To find it, go down the Thames from Limehouse, with the Isle of Dogs on your left. Pass through that frightening futuristic Thames flood barrier, and look to your right. There, just before you cruise into Galleons Reach, sandwiched between Charlton's dull tangle and Plumstead's duller marshes, is Woolwich. If you're in haste, as I always am, catch the Docklands Railway (don't worry – it's only the London tube poshed up). Or take the Woolwich Free Ferry. Or the Blackwall Tunnel, or the train from London Bridge. Listing them like this is an amazing history lesson. It teaches that all important roads once led to Woolwich and maybe, a little more secretly nowadays, still do. I zoomed there on the ferry.

You don't have to be Sherlock Holmes to detect Woolwich's once and future function. Its train station is Woolwich Arsenal. Walk idly for a few minutes and you find Ordnance Road, Master Gunners Place, Shrapnel Close, Artillery Place, Gunner Lane. Got it? It's the home of the gun.

A map surprises you – so much open space? So many playing fields, parks, commons? Well, yes, but soldiers and artillery needed to play. The names clue you more pointedly as you walk from the ferry – Grand Depot Road, Repository Road – until they become terse, blunt: Rifle Range, Depot. That's what I wanted. It took me a couple of hours to stroll where Footer had sketched.

For old times' sake, I paid a visit to the Museum. Though every planner in the Kingdom's had a go renaming it, everybody calls it the Rotunda. Its superb collections, beautifully displayed, show the artistry of fright. Flintlock weapons of mindbending cleverness – repeaters, revolvers, automatic safety built in – were there, with every art style imaginable in every precious metal mined from earth, representing every known country. Too much security, though. Well, you can't have everything. I made my way to the ferry.

By then I'd followed the dotted lines on Footer's map, grinning to myself that Woolwich Stadium was, naturally, more carefully drawn even than the Old Royal Military Academy and the Royal Artillery Barracks. Him and his football. It's a wonder he hadn't inked in the bloody goalposts.

The times of the security van's run from the library repository to the British Museum were given on a card, with probable variations for traffic density. Like I say, Footer's a pro. Wise old head. Shame about the rash.

I'm a master of indecision. Connoisseur of the dither, El Supremo of doubt. Uncertainty's my soulmate. My trouble is, each haver breeds subtype after subtype, all spawned to crowd the original spawner. Vacillation Man, me.

Sitting alone on my sleeping-bag, staring at the empty

grate, I realized I knew virtually zero. Nowt but doubt, my Gran used to say of me, recognizing a true champ. I was no longer sure of the Clayton-Meese axis, though no other explanation would do for Ben C's failure to send Seg on the vengeance trail after I'd burgled his exhibition. And Lorane had behaved predictably, returning to search my place – I hoped she had the sense to copy all my clues about the Celtic cross – after I'd speculated on doing an actual robbery.

Which set me wondering if there was anything I knew which they didn't. An hour's agonizing ponder yielded only one thing, and it was this: I, alone with Lydia, knew Countess Natalia was no uncomprehending ancient. If it hadn't been for the accident of my divvy sense I'd be like the others in thinking her a malleable old crone. I knew she was fluent, and a double shrewd clever, articulate lady behind her mask of incomprehension. OK, she was committed to a cause. To me that's a plus. It's a sign of life. Did Lorane, Meese, Vance, Max, know I'd even returned and chatted with her so frankly that tea-time? And if they did, would they care? Answer: no, especially if they thought her a dull octogenarian with hardly a word in her head. I still wasn't sure of Agafia. A bonny bird, but bonny birds have unreliable loyalties.

Another hour passed, me on the floor glaring at the grate. Bluetits hollered outside for me, cadging swine, but for once I let them get on with it. In fact I might actually have nodded off, because when I woke the light had begun to draw in and I was perished and peckish. I stayed where I was, though, because something important had occurred to me in that half-dozing state.

It was my People Game.

Odd, really, because I'd won, hadn't I? Q: What will she do next? A: Sleep with Parson Brown. *But suppose I hadn't really won at all.* Suppose Mrs Shrouder's love for Parson, missing believed dead, was merely a gambit? As meaningless as Lorane's torrid passion with me. A device to an end, no puns intended. Was the motive something far deeper? Maybe to keep Parson involved so that some greater scam could be enacted . . . ? Were Lorane the game's subject, it would be easy. She'd slept with me to hook me in. OK, so I was needed for the final filming in the Museum. But why? I'd not dug deep enough.

I phoned the Countess. They were in, and I was informed I could be received in an hour. I hurriedly collared Lydia's car and got on the outside of a couple of emergency pasties on the way. Couldn't expect a sumptuous ounce of Genoa cake every time I called, could I?

'Lovejoy! How delightful to see you! I wondered where you'd got to.' Countess Natalia was in the conservatory. It had seen better days. The plants were sprightly. 'Where's your lovely young lady? I like her.'

She didn't have to endure Lydia's criticisms. 'Everybody does, Countess. She's got a job on.'

'Is she too a divvy, Lovejoy?'

'A bit, for furniture.' They bade me sit down as Agafia rang for tea. A maid brought a ton of stuff on a tray, eats from here to eternity. I glowed. Only on Home Stores pots, but grub's grub. I kept trying not to look at Agafia, lovely in the subdued light. The Countess's conversation kept deflecting my attention. I was positioned by a handy table, to my relief. That genteel knee-balancing can ruin your appetite, especially when you're as clumsy as I am.

'You'd better start, Lovejoy. I feel we rather underestimated your appetite during your last visit.' She was civil, not laughing.

'No, no,' I protested. I wasn't clemmed, after the pasties, but hunger means any port in a storm.

'How is our grand design, Lovejoy?'

'The film? Oh, coming on, Countess.' I tried to sound enthusiastic. 'They said they've already done most. They've to film the balloon, and shenanigans in some hotels, then it's the big finale.'

'Which is . . . ?'

'Don't they tell you? The robbery. In the Museum. The last scene of the whole picture. After that it's –' I brought out my one movie slang word with pride – 'a wrap.'

'Ah. What have they decided on?'

'An entire exhibition. Armenian stuff.'

She looked slightly pained. 'Is there nothing better?' She said something in Russian to Agafia, who was already narked by my news. 'I'm displeased.'

'Well, I did tell you. The British Museum hasn't got much Russian heyday stuff, Countess.'

'For heaven's sake.' She and Agafia exchanged glances.

'I know where there's a special gold tea service. Belonged to some Tsar. Haven't seen it myself, but word is it's stupendous.'

The Countess smiled. 'My family has – had, perhaps I should now say – a milliard lovely things, Lovejoy.' A woman doesn't have to be young to be pretty. Her sweet countenance grew dreamy. 'You know what they said of Old Russia? That to be Russian was to carve wood. When Great Prince Vladimir of Kiev took on Orthodoxy in the year 989, all Russians became artists. We, as a great family, inherited some of that art.'

Agafia reached and patted her hand to allay her sadness. 'Don't be sad, Countess. This film might lead to a renaissance.'

'Might? *Must*, my dear.'

'What did you have, love?' I coughed. 'You see, I've not had time to go along to the exhibition.'

She smiled and was off, reminiscing. 'In the coffee-room we had that splendid iconostasis, not enormous, you understand, but the length of the wall.' A wooden carved screen, to separate off part of a Greek Rite church. 'The saints' figures were carved not quite in the round – statues as such are idolatrous to us Russians, you see, Lovejoy.'

'Did you have a metal table?'

'Not whole metal. A copper table top, yes. Long, for the dining-room.' She laughed, slapped her hands. 'Do you remember, Agafia, how we used to play as children, gumming into our reflections after the servants had burnished . . . ?' She sobered. 'No, Agafia. You weren't born. I forget.'

Russian copperwork was once supreme and unique. Their hanging lamps are real specialities for collectors. Copper candlesticks are another must, especially those florid compound three-candle pairs with birds worked into the fret. The only pair I've ever seen in my life were chucked out on a street barrow – not machined, modern or fashionable, you see. The rag-and-bone man went on a Mediterranean cruise from it, six weeks in the sun.

'We used to play with the silver bratinas.' Her old face was smiling again, but about to doze. Agafia moved but I caught her eye, sharply shook my head. This news was vital, life or death. Both, even.

'Bratinas, Countess?'

'You know, loving cups. Silver. Papa had ten.' She smiled, indicated the far doorway. 'Do take a look at your convenience, Lovejoy. They're in the display case. Agafia?'

'Yes, Countess?'

'I hate that great lumbering Prussian cabinet. Replace it with a proper Novgorod bureau.'

Agafia looked tearful, despairing, said, 'Yes, Countess.'

'Which did you like most, Countess?'

'Oh, the kovsh's shape is so wonderful to a child! It's . . . a scoop! We played in the sandpit. I'd have my three favourites, and my sister Elizabeth had hers. We'd fill all Papa's gold charkas, using the housekeeper's best silver cherpaks. Really naughty! Then we'd . . .' She faded, suddenly came to, abruptly lucid and bright-eyed. 'I do apologize. Have I monopolized the conversation?'

'Not at all.' I managed to speak. A charka – a quaich, drinking vessel – was common, but gold ones weren't. A cherpak's a ladle, precious metal for posh. She'd already showed me the last kovsh, seemingly one of many. They were the Tsar's traditional gift to some hero or favourite, as her ancestor's was from the inscription. Nowadays it's fashionable among the county set to buy a bratina, and use that wondrous ornamental silver loving cup as a punchbowl – not antique collectors' fault, really, since the Russians themselves started the ridiculous habit. I hate it. 'Were you happy, Countess?'

'Oh, Lovejoy!' Her eyes glistened rapturously. 'Idyllic! How often I have pretended things were unchanged!'

'Your mementoes, Countess. Did you bring all of, er, Papa's things?'

'Many. Dear Papa. He couldn't foresee the coming storm, though even we children knew change was in the wind.' Her eyes pierced me through. 'You ask me about antiques, Lovejoy? Agafia can provide you with as reliable an account as I. Quite a collection of jewellery, wasn't there, Agafia? And rather formidable Tula cut steel ornaments. Kiev cloisonné enamel pendants, earrings. Damascened wall plaques. Pottery figurines, sets of birds and horses. A group of flasks, really rather large and horrid with little feet . . .'

And on she rattled, a fortune in every breath. Vinogradov's early figurines of the 1750s, the faience wares of Kuznetzov – who later bought Francis Gardner's factory and outdid all China and the whole East with his delectable porcelains. And the lidded glass goblets from St Petersburg, the lacquerwork and lace, the embroidery . . . Just listening was a feast. (Tip: Russian antiques, and Indian, are tomorrow's moneybag finds, so keep an eye open.)

It was only when Agafia moved to take the cup and saucer from her lap that I realized how long she'd been going on, that she was calling me Ivan Ivanovich and occasionally lapsing into Russian. Agafia shushed the old lady into a nodding sleep and smiled a mute apology indicating that I should leave. Tiptoeing, I made a natural mistake, attempting to leave by the wrong door, which let me have a quick glimpse of the room Countess Natalia had indicated. No Prussian cabinet stuffed with rare bratinas, quaiches, kovshs. It was sparsely furnished, modern auction-bought junk.

'No, Lovejoy.' Agafia joined me. She wasn't taken in. 'We've nothing left. Only the kovsh you have seen.'

'Nark it, love. I don't know my way about, that's all.'

'Then allow me to show you.'

'Outside, eh?' I suggested. 'I've been cooped up all day.'

I waited for her to get a shawl. We strolled into a blustery wind and started round the house on the path. She slipped her arm through mine, pleasant. 'Of course, Countess Natalia has age against her.' That Woman's Mistake again: age acts *for* them, not against.

'Yet she made out a detailed list for Ben Clayton's exhibition.'

'No. She forbade any such list.' Agafia paused to point out a handsome piece of topiary work. I'm used to women's wiles so admired it, though topiary's tough on even a humble privet.

'But you made one out, Aggie.'

Her head raised, stung. 'I obeyed the Countess's orders!'

'Aye, love. The list?'

'Well.' She was defensive, walking us on. 'We didn't know this Clayton. He could have been anyone, any background. Nor Mr Meese and his thin angry girl, Lorane. It all happened so fast.'

'Who decided to hand over the Countess's heirlooms?'

'Why, the Countess, of course!'

'Ready for it, Aggie?' I waited for her to nod. 'Tell me this. How came they here? I mean, did they just arrive? A syndicated film company, complete with crew, writer, production team, plus Clayton, a roller-man antique wholesaler? What made them walk in your gateway with their megathink movie? Why nobody else's?' I stopped us, made her face me. I want to see eyes when my life's on the line. She met my gaze. I liked her.

'Because the Countess had the heirlooms, Lovejoy.'

It's embarrassing when a woman tries to be evasive and fails. 'Look, love. I'm a nerk but I'm not daft. You're not in the phone book. You're not members of the Women's Guild. You don't belong to the Village Wives. You don't do basketweaving at the Adult Education. You keep yourselves to yourselves.'

'Your quiet little apprentice researched us, I suppose?'

'What the hell's it matter who sussed you out?' I thumbed at the house. 'Many family houses like the Countess's are thrown open to the public, make money on the side, do a little souvenir-touting. But you don't.'

'We're refugees, Lovejoy. We have to be quiet.'

'Balls, Aggie. Sixty years ago, yes. Now? I ask you, love. Who cares about origins except maniacs?'

She stared over the gardens. It was a lovely windswept view, right down the estuary. I looked down at the grooves in the grass near a copse. The grass looked ploughed yet well nourished, really odd.

'The Countess wanted an estimate of value on some heirlooms. Thinking to make a money gift on a Russian immigrant foundation.'

'Tell me more.'

'No, Lovejoy. I'm sorry.'

I reached round her, an embrace just for closeness. 'Then shall I tell you? You got Sam Shrouder.' Her start told me I was on track. I kept hold, both of us looking at the view. 'Sam drove his bus in here, parked it there out of sight of the road, by yon copse, where the grooves in the grass are. He did an estimate. Maybe took an antique or two to work on, a bit of restoration. Then he started coming often. He did a deal of work.'

'Yes.' Her admission was so quiet it went with the wind.

'Then a lady came. Happen she delivered a piece of silverware one day, saying Sam wasn't too well. She was his wife.'

'Yes.' Almost inaudible. 'We were so afraid of burglars. Old Mikail's not strong.'

'And Mrs Shrouder suggested that the Countess capitalize on her heirlooms?'

'Yes.'

'She was the go-between. Then Sam stopped coming.'

'His work was finished, Lovejoy.'

And so was poor Sam. I let her go and we strolled on. 'When did you know something was wrong, Aggie?'

'Countess Natalia and I were talking it over. We

suddenly realized how vulnerable we were. We grew frightened. It had been so exciting, given our possessions from motives of true patriotism!'

That old con, still going strong. 'And Sam died.'

'We were so relieved to encounter you, Lovejoy.'

'Eh?'

'The way Lydia looks at you, the trust you seem to engender. And your divvying gift. The way you are . . . separate. We feel you're like us.'

Aye, missus. But when Parson vanishes or Sam gets topped it's me the Plod hauls in, not your posh countesses. And burglaries are pinned on my back, nobody else's. If that famous secret smuggler Thomas Chippendale were alive today, I swear the police would do me instead. Well, at least I'd now got most of the story, except Ray Meese's big finish. Maybe I'd better opt out of the last scenes, catch 'flu the day before.

'Right, ally,' I said. We'd gone all round the house and reached the front steps. 'Let's make two promises, eh? One: we tell each other, night and day, whatever happens. Agreed?'

'Yes, Lovejoy. And two?'

'You give me the rest of that grub. I'm starving.'

She exploded a laugh, pulled at my arm. 'See? Crooks don't think like you, Lovejoy.'

I stayed silent. Suddenly you can get too fond of a woman. When that happens, silence is a man's only denial. We went in to scoff the rest of the nosh. Maybe it was the analogy with fuel, or maybe only remembering the Rotunda, but suddenly I was thinking of a weapon. As in gun. Not for using, understand. Comfort.

A lawyer's messenger was at the cottage when I got back. He was posting a lawsuit through my door. It was from the building society, for nicking my own cottage deeds. Can you believe these people? And a note from Lydia to say that she'd spent every penny I was to earn over the next week on a private detective to ensure my safety, and had procured thereby some significant tidings – only Lydia uses words like tidings nowadays, so I didn't question the note's authenticity. Also she had obtained some sound furniture for me, cheaply, to render my cottage more comfortable. It would all be delivered next morning.

When it comes to wasting money, trust a bird.

Chapter 24

'Smoke,' I said aloud to nobody in particular.

Lydia was driving. Whether she didn't trust me with her mum's motor or simply wanted me on a short leash, I don't know. But today's decision was no Lovejoy behind her wheel.

'Smoke, Lovejoy? In what context?'

'Nothing. Sorry.' We were pulling into a breaker's yard in a village in Essex's wet lowlands. Cars were heaped everywhere, hollow hulls and rust-dried russet metal. 'I went to Woolwich, saw a rifle range. Reminded me they train riflemen with smoke blowing across the face of the target.' I looked about. We stopped beside the plank hoarding. It was broken in several places. A tavern stood opposite, the Cherry Tree. 'What are we doing here?'

'This, Lovejoy, is where Mrs Shrouder is having lunch. Her car is that small red Metro.'

'So? Getting peckish happens to the best of us.'

'We are here to recognize her companion.' She was sure of herself.

'Can't we just go in and have—?'

'*Lovejoy.*' Which shut me off. 'Why the concern with smoke on rifle ranges?'

'They used smoke at the studio.' I made a gesture to

show how it had fumed from machines on the floor. 'It's whitish mist, so cameras can see through.'

She found a notebook from her handbag. 'Do we need a smoke machine, Lovejoy?'

'No, love.' Bless her. She's absolutely no idea. But I kept wondering about those smoke canisters. Probably hadn't changed much since my day. I seemed to recall you pulled a tag on the top and stepped upwind. They were easy to carry.

'Attention, Lovejoy.' She indicated the tavern opposite. A long black limousine was arriving.

Ray Meese got out. Here in the wilds, miles from anywhere. Surprise, surprise. He entered the pub and the limo cruised away. Lydia was pencilling the time into her book. She passed me a bulky envelope, big and brown.

'You can open it now, Lovejoy.'

Photographs, with times, dates and locations on each reverse; typed sheets of place names alongside columns of initials. The penny dropped.

'This is why I haven't eaten for a fortnight?'

She flared. 'You've had quite sufficient, Lovejoy, and well you know it! Your expenditure on the private investigator was necessary!' See? My expenditure.

The woman was pretty, from any angle. It was her, the one I'd seen at Doc Lancaster's surgery the time I began my People Game. And at Ledger's police station. The photographs showed her with Ray Meese in a dozen places. Twice the photo was blurry, almost a negative. 'Those are taken at night, Lovejoy. A special camera. They . . . they appear to have stayed at the same motel.' A long pause, turbulent with difficulty. 'Possibly together, Lovejoy.'

Shock horror gasp. 'Who's the agent?'

'Eminently trustworthy. I obtained references from sources which need not concern you, Lovejoy.'

'I'm paying, yet they need not concern me?'

'Correct.' She coloured a little. 'There was a tape-recording . . . their nocturnal sojourn.'

'Any chance of getting hold of it, love?' I was sarcastic.

'No.' Cool as you please. Sometimes women take your breath away. 'I had it destroyed.'

I erupted. 'Of all your frigging nerve! Lyd, I swear one day I'll give you a sodding good belt! I'm paying with blood for this info and you—'

She faced me, fierce. 'That tape contained intimate, well, communications between them in, well, circumstances.'

'OK, love,' I said, broken. 'What am I allowed to hear?'

'This is an abstract.' She passed an envelope.

'Thanks.' Seven lines:

Mrs S.: He's got to be blown away, darling. [*a deletion*] Total.

R. M.: Who's telling me this here? It's all on. Truly, truly.

Mrs S.: It's pure genius. Then clover, honey.

R. M.: It's [*a deletion*] success. Truly megamax.

Mrs S.: No talk. Celebration time for my Oscar-winning [*a series of deletions*]

Translation: Mrs S. and Meese were in league, to put it at its most charitable. I said to Lydia, 'You said Meese has never come near an Oscar.'

'He hasn't, Lovejoy. She means he's about to.'

'From this film? Even the people on it say it's duff. What's deleted?'

She turned aside, colouring up. 'Intimacies, Lovejoy.'

'So for the sake of chastity we erase the most important and expensive bits, in love and vino being veritas?'

'Lovejoy, the evidence suggests that Ray Meese and

Mrs Shrouder are mutually enamoured, and that Lorane is being sadly deceived as to Meese's intentions.'

'Why didn't you just tell me this Jane Austenese gunge? Why bring me all this way?'

'You never believe me, Lovejoy.'

Narked, I looked away from her candid blue eyes. People who are right all the bloody time give me a real pain, and that's the truth. But I had bigger problems now than Lydia. To blow away = to kill. To total = ditto. Now, who on earth could they mean, I wonder?

'Let's go,' I said. I had a sense of things closing in slightly quicker than I wanted. Even on a good day I didn't want to meet Lorane. Once she found out Meese was two-timing her, I didn't want to be in the same galaxy.

The gold service was ready, Hymie sent word, so please collect. That meant the deeds of my cottage were due for redemption, or I was homeless. I was legally home-less anyway, so what the hell. The building society and Hymie could fight it out between them. Hymie knew I'd not default on the gelt, but he was covered anyway. Well, more or less – the Ruby was crisped, so his logbook was worthless, but is it my problem if aggropaths burn my car to cinders? People blame me for everything.

Lydia dropped me off at Castle Park. Sorry Malone arrived at the gateway as arranged. Sorry's a safe elderly locksmith who dresses like a taxman and only does one-off jobs, fixed price. He's called Sorry because he once broke into somebody's house in Romford only to find it was the wrong place. Quickly, he said, 'Oh, sorry,' to the astonished man and wife he found star-ing at him in the hallway, and left with an apologetic smile. I made our meeting a deliberate accident, literally bumping into him.

'Keep being glad to see me, Sorry,' I said. 'Give me something. Anything.'

'Oh, right.' He grinned, nodded, held my arm and rummaged in his pocket, passed me a penny. I pretended gravity, very theatrical, studying it on my palm but making sure I shielded our object from passersby. I returned it, pointing ostentatiously to the bus stop.

'Come to the cottage, soon as you like, Sorry.'

'What lock is it, Lovejoy? I've tools to bring.'

'A car, sort of.'

'That all?' He went off, chuckling. I went through the Castle Park rose-garden and round to the bus stop at the top of North Hill, calling in the Arcade as I went. I paused at the alcove stall temporarily belonging to our loudest mouth, Harry Bateman.

'Hey, Harry. You flog Sorry that Iserlohn box?'

'Me? No, Lovejoy. Genuine, is it?'

'Lovely. Really rare, in that form.'

'You buy it, Lovejoy?'

''Course I bought it. Well, genuine Adolph Keppelman, 1762. Mint, virtually.' An Iserlohn's only a tobacco container, decorated brass and copper. 'This has those lunatic Seven-Years-War characters on it.'

'How much, Lovejoy?' he offered.

I pretended to be narked. 'Gawd, Harry. Give me breath. He won't bring it to my place for a couple of hours yet.'

He rummaged into catalogues, notes, year books. 'Here, Lovejoy. I'll give you half the current catalogue price, eh? Only collectors are screaming for any tobacciana.'

'Take it easy, Harry.' I went all exasperated.

We settled on seven-tenths the listed price for a mint Iserlohn. Wondering idly where on earth I'd get one from, I took the money and caught the Maldon bus and got off at the Bell. Sorry could wait a while if he reached the cottage early. The Bell taproom was crowded. Several squaddies from the garrison were swilling and talking. I went in, carefully staying to one side, and meekly used the phone after glancing about. The man himself entered the saloon bar after a few minutes and came over. He wore a staff sergeant's uniform.

'Wotcher, Lovejoy.'

'Jock. All right?' I bought him a pint.

'Never better. Got another set?' Jock collects military medals of African campaigns before 1900. His mates think he's eccentric. Only he and I know how bright he is. When he retires he'll be able to buy his own army, what with the number of antique military decorations he's bought. He has a valuable and superb collection, and paid peanuts.

'Sorry, no. It's me. I need help.' I smiled a cheery disclaimer. 'Nothing naff. It's just that I want an effect. Children's pageant at, er, the girlfriend's village.'

'What, a couple of thunderflashes?'

'Er, aye. For a start, Jock.' I hadn't thought of thunderflashes, those big military fireworks. 'Strip-igniters, aren't they?'

'All sorts. What else?'

'Smokies.' He grinned at my use of the name. Back home in his Scotch shire a smokie's a fish. 'How many to blanket, say, a marquee?'

'Oh, two.'

'Four, then. Are they bigger than they used to be?'

'Aye, Lovejoy.' He was guarded with his next question. 'Can I let the old man know? He's strong on public relations.' His field officer.

'I'd rather not, Jock. Till it's over.'

'Cost a few quid, then.'

'Money's right here.' We haggled amiably, then I passed him Harry's money and went to catch the bus home. Jock'd get them to me during the candle hours. I'd paint them some flashy colour to match the studio gear, emulsion paint so they'd dry before dawn.

Sorry was waiting with his locksmith's patience at the cottage.

'It's round the back, Sorry. A bus. No word, eh?'

'Leave it out, Lovejoy.' We went round and I showed him Sam's bus.

'Open it, but give me a shout, eh?' I don't like watching Sorry work – his nose runs and he snuffles, blots it on his sleeve, snuffles, blots. Drives you mad.

'Right.' He undid his coat despite the chill. It clinked with merry metallic sounds. I left him to it and went to brew up. He rejoined me before the kettle'd even boiled. 'That all, Lovejoy?'

'Already open? Let's look.'

'I'll make the brew, Lovejoy.'

See what I mean? Careful, a real pro. I went out alone and tentatively opened the bus's rear door. Empty. I didn't know whether to be relieved or disappointed, but for sure there was no dead Parson Brown slumped inside.

When I say empty, I don't quite mean empty as in hollow. I mean nobody was inside. I climbed in. A workbench ran along one wall, lights positioned above it. Ceiling windows added to the illumination. A mark showed where some fixture had been wrenched from the opposite wall. A safe? Shelving had been torn apparently from high above the benching. No drawers remained – I saw where they'd been ripped away. All was gutted. Bolts had been fixed to the bench. A solid little metal chair, a few filings in a crevice, a faint pungent aroma, and that was the end of Sam Shrouder.

'OK, Lovejoy?' Sorry found me in contemplation. He stayed outside, holding the tea mugs invitingly.

'Aye, ta, Sorry. A good job. Can I lock this thing again?'

'Yes. Want a key?'

'Please, Sorry.' We chatted a bit. I paid him to let him go. 'Oh, Sorry. If folk get on to you about an Iserlohn, act thick, eh?'

'What's an Iserlohn?'

'That's right, Sorry,' I said. 'Keep it up.'

The bus yielded very little: wood dust, a single dot of umber paint, oil, by the bench a few gleams of silver. I went over it with a magnet and got metal filings. A third time, and found a fragment of pale papery stuff stuck to the underside of the bench. It took me a whole hour to recognize it as parchment. A stain by the bench lip was possibly Sam's homemade ink. Or maybe watercolour, burnt sienna? A three-pin power plug on the floor near the driver's panel bulkhead was hardly a clue; presumably Sam carried some sort of electricity, maybe a transformer, batteries. Finding which garage supplied him with sizeable batteries would be a needle-in-a-haystack job and anyway no use. I went inside to think.

And at long last put two and two together. It was a tandem job. With the genuine antiques from Countess Natalia alone, Ben Clayton would make a killing (apology). That exhibition was reportedly attracting collectors like flies. But any profit would be blotted up by the movie company's mounting debts. He'd only get his measly dealer's commission. *So he'd doubled it up.* He'd used Sam Shrouder's fabled skills to swell the genuine antiques by an influx of fakes. The undoubtedly genuine stuff – backed by the Countess Natalia's implied cast-iron provenance – would authenticate the whole. I'll bet the plan was to auction off the entire exhibition afterwards. Leaving Ben Clayton with a fortune. We call it a tandem job in the antiques trade – fakes plus genuines travelling on one set of wheels, as it were. And Ben had made Seg kill Sam, make it look like a possible accident, and ditch the bus where it wouldn't be thought misplaced. The reason: probably Sam got alarmed, realized he was in too deep. But this left me with a problem, for Sam was one of our greats. Faking was his job, his life. He'd certainly have loved doing the duplicates. A faker pulling a tandem job involving a single antique becomes famed in song and story. For pulling a tandem of an entire exhibition he'd become a legend.

Why had they killed the greatest, most cooperative faker? Well, maybe Sam disliked his missus cohabiting with Meese, Parson Brown. A problem, but love-lust creates these as it goes along, and needn't detain Lovejoy, superlogician. No. Leave that little hiccup aside. I'd reasoned a long way towards a solution. I was pleased with myself.

But.

Why did my mind keep on going over the same logic, and ending up with that nasty word *but*? My neurones should sit back and rest, put a satisfying QED there. Instead I was a mine of buts and hang-about-there's mores. I went to Sam's bus. I brewed up. I fed the robins. I filled the bluetits' net sock with nuts. Did the bus. Checked the birds' waterfont. I sat.

And it came, that oddity. Here was I, whole and fit as a flea. Seg and Ben never did do me over on suspicion of the robbery. Had my alibi been that convincing? Even if it had been, they'd demolish me on suspicion alone – *if the exhibition was the one true scam.* But they'd exercised restraint, and let me be. Now, even I know that homicidal psychotics aren't big on self-discipline. So Ben Clayton's tandem gambit was not the one true gig. It was relatively minor.

What, a fortune in antiques? Small fry? When Ben had topped Sam Shrouder? Probably topped Parson Brown too, all to protect it? Nasty instinct kept coming up with the cry, *yes*! – but the main scam must be somewhere in the movie, that drivel which was expected to gain Meese a hatful of Oscars. How? It was massively in debt, yet they believed it a box office supersmash. Even though it was dross.

Time was drawing in. Barmy to feel my heart thumping harder, faster, when I was only sitting in a remote cottage sipping tea and lobbing a sparrow crumbs. At the final filming I would certainly be well protected, Bracegirdle's security officers everywhere. The public would be on hand to ogle. A single close-up seemed to take a trillion technicians, who surely couldn't all be in on it, could they? And every move in the Museum would be monitored. And on film. Local police were already on triple tap, Footer'd said, on tippy-toes. And I wasn't to go up in the balloon. I'd got that down in elevenplicate, no cable-swarming for Lovejoy.

The only other thing I worked out was that Parson Brown, erstwhile lover of Mrs Shrouder, had possibly been disappeared because he – what? – proved dangerously superfluous? Discovered what was going on and foolishly tried blackmail? The more I thought it over the calmer I became, the more certain that I was safe as houses.

In fact I was so sure that I can't for the life of me understand why I went and got this gun.

Chapter 25

'You see, Ray.' I spoke quickly, while he was still sober. 'It's not that I'm greedy. I'm no crook, either. But being in a – no, *The* – Museum with the connivance of its security services is a sort of opportunity.'

'Is it?' he said between wheezes. He shouted to Vance to get a move on.

'Not for me, Ray. Good heavens, no. I mean, some crooks might see it like that.'

We were on the top of London University's Senate House. We'd arrived in daylight, and been busy doing nothing ever since. The stuntmen were readying guy ropes which sprouted from a structure hanging from a gantry. It was dark, eleven at night and windy as hell. Cold. Me and my oppos, Lofty and Nick were waiting in our black outfits to go and look menacing standing by these ropes. This, I assure you, was what I'd been terrified of. It was down on the studio's call sheet as Balloon Shooting/Senate House roof/9 p.m. There wasn't a balloon in sight. They simply rigged up a wicker basket on a small skirt of balloon material, picked it up on one of those little auto-motorized-gantry things, and pretended there was a whole balloon above us. When I'd tackled Lofty about it he rolled in the aisles. 'Silly sod,' he told me affably. 'They use a real balloon at the open-air balloon shoot. Not here, pillock.'

'What about the story?' I'd complained to Max and Vance.

'Oh, the story'll look believable, Lovejoy,' they'd assured me. 'It's got to.'

Got to. I was staying still, sipping coffee from a plastic cup and huddled down behind the wall out of the gale, when Ray Meese joined me and started this conversation. A trio of assistants hurtling to bring him vodka, gin, a selection of capsules. He consumed their offerings dismissively, sat to talk. He held a remote-button box, the auto-gantry controls. Only Vance and he were authorized users.

'How're you enjoying being a star, Lovejoy?'

'Do I get a psychoanalyst and a couple of sexy birds?'

'Nope. Only egomaniac stars get that. Ego country.'

'Rather them than me.'

He was bitter. 'They're Insecurity Inc., Lovejoy. Obsessed with how they look. Truly, truly. Status City. At my expense.'

'Speaking of expense, Ray. How marvellous it would be to use all this legitimate expense for something . . . well, a little less legitimate.'

'In what way?' No bitterness now. Just casual.

'Only imagining, you understand. Not in real life.'

'Oh no. Truly not, Lovejoy.'

That being understood, I spoke of opportunity. 'Well. I mean, we're in there legitimately. A few blokes would give their eye teeth for that chance.'

'What d'you think they'd go for?' Cool.

'Anything.' I could be as casual as him any day. 'I mean, I suppose this Armenian Exhibition itself is out, eh?'

'Bracegirdle's security people will be there, Lovejoy.'

He looked at me, his face shifting as electricians moved the lights. 'So who can steal anything?'

'The Roman stuff on the floor above isn't far off. And the Tapling Collection.'

'Tapling?' I swear he'd never heard of it.

'Stamps. It's the only stamp collection formed in the nineteenth century which is still intact, as one.' I signalled right. 'Come out of the Armenian place, dogleg into the King's Gallery. The big cases at the far end house it in great vertical window alcoves.'

'Is it valuable?'

'Covers 1840 to 1890, complete on all basic issues.' I groaned. 'And stamp collectors are the most unscrupulous collectors on earth. Easy to dispose of, quick money.' Stamps aren't my scene, though. Oddly, I was glad when he shrugged a disclaimer. I didn't want his scam to be some rotten old stamp album, however grand.

'Big cases, you say?'

'OK, then. The bronzes upstairs are a possibility. Or the clocks? They're a king's ransom each. There's silver. The Chinese gallery over the back door's too far, though the Montague Place entrance has a circular vent where most of the Chinese stuff can be lowered. The Japanese netsukes and the rest of the Hull Grundy collection's easily portable.' His expression hadn't even flickered. Another piece for my jigsaw.

'Interesting, Lovejoy.' He brooded a little. 'Look, your business is your business. What I don't see I don't know about, but no monkey business. My movie must remain pure. Get it?'

'OK if I ask a little cooperation – accidental, like?'

'Like what, Lovejoy?'

'Like, say, a prop – a genuine antique. To lend colour, sort of, to the set? See, if I have an antique which has been in a famous movie, I could sell it for twice the price.'

He pursed his lips. 'Anything in particular?'

'Well, yes. A Celtic cross.' We almost said it together. 'Genuine. Just read of it in the paper. Been dug up somewhere. Look great on film, Ray.'

'No comeback on us, Lovejoy?'

'Good heavens, Ray,' I said piously. 'What do you take me for?'

'OK, then. I'll tell Lorane to clear it with Bracegirdle.'

'I'm glad of that. I'm all for security. Hey, Ray. One thing.' I indicated the scene, cameras, surging assistants. 'D'you like all this pretence? It's a frigging yawn.'

'Pretence?' He gave me a look I know so well. Seen it the world over. The addict, the obsessed. 'It's all there is, Lovejoy. What the camera sees is real. Everything else is myth.'

Funny. I say the same about antiques.

He rose, bawling reproach and unhappiness at people on the ropes, and moved off across the flat roof to the cameras.

Well, well, I told myself. Odderer and odderer. A scam, and the main perpetrator cares not what scam it is? I started to do a little brooding myself.

In a lull Renny, a props bloke, fetched an antique for valuation. He was the sort who dresses in coloured tat because it's trendy, and who goes at women simply because they're handy mammals. All the insight of a bandsaw. By now I was getting used to these impromptu antiques roadshows and took the little magnolia-coloured statuette to a light. Soft paste. She was the Chinese goddess Kuan Yin, all serene.

'Has it got the mark?' *FF* was incised at the back, which made it from the rare G. G. Rossetti factory in Italy about 1740. But the word TORINO in underglaze blue was inside the base edge. I almost fainted. There's only one other of these known, and the British Museum's got it. The two others with similar marks are small glazed busts on rather ugly little pedestals in the Palazzo Madame, in Turin.

'Cherish it, Renny. It's your heirloom.'

'Really, Lovejoy?'

I looked at him. Now, the one thing people don't ever do is look dispirited when you break the happy news that they've suddenly collared a fortune for a groat. They're over the moon, ecstatic. He wasn't.

Oh, he instantly put on a happy expression, told me some cock-and-bull tale of an auntie from the Far East bringing it home as a gift, the whole drossy rigmarole. But false. Probably not really his at all.

Things were looking up. We only had to wait three more hours, eight in all, before the cameras actually started up. Really breakneck.

Lydia met me off the train, white-faced. I'd slept all the way in spite of some old dear telling me about some bulbs she'd just planted. Why can't people leave gardens alone?

'Lovejoy?' She didn't drive off, so we just sat in the station car park. 'What is this lawsuit?'

I gave a horrified gasp. Well, I did my best, knackered as I was. 'Lawsuit, love?'

'The building society called. You're to attend court on the sixteenth.'

'Goodness gracious, Lydia!' I cried.

'Not only that, Lovejoy.' She was trembling. 'Hymie sent to ask the whereabouts of your old motor. He seems to believe it's now his property.'

'Hymie? Of all the nerve! Let him get his own—'

'As do three other people, Lovejoy. Harry Bateman also called for some antique tobacco box you sold him.'

'I'm sure there's some mistake, love . . .'

She sat there, pale. 'Lovejoy. Are we in serious trouble?'

We. So she wasn't resigning. I was relieved. 'Aye, love. I'm sorry. Especially as you've been so marvellous all along.' I brightened. 'But we've got a gold samovar set.'

'Solvency's as much in the mind as in external reality, Lovejoy.'

Eh? 'Well put, love,' I said lamely. She's a mine of forgettable aphorisms. 'It's just that I've landed in a tangle, trying to help the old Countess.' Wisely I didn't mention Agafia. The Lydias of this world don't understand the problems of trying to survive in a malicious world. They simply can't see evil. I sat unhappily in silence waiting her judgement.

'I'm afraid I have been dilatory, Lovejoy,' she said quietly.

'You have?' I was baffled.

'I should have advised you better. I can see that now. We must take remedial action.'

'Action, love?' I was apprehensive. More help?

'I with your finances, Lovejoy. Until we are out of this.' She faced me in her seat, a lovely tempera painting, glossed with colour. 'Do you agree?' her luscious lips said, moving.

'Anything you say, love.' I even sounded weak.

'Very well,' she said decisively, starting the engine. 'Now. There's a small Queen Anne bureau at Asquith's auction house. I suggest we acquire it on my credit, and ship it instantly to London for an increment of eighty per cent. Your hand is on my knee, Lovejoy.'

'Sorry. About the bureau?'

'Well, it has a minor blemish . . .'

She's good on furniture, so I let myself be persuaded.

* * *

Brad's our gun man. That is to say he isn't a gunman. He lives down in Wivenhoe by the water, our tidal navigation limit and all that nautical stuff. The reason I say he's a gun man is that he deals in antiques. Ask him about Napoleonic weaponry and he's fine. Civil War flintlocks are his home ground. Ask him about a new Belgian A101 SLR and his eyes glaze. He doesn't know, nor does he want to. Guns ended when mass-produced cartridges came in. And firearms started when guns ended.

He was cleaning a Nock flinter when I arrived and told him I was desperate for a percussion handpiece, Barratt of Birmingham preferably.

'How soon, Lovejoy?'

'Now.' No wonder you get narked. I'm scared and the world's suddenly laid back. 'Immediate, forthwith, Brad.'

He looked up, surprised. 'I've eight or nine small arms upstairs. I'll bring them down.'

I waited respectfully. In two journeys he fetched his weapons and laid them on a blanket. A couple of Spanish pinfire pistols, a lovely cannon-barrelled Queen Anne flintlock worth a small car, an officer's holster pistol, three Tower service percussions (forget these; they're very mundane), a relic – this only means derelict in the trade, nothing holy – flintlock barely clinging to its fractured walnut stock, and a pepperbox.

This last is a precursor of the revolver. Imagine five or six barrels moulded into one cylinder and you have it. You stick a small percussion cap over the nipple of each barrel. The cylinder revolves when you pull the trigger. Of course you have to load each barrel separately beforehand, but that's a cheap chore when you think of what you gain – a pistol which fires a handful of separate shots.

I bought it after haggling over the price. I got Brad to

accept the motor – Lydia's mother's – as pledge for the pepperbox. I signed, promising to hand it over as soon as I'd been to see my sick uncle. I also got a few ounces of black powder and a few spherical lead bullets, saying I wanted to demonstrate its firing mechanism to the customer. I left really pleased. You can't be prosecuted if, as a *bona fide* antique dealer, you transport your wares. And a genuine percussion pepperbox handpiece is not a firearm within the meaning of the Firearms Act, so I could carry it about. This, for no reason I could think of, was an odd satisfaction.

Later, I began reflecting on that exquisite eight-inch statuette of Kuan Yin. And totting up the number of antiques, real or alleged, which I'd been brought by the film crew. The 1860 dress. The Scottish dirk. The darning sampler. The revival clock. The others, some dud. But they mounted up. And at least a couple had carried marks or areas tacky to the touch. Had some come from auctions? Or all, even? I thought some more, and finally asked myself, were they sent from *one* source? Like, say, Ray Meese? Rotten question, but a worse answer.

Chapter 26

We were assembled in a field near Cheshunt. Lighting cameraman Jim Boyce explained how, on film, early dawn could be made to look like a dark London night. I was so captivated I almost nodded off. A balloon, hired along with its six attendant loons, was taking hours to fill. We resembled a stranded circus, vehicles everywhere. For the first – and hopefully the last time I saw myself described as 'artiste' on a movie call sheet. I swiftly quelled my surge of pride. There were already too many egos around.

Hooded up, me, Nick and Lofty were readied and told to haul on the balloon's ropes. It wasn't even vertical, just lay there on the grass puffing and flopping while people fired hot air from an engine into its rubbery mouth. Lancelot Lake joined us for the first time, also garbed in black but hoodless. He merited three cameras and ninety per cent of everybody's attention and seemed obsessed with the focusing abilities of the cameramen on his visage.

And that was it, freezing in a field dressed like a synchronized swimmer minus the grin. The only thing worth noticing was the antiques. By now I was the studio's focus for stray antiques. Ever-hopeful technicians were always showing me wares they'd picked up down The

Belly, London's nearby Portobello Road antiques market. I was glad. I honestly don't mind antique bargain hunters, though I sometimes think they'd be better off stalking modern trophies like the country paintings of Arthur G. Carrick (the terribly secret pseudonym under which in 1987 Charles Prince of Wales started entering his masterpieces at the Royal Academy Summer Exhibition), or trying to track down the parchment whereon the Bostonians' delegation in the 1770s offered Bonnie Prince Charlie the throne of America (declined, incidentally). Still, each to his own.

At this barmy balloon shoot I was offered a bonny flat leather-covered case, two inches only, containing minute glassy discs.

'They're earrings,' Charmain said. I vaguely knew her as a dynamic and thirtyish organizer of mobile ladders, to no clear purpose. 'But I can't find the clips.'

'Early contact lenses, love.' I tapped them with a fingernail, listening. 'Probably American. They came in around the 1940s. The Czechs developed the soft modern ones in the 'fifties – no sharp sound against your finger, see? Cherish them. Another five years museums will be crying out. They're rare.'

'Ergh!' She went, practically holding them at arm's length. You have to laugh. Earrings are pretty, old contact lenses disgustingly medical – even though Leonardo da Vinci worked out their optics over 500 years back. Why don't antiques gold-diggers save themselves all this disappointment and go for sheer investment potential outright, like old port or something – up nearly 5000 per cent in 25 years? Still, no passion in port, whereas antiques . . .

'That's it, paisanos!' Ray Meese called after only sixty takes of us standing, hauling. 'You were super-boy, Lancelot!'

Eleven hours and double pneumonia. Cheap at the price.

Strangely, as the final week approached my fear was that Three Wheel Archie would default from Monday's filming in the Museum. I checked on him so often he asked what the hell.

'OK, Archie. Sorry I asked.' I'd chased after him in the Saturday market.

'Lovejoy. You phoned me four times yesterday. You've sent seven messages. I'll be there.'

'Right, Archie.' I gave a sheepish grin.

'Now leave me alone!'

'Right. Sure. See you Monday, Archie.' I waved him off. Then I told Tinker to keep track of him.

Over the weekend there was to be a studio party, after the residue of the set-piece filming. I went to see the Lake Bayon wagons cause pandemonium outside a Bloomsbury hotel while Meese and forty minions filmed hostage-taking, but the presence of a smiling Gabriella and at least five of Bracegirdle's navy blue Security uniforms got me down and I came home.

Friday night I tried the pepperbox. Its spring was slightly weak, but the percussion caps worked well and the black powder did its stuff. I dug the spherical bullets out of the garage door and restored them to spherical. I didn't reload it immediately in case I started worrying about how the wadding was getting on. Plenty of time.

That night I painted my smoke canisters. Emulsion paint dries quickly, so the cardboard sleeves I adapted to contain them didn't stick. Authentic labels I got from the theatrical equipment shop by Long Acre, soaked off legit small-fry stage smokies. I transferred one to each of the larger variants Jock had left for me. Then I cut a paper stencil and did a lookalike warning on the canisters themselves. They'd pass as studio kits. I hoped.

As it happened I didn't attend the party. I went to the rah-rah session at Sunday noon, though. The Lake Bayon mob had hired a motel place in north London. I suppose they felt they could let their hair down outside the studio. It worked, because everybody whaled into the booze and the scheduled 'quiet drink and chat' was a riot.

No sooner had we got going than Ray Meese came out on a raised platform, wheezing, glasses gleaming, his large form glistening. Whenever and wherever he stood up spotlights sprouted. He stood in a pre-battle Patton posture. Everybody whooped, clapped. It was sickening. Vance quietened the hysteria by a wide-armed appeal.

'Friends,' Meese boomed. His throat caught as he blotted a tear, recovered magnificently. 'I mean, heartfelt truly, not merely friends. I mean . . . *friends*.'

Wild applause. I looked about. They were exultant.

'We've come a long way – long? We've travelled *worlds*, friends. And we're still here. Need I say more?'

Hysteria, a pandemonium of adulation. He left the stage weeping. Vance shuffled on sideways to announce praise for all concerned.

'Monday's the big day,' he said, taking hours to say it. 'Last scene. And I know we'll wrap the greatest, most memorable megabuck movie of all time. Monday's completion is movie *launch*.' He got only scattered thin applause.

'I'm disappointed about the balloon,' I told Max, still wearing his duffle coat.

'But it went beautifully, Lovejoy.' He was puzzled. 'Lancelot Lake looked absoluto ultimo.'

'Bit of a fraud, though.' I told him I'd said as much to Ray Meese. He was appalled. 'I expected to see a hot-air balloon take off from that Senate House tower and get pulled on cables from those hotels—'

He still couldn't see. 'But you will, Lovejoy. On film.'

'No.' You have to be patient. 'I mean us, in real life, not just on the picture.'

He stared at me. 'That film is the real, Lovejoy.'

'Did you do the hotels? Gunmen, hoods, the winches?'

'Yes. You saw us, the Wembley studio.'

I gave up. Another nutter who thought nothing existed except what you saw in the movie. Even reality wasn't real if it wasn't on screen. Talking to these lunatics gave me an eerie feeling. I mean, I might not exist at all. I wasn't filmable, not really, so wasn't I simply coincidental? I might not really be here. Weird.

Hank the stunt arranger passed a few words. 'Not worried about tomorrow? It's going to be falling off a log.'

'No falling, Hank, please. What do we do?'

'Same as the studio work. Remember? Run from the Exhibition room carrying sacks, firing our toys. You kill a security guard. He falls from the balcony, splat!'

'He be OK, will he?' I asked uneasily.

Everybody in earshot laughed. Hank said kindly, 'We've already shot the fall two days back. Remember? And last week we did the smashed window, an outward prat. It went great.'

People in earshot reflexly praised it. 'Magic, Hank. Best stunt ever.'

'So it's all done?'

'Yep. You shot him dead centre, Lovejoy.' Everybody laughed. My eeriness worsened. I hadn't shot anything, let alone anybody. 'The balloon scenes were mega mega. We lost Clack. Broken leg, but he's replaceable.'

'Cinema art! Magic movie moment, Hank,' people chorused. I swear they didn't even glance our way. It was all automatic, stroking one another's egos continuously. I thought on this news. I'd already shot the security guard? I'd done it? It was on film, which proved that it really was so.

'Hank,' I said. 'We all stay together tomorrow?'

Hank refilled our glasses from a bottle nicked off a passing serf. 'Yes. You, Nick, Lofty and Lancelot Lake. The baddies. Vance'll give you the details.'

'Hardly seem worth bothering with.'

The world turned and stared. Hank grinned to ease things. 'Movies *are* life, Lovejoy. You'll see, in the finished movie. Just give Saffron and Honor their moments.'

'Their what?'

'Don't get in their way when they shoot you.'

Hello, I thought. Here we go. 'Shoot? As in bang?'

'Don't worry, Lovejoy. My stunt lads'll do the falling down. Just go and stand exactly where you're told.' He refilled our glasses. Mine had inexplicably emptied, yet my mouth was dry. 'The plot getting to you, Lovejoy? Come and see yourself fall out of the balloon.' He grinned at my expression. 'Only joking, Lovejoy. They're going to show us the rushes.'

Rushes? We went to a small cinema in the motel complex to watch snippets of our magnum opus. They showed – no sound, really odd – a few disjointed snippets of the film. One showed what we'd done on the University's roof in darkness. Me, Nick and Lofty tugging ropes. We climbed into the balloon basket. Nick and Lofty did the dangling. I just stood there, pulling. Lancelot Lake was specially featured in close-ups. (He got to rip off his hood, wipe sweat from his forehead, grimly move his soundless lips, light a fag.) Somebody's hands – Nick's I think – slickly checked a machine-gun. It was disorientating. The film was made up of bits filmed in half a dozen places, spliced together. Hank told me they added the sound later. I was disappointed. I could hardly recognize myself. It could be anybody in that black overall. In fact, it need not be me at all. I needn't be there. Or did I mean have been?

That eerie recurring thought: so why *was* I here?

Then somebody, one of us hoods, tumbled spectacularly from the basket, miraculously saved himself in freefall by grabbing a trailing rope, then fell. Presumably Clack, breaking his leg in a good cause. I gave a shiver. The few film people who had bothered to come in burst into applause, which Hank accepted with modest grins.

The last rush was a series of dark shots of small wall cases containing phoney Armenian items being wrenched away, with much flashlight flickering and shadowy to-ing and fro-ing. Lancelot, clearly identifiable by an incomplete hood which permitted his famous sneer to show beneath his gimlet eyes, did another snarly close-up. Heavy-duty sacks earned a detailed screening. 'Weight and content all implied, see?' from Hank.

'Great,' I said. *It needn't be me.*

The screen blotched as the ratchets slowed. Lights came on, to applause and exclamations of ecstasy and admiration.

'Staying for the party, Lovejoy?'

'Me? No, ta, Hank.' I tried a grin as easy as his. It didn't work. 'I've a hard day's filming tomorrow.' He laughed, and I moved off.

It needn't be me. Up there on that big screen it could be Joe Soap. Yet everybody on earth was bending over backwards to keep me in – employ me, flatter, seduce me, consult my divvying expertise. Why?

Ray Meese, Vance and a million minions were holding court, listening to supplicants. Stef Honor was moaning about the number of close-ups Lancelot Lake was getting. Saffron Kay was dithering weepily on the outskirts of the mob. I pushed through.

'Great, Ray,' I cried like the rest. 'Great.' And I added as he rotated into this unexpected beam of adoration, 'Pity, though.'

'What?' he wheezed into the spreading silence.

'It'll look sparse, bare, unadorned. Maybe even cheap.'

People grabbed me to lob me out, but Meese stopped them with a frown. 'Do I hear opposition?'

'Not opposition.' I tried to look eager and waggy like the rest of them. 'Only, a great museum saloon – well, Ray. Anything duller to the average bloke? And it's death to birds.'

Meese intoned, 'Have I been wrongly advised, O Universe?' People paled and edged away.

'Needs a bit of colour, Ray. Don't spoil the ship for a ha'porth of tar.'

'What's this particular tar, Lovejoy? And its cost?'

'Free, apart from transport.'

He held out a hand, passed a palm over his closed eyes. Some panicky girl rammed a filled glass at him. 'Arrange. Consult. Beaver. Strive. Gogogo!'

'Ta, Ray,' I said, and went with Vance to arrange, consult, etc. A Celtic cross wasn't much of a problem for our overnight wagons. The gold samovar set I'd get Lydia to fetch.

Off home. That nasty why was getting on my frayed nerves. I was close to deciding to chuck it all up, risking Ben Clayton's ire, Seg's homicidal rage, Big John Sheehan's vengeance, let the world down, when I found the first glimmerings of an answer.

When it happened I was waiting for this train at Liverpool Street. I went into Platform 9's grotty nosh bar for a pasty – none available, of course. Gnawing at a cheese boulder, I went to sit outside the bookshop. A couple of blokes were moaning about travel. 'It'd be all right if I worked normal hours. Sunday travel kills me.' His oppo was equally grumpy. 'Same here. Look at tomorrow. Bloody Bank Holiday. Everything shut, travel slowed to a crawl.'

My train limped in about then. I'd got settled with Savage's *Forgeries* before the travellers' grouses seeped into my soporific cells. Tomorrow a Bank Holiday? Everything shut, traffic at a creep? Yet we were filming the big punch-line at the British Museum. I stared into the tea puddled in my plastic cup. Nothing to worry about there, eh? I mean, Gabriella told me the Museum had allowed forty movie companies to shoot their pictures during the past year. And why not do the filming when the Museum was closed? Better security, fewer problems with public oglers, less chance of people falling over cables . . . Sensible, I'd say. Film when there's least hassle.

Fewer witnesses.

That evening I caught Tinker at the Welcome Sailor. He was indignant at being given a job on Sunday night.

'That's bleedin' impossible, Lovejoy.' I poured three pints into him in a corner of the taproom before I got him quiet. 'Find out what?'

'Here's a list of antiques, mostly fingers.' I'd written it out on the train, a complete account of all the antiques Ray Meese's film crew had occasionally brought in. The descriptions were as full as I could make them. A finger is an antique small enough to be held in the hand, as opposed to so-called 'lifters' – furniture and the like – which require vans for transportation.

'Gawd Almighty.' He gave a prolonged bubbly cough

of dismay. His chest is always ailing – 'Aleing's my medicine,' his joke – and his cough is notorious. I ducked the spittle flecks. He came back to earth, puce and racked.

'I need the answer tomorrow, Tinker.'

'You're off your bleedin' nut, Lovejoy.' He took three more pints and two coughs to recover.

'Find out where they were sold. I think they were all flogged off together a few weeks since.' I looked around, skulduggery in mind. 'North London to the Eastern Hundreds, inclusive.'

If they were from one source, and that source Ray Meese or thereabouts, then my suspicions were well founded. They really had gone to extraordinary lengths to get me to that last big scene. 'Find Lydia. Tell her—'

He cackled an unexpected laugh. 'Her? She's at the cottage, Lovejoy. Friggin' Snow White, she is.' He went suddenly indignant. 'Know what the silly cow did today? Hauled me out of the Marquis of Granby, asked if you'd like some poxy-coloured rag for curtains. Stupid mare.'

I sighed. That's Lydia. Death, prison, all hell looming and she was matching chintz. I saw Brad and Hymie, creditors both, enter just then and hurriedly eeled out of the taproom through the bar. The safest place for the moment seemed to be my cottage. I got the bus and luckily made it without help or injury.

We sat on the divan, opposite ends and knees together. It had that uncompromising firmness of the new. Lydia had made a meal of scintillating taste and substance. I didn't doubt its wholesomeness. My cells shrieked lustily of health as vitamins and longlost trace minerals surged in.

'Did you like supper, Lovejoy?' Lydia had washed up and brewed coffee.

'Great, love. You're, er, skilled.'

'Cooking is enormously satisfying,' she said, all smiles.

Then why do women come for you with a cleaver if you're late for grub? 'Look, Lyd. Who pays for all this?' I'd now a small usable oven, a bucket chair and a tiny kitchen table. Oh, and a divan bed.

'You, Lovejoy. In due course.'

True, true. 'What I mean is, where's the dosh come from?'

'It's a loan, Lovejoy. That explanation will suffice.' She poured more coffee, not looking. 'I am very pleased this film ends tomorrow. It's time we re-established our antiques trade.'

'Me too.' Is the antiques trade normally tranquil?

'These individuals are untrustworthy, Lovejoy. They constitute risks—'

I gasped in affront. 'Lyd! That's most unlike you, to—'

She turned, defensive but with spirit. Women have a yard start in indignation. 'Why have you acquired a gun?'

My indignation evaporated. 'A what?'

'The pepperbox multibarrel. Hidden in the cistern.'

That's Lydia. Only she'd scrub a cistern before installing new furniture. 'Oh, that old thing!' I chuckled a merry chortle. 'Notice the chasing? Lovely. Now that six-chambered percussions have gone through the roof we'll make a . . .' I nearly said a killing '. . . good profit. It's mint.'

'It is not. But it *is* loaded, Lovejoy.'

'Really?' I was thoroughly shocked. 'That'll teach me not to check. Brad says—'

'That you traded my mother's car for it. Bullets, percussion caps, black powder.'

'He did? It's not worth that. Your mother's motor's worth—'

She moved towards me. Independent observers might not have noticed any motion, but I did. It consisted of a slow inhalation, a pursing of the lips, a gentle lift and resettling. For Lydia it took the exertion of a pole vault. Then, a miracle, she actually reached and touched my hand. A robin's breath.

'My antipathy towards Ray Meese, Lorane and the others is not what makes me fear for your safety, Lovejoy. It is your lack of perspicacity.'

'What have you done with the handarm?' I spoke carelessly. If the silly cow'd moved it I'd—

'It's here.' She brought it out after a lengthy handbag rummage. 'I take it you'll need it tomorrow.' The black powder was still bagged up in plastic. And the lead spheres. And caps.

'Well, I might take it.' Offhand.

She looked edible, succulent. 'Would you rather I went to the Museum with you, Lovejoy?'

The question hung, implying was it really worthwhile driving off home when we needed an early start.

'Maybe, Lyd. I'll take the gun.' Odd juxtaposition of words, but she somehow got the point and nodded.

She rose, tidied away a couple of pots so they'd be untraceable once I was alone, and said, 'Oh, Lovejoy. The strangest thing.'

'Yes?'

'Those antiques you mentioned. The ones the camera crew and assistant people keep bringing to show you.'

'What about them?'

'They're mostly from one job lot, and all from one auction. In Maldon, at Baskerville's. The week before the St Edmundsbury exhibition began.' She did her face, mouth, examined her eyes, put away her lipstick. 'Isn't that a curious coincidence?'

'Extraordinary.' That's why she'd come, searched the cottage for weaponry. To see if I felt the same unease.

'Isn't it, Lovejoy?' She sat, closer. My breathing went odd. 'As if they bought the antiques so you wouldn't become bored. A carrot, to keep you there.'

'Me being so indispensable, you mean.'

'But we both know you are not indispensable,' she said calmly. 'You are probably the one person who is superfluous by any criterion, Lovejoy.'

'Here. Nark it.' You can only take so much.

'It's true, Lovejoy. You are dispensable to the film company, the film, the British Museum.' She rose and stood, lovely in her smart suit. 'You're *in*dispensable, however, to me.'

I thought I'd misheard. 'Eh?'

She faced me sternly. 'We must accept that affinities do occur between people, Lovejoy. Strange, for we're really rather different. It implies obligations.'

'It does?' I was still bog-eyed over that Really Rather Different.

'Indeed.' She gathered her things, coat across her shoulders. 'After tomorrow, no later, we must discuss the implications.'

'Very well, Lyd.' The filming was tomorrow.

'Lydia, please.' She took a slow pace, solemnly put her mouth on mine, very inexpert. Our eyes stared into each other's, both sets astonished. She stepped away, breathless. 'This is all very well, Lovejoy. But I have a great deal to do.'

'Er, tell Tinker no need to hunt that list of antiques down.' I shrugged when she turned and gave me a look: So we both suspected the same thing, Lovejoy. 'And get Hymie's gold Russian set by breakfast-time. Come to the studio, props division.'

'Very well, Lovejoy.' I went with her to her car. She wound the window down, her face serious and half-frightened in the diffused headlamps' glim. It was dark and spattering rain. 'Lovejoy. May I ask your first name, please?'

Bloody nerve. 'Mind your own business.'

'Mine's Lydia,' she said, nearly practically almost smiling as she pulled away. A Lydia joke. Things were more desperate than I'd thought. I watched her lights recede up the lane, then went inside. They don't leave you alone even when tomorrow's your hanging.

Chapter 27

Dawn. The British Museum wore its Bank Holiday face, in a faint gold on grey. Me and Three Wheel Archie sat in Lydia's motor watching the world appear, him perched on a stack of cushions.

'Like warpaint, them great pillars.' He too had noticed the resemblance. 'Great rectangular eyes.'

'No people.' A newspaper blew idly along the street, occasionally pausing at parking meters like a peeing dog.

'You're always on about people, Lovejoy. What difference'd people make?'

'Witnesses. Hiding places. Easier all round.'

'You're barmy.' He has one of these merry medieval visages, humour everywhere. 'Three hours you've been moaning, no people, why's it a Bank Holiday. Look on the bright side, Lovejoy.'

'I asked about the smoke cans,' I gave back indignantly. Cheery little sods nark me.

'Eleven times. Yes, Lovejoy. I did sneak into the studio and put your four tins in the pantechnicon. You drove me there at two a.m. Remember?'

'With the studio's smoke guns?'

'Shut up, Lovejoy. You're paranoid. Is there no way of getting a bite?'

'Nothing open.' The world closes on Bank Holidays. Nobody works. The tube dozes. An occasional London bus drifts past for the sake of appearances. We were the only motor in the street. A couple of tramps were still asleep on Russell Square's park benches. One taxi had passed us in two hours.

'We going to starve all day, then? Thought you don't start filming till five.'

'We don't.'

'So why're we here before cockshout? Seems daft to me.'

'Because I'm—' I'd almost said frightened, stopped myself in time. Archie was looking at my knuckles, white on the wheel. 'Early,' I finished lamely. It sounded pathetic.

'Tell you what,' he said after a minute. 'Let's see if anything's open by the tube station, eh? Have some grub, hot cuppa.'

'Good idea.' Shamefaced, I locked up and we walked towards Bedford Square. 'Got any money?'

'Less than twenty wagons, mate, it's them television pillocks.' Everybody in earshot laughed at the Cockney electrician's humour. I'd expressed astonishment at the cavalcade. It looked like an arriving army. Vans, huge closed pantechnicons, lorries with trailers, caravans, lined the road as far as Southampton Way. 'Over forty, it's us proper movies.'

'What's twenty to forty, then?'

'A frigging traffic jam.'

I laughed along, synthetic. The Museum forecourt was crammed with motors, strewn with cables. Men were pushing and hauling equipment. I'd already seen three of the small forklifters file, whining on their heavy batteries, down the slope into the basement from the north entrance. We could have fought a war if we'd had a weapon or two. Speaking of which, here came Lydia, minus Three Wheel Archie.

'Lovejoy! Those guards refused me entry when I said I was your apprentice!'

'My name changes continents, love,' I said drily. Gabriella was conversing with the uniformed gatemen. She flashed me a winning smile. 'Bring it?'

'Yes, Lovejoy. And I had to hire another car, because—'

'Thanks, Lyd. I'll remember your self-sacrifice.'

'Yes, well. And it's Lydia.'

Gratitude won every time. I was getting the hang of Lydia. Three Wheel Archie was guarding a small saloon across in Museum Street by the tavern. I could just see him between wagons. 'Love, have two security guards carry it in, please. It's to lend authenticity to this shack's heap of crud.' That'll be the day. 'Gabriella over there'll lend you a couple of husky lifters.'

'Very well, Lovejoy. Shall I be permitted to watch?'

'Doubt it, love.' I added as she turned, tutting, 'And tell Gabriella her men must stay beside that gold set until it's all over, eh? And tell them to keep their nasty digits to themselves. I don't want any gold filed off while I'm not looking.' I deliberately spoke loudly to nark the security folk, and was rewarded by a sharp annoyed lift of a uniformed girl's head.

'*Quis custodiet ipsos custodes?*' Lydia agreed gravely, trotting towards Gabriella at the gateway.

'Indeed, Lyd, indeed.'

'Lydia,' drifted gently back. Nothing for it now. I just hoped I'd kept Lydia talking long enough for Three Wheel Archie to do the necessary with the little package I'd slipped him. He'd had hours by now, for God's sake. A full minute at least.

'Lovejoy,' somebody called. The world converged on the main entrance, Max loping, Vance shuffling, Hank striding.

'Coming, coming.'

No escape now. Doom is depression. I walked at a creep towards the milling crowd. I'd done what I could. Cattle on their last round-up must feel this why-me degradation. It's a horrible sense of void, where malevolence rules and even legitimate explanations are impotent.

'Hello, Lovejoy,' various cheery loons cried as I joined them. 'Great day, eh? One-take finish!'

'Great,' I said. 'Truly, truly.'

'See where they've put the dressing trailers?' Lofty asked. 'And the honey wagons are out fucking side! I've heard of security, but this is crazy.' Honey vans are mobile latrines.

Two hours later nothing had happened. My rapid heartbeat had slowed to a nod.

'We'll be lucky getting home before morning,' Nick gloated. 'Overtime's money . . .'

He kept nipping out for a smoke while we stood about or sat on the floor of the main entrance hall. I noticed he was closely searched every time. A dozen more plans went out of the window.

There must have been sixty, seventy of us, but even waiting didn't go smoothly. Pal the firearms expert had three men, like the rest wearing identity tags with full-face photos. He wanted to take his toy guns in through a separate entrance and was sternly overruled. Stef Honor had a tantrum over his accommodation – a small canvas shelter pushed like a wheelbarrow on rubber wheels. Saffron had a prolonged weep over something. Vance oscillated between gloom and hypermania, constantly doing surreptitious magic with a tiny box and bulky cigarette papers. Major Bracegirdle was everywhere with his ha, pause, ha, laugh. The thought crossed my mind of passing him a secret message begging for protection, but the nerk would probably have read it aloud as a witty joke.

A wide flight of stone steps ascends left from this main hall. Three of Gabriella's Museum heavies stood impassively abreast on the tenth step, arms folded. They weren't to be blown away by a chance draught. Idling among the mob, listening to technical talk of cameras, electronics, money – always money – and other people's disastrous movies, I sussed the hall out. Two shops to the left, and ladies' loos. Straight ahead, the heavy pale wooden doors leading to the famous Reading Room with its labyrinthine subterranean bookstacks. Going right, a closed cloakroom, men's loos, a lift, some telephones. Then, under the clock, vast double doors opening directly into the Grenville Gallery of illuminated manuscripts. All loos were shut, barred. Carry on right and you're in the historical document Saloon with its bookcase walls and high railed gallery.

It was in there that it would all happen. Into the broad Saloon me, Lofty and Nick would follow Lancelot Lake in our mad criminal dash, after so-say harvesting the Armenian antiques into our black plastic bags. Cameras would be on the red-eyed go, silently cooking our mayhem into a permanent record to enthrall the paying millions. Theory, of course.

As the hours passed my heartbeat took up a steady dryish sound, thudding its way into the early afternoon and maintaining its exhausting I'm-ready-when-you-are shoves.

We left, were searched, had an astonishingly sumptuous hot nosh standing beside the food wagons in the street, surged back again to be searched and start waiting some more. A tense girl called Laurie with a clipboard and two querulous assistants came to brief us.

'You all here?' She ticked us off on her list. 'Now, before we can go through the Grenville Gallery to the shooting lot, you'll need these.' Her team tied tight plastic bands round our wrists, one each. Our photos, identity card, and a nasty little cold metal button. I glanced round, caught Gabriella's innocent gaze and nodded wryly. We were bugged. Upstairs, security control would follow us on their horrible greeny screens. Footer said the security men tone the colour down for clarity. Another useless fact.

'Now! An Italian run, OK?'

'A quick run-through, Lovejoy,' Lofty translated.

As cameras and cables were trolleyed past and assistants barged through to be admitted to the long gallery Laurie and her two began to instruct us. 'Lancelot and you three are skulking in the Russo-Armenian Exhibition, right?' She lowered her voice, skulked about. 'You've stolen the riches, right? The goodies are in your bags, right?' Pause. 'Right, Lovejoy?'

'Eh?' Three Wheel Archie was between two guards, in the search barrier, being tabbed, labelled, bugged. Two others were pushing a Museum trolley on which Hymie's lovely gold samovar set shone resplendent. 'Oh, right, Laurie.'

'Pay attention, please. This is a one-shot scene. No going back, no re-runs, no retakes, OK?'

'Right, right,' everybody said.

Except me, who said, 'Why not?'

Laurie went thin-lipped. 'Ray says so. It's to have spontaneity, vivacity, everything.'

'Right, right,' chorused Lofty, Nick, our four helpers, the world. Except me.

'Didn't the phoney balloon scenes on the University tower have those, then?'

'Sure they did, sure,' the unbiased world said.

'We repeated those twenty times an hour,' I said, unrepentant. I mean, it was me going in where Hank's toy guns were blazing in the smoke. 'Why can't we repeat today's?'

'Artistic need, Lovejoy.' Laurie was annoyed. Those were edicts from the Almighty, and not for antique dealers like me to question. 'The need's imperative. Vital. Total. Truly, truly.'

'Right, right,' from everybody e.m.

Because what's on the film is the truth. Wasn't that their whole and total all-encompassing creed? We'd lived weeks of non-balloon balloons doing non-flying flights. We'd done non-ascending ascents, no-death massacres, fired non-firing guns. Unassaulted assaults on non-hotels. The whole movie was a non-theft of non-valuables in a cardboard cut-out mock-up room in Wembley. And whenever I'd asked why such amazing phoneyness they'd all trotted out the same old answer: *It's only real on the screen.*

And, suddenly, I had it.

Right there in my jumbled mind I had it. Countess Natalia's faded fortunes, poor old Sam's death, greedy Parson Brown's disappearance, my sudden unhealthy immunity from Seg's batterings, the confidential antiques consultations every time I showed up at the studios, my unexplained job as an extra, why this movie would gain every award under the sun and gross a trillion on release. *And why me.*

'Right, right,' I said, looking about in the press for him now I knew. No, nobody who shouldn't be there. He couldn't be delayed by the traffic, for sure. Apart from studio convoys we'd hardly seen a car all day, London lifeless this Bank Holiday. But he'd come.

'Good. Now,' Laurie surged on brightly while Museum

security men pushed and unscrewed and peered at a tiny studio rubber-wheeled forklifter. Footer was right. They always do this to everything except to priceless antiques, like my gold samovar. 'Lancelot first, OK?' Laurie pointed with her pen. This indicated that we hoodlums should charge from the Exhibition Room. 'Guns ready, dragging your sacks, you run – that's *run* – out from the desecrated Exhibition, OK, into the open Manuscript Saloon. Smoke, smoke, gloom, lights, shadows, cockalorums spreading shadows, desperate stuff, OK?'

'Cockalorums,' Lofty explained low-voiced. 'Big square light reflectors up on poles.'

'Lancelot, Nick, Lofty, run forward-left. Stef and Saffron are on the balcony above. They fire. You three fire back. Lofty gets hit, goes down—'

'Er,' I said. 'Sorry?'

'—Firing up, Nick, with Lancelot yelling, "Come on, men," firing, firing. Stef flings himself in front of Saffron, who's falling. Bravely he keeps firing – stop those crooks, goddammit! Really real, right?'

'Er, Laurie—'

'You, Lovejoy, dash left and—'

'Er, sorry, love. Why don't I follow the—?'

'I'm telling you.' She spoke exasperatedly. The rest laughed, shaking heads at me. 'You hear shots, see the rope-ladder Stef and Saffron have climbed to reach the balcony. Right? With your sack you rush—'

'Isn't that long case in the way?' These manuscript display cases are immovable and stand chest high. 'Hit one of those running you won't get up for a week.'

'No, Lovejoy.' All patience. 'Make a ninety-degree angle left and you'll avoid it, OK?'

'Anyway, you'll still see a bit,' Nick said. 'How fast, Laurie?'

'Fast as shit,' she replied elegantly.

'Do I climb the rope-ladder?' I asked, knowing the answer.

'No. Stef shoots you and Nick.'

'Nick right over there, and me a mile to the left?'

'You've got it, Lovejoy.' She turned a palm down. 'Just as you reach that big case you're got in the chest. You make a grab, hold on, groan, look up. You're shot again. You shoot back, bam bam! Just as you've rehearsed it.'

'Then?'

'Then you die. Crump. Just like you practised.'

'What happens to Lancelot?'

'He makes to shoot Stef when Saffron raises herself, wounded, shoots Lancelot, saves her lover, saves the priceless Armenian cultural heritage. It's sweet. Truly.'

'Good, eh?' Lofty was chuckling. 'We call it an Eddie G. finish. You know Edward G. Robinson? On the steps of that church, gunned down with visions and a heavenly choir.'

Nick grinned. 'I knew an old stunter once, worked on that Yankee stunt feature. Reynolds did the lead. And—'

Laurie cut them short. 'We'll have a few run-throughs, Lovejoy. You'll be able to do it blindfold.'

'Question of timing,' Nick said.

'Right, everybody?' Laurie called. 'We'll start the walk-through.'

'Speaking of rope-ladders,' Lofty began, 'I knew an old bloke once. Said he'd worked on *Khartoum*. Well, he reckoned that in those long drifty Nile shots, the gunboat was—'

'Stand still, sir, please,' the Museum guard said at the gallery entrance. 'Just a quick security check.'

'Take particular care with this one,' a voice said from inside the doorway. The voice I'd been waiting for.

'Aye,' I said. 'I've ten howitzers under my armpit.'

The Museum guard chuckled. 'Now, sir. No jokes like that, please. Not until your picture's over and done with.'

'Best make sure, Lovejoy, eh?' Seg said, helping to frisk me. He wore a dark blue uniform with Sec-Gard flashes and what seemed a number of black leather belts with pouches. And a holster.

'If you say so, Seg.'

The Museum guard motioned me through. 'Stand inside a moment, sir. Then all go in together. Security in numbers.'

Thought it was safety. But I let it go, and did as I was told. Safety had had it for good, for now, for somebody.

Chapter 28

'One more time everybody.'

'Christ,' Lofty groaned. 'How many more?' We clambered to our feet. It took effort. I was knackered, in no state to fight for my life. The all-black sweat suits were exhausting, even though we were only sitting in the enclosed Armenian Exhibition, Room 31. I was beginning to hate it. The walls and its exhibits were covered by a mock-up panelling with pale, scagged areas showing where we were supposed to have raced in and ripped the precious items away. The genuine exhibition was of course still complete and untouched behind our false panels. So what would be nicked?

'Extras! Where the hell are the extras?' Vance was in delirium, giggling and talking to himself. Only rarely – when terrified by Ray Meese's approach – did he descend to earth.

'Here, here!' Laurie yelped. She lived on nerves, her own as well as Vance's, Lorane's, Ray's. 'They're here, Vance.'

'He'll snort his way to paradise,' Nick prophesied, reaching for his submachine-gun. I'd kept mine clutched to myself throughout these rehearsals. Lofty tended to nod off between the walk-throughs. I'd have done the same, but I was frightened.

'OK, crooks?' Pal Trevelyan had already issued our weapons, but kept doing repeat checks and getting in the way.

'Right. Final walk-through.' Laurie hovered, dithering, calling anxiously as we filed into the large Manuscript Saloon.

The place was crammed all round its periphery by cameras, lighting equipment, lift gantries. I'd no idea movie gear was so tall. Tubing, scaffolding, floodlights, people even, stood almost as high as the balcony which ran round the Saloon. Good old loyal Three Wheel Archie was there, ready to snap into action with my superb Save Lovejoy plan. Friendship, that's what counts. No question.

'Right. Out comes Lancelot Lake, bam bam bam upwards.' Laurie was reading from some gospel they'd chained her to. 'He pauses, OK? Then cries, "This way, men." Sack in your right hand, Lovejoy. All others left.'

'Not left?' I changed over.

'Sixteenth time, Lovejoy,' Vance crooned.

'Right.' I kept trying it on, but Laurie caught me every time. I'm right-handed, and the lovely gold samovar would be on my right if they left it where it was. 'Laurie, love. Wouldn't it be easier if I—?'

'Leave off, Lovejoy,' Nick said wearily from in front. 'Why the frigging hell d'you keep *on*?'

Technicians, assistants, camera people were watching. A camera was rolled with us on rails as we walked. Another rose on its tubular neck, a hunting creature wary at the approach of strangers.

'Remember this entire sequence is only twenty seconds long. Got it? That's two-oh seconds. No time to tie your shoelace, OK?'

'Right, OK.'

'Nick follows Lancelot oblique ahead, OK? Bam bam! Lofty makes a run dragging his sack, same direction. Bam bam, OK?'

'OK.' Lofty moved after his mate, heading for the King's Library's giant sealed door. 'One, two, three.' He counted paces.

'Lovejoy, move left.' Laurie pointed.

'Do I shoot?'

'You *know* you don't, Lovejoy. I've told you – wait for Lofty to fall. Keep moving. Bam bam bam. Stef and Saffron up above motionactionbam and down goes Saffron, blood shock horror, OK? Bam bams, plenty bambam. Lovejoy?' She was sarky with me because I was walking in slow motion like Nick and Lofty, saying nothing.

'Sorry, Laurie. Bam bam?'

'No, for Christ's sake. Bam bam *bam*. OK? Exactly alongside that yellow urn thing, shoot up and round it. OK. OK?'

'OK,' I said. Yellow urn thing? Hymie'd have a fit.

It stood a few feet from the long central display case. Vance had finally decided it should be seen by the camera when it swung to follow the action. My heart kept going funny every time we got to this bit, me slowly reaching the central case. My chest did its bonging and each breath took ages. This display case is fourteen feet long maybe, six or so wide, about four tall, and has four glass-covered compartments to each sloping side. In each compartment is a manuscript, contained in a kind of plastic frame. Wired for sound, alarms, atmospheric pressure, humidity, and everything else including passing robbers. I reached it, fifteen of my slow motion paces after emerging from the Exhibition doorway.

Laurie was stepping backwards, reading from her clipboard. 'Bam bam up there, Stef, OK? Nick dies. Then you, Lofty, bam bam bam and glasscrashshatterkaboom. Props, OK? Leaving Lancelot.'

'And me,' I said anxiously. 'And me. Am I right, here?'

'You're OK there. At the long display case. Exactly spot X.'

Spot X. 'Bambambam upwards?'

'No, Lovejoy,' wearily. 'Like in rehearsal. Security man comes forward. You bambam him. He bambams you. You fall, multo glasscrashshatterkaboom – got that, Props? You know how, Lovejoy. You do it great.'

I halted motionless to show I agreed I was dead. Spot X.

'Now Lancelot's alone, smokecrashbambam. Candice, you get all that? Where the fuck's Candice gone? Stef's wounded, disarmed. Lancelot raises his gun, when Saffron . . .'

They prattled and paced on, bambamming and pointing. Me on Spot X by the big central display. I leaned on the long case, listening casually. I'd got it all pat. Spot X was where I'd fall, then I'd be out of it. That was the plan. I'd be dead, killed. And not merely on film. In the truly-truly real life that mattered only to me.

Minutes away. I'd be filmed in the ultimate snuff movie, a real killing caught in gruesome reality. A legitimate snuffle. An attempted robbery, genuine – after all, I was a born crook, wasn't I? A shady antique dealer with a police record as long as your arm. No wonder Meese had hired me – instead of some safe, trustworthy dealer. And when they killed me, there'd be panic over my very real death. As technicians rushed to help and assistants coped with the disaster once they realized there had been a ghastly real topping among all their let's-pretend phonies – a very real heist would take place. During the ensuing hullaballoo Ray Meese or somebody close to him would nick what the whole film was about, this central displayed item. No question. It'd be the most famous and talked-about film in movie history. Whatever the artistic demerit, its cackhanded writing and faulty photography, all known prizes would hurtle its way, in this industry where reality and movies collided with an ultimate clang. Truly, it'd be the very last gambado they dream about.

'Sir,' a vigilant Museum guard called from among the forest of equipment. 'Please don't lean on that main display case.'

'Sorry,' I said, straightening up. It took real effort not to glance down at the Magna Carta. 'We done with the walk-through?'

'Right. Stations everybody.' Laurie flagged us back. 'We'll do a few time runs, then a full rehearsal. OK?'

'OK,' everybody said. 'Great.'

'Right on, man,' I said. Lofty looked surprised and grinned as we returned to sit in the Exhibition Room.

'Getting a taste for this life, Lovejoy?'

'Never,' I said back. 'I think you're all barmy.' Not me, note. Them.

But Three Wheel Archie had been watching near a cluster of suited executives chatting with Ray Meese and Lorane. And he'd given me an oh-so-innocent thumbs up sign. Good old loyal safe Three Wheel. Now all I'd to suss out was where Seg would be when he made his attempt on my life. After that it'd be up to me to scarper, intact as ever and fleet of foot.

We did six sprint-throughs before Lancelot Lake, immortal star of stage, screen and faded B pictures, deigned to appear. He did nine runs and insisted on twenty-six changes, which is two point eight script alterations per rehearsal. 'The bastard averages ten hysterics a take,'

Nick whispered. 'Yesterday's news trying to be awards material.'

Between practices I asked Lofty if Lancelot really was no good.

'Him? Unemployable.' He cast about, made sure all the directional mikes pointed elsewhere, whispered, 'After that barney over that American gaolbait? Did a stretch for it.'

'Then why did Ray hire him?'

'Gawd knows. Old Pals Act, they say.'

Gulp. A gaolbird on the team now. Was it him? Him scheduled to be my killer, and psychotic Seg only a decoy? Or was Seg going to blam me, while Lancelot Lake sauntered off with the Magna Carta? I gave up and slumped beside Lofty. Out there in the great Saloon Lancelot was posturing and complaining. Ray and Vance were placating. Lorane was ballocking Laurie and somebody called Edna. A girl was sobbing, wailing feeble excuses for some calamity. Nick idled to the door and called could he knock off for a fag, please, was told no. He settled down to watch the egos riot. 'It's getting on for eight, Lovejoy,' he said, 'we'll break for supper soon.'

'Great, Nick.' Tina brought me an old pen. It was one of Alonzo T. Cross's famous firsts – the 1879 Stylographic Pen, precursor of the ballpoint. I wasn't up to it, I'm afraid. I just told her it was worth a fortune, listened to her fake enthusiasm, and slumped to wait out the remaining few minutes of my life.

No wonder poor old Sam Shrouder had finally rebelled. Superb faker as he was, he went along with them, all in the interests of honest skilful fakery. But he'd learned that the scam was to nick the Magna Carta itself. And he'd demurred. The rights of everybody in over a hundred nations were established on that ancient slip of scrawled parchment. It only measures one foot by one-and-a-half, but it spelled the beginning of the end for government by whim. The start of mankind's hope, to live in order. Two-way rights began to take over from one-way obligation.

Funny how you can miss the obvious. The Articles of the Barons preceded the Magna Carta. They were a kind of rough draft, a let's-do-it-thus-lads prototype. These Articles are in Compartment No. 1 of that long central case. Meese's plan could have been to nick that priceless parchment, yes indeed. But the world hasn't got the Articles indelibly into its mind and soul, not like the Great Charter. All right, there are two other 'exemplifications', as historians call these original parchments. One's in Lincoln, one in Salisbury. But to us mere people, all mere humanity, there's only one true Magna Carta. And that's in Compartment No. 4, of that long central case in the Manuscript Saloon, Room 30, the British Museum. Just thinking about it gives your stomach a high dive. How could I have missed it? Easy: you never notice wall-paper much, weather, traffic noise. They're all normal background. And nothing's more ingrained in our interstices than that one scrap of wriggly writing. Now, I'm no hero. If it came to the Big McGuffin or me there'd be no question – me first, every time. Lovejoy, masterblind. Idiot. Nerk.

The arguments outside diminished. Lots of making-up took place. Several people suddenly became lovie, honey, darling, instead of slags and cretins. We three came to. Lofty woke, blinked his eyes, replaced his hood. Nick made way. Ray Meese came in, embracing Lancelot Lake.

'Lancelot. Everything, every breath – it's you. Did I ever admit it, shriek it from the highest Everest? This movie – truly, truly – is you, Lancelot. And you, lovie, are this movie.' He faced him, staring soulfully into the actor's eyes. Tears of emotion streamed down the director's cheeks. 'I kneel in worship, Lancelot baby. As will the universe – Did I say universe? The galaxy's all-time history, as far into the future as Man can foresee.'

God, I thought, appalled, don't really kneel. But it was only filmspeak, stupidity.

Lancelot was mollified. 'It's an honour to work with you, Ray. A delight, an education, to serve the man with the vision.' He choked, bravely continued. 'I . . . I . . . respect you, Ray Meese.'

There was more, all of it so convincing that I nearly filled up myself, listening to the crud. Ray recovered from his angst and went, blithely calling to his merry band. Lancelot turned, casually nodded to us three nerks. His eyes fixed on me.

'Hello,' he said, magnanimity time. 'You're new, aren't you?'

'Lovejoy,' Nick said. 'The antique dealer.'

'Hi, Lovejoy. Antique dealer, eh? I've an antique cupboard needs a bit of restoration. Some veneer stuff's fallen off, flowervase design. You can look at it for me.'

He really sounded not bent on killing me for the sake of fame. I warmed to the man, glad he hadn't thought of me as a sacrifice. Well, actors, publicity and all that.

'Certainly. Where'd you buy it?'

'Ready for another run?' Laurie called. Vance mumbled. People called for quiet. The pre-run shouts began. Where's the key grip, the forklift controls, straighten that auto-gantry, hold everything for a second, Christ, is there a hair in the gate, all sorts of incomprehensible folklore lingo.

'Go again. Run through.' Laurie poked her head into the Exhibition Room, nodded, ducked out of the way. 'Go go go!'

We lumbered out, dragging our sacks, shouting our bam bam bams. And Three Wheel Archie had gone. Everybody and everything else was still there, same as ever. But my one hope, my loyal pal whom I'd helped time and again in the past from sheer heartgoodness, had vanished.

Life being what it is, the instant Three Wheel Archie disappeared our rehearsals became trouble-free. We were instantly fast, slick, accurate. We actually used our toy guns, doing it right, too. We sounded like the Battle of the Bulge. I thought we must look really great. And each time things improved, worse luck. Cables untangled, hatreds evaporated, bambams synchronized. And Three Wheel Archie didn't come back.

An interruption for feed, smokes, a pee, and we got the final word.

Our run-throughs were perfect. Next time was the big gambado, and me alone.

Chapter 29

Midnight on the set. Anyone else would have found it magic, even exciting. Me, heading to doom, all I could think of was where's Three Wheel Archie? That's what comes of trusting midgets. I'd kill the treacherous little nerk. When he was in a mess over the small 1780 Chippendale Haig & Co. breakfront bookcase, who'd bailed him out? Me. And when—

'Ready for go. One minute, okayee?' from Laurie and her sweatshirt acolytes.

'Okayee,' we all said. I peered out, pushing past Lancelot Lake. He'd just been made up again. No Three Wheel. I'd murder the disloyal little sod. Another auto-control camera gantry was now by the central case. Seg was by it, standing, still in his Sec-Gard uniform. Something was wronger, different.

'Places, places. Go half minute.'

To my dismay shouts of okayee rose. Where when I needed them were the lost junction boxes, those faulty connections, the petulances and hatreds? They alone could postpone my demise. I looked again towards Seg. He was made up, cosmeticked to the eyeballs. That's what was different. A make-up girl was replacing her grimy sticks and powder puffs in her horrible plastic toolbox – *Seg? In the movie?* He was standing where amiable sweatshirt assistants had been. Throughout the rehearsals the security man – the one I bambammed and who'd bambammed me – was represented by anybody handy. I hadn't given it a thought. Now, suddenly, Seg was the extra. It was him I was to close on in the smoke, firing my toy gun. He was to fire back as I reached the Carta display case. I was to fall in a semblance of death. Jesus.

Sickened, I went back in line behind Lofty, almost vomiting from fright. Seg was the film extra, the security guard. Who'd kill me, there in the smoke. What was it Laurie'd said? *You bam him. He bams you. You fall, multo glasscrashshatterkaboom* . . . My movie demise would take place in a cacophony made by the sounds unit.

The autoforker was waiting silently in position. Whoever held the control box need only move it forward two yards, raise its two prongs, and the locked and sealed cabinet's top-hinged glass would be ripped up. The Carta would be exposed in its small picture frame. It was wired to the world's security alarms – so what? The assumed culprit, Lovejoy, would be dead. His body would be proof the scam was nipped in the bud. The smoke would need time to clear, the pandemonium time to lessen. Only then, in the debris, would somebody inspect the display case. And might they have a perfect Shrouder-made replica somewhere to drop in the cabinet, to make everybody believe that no theft had actually occurred? By the time Gabriella's security people recovered the trail would be hopelessly obscured. These movie people talked forever of planes to catch, where they were going next, jobs overseas . . .

Smoke. No Archie. Plus impending doom.

'Counting,' Laurie called. 'Everybody? Ten, nine—'

I went for it. 'Why've they shifted all the lights, Lofty?' I said loudly.

'Shhh, Lovejoy!'

'Five, four—'

'They'll see bugger-all of Lancelot's face—'

'Two, one—'

'Hold it.' Lancelot stepped out of our doorway, God bless his ego. 'Hold it. Ray? Where's Ray?'

'What the hell—?'

Screeches began, a riot of detumescence and deflation. People yelled. Lofty and Nick were staring at me. Lancelot, Meese and a reeling Vance were bellowing in a mêlée of assistants. The camera people were mostly holding hands over their faces.

'What the frigging hell, Lovejoy? No light's changed.' I swear Lofty nearly took a swing at me.

'Sorry, lads.' I was so apologetic. 'When I saw they'd shifted the lights I got scared I'd fall over and ruin it all.'

Nick slumped. 'We'll be fucking hours now, Lovejoy. You couldn't have said anything worse.'

Or better. 'Sorry, lads. I'll go and apologize.'

'Yeah, do that,' bitterly from Lofty.

Trailing my sack I passed the Lancelot-Meese maelstrom, went to sit by Props. It's strange how dedicated these folk are. People grumble about show business, the money they get. Believe me, for single-minded get-it-done conviction they leave whole industries standing. Props numbered a dozen or so, really down. I sat beside a lass on the floor.

'Sorry, love,' I said. 'I tried persuading Mr Lake.'

'Bastard actors.' She was laconic, 'Gone midnight and it's will the world spot Lancelot's missing eyelash. The hours we waste.'

'Terrible.'

Somebody called her. She pulled herself up and entered the mob. Nobody was looking my way. All attention was focused on the contumely.

Eight smoke cannon were placed about the Saloon. After we'd been readmitted, the lofty Saloon doors to the Grenville and King's Galleries were closed, two uniformed Museum guards standing mutely before each. We were boxed in. And so was I.

A mound of equipment lay beside the wall. All walls were glass bookcases, reaching as far as the ceiling, ancient folio tomes peacefully ranked behind glass. This was where Three Wheel had been standing, my reason for coming. Idly, I raised a flap of the nearest box. Archie must have stood on it to see over the heads. My four smokies, thank God. Action now? Or later? Watching the arguments subside about Lancelot's best side, lighting, where the cameraman was focused, the jaw angle, eye lines, I tore my plastic bag near its gathered neck. It was difficult. Try to keep the damned bags intact to line your dustbin and they fall apart. Actually try to pierce one and it shreds your fingers. I heard somebody say, 'Truly, lovie,' and lifted one of the canisters. Seal intact. I pretended to examine it, casually dropped it into my bag through the slit. Another. Nobody looking. Reconciliation raised its rose-tinted head. People were walking back to their positions. Lovie, darlings, angels, resounded.

'Lovejoy?' Laurie.

Oh hell. I dithered. Time for a third? Or did I release the smoke now, make a run? But Seg was in view. I rose as Laurie's podgy helper pushed among the equipment to find me.

'It's places, Lovejoy,' she said sternly. Her eyes misted in rapture. 'We're going for the take!'

'Great. Okayee.' I hauled my bag to my shoulder. Nothing fell out. 'I'm glad it's finally come.'

'So'm I.' She guided me among the gear towards my least favourite doorway. 'Isn't it . . . oh, simply ecstatic? Imagine how privileged, honoured, you must feel! Part of this great enterprise.'

'Aye, Laurie. Imagine.'

'Did they change it, Lancelot?' I asked, worried, now I was the one who wanted no interruptions.

'Bastards,' he said. 'Directors, producers, extortionist blood-sucking swine.'

'Er, right, great.'

Lofty gave me the bent eye so I abandoned diplomacy and stood in line. Fourth hoodlum, after Lancelot, Nick, Lofty. Lancelot carried no bag, so he could rip off his hood and do his close-up sneer and die dramatically for his Oscar.

Outside in the Saloon shouts were being raised for coordination, readiness, a last-second stand-to. I nudged Lofty, not believing my question, his answer. 'It's go this time, eh?'

'This is the one take, Lovejoy. Just keep going.'

'Now hear this, Planet!' Ray Meese's amplified voice cackled. 'Whatever, it's the one true take, truly, truly. We go, and keep going no matter what. No turning back, O World. Okayee?'

Whoops, cheers, moviespeak praise, arose in a crescendo. Ray must be loving this, his moment. All was on course for the greatest achievement in movie history. Real life and storytelling would do the ultimate: step into each other's existence, do a miracle interchange before everybody's very eyes.

'Stand by, everybody. Where's Josephine?'

'Stand by. Hoods okayee in there?'

'Okayee.'

'One minute soon, Lovejoy,' Lofty's black hood said kindly over his shoulder, white eyes blinking roundly. 'Just do exactly what you did at rehearsal.'

'Ready, Lofty. And ta.'

He chuckled. 'Bag in your left hand, daft bugger.'

'Oh, aye!' I made a joke of it, only falling silent when the crews' shouts achieved unison. We all quietened.

'A minute, everybody.' The deep voice of Jake, Vance's fourth assistant. Or was it fifth? A hairy gorilla of a bloke, always after Laurie. Rumour said she turned him down every time.

I checked my gear. Neck of sack grabbed in my left, submachine-gun in my right. Hank had renewed its magazine. All on course. Nick's gun clacked against the panelling. He moved aside, no panic. Lancelot's hood was nodding gently, him going over his movements.

'Half a minute, everybody,' from a high-pitched nerve-jangled Laurie. 'All in? Negatives only, everyone. Fog us up. Slow on. Ted? Sadie? Vernon, that far side . . .' Names, mutters, a clatter as somebody dropped something.

My hands were wet. Lofty hitched at his hood. I used my arm to clamp my toy gun to my side, and slowly stooped. The others obscured me from the pale faces outside, all still and watching. The lights were blinding. Hand inside my bag's slit. Slow-motion rummage, one canister in the hand. Slowly out, on the floor between my feet.

'Twenty seconds, World. Still and quiet.'

Hand into the bag. No second canister. A slightly faster fumble, heart banging. Canister, cold and capable, falling into my palm among the dross of secondhand picture frames and polystyrene cubes in there. Out. Between my feet to join its pal.

'Fifteen seconds. No going back. Stef Honor?'

'Okayee, okayee.'

The canisters have a seal. You pull it, very like a ring on a beer can and that easy. Sickened, cursing faithless Three Wheel Archie to hell, my hands sweat-slippery, I heard the seconds ticked off, heard the faint chug of the smoke guns start, saw ahead the opalescence beyond the doorway, heard the assistants' call, wait for it, wait for it. I'd been in an army last time this horrid nausea froze into my belly. What was I doing here among these maniacs for God's sake? They were all mad, mental.

'Two, one, on hold for action everybody. And . . .'

Lofty's elbow nudged me. Any second. Sod them. I changed hands, bag under my left arm, toy gun in my right. I waited. I was suddenly vaguely disappointed they didn't shout 'Lights! Camera! Action!' like on old black-and-white Tuesday night re-runs. But was that maybe just setting the mood? I'd have to look it up properly to find out. Or happen Lofty and Nick knew, my mind babbled. They all seemed immersed in the folklore of movies. How odd. Me thinking movie instead of film. The American influence perhaps? Altogether—

'Action!' somebody screeched, high-pitched, desperate, and all hell broke loose. I was astonished. Guns were firing. My finger ripped the canister rings. Lake, Nick, Lofty, were diving out of the door. It was here. Now. Action.

'Gawd Almighty,' I muttered, then remembered I wasn't to speak, just leap out, go left, shoot bam bam bam.

It can't have been more than half a second, but it was centuries long, that gap before I had the sense to sling two tin cans. Sounds easy, but isn't. Try it, clutching a plastic bag and holding a toy gun, simultaneously trotting forward into pandemonium. I must have emerged like Quasimodo, hunched, trying not to drop anything. And immediately I couldn't see a bloody thing. I'd forgotten. These military smoke cans don't just leak a tiny plume. They sort of explode, shooting out a tremendous opaque brown smoke fountain with a ferocious hiss. It spumes out, spitting, for all the world like a pipe sprays water. Panicked, blinded, by two uncontrollable canisters hosing cloud, I blundered forward into the door jamb, nearly dropped my bag, caught sudden sight of a brilliant light with Lofty's hooded noddle bobbing in silhouette, guessed a direction and slung a canister along the floor that way as I leapt out. I inhaled a lungful of smoke directly from my remaining can about then, and ran to my left retching. I had the sense to duck low, skim the other canister like a bowling ball along the wooden floor at my Spot X. Lancelot started shooting, then I heard him, 'This way, men!' A snapshot glimpse of a figure in security uniform in the smoke, Seg facing me by the central cabinet, waiting.

Nick and Lofty were firing now, Lofty dragging his sack, and shots deafening. Me to move left, not firing. With all the lights foresting the Saloon I was blinded. In country fog you look up, take direction from trees. Astonishing to see the ceiling clear as day, brilliantly lit. Gunfire. Somebody thumped down in a terrible clatter – Lofty getting pretend-killed.

Shots from above ahead, a whimper and thud. Saffron getting wounded, everybody's guns bamming except mine. I dropped the thing, felt along the nearest display cabinet and mercifully there was Hymie's samovar, cold, gold, richly meeting my hand. Smoke was impenetrable, my brown stuff hosing everywhere, instantly thickening the feeble pallor of the Props' mist into solid umber. Faint patches of ochre showed where the big lights struggled to transect the air.

The fucking lid wouldn't come off. I whimpered in the gunfire, the thuds and bambams, turned the top, managed it, dropped the precious gold cover any old where, grabbed inside, extracted the cloth-wrapped heaviness, lost my sack, heard Stef's submachine-gun start up from above and Nick thump to the floor, tremblingly unwrapped the six chambered percussion handarm and moved at a fast crouch, gagging on the brown smoke.

Two of Laurie's glassclattershatters sounded almost simultaneously. I knew where I was to an inch. Lofty was one crash, finally dying from Stef's balcony shots. The other was unscripted, the autoforker vehicle ripping the Carta cabinet's wood and glass cover. That faint creaking within was the metal reinforcement concealed in the wood. Clever, but even strip steel's no use against a device that can raise tons. Two yards away, duck left and run blindly, halt. Spot X must be a yard to my right. Seg would be within arm's reach. I thought, Oh sod it. Him or me. Well, I honestly didn't think, just held out my percussion piece honestly without any notion of hurting anybody, simply in sort of blind despair, and pulled the trigger.

These pieces recoil badly. I felt my elbow whine with sprain. But something thudded practically next to the muzzle. Something stabbed at my cheek under my right eye; the copper percussion caps always splatter back at you. Horrified, I felt my trigger finger pull. A second flash, thump.

Something groaned, nudged my foot. A weight slumped at me, Seg's body. I shoved it away, going 'Argh' in fear. And reached into glass fragments, felt, grabbed, hauled at the picture frame which held the Carta. I had to lever it with the percussion's stock because of wires, realized alarms were suddenly whooping and wailing in pandemonium. I'd got it. And stood flummoxed, blinded, frightened. What now, for God's sake? I heard somebody start coughing, practically in my face. My percussion boomed a third time, cracking my elbow, the noise also lost in the other shooting and the howling sirens, me catching a lash of copper fragment on the forehead.

Shakily I checked my position from the ceiling, dived through the smoke. The place was darkening. Were they dowsing their lights? Hardly. A bambam sounded, Lancelot dying away, gamely sticking to the script though by now everybody must know things were going wrong. Choking and wheezing, I scraped along a wall, almost yelped when it hit me in the face. The rope-ladder. I'm not good on muscular coordination but fumbled up it. It's your feet which have the difficulty because the damned thing swings about the more you climb. And I had to keep hold of the Carta in its frame. It was only small, but too big to stuff into my body suit as I had the six-chamber. Of course Stef and Saffron hadn't had to climb, idle swine. They'd gone up the staircase which is concealed in the wall bookcases near the Grenville entrance. Skilfully banging my head on the bottom of the balcony I clambered over the railing and peered down. It was a mess.

The great Saloon was a sea of brown mucky smoke, still billowing up from two areas, one in the centre and another almost immediately below. Huge floodlights stuck out of the smoke like monsters questing from a primaeval swamp. Swirls showed where people moved. Two people were above the smoke level on gantry chairs. Ray Meese was one, Vance the other. The alarms were deafening. Somebody was thumping. Sirens were rioting outside.

'Cut,' somebody yelled. The call was echoed everywhere. Time to go. I groped, hauled out my percussion piece, and turned along the balcony when somebody touched me.

'What happened?'

I screeched, leapt a mile. Stef and Saffron were standing beside me, puzzled. She was bloodstained, only a shoulder wound from a Props blood capsule.

'You stupid burkes!' I yelped. 'I almost shot you.'

'Is it a wrap?' Saffron asked, silly cow. I ask you. I pushed past them. Everybody down there was coughing. A camera poked up through the filth to give me another scare but I was being scared for me now, not them, and scurried round the Saloon balcony like a rabbit. Getting round the corner proved difficult as Footer had predicted. Security had locked the glass door, but I could stretch round to grab the far rail and managed to slide the frame on to the balcony first before climbing after. After that there was only one way because there's a huge fixed glass door barring the way from the Saloon on to the Grenville's balcony, and that was to break it. I nearly broke my foot trying to kick through, so I stood at an oblique angle and shot at the glass from a distance of inches. Somebody below in the hullabaloo screamed, 'What the fuck's that?' I was past caring. The window didn't cave in as I'd expected. Two shots to do it, would you believe, and each one of solid lead. I was enraged. Security swines had even used reinforced glass at balcony level. No wonder Footer gets annoyed. I struggled through the opening, cutting the back of my thigh.

'Pssst!'

Startled, I looked down from the balcony into the tranquil, well-lit, smoke-free Grenville Library. A Museum security man was gazing up at me, worried.

'Are they finished in there? Those alarms—'

'Yes,' I said. 'I'm the last. It's done now.'

He held up a clipboard. 'Only there's nothing about fire alarms down here.'

Another security man was by the barred exit door. 'That glass really broken, is it?' he called up, interested. He too was caught up in moviedom's trick, no longer knowing what was real.

'Best ask Gabriella,' I suggested, walking to the first rectangular window. Brown smoke poured through the opening behind me. 'Major Bracegirdle's on his bleep, somebody said.'

'Right.' He sounded relieved, started tinkering with his intercom. I gnawed through my ID tag, whizzed it back into the Saloon's smoke.

I lifted the Venetian blind away from the window. Pitch black outside, of course, in the central quadrangular space bordered by the Museum's enormous structure. I had one shot left. Hang the consequences. I pointed, pulled, whimpered at the pain as my arm took the recoil. This time the glass completely shattered, cascading all over me. I dropped the percussion and clambered out into the night air. One uniformed bloke called, 'Here, mate,' and 'You there!' I heard somebody running, orders given, people shouting. Reality was intruding.

The great building's inner face is unadorned, not like the lofty pillars and smooth slabs of facing-stone on the outer street-side aspect. This meant drainpipes and brickwork. And ledges. I found myself standing on glass fragments on the sill. I didn't move, pulled off my hood and forced the manuscript frame into it, took the corner in my teeth, then sidled along the sill until I happened on a drainpipe. The darkness wouldn't reveal how far from the ground I was, but guesswork said about forty feet. Where would I be even when I got there? More shouts, a whistle, a wahwah car siren.

London's faint skyglow etched the Museum's bulk for me. The enormous central dome of the Reading Room loomed in front. I'd make for the base. But hadn't Footer's sketches showed treacherous glass-panelled sloping roofs in some places in this vast quadrangle, the Map Gallery for instance? I'd no torch. Action, into the great unknown. I shinned down the drainpipe. Odd that it was rectangular in section, Edwardian decorative classiness showing, I suppose. I was glad. It makes for difficult shinning, though.

I'd no way of telling what I was standing on. I felt around. Naturally, it had started to rain the instant I'd broken out. Just my luck. The ground felt stone slabs, not glass. Feeling my way two-handed, I struck out on all fours. There's no one public spot in the whole British Museum from where you can see inside the quadrangle – further evidence of the nasty minds these security folk have. I'd no idea how far I'd have to go before . . . before nutting my suffering head on this wall. Windows, a yard or two along, at knee height. I broke in by lying on my back and kicking a heel at it. A latch, and I was inside, among ordinary prosaic furniture. Somebody's office.

By now a light was on in the Museum building, a row of high rectangles partially blocked by a low roof. No smoke showed, but wahwah motors chorused in the distance. Fire engines, peelers arriving? I did the interior lock by simply trying it before smashing it with a chair. The incumbent must have felt so secure, carefully locking his office from the corridor side as he'd departed – folk don't break out after all, do they? Only in. I had a little glow to help, but it's always easier looking from dark into the less-dark. I set off down the corridor, reached a staircase. I knew what I wanted, and kept Footer's pencilled map in mind. Trouble was, the Museum building's ructions outside had begun to dwindle. Frequently I stopped to listen and each time got colleywobbles. Analyses were taking place. People were being counted. The smoke and its canister cases were being removed. Seg would already be in hospital. If I'd hit him at all.

For a moment I was tempted to drop It just anywhere and clear off. Or go back upstairs and own up. That's typical me, sacrifice anything for an easy way out. But self-disgust won. I pressed on. This way was harder, but it'd keep the Great Charter safe – at least until I knew who was doing what. And moving It from one part of the Museum to another wasn't stealing as such, was it? Which might get me a year or two remission of sentence.

More by luck than good judgement I found the place. Only two locked doors, and only one of those I actually had to damage so you'd notice. The trouble with security is that it's its own enemy. It fades as more security is established. Like I mean a castle keep's lived-in interior must have been less vigilant than the outer walls, right? The deeper I went, the less troublesome the security obstacles, the locks, the infra-red beams which burglars call stiles. I hit the book-stacks after what seemed an age, yet I couldn't have taken more than ten minutes. They're the enormous subterranean library shelves, mile after mile, sealed under London's streets and inaccessible except from the oh-so-secure Museum's centre.

Once there I surpassed myself, only making five false starts before finding the loading point. I risked a quick switch of a light to check, spotted a couple of massive volumes waiting by the bay. No way out to the bright safe streets of London beyond, of course, but I didn't need one. The Magna Carta, in its little frame, did. Light off. Apologizing like mad to the bigger tome – it was diagrams of some architectural monstrosity – I put my precious frame aside and began tearing out the pages' centres, leaving a rim. It sounds easy, and isn't. Easy with a Stanley knife, rotten with your fingers. It seemed to take an age before I'd ripped the damned thing enough. An hour? A few minutes, eleven at the most. I risked a flick of the light switch to see the books were aligned right, and put my bundle of excess diagrams on a topmost stack under a rank of volumes, all by feel.

Unhampered at last, but there was eerie flickering at the windows from lights in the central areas. I finally broke out on the north side – no, that's too dramatic: I stood on a chair, opened the window and hauled myself up. I replaced my hood for the sake of all-blackness and skulked slowly across the open rectangular space to the north wing's great windows. No lights in the Map Gallery's long glass roof, so Footer's hateful turn-screw doors were still presumably sealed. The Museum's metal-framed windows are ordinary glass, old as the hills – well, maybe forty years or so. Wired for sound of course, half way up their tall lengths they have crisscross locked metal gating linked to London's vigilant central Plod and Holborn police. The question was, could it stop me? Answer, hardly, though my exit would scarcely lack spoor.

Worn out and wearily past caring, but now unencumbered, I climbed to the first available sill. The hullabaloo, fading into a steady racket of shouts and whistles, was on the south, opposite, corner. I elbowed the glass in, put in a hand to try the catch. It was painted shut by layers of lazy painters – or decorators thoughtfully working to order? Another clamber. I heard somebody yell and another bloke answer as they searched the interior quadrilateral. I almost castrated myself on the points of the window gates, was saved by the many footholds on the inside, and dropped easily into the enormously long 34, the principal Oriental gallery. It runs the entire length of the Museum's north side. Alarms sounded, but what was one more siren among friends? Now there was ample but weird light slotting in from the orange lamps of Montague Place.

The way out was a mirror image of the way in: cross among the Chinese jades and ceramics, haul myself up the window's gate, smash the glass and climb outside. This time I used my hood wrapped round my hand to avoid cutting myself, which I'd done with monotonous regularity. Facing Montague Place there's a huge cellar-ditch, like an unfilled moat. That made me edge nervously along until I reached the north entrance's fancier architecture.

I lowered myself into the street. For a second I almost fell from exhaustion. I hadn't realized how drained I was, utterly spent. I was free, safe, in a London street: Dressed like a night-stealing Arab still, but self-rescued and whole. Civilization.

The one car parked along the central meters fired its engine. I walked over and got in, driver's side of course because my least favourite titch's legs were too small to reach the pedals.

'I knew you'd make it, Lovejoy!' Three Wheel Archie was so anxious to please.

'Don't give me that gunge, you treacherous midget.'

'Lovejoy. What could I do? I had to scarper. I could see you were going to do some real shooting. I had to, mate.'

'Don't mate me, you two-pint pot. You left me in there to get topped, you burke.'

'Honestly, Lovejoy.' All traitors wax indignant. It's their only defence. 'Who put the iron in the gold samovar? Who stuck by you all through that barmy filming, that—?'

'Archie.' I laid my head back on the rest, eyeing him.

'Just shut up. OK? One word. And turn that frigging engine off.'

He obeyed, reaching over and subsiding into a pained silence. He lasted an hour before he risked asking. 'Lovejoy?'

'Yes, friend?' I hadn't slept, just thought thoughts.

'Why don't we zoom home?'

'Because we'd not get ten yards. Friend.'

He was mystified, looked about nervously. 'How come?'

'Because they're not that thick. Friend.'

'Don't, Lovejoy.' He sounded broken. 'I got scared. I hid in one of the smoke-gun containers.'

'Good on you. Friend.'

Another pause. Then, 'Lovejoy? What happened?'

'Somebody shot somebody. They'll say it was me shot Seg.'

'Dear me.' He never curses, swears. A real gentleman.

'And somebody pinched something.'

There are pauses and pauses. He tried for a brief one, failed, finally cut a thirty-minuter. 'So somebody finally did the big one, eh? Who'll they blame, Lovejoy?'

'Guess, Archie.'

'On your tod, or with an accomplice?' His gravelly voice practically went falsetto.

For the first time I grinned, patted his leg. 'Give you one more guess. Friend.'

'Oh my stars,' he croaked. 'They'll crisp you, Lovejoy.'

We didn't speak again until they came. The motor's clock said five-thirty a.m., and London's traffic was beginning to roll about in eager bits.

Chapter 30

The cop shop in Bow Street's better outside than in though they all are, aren't they? It took eight peelers to take my statement, plus two secretaries with pretensions to learning, and four witnesses including Ray Meese. He was apoplectic with hate and rage.

'That killer murdered my movie!' he kept screaming until they took him away. Vance, Lofty and Nick remained.

I told a simple tale. Yes, I'd snuck in two army smoke canisters. Yes, I'd spoiled the film, admitting to a king's ransom in damages. I was outraged and astonished when the inspector asked me about a real weapon. Shoot with a real gun, albeit percussion, at a living person? Not me. Kill anyone? Never! Intent to commit murder? What on earth for?

Sixty-nine questions later, all oft repeated, I signed my statement. They took my fingerprints. They showed me the percussion piece, and I said I'd never seen it before. Lofty and Nick, still not knowing what anything was about, were released about midday. They let Three Wheel Archie go home, after questioning him separately. He tried to have a word but they stopped him. I heard him shout so-long from the corridor. That must have been about six o'clock, twelve hours or so after they'd arrested me. And nobody had mentioned any robbery. Especially, nobody'd mentioned the big MC.

Corrigan, the boss, and his oppo Welch conducted me to view the body. I suppose they videoed the scene, me coming in all queasy into the King's Cross mortuary and standing there sick as a dog while they uncovered Seg's corpse.

It had a central chest wound and an additional one in the throat, complete with charred flash burns made as a percussion weapon had flung its heavy spherical missile into the flesh. The body was very, very deceased.

Only it was Lorane.

I surrendered after that. Not to them. To fatigue. I must have slumped because that was it as far as I was concerned.

When I came to, Wednesday after the Bank Holiday Monday, I read that the British Museum building, with its enclosed Reading Room core, remained closed. Normally I don't read newspapers or other comics, unless they're antique and therefore of interest, but that Wednesday I devoured the duty copper's morning paper in my cell. I wasn't named. Interviews with twenty or more Lake Bayon people were reported in gaudy detail. Hype ruled.

About the Magna Carta? Nothing.

Late that night Major Bracegirdle came, MacAdam alongside with two local blokes I recognized. It was an attempt to be friendly. I was offered a deal, cloaked in many hints of leniency, turning State's evidence, an amnesty. All balderdash, because they aren't empowered to offer bargains on behalf of the judiciary. I expressed eagerness to help, but couldn't tell them more than I knew, could I? And a deal? About what? I asked innocently.

Nobody mentioned it.

'You see, Lovejoy,' Bracegirdle said, 'Seg's turned Queen's evidence.'

'Against Ray and—?' I stopped. I'd nearly mentioned Clayton.

'Against you, Lovejoy.'

'The crux is,' MacAdam said from the doorway after a fruitless hour, 'we know you were after something in the Museum. Nothing's reported missing so far. The one extra valuable – that gold teapot and things – you own, it appears. And you hired that hide-away Celtic cross, but all legit. Nothing to charge you with.'

'Except murder, eh? Seg escaped, did he?'

'Abdominal wound. Gunshot. But yes.'

'Pity,' I said evenly. I'd downed two out of three.

'But it's completeness, see?' MacAdam said. 'Loose ends irritate.' One loose tag was Seg's real handgun. Of course, any number of accomplices would have vanished it in the uproar.

'When are they opening the Museum again?'

'Tomorrow, Lovejoy.' He waited. 'Want to pop along?'

'Wouldn't mind. Better than here.'

'Any particular reason?'

'Tell you when it's open, Mac.' And as he made to leave, 'Any other weapons found there? Besides that antique muzzle-loaded percussion you mentioned?'

'I never mentioned muzzle-loaders, Lovejoy. I only said percussion.'

'Well, whatever.' Mistakes are my forte.

'Why do you ask, Lovejoy? Drop a couple of modern automatics as you bashed your way out?'

'Never mentioned automatics, Mac.'

'So you didn't.' He didn't look back as he left. I was put into my cell by a bobby who was disappointed I refused to play him at snooker.

Gabriella arrived next day. It was her turn.

'Not before time,' I said. The Bow Street mob have the dullest interview room in the known world. Talk about decor. Graffiti'd be an improvement.

'Good morning, Lovejoy.' Gabriella was pale, charming. 'I've come alone, you see.'

'Is the Museum open today?' First things first.

'Yes. All services.'

'Routine operations all round?'

'Yes.' She'd cottoned on that that was what I'd been waiting for.

My sigh of relief felt unending. I relaxed, sat back. We were on chairs six feet apart.

'I thought you'd never get round to it, love.'

'Where is it, Lovejoy?'

I glanced at the clock. Nearly midday. 'Woolwich. Unless the traffic's bad or your van driver got 'flu.'

Her eyes closed. She nodded. 'The vehicles are garaged external to the Museum. But you couldn't have got it there, Lovejoy. We had your car and Three Wheel Archie on night scopes in Montague Place.'

'On record, I presume?'

'It's not only film makers who own direction microphones.' She caught my interrogative glance and reddened. 'No, Lovejoy. This place is tap free. We're off record. I give you my word.'

'Ask away, then.' She was lying, of course. Nothing immoral; it's just the way they are.

She asked, and I told her how I'd grabbed a priceless treasure, and where It lay snug in a tome of architectural drawings. 'By the van loading bay. I reckoned they'd be loaded up and driven out as usual when you resumed normal activities.'

'Why not tell us before, Lovejoy?'

'Who?' I asked, matching her real anger. 'Who should I tell? You? Bracegirdle? Don't make me laugh, love. I had to wait until the bloody thing was safe in Woolwich Arsenal – you cackhanded Security people might let a deadbeat like me nick it, but once it's in the army's tender care not even you could lose it.'

'Of all the offensive, nasty-minded—'

'Give it a rest, you silly cow.' I rose, walked about in fury. 'You make me sick. How the hell could I've trusted you, straight off? You were pally with Meese, Lorane, Vance. Christ, you even let Seg in – psychotic murderer – as an extra! I just don't believe you nerks.'

She was on her feet in rage. 'That's unfair, Lovejoy!'

'Unfair?' I yelled. I could have given her a thrashing, stupid bitch. 'Unfair? It was frigging *me* Seg was going to top, love. Not you Admin coffee-drinkers playing whist in Security. And much you did about it!'

'I should have expected this rubbish from a thief, Lovejoy!' She was blazing, hands clenched. We competed decibel for decibel.

'Thief, am I?' I bawled. 'You admit murderous thugs, let them rip open the frigging Magna Carta's cabinet, nick it, let them try to kill me, then have the frigging nerve to . . .' I petered out. She'd gone white, almost reeled.

'The *what*?' Her lips were blue. 'But it . . . it's undisturbed, practically.'

'You didn't know?' I closed my eyes.

'We . . . we assumed that you . . .' She was speechless. Then almost whispered, 'The smoke bombs. You're on film throwing them. The autolift control was in your bag.

The Magna Carta's frame was almost pulled clear, but quite intact. We thought you'd been stopped in time . . .'

Good old Lorane, Vance, Meese, Seg.

'We simply remounted the Great Charter.' She began to shed tears. 'An auto-gantry had hit against it. The frame was honestly intact, Lovejoy. It had only been pulled free of the security wires . . .'

What had I done? I remembered I'd fired twice, lifted the frame, fired again at somebody coughing close, then somehow scrambled to the balcony. Either Seg or Lorane – whichever one I'd hit last – had been holding Sam Shrouder's perfect replica concealed and ready to hand. Hearing the shots and somebody's body tumble down, they'd assumed that I'd been shot as planned, and slipped the replica into place. So Lorane and Seg had been in collusion. I was in the clear. They'd both been part of the Lovejoy annihilation squad.

Good old magic Sam, he of the miracle hands, to create a replica which took in this lot. I was proud of him.

'Sit down, love.' I led her gently to her chair, pulled mine within reach and sat while she blubbered.

'Lovejoy. Tell me what happened.'

'Ready?' She nodded, blotted, sniffed. 'Here goes, love. Listen carefully.' I sat back, hands behind my head. 'Once upon a time, there was a deaf old coot name of Sam Shrouder. A genius faker. He had a pretty young wife who hatched a scheme to rip off the greatest museum on earth. It would be the ultimate scam, the very last gambado . . .'

'Ray Meese, Seg, Ben Clayton and Mrs Shrouder? All in it?'

'Plus poor Lorane, two-timed throughout.' Why poor Lorane? She'd been helping to blam me.

'And the Magna Carta's—?'

'Told you. In your own Repository by now. The one in the Woolwich army garrison.'

She straightened up, quickly recovering her composure. 'Actually that's not quite true, Lovejoy.' She smiled. 'I lied. The Museum's not yet open. Major Bracegirdle and I decided it would be injudicious to allow the public in when we were still uncertain whether anything had been stolen or not.'

'You lied, Gabriella?' I said, straight out of a Victorian melodrama. I even grabbed my lapels, very formidable, wished I had a moustache.

'Lies are sometimes necessary, Lovejoy.' So sweet.

'Like about this interview, not being recorded?'

She smiled, fetched out a powder compact and did her face. 'Of course.'

Well, that seemed to be it. I said conversationally to the ceiling, 'Did you get it all, Mac?'

'Aye, Lovejoy,' a voice said from the light fixture. 'All of it.'

'Lovejoy!' Gabriella blazed. 'How dare you! *You* suspected *me*? You got the police to bug *my* interrogation?'

'Why not? You're now in the clear, Gabe,' I told her magnanimously. 'You didn't even know it was the Great Charter until I told you.'

She snapped her compact away, ice. 'Lovejoy. You are repellent, ridiculous, horrid.'

'Gabe.' I was suddenly worn out. 'Stay in Security, love. You're too dumb to do a real job.'

Chapter 31

A wet Tuesday and the auction crowded. I went into a hail of hails, all derision.

'Wotcher, Lovejoy! How long're you out for?'

'Bribery still works, eh, Lovejoy?'

'Shot any good dealers lately, Lovejoy?'

Old Midwinter the auctioneer is straight out of *Little Dorrit*. Bottle lenses, waistcoat, winged collar, an Adam's apple that works at silent yodels. He peered down at my arrival, scribed a note which he passed to Dan, his nearest whizzer, who was desultorily shifting the dross on offer. I knew what the old sod was up to – ordering me slung out as undesirable, which is a laugh. Blackening an auctioneer's name is lending Satan sin. Tinker's melodious cough ripped through the smoke-filled fug, music to my ears. He approached, grinning, as the auction droned on through the clag of fakes and duds.

'Hiyer, son. I heard you got orf.'

'The innocent do, Tinker.' A lie. Innocence is luck, a terrible truth Law ignores. 'Anything in?'

'Funny teacup, for blokes with a tash.'

Interesting. 'Moustache cup? If it's for a left-hander go for it. They're twice as valuable as right-handers. Owt else?'

'Funny teapot, sailor with three legs. One leg's the spout. Horrible.' It wasn't the teapot's design made him shudder; it was the thought of actually drinking tea. Tinker growled, hawked, spat on the bare flagged floor. 'They're going mad over it.'

'Don't touch it, Tinker. It'll be a Stoke-on-Trent novelty pottery piece made for the Isle of Man.' They're tin-glazed, trying hard to be old Italian. People talk themselves into paying highly over this 'English majolica' – even a perfect specimen deserves only a week's wages. 'Hopeless buying that rubbish until the American dollar steadies up.'

'Lovejoy.' Dan stood by. Dealers watched with interest. My evictions always receive popular attention. 'Out.'

'Very well, Dan.' I sighed heavily. 'I'll take it to Gimbert's or Seeley's.'

'It? What's this it?' Dan asked, undecided now. He glanced from me to the auctioneer. I'd spoken loud enough.

'You've read in the papers about a famous gold samovar, I trust? Come on, Tinker.'

Midwinter called, 'Daniel. Is that gentleman a *bona fide* customer?' A gaolbird plus a pricey gold antique equals a gentleman. See how their minds work?

'Well, sir . . .' Dan was on the spot.

'Then leave him alone, please.' The cunning old devil changes his tune at the first whiff of gelt. 'Now, continuing with Lot One-thirty. A handsome bronze, a wild boar attacked by dogs. Offers, please.'

'Cheers, Dan. Enter my samovar for next week, OK?' I passed him a description, let him go and whispered to Tinker, 'Bid a month's average wage for the bronze. It's a Fratin.' This French bloke was a pupil of the painter Gericault, the flavour of the decade now collectors are learning to read. Tip: Fratin bronze prices are bound for the stars.

'Right. Here, Lovejoy. You clear for good?'

'Aye. Parson Brown was arrested last night. He'd gone to earth in Wimbledon, scared after Sam Shrouder got topped.'

'Wimbledon? Poor sod.' He spat a volume. I looked away, queasy. 'Here, son. Your bird, the one with the big bristols. She wants you to sign something.'

'Lydia?'

'And Suki Lonegan. And some foreign tart, smelled posh.'

Bad news all this. Just when I thought it was safe to go back into public life. I muttered a good luck with the bidding and ducked out. And bumped into a familiar figure on the pavement.

'Good morning, Lovejoy.'

'Oh, er, Lydia, doowerlink! How marvellous!'

She looked lovely, smiling. My eternal question recurred: does she dress prim from innate demureness, or because she knows it's fetching? I have my suspicions. 'Do you have a few moments, Lovejoy?'

'For you, anything.'

We crossed to the Tudor Rose café for a quiet table by the old-fashioned windows, from where I could see on to East Hill behind her. She settled, ordered tea and toast, brought out a sheaf of papers. Her tiny handbag's like Merlin's sack – contains umpteen times its own capacity. Out the stuff came, yards and tons of it. I watched her curiously. Her skin is a-bloom, smooth and fruitlike. And her mouth really is bow-shaped, straight off a Victorian painting. Her figure is voluptuous in those reserved lace blouses she wears. Her hair was so precise about the temples you can't help wondering how it loosened . . .

'Eh? Sign where? What?'

'Here, Lovejoy. And here, please.' She smiled, I obeyed, she put the papers away. 'There! Now we shall have a celebratory cup of tea!'

Pity Tinker wasn't here to riot along. 'Er, celebrate what, Lyd?'

'Lydia, please. Your cottage, Lovejoy.' She held my gaze, but shyly. 'Well, not exactly yours. Mine, actually.'

Headache time. I closed my eyes. 'Yours? My cottage is yours?'

'I knew you'd be thrilled. I re-mortgaged my own flat. Its value has increased inordinately. With the proceeds I redeemed your deeds.'

'From Hymie?' I said weakly. Behind her, a long saloon car drew up opposite. Agafia Potocki descended, elegant and affluent.

'Certainly. I returned his samovar, of course.' She sighed, a woes-of-the-world sigh. 'It was only leaded bronze, gold-plated. Hymie was so unwilling to be prosecuted and involved in the Museum trouble that he quite forgave you your foolish deception.'

'Fake?' My vision blurred. I'd kill Hymie. 'He diddled *me* with a fake?' I'd marmalize him. My hands clenched, nails into my palms. He'd defrauded me, just because he knew I'd cheat him over my cottage deeds. And him a friend.

'He couldn't deceive you with a fake of an antique, Lovejoy. Only with a fake you knew was a fake.'

I'd still throttle him. 'So my deeds are . . . ?' What had the crafty cow got me to sign?

'Are actually mine, Lovejoy.' We held a silence. I saw a voluptuous over-dressed young lass emerge from the auction rooms doorway with Tinker. He pointed into town, graphically mimed a just-missed-him, nodding.

She clacked off, stiletto heels stabbing and skirt wobbling erotically. She wore chunky jewellery on every limb. Gulp. Lavina, Parson Brown's daughter. Trouble. Exquisite trouble.

'Love,' I said quickly to Lydia. 'Thank you. You've done really superbly. Now I'll just pop across, give Tinker a message . . .'

'No, Lovejoy. You won't.'

'Eh?' I said, narked. I suddenly didn't like her steady blues. 'It's about an important bracket clock—'

'There is no bracket clock in today's auction, Lovejoy.'

'Isn't there? Good heavens! I meant at Seeley's.'

'Lavina Brown's the least of our difficulties.' She smiled at my astonishment. She hadn't even turned round, not even glanced at the street. 'That young lady has loitered – I can't in all charity use a kindlier description – ostensibly wishing to thank you for indirectly helping her mother.' She stirred her tea briskly. 'I doubt her intentions, Lovejoy.'

So did I, thank God. 'Yes, but—'

'And Gabriella has taken up temporary residence in the George Hotel, Lovejoy, looking for you. And that Laila keeps telephoning offering you a cheval mirror.'

'That bad, eh?'

'That bad indeed. We must be careful.' Behind Lydia I saw Agafia leave Midwinter's, beckon her chauffeured saloon and be driven off into town in grand style. Things must be looking up at Condor Hall. 'And Agafia called repeatedly – some proposition involving the Russian Exhibition. It seems that the entire Exhibition's contents have been repossessed in Countess Natalia's name. I am arranging a contract for you to sell the items excess to Countess Natalia's requirements – properly authenticated – at ten per cent commission.'

I brightened. Chances of delving commission don't come that often. To delve is to sell an antique for a phonily low price, say four-fifths, the true market value *x*. You receive an illicit one-tenth of *x*, plus the commission on the whole of *x*. Work it out, and you'll see it's a worthy little bringer, as long as nobody—

'We'll take firm precautions against delving, Lovejoy. Some dealers are unscrupulous.'

Like I was saying, as long as nobody gets an attack of honesty. 'Good thinking,' I said miserably. I'd have to work on Lydia, somehow erode this all-bran aerobics morality of hers.

'And Mrs Lonegan has called, proposing a partnership with her in antique jewellery and silverware. I had to disabuse her in no uncertain manner.'

'Er, about what?'

'About your new partner, Lovejoy.'

She'd lost me. 'Tinker'll never make a partner in a million years, love.'

'Not Tinker, Lovejoy. Me.' She blushed, pretty, into her tea. 'Tinker approves wholeheartedly, I'm pleased to say.'

Aye. He would. He'd turn Buddhist for a pint. A new headache pressed behind my eyes. 'My new partner? Er, you?'

'You've just signed our partnership contract. Remember?' That's a woman for you. I've never known a bird who isn't two jumps ahead. Lydia's three. 'The Russian contract discharges some of the debts you incurred, Lovejoy.'

I reached for her hand and tried a fond smile. 'Look, doowerlink. I couldn't possibly burden you with my debts.' Hang on. Why not, Lovejoy? Give one good reason.

'You haven't, Lovejoy. The bonus—'

Another headache moved in beside its pal. Nobody

gives me bonuses. The world expects me to bring the handouts. 'Don't joke, er, sweetheart.'

She withdrew her hand, reddened. 'Please remember we're in public, Lovejoy.' In public? The Tudor Rose was empty except for us. 'Big John Sheehan arranged for many local dealers, including Brad, to reschedule their credit balances for us. Wasn't that kind?' She smiled. 'He took a great deal of persuading. But when I pointed out the risk and expense you went to, to remove Clayton's influence from the local antiques trade, he was very impressed.'

'He was?' I was now a multi-headache man. Lydia, negotiate with Big John Sheehan? A kite negotiating a change in the wind.

'Sheehan was rather disappointed the cameramen failed to photograph Mr Seg's mishap, all that smoke. He longs to have it on video, though he admits that isn't your fault, Lovejoy.' Thank Christ for that. 'He's somehow acquired a container shipment of assorted antiques. Our bonus is to be one-third its wholesale value.'

It was probably one of Ben Clayton's loads. I'll bet Big John's lads drove over and simply nicked it the instant Ben got arrested, in the manner of their kind. Well, cross that bridge. I didn't like this 'our bonus' bit. Why not mine alone? Who'd risked life and everything, entirely unaided? Suki Lonegan walked into Midwinter's opposite.

'Look, doowerlink,' I said brightly. 'Would you mind just waiting here a sec? Only, I promised Tinker—'

'Mrs Lonegan's husband has returned, Lovejoy,' Lydia said evenly. She was gazing beyond me. I turned. An ornamental mirror on the wall gave Lydia a panoramic view of the street. How sly can you get?

'Lydia!' I did my gasped outrage. 'You're surely not suggesting . . .' etc., etc.

'Lovejoy. 'Morning miss.' He sat, unbidden, looked disappointedly for a spare cup.

'Hello, Mac. We were just going.' I'd seen enough peelers lately to last a lifetime.

'Sorry, Lovejoy. The station calls.' He thumbed at two helmets beyond the frosted glass. 'Now.'

Wearily I rose. Some years can ruin your whole day. 'Try for bail, Lyd.'

'I shall indeed!' Lydia came with us, expostulating furiously. Not an all-time first. 'I shall contact the Lord Lieutenant of this county . . .'

'Lovely bird,' Mac said in the police car. 'You don't deserve her.' I didn't try explaining how things are between Lyd and me. The Plod only think genitalia and other weapons. 'Stop here, Fred.' The war memorial, by the Castle?

'Sir.' The driver pulled in.

A huge saloon waited alongside the rose garden. Was Agafia's motor maroon? Anyway, it looked familiar.

'Out, Lovejoy.' Mac walked with me, bent and spoke through the chauffeur's window. 'Here he is, lady. Would you confirm his identity?'

'Yes. It's him.' The door opened. Agafia was serene, fragrant. 'It's so unfortunate, Inspector. The missing silver was the only original piece left, you see.'

'Missing . . . ?' I gaped. 'I'm the one who saved your fortune, remember?' But I'd nicked that silver Tsarist tea set, St Petersburg. And its whereabouts were still known only to Big John Sheehan. I smiled weakly.

She pondered. 'Mr MacAdam. Would you mind releasing Lovejoy into my custody? Perhaps together we might remember where it is. Only, in all the upheaval we might have made an oversight.'

Me leave what, where? I gave up, stood forlornly with

my load of headaches while they talked. I was duly handed over into the perfumed interior, plush gentility with prospects. We moved off. I was vaguely surprised Agafia didn't give a royal wave as Lydia's motor burned blindly past towards the police station.

'Wrong way,' I told her. 'This street runs west.'

'Does it?' Agafia said calmly. She lit a pungent Russian cigarette.

Watching the shops glide past, I thought of Agafia's position as sole go-between for that assortment of Tsarist antiques and Sam Shrouder's fakes which comprised the St Edmundsbury exhibition. Her hip pressed against me as the saloon swung out on to the dual carriageway and the umpteen-miles-to-London signposts began.

She moved away a little. 'Lovejoy. Countess Natalia wondered if you would help us start an antiques business in Chelsea. Nothing costly, you understand. Nothing too showy.'

I swallowed. 'Using what, love? I'm broke.'

'We have repossessed the Rumiantzeff possessions.' She looked into me. 'Plus a large number of unfamiliar Russian additions, the origin and provenance of which I'm rather uncertain. Including an enormous Wedgwood dinner service, scores and scores of pieces.'

'Good heavens.' I went giddy. In 1774 Josiah Wedgwood himself made an 800-plus dinner service for Empress Catherine II of Russia. Surely Sam couldn't have . . . ? The saloon was cruising now. The houses were fewer, traffic lights ended. 'You didn't tell the police the extra items weren't yours, then?'

'It slipped our memories, Lovejoy.'

At least eighty fakes, all made by the great. Sam. All delivered by the unsuspecting Old Bill into our hands. Plus all the Rumiantzeff originals. Well. There might be rumblings from Big John, and wasn't Chelsea Bill Sykes territory? But there'd be no desperately honest partnership contracts with Lydia to restrict my activities. And London's so liberating – it doesn't confine like rustic old East Anglia.

'Well, it could be done. Need close working.'

'I'd welcome that, Lovejoy.'

My throat was getting drier and drier. Her cigarette, probably. 'It might need a bit of careful delving, Ag.'

'Please, Lovejoy. One thing.' Her hand rested lightly on my knee. 'Agafia. Not Ag, Aggie, nor Ags. Ag-a-fi-a.'

'Agafia.' Women are odd about names.

'And what is this delving, please?'

The sun came out, spilling brilliant dazzling free gold on to my poor moth-eaten world. I smiled, slipped my arm round her.

'You don't know? Well, Ag doowerlink, it's like this . . .'

Our grand saloon purred smoothly towards the London sunshine.